Another Word for Sister

CHERYL IRWIN

GVP

Another Word for Sister is a work of historical fiction.

Apart from the place names and the name of the ship, all names,

characters, and incidents are the products of the author's imagination or are

used fictitiously.

National Library of New Zealand Cataloguing-in-Publication Data

Irwin, Cheryl, 1960-

Another Word for Sister / Cheryl Irwin

ISBN 978-0-473-26921-0

2013 Goddess Voice Publishing

www.goddessvoicepublishing.com

ISBN 978-0-473-26921-0

Printed by CreateSpace, an Amazon.com company

Cover photo by www.billirwinarts.com

www.goddessvoicepublishing.com

For My Sister

Acknowledgements

I would like to thank my husband, Bill Irwin, who encourages all my creative endeavours, no matter how wild or costly, and my first readers, Rachel Irwin, Lizzie Barwell, Leslie Russell, Cindy Macho Johnson, Sandra Marr, Sonia Molloy, Vashti Johnstone, Cath Roderick, and Mary Ralston whose suggestions and enthusiasm inspired me to publish *Another Word for Sister*.

A special thank you to Grace Spampinato for her editorial expertise.

I would like to thank all my writing teachers, especially SARK (Susan Ariel Rainbow Kennedy) for her WINS program and introducing me to the micro movement wheel. *Another Word for Sister* is a product of the 'one tiny step at a time' process. Thank you for helping me keep the faith.

Another Word for Sister

Prelude

1858~Creggan, County Armagh, Ireland

"Take this one, Annie. Here, wrap her up, hold her tight. Don't worry about cleaning her; just get her warm. Move closer to the fire." Annie moved and jiggled the baby in her arms, trying her best to do what was expected of her.

Katherine Donnelly's right hand disappeared back into the bloody slit that was the new entrance to her daughter's womb.

"I've got it! I've got the other one." Katherine pulled, and the tiny body made a sucking noise as it left its wet cocoon. "Another girl."

She wrapped the baby quickly and, holding her tight, bent to her daughter.

"Lillian! Lillian! There are two. You were right all along. You have two beautiful daughters, Lillian. They are strong and healthy; they will live." Holding the baby with one hand, she reached for her daughter's wrist; the pulse was slow and weak.

"Lillian, can you hear me? Clasp my hand if you can hear me." There was the tiniest of movements.

"Go with God, Lillian. O, blessed Danu, take this woman. Free her soul to fly once more." Katherine motioned to Annie and they laid the babies in the crooks of Lillian's arms. With her hand on her daughter's forehead, she intoned, "Behold, woman, the children of your womb, the precious life you have created. I call upon Danu and all that is good, take this woman, but leave her power for her daughters who, through her power, will know her love. Let the circle remain. Let the circle remain."

The small house became silent then. Even the blazing fire seemed to quiet itself. Annie had always gone along with her own mother to the secret rituals and celebrations that Katherine and Lillian had led, in the hills behind Creggan, in the grove of ancient oak trees near the stones. She liked going, liked that they needed to keep their meetings secret. But this was a little too much. She could just about see all the spirits dancing around, leaving bloody footprints.

Lillian made a sound, as if she were going to speak to a large crowd and needed to clear her throat first. Her shoulders moved, then her elbows, and finally her hands. She was trying to hold her babies closer. *This is so sad, so very sad,* Annie thought. But Lillian's voice wasn't sad at all; it was brave, it was beautiful, it sounded so strong.

"Maiden. Mother. Crone."

Katherine smiled as her daughter invoked the Triple Goddess. Lillian had said once that three women together could sort anything out.

"I have travelled the great wheel of death and rebirth many times, and now it is time for me to return to the world of spirits. Please welcome me." Lillian paused as she struggled to breathe and her voice wavered as she continued, "Here in the physical world, I leave my two daughters, Lily and Rose. Please bless them, and throughout their earthly lives let them know of my love."

Then she took her last breath.

Chapter 1

1875~Lily

We had no reason to stay. There were no prospects for us in the tiny village we called home. People knew too much, or not enough if it was the truth they were after. Under other circumstances it might have caused more of a commotion—two seventeen-year-old girls leaving Creggan to go to New Zealand—but not now. It seemed that everyone else had already left or was busy packing. Still, it wasn't easy for me, leaving the life I knew behind.

I wanted to leave. I wanted to get away from the people who only knew to judge me. I wanted to leave behind their questioning looks and mistaken ideas. I was tired of being misunderstood. Mind you, the idea of travelling all the way to New Zealand by sea and then establishing ourselves there was daunting, but both Rose and I wanted to start again in a new place. We wanted to be happy.

We had heard the New Zealand government offered free passage to all single female domestic servants. So that is what we had become. We were excited about our journey but also very nervous. Everything was new to us. All free and assisted immigrants departing from London had to report to the New Zealand Immigration Depot at Blackwall on the Thames. We had come from the outskirts of our small, quiet village in Ireland to the busy, noisy and smelly wharves of London. The smell was the hardest thing to get used to. A dank river aroma underlay all the less than savoury human ones. It unsettled us.

The accommodation block was crowded. It was one very large room, with a partition down the middle with rows of bunks down either side and along the outside walls. The bunks were just barely wide enough for one person and had mattresses stuffed with straw. We were each given a pillow, a blanket, and a sheet, which we were to take on board the ship with us. The men were on one side of the partition and the women and children on the other. Rose and I were happy to be assigned bunks next to Mrs McGregor and her five children.

People were everywhere. I could sit on my bunk for hours and just watch and listen. There was so much to see, so much life to appreciate.

I liked watching for the husbands. During the day one would, from time to time, appear around the corner of the partition. His eyes would search the bunks for his wife, and when he found her, his body would relax with recognition. He'd call out her name and she would turn towards him smiling. He'd smile back, while he waited for her to gather up the children and come to him. It was as if some great unease had been relieved at the sight of his family. Of course, Rose and I then found ourselves anticipating the return of these same families, as we became more and more intrigued with normal family life. Sometimes the husband would come all the way into the bunkroom with a sleeping child in his arms before relinquishing the child to his wife; he'd whisper in her ear and kiss her quickly before he left.

Although we had to wait for our papers to be processed and for news of when our ship, the *Crusader*, would be ready to sail, we were not too impatient.

"Have you boys seen our ship?" I asked Johnny McGregor on the bunk beside me. He looked at me blankly but his older brother Mick piped up.

"No, ma'am, haven't. But hopin' it goes soon."

"Day after tomorrow, they are saying now," I replied.

"Good. Then we'll finally get some fresh air. Johnny, don't jab me! I'm talking to the lady here." Mick McGregor elbowed his brother while trying to speak.

"Ask your mother if you can come out for a walk with us. We can get some fresh air right now." I stood up and looked around for my sister.

I had liked Mick McGregor right off; he was fourteen and not at all like his father. Where his father was thin and bookish, Mick was muscular, robust, and tanned. Mick liked to laugh; he had a lopsided smile and eyes that twinkled with humour. His father was grim, dutiful, and moral to the point of being sanctimonious. I could tell Mick found it hard work being the Reverend McGregor's firstborn son.

"Where are we goin', Rose?" Mick asked my sister as we all gathered. Rose had a gravy spot on her white cotton apron, which I think was how he told us apart. Rose took hold of Johnny's hand, and Mick took five-year-old Jamie's hand, gripping it tightly.

"To the East India Dock," Rose answered, and we headed out the door to walk along the edge of the river. The day was bright; the air did feel good and was cool on my skin. Though smelling of fish and too many people, the air was still lighter. I lifted my face and smiled as I savoured the occasional whiff of salty sweet freshness coming to me on the breeze.

Mick was walking beside me and I kept catching him looking at me. He didn't stare the way the people had at home; there was no fear in his eyes, no judgement, just curiosity. I think he was searching to spot a difference between my sister and me.

"What?" I asked, smiling at him.

"Nothin'."

"No, really, it's all right." I walked closer to him.

"Well," he took a deep breath of the fishy air and then looked like he thought better of it. He glanced from me to Rose and back again several times. I think we confused him more because now Rose was lifting her face to feel the breeze and smiling with enjoyment just like I had.

"Are you fairies?" Mick blurted out. I watched as red crept up his neck.

I smiled, "No, but I wouldn't mind."

"Wouldn't mind what?"

I turned towards Rose. "Mick just asked if we were fairies."

"Well." Rose and Johnny stopped. She took Mick's free hand and the red deepened. She laughed. "What a lovely compliment! Ever so much nicer than being called a witch."

"What?" Mick tried to extract his hand, but Rose held on, still looking amused. Mick smiled back at her, shrugged his shoulders, and they continued walking, the four of them taking up most of the walkway in front of me.

"I think that might be it," Mick said excitedly. He suddenly sped up and pulled Rose and his brothers behind him. "That's our ship! That's the *Crusader*! Look, they are putting stores aboard." We all stood on the dock, watching the men load the ship that would be our home for the next three months.

The ship was a beautiful sight. Sitting there at the London docks it very much looked as if it were resting, catching its breath for its next run across the high seas. I sighed and tried to quell my anxieties about going to sea. I looked closely. The *Crusader* had three very tall masts rising out of its iron hull and looked imposing and oddly trustworthy. I imagined this ship looking down its nose at the wooden ships sitting nearby. Rose was frowning at me. She took my hand, and instantly I knew exactly what she was thinking. "No, it shouldn't sink," I told her and we both smiled.

"Do you think that might be Captain Renault?" Mick asked us as a tall man made his way down the gangplank past barrels and boxes of supplies and stepped onto the dock.

"I don't know. I suppose we could ask him," I said. Rose nudged Mick forward as the man continued towards us.

Mick squared his shoulders. "Excuse me, sir, are you the captain of the *Crusader*?"

The man slowed his pace and smiled, taking in the three boys, Rose, and me. Then he looked back and forth from me to Rose and back again. "No, I am First Mate Brian Donnelly. And you, sir?" He extended his hand to Mick.

Rose interrupted. "Donnelly! That is our grandmother's name. Where did your family hail from in Ireland, kind sir?"

"Oh, my parents moved to London before I was born. My father, being a seafaring man, never called any place home, and I, well, I am much the same. And you, lass, what brings you dockside this fine afternoon?"

"We are sailing to New Zealand, sir," Rose told him.

"On the *Crusader*?" Mr Donnelly looked us up and down.

"Why, yes. This is Mick McGregor and his brothers Jamie and Johnny. They are travelling with their parents and two younger sisters. This is my sister Lily." Rose held up our still joined hands, "Lily and I are going on our own. We have no other family."

Mr Donnelly shifted uncomfortably at Rose's announcement. "Ah, well, we have single women's quarters on board. See that you keep to them. There'll be a fair fight amongst the unmarried men when they catch a glimpse of you two," Mr Donnelly warned us, "and maybe do something with those curls." He said the last bit under his breath.

"What?" Rose asked, "What did you say about our curls?"

"Hide 'em," he stated firmly as he walked off.

Rose and I simultaneously raised our eyebrows as we watched the back of Brain Donnelly continuing on his way to the Shaw, Savill and Albion Company's shipping office.

~

"We did it, Lily, we did it!"

I didn't answer. I was busy squinting, trying to see through the foggy mist. I wanted one last glimpse of land. I sighed, shrugging my shoulders, thinking, *that's it, it's gone. Goodbye, England. Goodbye, Ireland. Slán go Foill.*

"Lily, you aren't listening." I was gazing out to sea.

"Lily, are you all right?"

"I was just saying my goodbyes." I turned from the ship's railing towards Rose and her sparkling blue eyes and wild dark curls blowing in the wind. I saw a mirror image of myself, and I smiled in the hope that the reflection would smile back at me. She did and I instantly felt better. We'd always been so in tune with each other. Nana Kat used to say she didn't know where one of us ended and the other began. The truth was, sometimes, neither did we. Nana Kat, even with her intuitive powers, could not tell one of us from the other once we were old enough to take the ribbons off our wrists. She said our mother was at fault. She had named us on her deathbed but hadn't told Nana Kat which one was which, so how was she supposed to know? So Nana Kat would say, "LilyandRose, you hurry and finish up there," and as she got older it was just LilyRose this and LilyRose that, as if it were just too much effort otherwise.

"It's getting cold." I put my arm around my smiling sister.

"I'm not cold; I'm so excited! We're going to New Zealand, Lily. New Zealand!"

"I know," I murmured, hugging my sister closer, and shivered as the enormity of what we were doing struck me.

"*Ni neart go curle cheile,*" Rose said softly, taking both my hands in hers and clasping them to her heart. I breathed deeply in and out and looked into my sister's eyes.

My voice was strong as I repeated back to her the old Gaelic saying that Nana Kat had taught us long ago, "*Ni neart go curle cheile.*"

There is strength in unity.

~

"My dear, you look very white. Are you not well?" Reverend McGregor asked his wife as we finished settling into our very cramped quarters on board. We had been invited to berth with the McGregor family, in a cabin with four sets of bunks, two on each wall, and a small aisle running between them.

"Oh no, I think… Oh dear." Leticia McGregor reached for the chamber pot and scurried to the corner for what little privacy she could secure as she stood and retched.

"Mother? Mother, what is the matter?" Mick rushed to his mother's side.

"Mick, there now, boy. Your mother is fine. Leticia, you are all right, aren't you?"

Mrs McGregor shook her head and continued retching. I held the pot for her. Her hands were trembling.

"Sebastian, I'm quite sure, that I'm…"

She paused and looked at me and Mick, then shrugged her shoulders. "Sebastian, I am in the family way again," Mrs McGregor just managed to say the words. "Oh, the thought of a sea voyage, the very thought…" She retched again, putting her cold hands on top of mine on the edge of the pot to brace herself.

I could tell by his expression that this was not what the Reverend McGregor had planned and that he was one of those people who very much liked life to go according to his plans—his and the Lord's.

"Leticia, you'd think, wouldn't you, that once, just once, we could…" He looked at me and Mick standing right beside his wife. He paused and then shook his head, his voice softening. "It is a woman's place to bear the consequences, I suppose. The Lord will see us through."

Mrs McGregor told me later that the Lord did see her through in the form of Lily and Rose Quinn, two angels sent straight from heaven. She said she would never have managed without us.

Rose would get up when the third mate bellowed "Water!" early each morning and stand in line with the jugs to get the day's water rations. At the same time, Mick or I would stand in line in the galley waiting to collect our morning porridge. Later, we'd take Mrs McGregor's two little girls in our arms, and with Johnny and Jamie trailing our skirts, we would walk slowly around the common room in the passenger hold. Then, if the weather and the captain allowed, we would all climb the ladders to the deck and do a slow circuit there. In between these excursions we would gather the children in a circle. Rose and I would take turns telling imaginary stories, playing guessing games, and sometimes recounting old Celtic legends to the children, ones from Nana Kat's old book, many of which we knew by heart. Rose was better at storytelling than I was. We had quite a following amongst the children on board; almost all seemed to enjoy the mythical tales. Once, the Reverend mentioned that he thought it might be more appropriate to read to the children from the Bible. Rose told him that would be fine and he was most welcome to read to the children any time he wished.

Life at sea suited Rose and me. We relaxed once we got used to things. Oh, there were concessions to make; we weren't at all used to being close to so many people. We were curious though and enjoyed watching and listening. In some ways we felt more a part of life than we ever had. The food was better than we were used to, appearing magically at regular intervals. We were not accustomed to these circumstances at all. We also had the luxury of being able to read for leisure. A fair number of books on board were traded amongst the literate passengers. The first class saloon had a shelf full of books, which the captain said could be borrowed by the steerage passengers if the understeward fetched them. I read *Amelia* by Henry Fielding and *Silas Marner* by George Eliot and a few plays; we wanted to read everything there was to read. *Pride and Prejudice* by Jane Austen was one of Rose's favourites. She read it three times and then told me about her very detailed dreams of her own Mr Darcy.

I quoted Jane Austen back to her, "'A lady's imagination is very rapid; it jumps from admiration to love, from love to matrimony in a moment'."

She laughed, "Ah, but you cannot tell me that you don't wonder, Lily, what it would be like to have a fine, strong man, one you could call your own?"

Oh, aye, I'd thought about it. The truth was Rose and I dreamed the same dreams.

~

I had time to sit and watch the sea, sometimes placid and inviting like a cool clear lake and at other times angry with waves attacking and threatening us with a watery grave. The floor would pitch and lean, confusing my feet. Instead of reaching for the nearest bunk or the ship's rail, Rose and I would lurch towards each other, assuming that it would help if we clung together. We'd laugh, swaying but unified, and make our way towards something more stable. I did miss the earth under my feet.

I was intrigued with the sea life. Every now and then something came visiting: porpoises, dolphins, whales or seabirds—like gulls, stormy petrels, mollymawks, or cape pigeons. It was as if they too needed the reassurance of company to cope with the vastness that surrounded us all. I didn't like the sharks, which were always edging in like they were looking for something worth eating. But I loved the Portuguese-man-of-war, a jellyfish with purple water lily translucence that would expand and swell, like a magical heartbeat, in tune with the wind and the waves. Once, a flying fish appeared. I presumed it had leapt out of the water and glided onto the deck. By the time I caught sight of it, it was being stuffed. It reminded me of an oversized dragonfly.

Whenever there was a commotion on deck, it paid to investigate. Every now and then we sighted outcroppings of land in the misty distance, either a renowned landmark or some uninhabited, strangely named islands; the excitement seemed to be the same no matter what it was. Sometimes we would pass another ship; the country of origin would be determined, the type of ship discussed, and surmises made about the destination.

Occasionally, when there weren't too many people on the deck, Rose and I would organise games for the children. We would play leapfrog or hunt the slipper, or we would have a competition to see how long the children could keep Johnny's top going. We would do anything we could think of to pass the time. We knew we were on the way to where we wanted to go, but it was most certainly going to take a while.

The McGregors were good to us. Because we were not bunked in with the other single women, I think the single men overlooked us the first few weeks of the voyage. But as the days wore on, the looks we got from some of the men on board began to intrigue us. Rose and I had been used to our own company for so long that this attention made us curious—and confused, because it seemed they were judging us favourably. But we continued to be surrounded by children throughout the day, and in the evenings Reverend McGregor made it clear that the nursemaids in his employ were to be left alone.

And we were.

Until the dance.

After the rhythm of the voyage fell into place, the instruments appeared. At first it was just Mr O'Leary and his fiddle, then Rory joined him with his bodhran, and Mrs McMurphy astonished everyone with her proficiency on the flute. Johnny even got up the nerve and joined them with his tin whistle. All of us were drawn to the music and the entertainment it promised.

One perfectly exquisite, still night, the sailors organised a musical evening. They formed a semicircle and sang. Song after song, thoroughly nautical yarns that went on and on, and finally, after very patriotic renditions of "Rule Britannia" and "God save the Queen", they started to disperse. The travellers, however, had just warmed up. Listening to singing was all very well, but obviously the urge to dance to music was too strong. It was a new experience for me. Of course, I had heard music before, but in the past few years it had always been from a distance. I wasn't prepared for the emotion. Our fellow voyagers danced around, letting themselves swim in the music—diving in, barely coming up for air—taking me by surprise. At first I just watched, feigning nonchalance, but my eyes darted around as I watched the intricate footwork of the ancient steps. Rose's fingers were echoing the measure of the beat on her thigh, and I found my toes keeping tempo with the tune. I looked at Rose. Swaying, her eyes were closed, then her hand reached out to me. I took it. Together we moved into the space cleared for dancing.

We had no choice.

Once our hands touched, there was not a single moment of hesitation as we gave ourselves to the primal pulse of the music. We threw our heads back and we danced. Deliciously beautiful feelings swept through my body as I moved. My cap slipped off my head and was only held on by the ties at my neck. My hair flew loose and I didn't even care. Rose kicked off her soft fabric slippers and then I did too. Rose's shiny, flushed face was alight with joy. Her brilliant blue eyes were glistening, her smile was radiant, and her long dark curls flew around her as she moved. The rhythm was infectious. As it coursed through us, Rose's body magically echoed my exact movements. She looked so alive, I thought, and so exquisitely beautiful. I looked at her in her plain brown linen dress and then down at my own, unable to accept that I must look exactly like her. I shook my head in bewilderment, and Rose grabbed my hand as we twirled around, attempting to follow the steps of the dance.

"Yes, yes, Lily!" Rose said, as if I had asked her a question, "Yes!"

I did feel like I had never felt before, like we belonged, finally, but

I wasn't sure to what. I was aware of people watching us and caught glimpses as we spun around the room.

First Mate Brian Donnelly's look was one of reverent awe.

Sean O'Hennessey turned to his friend, Jimmie, and firmly placed his palm under his chin and shut his gaping mouth for him.

Reverend McGregor's eyes were narrowed, but still he watched.

Two of the crew elbowed each other and smirked.

Rose was not aware of any of this; she was lost in the dance.

~

Later, when the deck had cleared, I stood alongside the railing and stared out at the bottomless blue sea. All I could think about was how free I had felt dancing with Rose, like I had finally let go of something I had been hanging on to. I wiggled my toes and spread them in my soft canvas shoes and took a deep breath. Then I lifted my heavy hair and let the cool breeze caress my neck. I arched my back to stretch as I gathered up my hair and retied the ribbon higher up. I could still feel the energy of the dancing coursing through me. I looked up at the sky—the stars were glittering—then back again at the sea, endless in every direction. I leaned, elbows resting on the painted metal railing, and let the peace of the world seep into me. It was as if I had danced away some of my fears, and everything around me seemed a notch more beautiful.

"Rosie, Rosie, I knew you'd meet me," I heard suddenly from right behind me. The same moment large hands grasped the rail on either side of me. I tensed in fear.

"What are you doing?" I turned around to see Sean O'Hennessey.

His words came thick and fast. "Rosie, you can be my wife. Would you, Rose? We'll work a while and then buy land. We'll have a farm. Would you like that, Rosie-girl?"

I relaxed a little, I knew Sean. I liked his cheerfulness and the roguish grin that seemed in permanent residence on his handsome face. I also knew he had a sense of humour.

"Oh, and what have I done to deserve such a proposal, Mr O'Hennessey?"

"You could give me another kiss, that would surely seal the deal," Sean wiped his hand across his forehead and moved his tousled brown hair out of his eyes and then bent his head towards me, and his surprisingly soft lips gently brushed my cheek.

"There is no deal, and I'm not Ro…" Suddenly his mouth was on mine and his arms left the railing to enclose me tightly, very tightly. I could not move. I did not know what to think. I gasped for air, unsuccessfully, in an effort to explain, but I finally resorted to kicking him in the shin. "Sean, honestly, listen to me. I'm…"

He finally pulled away. He raked his hand through his thick, dark hair again. "Ah, Rosie-girl, I am sorry. It's just that, well, you're the sweetest-looking thing and to think that you might consider… Well, I just got carried away. You will accept my apology?" His usual grin deepened further, and he held out his hand. I took it.

"Now listen, I'm not your Rosie-girl. Got that? I'm…"

Suddenly I heard Rose. "Lily, there you are!" She looked confusedly at Sean and me as she walked across the deck; she did not know what to think either. "Why, Sean O'Hennessey, what do you think you're doing?"

I could tell that Sean O'Hennessey was not a man to be easily embarrassed, but he dropped my hand and looked down at his feet. "Damn it," he mumbled and blushed red. "Rose, there you are," he said sheepishly, kicking the deck with his boot. Rose raised her eyebrows at me, but I waited for Sean to explain himself.

"I was just passing the time of day here with your sister. Your sister who looks exactly like you, I might add. In fact so much like you," he was on a roll now and his demeanour changed as he attempted to clarify the situation, "that I mistook her for you. Yes, that I did, even kissed her, thinking it was you!" He looked from Rose to me and back again, squaring his shoulders.

"He also asked me to marry him!" I interrupted. "Well, marry you, Rose, actually, before he kissed me, I mean you. You know what I mean." Rose and I were both giggling now, enjoying ourselves.

"Well, Sean, maybe you might want to try that again sometime and make more of an effort to get the right girl," Rose carried on. "Fancy that. Whatever were you thinking?"

"I'll tell you what I'm thinking, Rose Quinn." He looked right at her, "I'm thinking that it's not a joking matter. I'm thinking…" Sean was getting wound up; his hands were clenched at his sides.

Rose stopped smiling. We both stared at Sean. He was suddenly very serious.

"Actually, I'm tired of thinking," he said, stepping forward, taking Rose's hand, and tugging her towards him. She lifted her face, her blue eyes shining brighter than the stars above her head, and they kissed. Sean's free arm encircled her and drew her closer to him. Standing so close, I could feel what was going on between them—all my senses fully aware of the lovely sensations invading Rose.

"Rose, we aren't dancing," I managed after a moment.

Their kiss lingered on for another moment, and then Rose slowly turned towards me. She smiled and happiness radiated out of her.

"Ah, but it's a different kind of dance," she murmured, pulling away from Sean, "and one we don't know the steps to."

"Oh, Rosie-girl," Sean shook his head in dismay as Rose took my hand, and we stepped away. "You two parade around with the children all day, but you are women, and every man on this ship knows it."

~

I listened for the Reverend's gentle snoring. He seemed to be asking questions of the inky blackness, and funnily enough, they were eventually answered by Mrs McGregor's soft, even breathing. I climbed in beside Rose into her little bunk. It wasn't much narrower than the bed we shared in Nana Kat's cottage. We wrapped our arms around each other and whispered in the dark. Then we got sleepy and relaxed, and our breathing deepened.

It was instantaneous.

We just knew.

Everything we were thinking at that very moment would pass between us. We could share our thoughts without speaking at all.

Rose's memories from this morning—when she had first kissed Sean O'Hennessey—flooded into me: how she hadn't given him a thought before then, but the day was so beautiful, the sky so clear, and she was curious, and so she kissed him, and she liked it. Rose felt like she was floating. We remembered Nana Kat's stories of all that can be between a man and a woman, and we agreed the stories were true. We held each other tighter as we became more conscious of the thoughts and feelings coursing through us. Then the realisation dawned that we could not continue to cling to each other so tightly.

"No!" I whispered in Rose's ear, awakening at the thought of separation. "No, *ni neart go curle cheile*, LilyRose."

"Yes," Rose whispered back gently, "but not for a while."

I relaxed again in her arms.

Chapter 2

1875~Rakaia, Canterbury, New Zealand

What was he waiting for?

A moment before, Liam McCann had turned the corner and stopped the wagon in the middle of the road. He now sat there looking around him and, for some inexplicable reason, counted the cabbage trees; there were fourteen.

"Fairfield," he said the name of the farm out loud and smiled. He wasn't sure where the name came from, but it had come into his head unbidden and stayed, so he knew it was meant to be.

He slowly drove the wagon off Back Track, smiling at the comical connotations of the name of the dirt track that bordered his acreage. He drove over clumpy tussock and grass towards a slight indentation in the land where he stopped again. The Southern Alps stood on the horizon—distant sentinels—still in their dress whites. Dogs were barking in the far distance and the odd bird twitter, but otherwise, it was quiet. An agile young man, he jumped down from the wagon, paused, then squatted, and reached out to touch the ground. He raked the grass with his hand and then dug into the soil with the tips of his fingers, leaving tiny little furrows, smiling as the earth yielded to him. Then he laid his hand still and flat against the ground as if he were waiting to feel something, a heartbeat maybe. Eventually he stood again, uncurling his tall, lean, muscular body. He brought a handful of soil up with him, inhaling the earthy richness before letting it slide through his fingers and watching it fall back to where it belonged.

Liam looked around, still smiling. For as long as he could remember his dream was to own land. As a boy helping his father on their small holding, he had known without question that he was meant to tend the land. The bounty he could coax from the earth never surprised him, just affirmed his place in the scheme of things.

His was not a dream that could be realised in Ireland, not with four older brothers and the economy the way it was. After reading pamphlets and attending lecture evenings, he chose to emigrate to New Zealand. The newness and the ruggedness of the place seemed to issue him a challenge.

Liam's mother had worried about the wars and the unsettled natives, but Liam assured her he would go directly to the South Island to avoid the turbulence on the North Island. When he first arrived in Christchurch in 1867 he wrote to his parents describing the city and all the accoutrements of civilised life that his mother was so sure he wouldn't find. After several years clearing bush in North Canterbury at a place called Glentui and then working building roads, he had still neglected to give his mother exact descriptions of the conditions of the camps he lived in. But he worked hard and was eventually able to save enough money to buy land and pursue his dream.

The Canterbury Plains where Liam finally chose to settle were true to their name—flat plains, still mostly virgin soils that caught his farmer's eye. At one stage, the land had been divided into large sheep runs that ran from the Rakaia River to the Ashburton River, the native scrub burnt to make way for pasture. It had pleased and delighted him to buy the land, covered with clumps of grass called tussock and dotted with tropical-looking cabbage trees.

Liam looked at the day moon and then the wagon loaded with supplies. Before nightfall, he had fashioned a shelter of sorts—a large piece of canvas, tied and staked to the side of the dray and the ground. He organised a fire with the wood he'd brought and watered the horses and the cow from the oak barrel on the back of the wagon. From now on he'd be going to the foothills for firewood and down to the river for water. As soon as he built a house and a few sheds, he could collect the rain water off the roof.

Sleep was elusive. Liam lay on his stomach with one arm bent under his head and his other hand flat on the bare ground. He breathed in again the earthy scent of the land. His mind raced, organising priorities, concentrating on the practical things he needed to do. His hand dug like a small cultivator, furrowing and then smoothing, furrowing and then smoothing. He liked the feel of the soil under his nails. He imagined the house, his home, and building it with no one else telling him what to do or where to do it. He turned over and wriggled, moving out from under his canvas tent to look up at the stars. The sense of freedom was almost as overwhelming as the sense of promise. This land of his made him feel stronger, more sure of himself.

Liam woke up with the sun and a restless energy, anxious to start the day. He took deep breaths of the cool morning air, remembering how his mother had held him close and murmured in his ear, "Take care, Liam. Be happy." The memory made him smile. He must write to his parents and tell them of his good fortune.

Liam started building boundary fences first, driving to the bush line in the foothills to fell timber and hand sawing it into suitable posts. It was slow laborious work. When he needed a change of pace, he would work on his house, using timber purchased from the sawmill in Ashburton. When he tired of sawing and pounding in nails, he worked on clearing the land he planned to cultivate for crops. He would dig, pulling out big clumps of grassy tussock, their roots too moist and embedded in the soil to burn.

Every week or so Liam would ride his horse Smoke to Rakaia for supplies, buying enough meat and flour to see him through. On each trip he checked to see if the new plough he'd ordered had arrived. He was anxious to start cultivating his land, and spring was well on its way. On one trip, after he had been disappointed again, he paused outside the new railway warehouse.

"She's a beaut." A man yanked on a Border Collie's leash, turning its head. "She'll do you right," the man added in his effort to make a sale. Good sheep dogs, well, any sheep dogs were hard to come by. Liam hadn't the need for a dog just yet, but this one looked up at him with a sort of 'rescue me' look, still maintaining a sense of pride. Liam recognised the look and bought the dog. She was called Pearl. After he patted her and bought a few bones for her at the butcher's shop, he removed the leather strap and the dog trotted along behind Smoke all the way back to Fairfield.

Pearl was good company, if a person didn't mind one-sided conversations about the changing state of the weather or the straightness of the latest fence line. And even though he was certain that Pearl did not understand his exact words, he had the suspicion that the dog did indeed actually know how he was feeling.

As the days went on, he felt an underlying sense of unease. It was very vague at first, but grew as the days passed. Liam was alone, very alone. He had grown used to the easy camaraderie of the work gangs. Well, it wasn't always easy camaraderie, but even when there had been trouble it had been interesting. And, of course, there had been his mate Frank. Good ol' Frank whose life's mission seemed to be to keep those around him smiling. Liam realised he missed people and the only solution was to make an effort to meet the neighbours, the English neighbours. It seemed that Liam McCann was the only Irishman around.

~

The next Sunday, after his usual wash in the cold river, Liam put on his only clean shirt with his everyday moleskin trousers and his wool waistcoat. Instead of riding home, he rode up the long drive to Avonlea. Avonlea was the home of George and Elisabeth Lichfield. George Lichfield had worked as an engineer and had overseen the building of the Lyttelton Tunnel between Christchurch and the Port of Lyttelton. Avonlea had been gifted to him by the Crown in lieu of payment.

An older well-dressed man was just coming out of the stables; he was wiry looking with hair greying at the temples and kind eyes.

"Hello, there, what can I do for you?" He seemed friendly enough.

"Hello, I am a neighbour. Liam McCann, sir." Liam dismounted and stretched out a hand.

"A neighbour, well, we haven't as yet had much experience with neighbours." George Lichfield prided himself on his ability to judge people, and he liked the look of this man. He was solid and strong, with honest green eyes and an engaging smile. "I'm George Lichfield. Please call me George." They shook hands.

"Just over at the corner of Back Track are you?"

"Yes, sir."

"I saw a wagon parked up there just the other day. What are you going to use the boulders for?"

"I'm using them for the foundations of my house."

"Should work, I guess," George thought for a moment. "You might have some subsidence though, after fifty or sixty years."

Liam smiled, "I guess I'll worry about that then."

"Come on, come in! We'll have a drink."

Liam tied Smoke to the railing in front of the stables. George led Liam through the young garden to the terrace in front of the large wooden house. They went in through French doors, with pane after pane of bright shiny glass, to a billiards room. Liam blinked; the huge billiards table looked surreal, nonchalantly sitting there, just as if it were in a pool hall in the middle of Dublin.

"How on earth?" Liam tried to be casual and not think about how he was living under a tarp in the middle of an unfenced paddock. The very idea of being able to play a game of billiards was almost beyond his comprehension.

"Have you met Richard Elworthy? They're up river, on the crest there. Call the place Worthington."

"Just heard of them."

"Well, he's in shipping. He'll bring anything out, if you pay him enough. He brought me this table. I'll introduce you to him. You play?"

"Haven't in a while." Liam smiled as George handed him the cue stick.

George knew quite a bit about farming in New Zealand; Liam figured that out right away. He'd also had some experience with raising sheep. Although he hired men to do the work, he knew where to buy, when to sell, and what to do with them in between.

"Longbeach is where you want to go, other side of Ashburton, towards the sea. Fellow by the name of John Grigg, best sheep breeder around." George hit a tricky shot and missed. "Tell him I sent you." Liam liked the sound of that, but had to get some more fencing done before he could purchase livestock.

"Do you have a family?"

"Of sorts." George angled in a difficult shot. "I have a wife, Elisabeth." He looked up at Liam as if he were deciding how much to tell him, "and Elisabeth has a son."

"Oh," Liam was not sure how to respond. He reached for his whisky and had a sip. George knew his comment was vague and carried on hurriedly, "Elisabeth is in Christchurch, staying at Warners Hotel, shopping mostly and hiring more help, I believe. She says she is visiting friends, but really, she has very few. She loves to shop, however. I think that might be the only thing that makes her happy." Liam looked down at the whisky in his glass.

"Don't worry, my man, we came to an agreement some time ago. We actually get along quite famously."

"What about the boy?" Liam wanted to change the subject, and that was the first thing that came to him.

"Oh, well, he is a big part of our unspoken agreement, but that is another story. I might tell you about it sometime." George sipped his whisky and then thought he'd tell Liam the basic details. "His name is Henry. I've sent him to school in Christchurch, mostly because I don't know what else to do with him." George abruptly changed the subject. "Tell me about yourself. How did you come to be at the end of Back Track?"

"Fairfield, sir, I call it Fairfield."

"And so you do. Please call me George."

"Well, George, I came from County Armagh in Ireland, a little place called Richhill...my family being Ulster Scots. I got here '67. Didn't have much to call my own. I've been working clearing bush, building roads. That type of thing. Got enough together a few years ago to put a deposit down on the land and just lately felt like I have enough behind me to start farming it."

"Good, that's good! Ambitious, ambitious and hardworking. New Zealand would suit you just fine, aye?"

"Yes, sir...George. Yes, it does! Suits me just fine." The men polished off what remained of their drinks.

~

Liam McCann's life settled into a satisfactory routine. He worked from dawn until dusk six days a week, learning to get by with Pearl for company. He worked on building his home, clearing land for his crops, and fencing paddocks for his stock.

On Sundays he would meet up with George Lichfield. George's wife Elisabeth was quite charmed by the handsome young neighbour and his friendly demeanour. Sunday afternoons would be spent in their sitting room making polite conversation. Sally, the young English housemaid, served them Madeira cake and wine and then later tea and small savoury pies. However, Elisabeth soon realised that her feminine charms had little or no impact on Liam. This disheartened her considerably. Even though he wasn't English and had no title, still he was a neighbouring landowner and had a gentleman's manners. She deemed him to be exceptionally handsome and had felt a mild flirtation would have done nicely. But George and Liam's conversations would invariably turn to the intricacies of clearing the land for successful farming, the particulars of profitable sheep farming, or the vagaries of the climate. So it was by mutual agreement that the men were left to their own devices, which consisted of the billiards room and the whisky bottle, and this suited them just fine.

"George, I have a favour to ask you." Liam sunk the eight ball, "I'm going to Christchurch for a few days and wondered if you could spare someone for a couple hours to check on my stock, milk the cow, and give the dog a run?" Then he added, "I'll pay of course."

"Sure, Liam! Oh, don't worry about payment. I'll do it myself; it will be a nice change of pace, riding over to your place."

Liam was taken aback, but smiled. "You sure you could milk a cow?"

"Oh, you'd be surprised what I could do," George chuckled good-naturedly. "Might have a few things you could do for me in town, actually. Would you mind? Damn!" George swore as the cue ball gently followed in the two balls preceding it.

"Of course not." Liam felt a mixture of comfort and satisfaction, a good feeling that reminded him of home—and family.

Later, Sally watched Liam saddling his horse as she took washing off the line. She couldn't help being intrigued by the way his large hands moved so deftly over the buckles. She heard him murmuring encouraging words to the animal. She liked the gentle tone of his voice and for just a moment imagined him speaking to her like that. She shook her head and reached up high to grab a clothes peg. No, she didn't want some sod farmer, however fine-looking. She watched again as he gracefully mounted his horse. There was something about the way he moved—his masculinity so assured—that reminded her that Henry was hardly more than a boy. She shook her head again as she shoved the sheet into the wicker basket. No, she knew all about struggling with the land and was sick and tired of it. No, she'd already set her sights and was making very good progress with her plans, thank you very much.

Chapter 3

Lily

The conditions aboard our ship the Crusader were generally adequate, but still began to take their toll. Some of the babies succumbed to dysentery, and it soon spread to the younger children. Several died. One small girl named Sarah Jane, who had clung to my skirts when we walked on the deck and listened to Rose's stories with the most intense concentration, had been there one day with the rest of us and the next day was a small bundle being gently lowered into the cold sea. Reverend McGregor said a few words and referred to 'God's will', but I couldn't find any comfort—which I thought was odd, because when Nana Kat died, I had found solace in God and felt he was merciful.

Mrs McGregor was the first adult to weaken. Apparently she'd made it through several of her harder pregnancies by sipping sugar water, but their private supply of sugar dwindled rapidly. Mint and chamomile were Nana Kat's answers for unsettled stomachs, so Rose and I made her tea with some of our dried herbs, which seemed to help. The ship's doctor, a kindly man by the name of Dr Langford, was of no practical help.

After we had been sailing a good two months, the ship began to take on water, as much as two and half inches an hour, although the pumps seemed to keep on top of things. The Reverend told us that Captain Renault wanted to put in to one of the ports on the South American coast, but Dr Langford advised against it because yellow fever was rife in those places, and he did not want to take the risk of an epidemic on board. So Captain Renault continued on. By the time the ship neared the Cape of Good Hope, the leak appeared to have stopped and it was decided that there was no need to put into port. But after the ship passed the Cape, and it was too late to head back, the leak got worse again. Rose and I were not afraid, but we were anxious.

The craving for earth under my feet got a lot stronger. I tried not to let the power of the sea bother me, but we were such a tiny little dot in the hugeness of it all. I trusted the Crusader to keep us afloat, see us safe.

Owing to the amount of work the pumps had to do, the next situation to be dealt with was a shortage of pump leather. One day an American ship was sighted, and the Crusader signalled her asking for some leather. But not the slightest notice was taken of the flags, and so we had to use whatever could be found. Some of the first class passengers had leather bags that were the right thickness. They were unceremoniously cut into pieces for the good of everyone on board.

Eventually a bucket brigade was formed among the emigrants to supplement the pumps.

"You girls go back to your quarters; the menfolk will handle this," First Mate Brian Donnelly said to us as he organised another shift of passengers to man the buckets.

"Oh no, we can help," I asserted. "We are strong, and we love the fresh air." I stepped up to the line of men and took my place. The wind was cool on my face, with the sun peeking through the clouds.

"Well, don't strain yourselves, and have a break when you feel tired," Mr Donnelly replied from beside me in the line. Rose ended up further down between Reverend McGregor and Sean O'Hennessey, with whom she was engaged in quiet conversation. Rose had eventually thanked Sean for his offer of marriage, but explained that we were going to focus on getting to New Zealand and settling there before she made any decision about her future. But I didn't think Sean had given up hope.

"So when you get to New Zealand, do you just turn around and sail right back?" I asked the first mate, as he handed me a full bucket.

He paused and seemed to look me over; his eyes smiled when he did. "Well, first we organise provisions and then we fill the ship's hold with freight to take back to England. It takes a few weeks usually."

"What will you take back this time?"

"Oh, I don't know for sure yet, usually some timber and quite a bit of kauri gum."

"What's kauri gum?"

"Well, it's the sap from New Zealand kauri trees. They tap holes in the sides of the trees, and the sap collects in big lumps where it bleeds from the trunks. They knock off a lump and process it, and then it gets sent to England to make all sorts of things."

"Like what?"

"Oh, they make it into varnish for wood and linoleum. I'm not sure what else, really. I'll ask the captain and let you know," he said earnestly, as if for some reason it seemed important to him to satisfy my curiosity.

I summoned up the courage and asked the question that had been on all our minds for weeks. "Do you think we'll sink?" I handed him an empty bucket on its return trip. Mr Donnelly bent his head to answer me.

"Ah, no, I don't," he smiled gently with that twinkle in his eye, and I smiled back. "It's an iron hull, and strange that she'd spring a leak to begin with, but it's not getting any worse for all that. We'll get to Lyttelton in a matter of weeks, I would think."

"Oh." I took a deep breath, relieved. I imagined my feet on dry land again. We passed the buckets in silence for a while.

"Lily?" Mr Donnelly's voice was kind. "What are you going to do when you get to New Zealand? Do you have plans?"

"Won't need any plans!" A rough-looking man by the name of Seamus interrupted. "There's a shortage of womenfolk there. She'll be able to take her pick, find a husband straightaway, have young'uns. That's what any new country needs. Far too many single men." I turned and edged closer to Mr Donnelly, flustered.

"I was talking to the lady here," Mr Donnelly said sternly. "If we wanted your opinion we would have asked for it." He took a long hard look at the balding, pot-bellied man who had interrupted us. I didn't think the man could possibly be as stupid as he looked. But he was bored—bored and itching for a fight, I could tell.

"Well, that's too bad, because I'm in a mind to give it. A girl looking like that," he leered at me, "should get herself married for her own good."

I stepped up. "For your information, Mr..." I had no idea how to address him. "For your information, my sister and I have a job, and we have plans, and we will get married when we feel like it and not before. And furthermore..." I said 'furthermore' very loudly, "It is absolutely none of your concern." I was annoyed that his comments made me doubt our plans. And he smelled.

"You heard the lady!" Mr Donnelly joined me in looking severely at Seamus.

"Won't be a lady for long," he responded. Well, Seamus was

really itching for a fight to say that.

"Why you…" Before I knew what was happening, Mr Donnelly had swung, but Seamus was ready and surprisingly agile, considering his physique. He danced out of range as Mr Donnelly pulled up his sleeves.

"How dare you so blatantly insult Lily…a woman," he quickly added, then apologised to me with his eyes as if he didn't want it to be personal. Suddenly Rose grabbed my hand and pulled me away from the men.

"Lily, come away."

"Girls! Back down to our quarters," Reverend McGregor called sternly from behind us.

But we were not about to miss any of the excitement. The men on deck had quickly formed a circle around Seamus and the first mate. The tension was quickly replaced with a carnival atmosphere as the entertainment value of the fight was recognised and bets were taken. We did move away from the Reverend towards the main hatch, so it would look to the others like we were following orders.

I stood on tiptoes in an effort to see the action. It seemed that the fight was pretty even, and the crowd was equally divided between the sailors who were cheering for their first mate and the single emigrant men who didn't mind if old Seamus showed him a thing or two. Further back, there was a group of more respectable men, including the Reverend and Captain Renault, who were endeavouring not to show too much interest but who would call a halt to the proceedings if things got out of hand. It reassured me to see a straggly line of people still dumping buckets of seawater overboard, when they appeared at the after hatch.

"Rose, I didn't ever imagine anything like this, did you?"

"Ah, men fighting over your honour? I have, I have."

"You have what?"

"Imagined it. I have Lily," she stated quite firmly, though she must have seen, by the look on my face, that I was worried.

"We'll be fine. We'll live with the McGregors and look after the children, and if any man wants to come calling…" Rose paused as Mr Donnelly staggered from a well-placed blow and almost fell, "they'll have to ask our permission. And if we say no, well, I'm sure the Reverend will send them on their way."

"Who will he send on their way?" Mick had sidled up to us, also trying to avoid his father's attention.

"All Lily's admirers. From the looks of it, she's going to have quite a few."

"Ah, and you, Rose, you and your proposals of marriage, goodness me!" I laughed nervously and then winced as I saw Mr Donnelly's fist connect with his opponent's chin, causing the man to slump to the deck.

"I haven't had a proposal yet, if you recall?" Rose said loudly as she looked sideways at Sean O'Hennessey who was within hearing distance. He glared back at her.

I shook my head, but I was smiling. "Ah, Rose, do be careful. You'll start another fight."

~

"I keep thinking we must be over the worst." Rose handed me her hanky.

"And it's February. Fancy it being this hot in February!" I wiped the sweat off my forehead. I untied my bonnet and took it off, seeking relief.

"You'll get freckles." Rose reminded me with her bonnet still firmly in place. We were tucked into a large dray that was slowly making its way through the steep tussock-covered hills from Lyttelton, where the Crusader had docked, to Christchurch. We were dusty, thirsty, and tired. Our previously white cotton pinafores had turned a browny grey, almost the same colour as the linen dresses we wore underneath them. We were so tired of washing ourselves and our clothes in seawater.

When we first got off the ship in Lyttelton, I kept losing my balance. I couldn't seem to take the firmness of the earth for granted. This trip wasn't helping. I wiped the hanky over Mrs McGregor's brow. She was not looking well, not well at all, I thought, as we rounded a bend.

"You'll stay on, then?" Reverend McGregor asked Rose.

"I'm so glad you two are here to help us," Mrs McGregor said quietly, squeezing my hand.

"Well, yes, we thought we would. We are grateful not to be on our own." My eyes met Rose's as she spoke.

"Ah, yes. Well, good," Reverend McGregor answered. "We'll get some lodgings for the night. I'll leave you two in charge while we set about finding the whereabouts of our permanent accommodation."

"Oh, look," exclaimed Mick, "Look... That must be Christchurch."

I squinted at the plains stretching before us and the buildings in the distance. I looked at Rose. *It will be all right.* We smiled at each other tentatively.

"What? Oh, you're doing that again." Mick looked at me carefully and then at my sister. Sometimes he seemed to be aware of our silent communication, but how could he be?

"Hmm, so that's Christchurch," Rose murmured.

I could see a collection of buildings on the plains not far from the sea. They were divided into blocks by wide straight roads. A river wound through the rows of buildings as if in defiance of the order the roads were trying to impose. Large patches of swamp land and stands of messy-looking forest stood just at the edges of the civilisation. This created a tension—some of the structures on the edges looked so insubstantial and tired that it seemed like any minute they might revert to swamp once more, the effort of being civilised too much for them. I saw that the outlying areas looked to be mostly cultivated and made a comfortable patchwork, which held promise. All in all, it did not look particularly inviting, but the voyage was over and the sun was shining. *It will be all right.* I met Rose's gaze, and Mick, looking on, grinned and nodded, giving me the strangest feeling that he knew exactly what we were thinking.

We drove into the town, which was much busier than it had looked from a distance. We unloaded the older children from the rented dray for a walk, while Reverend and Mrs McGregor and the girls carried on looking for accommodation. I was hesitant to leave our small sea chest on the wagon. It was full of precious books and objects that had belonged to our mother and our grandmother, some we had only discovered after Nana Kat died. I watched them drive away.

"Rose, wait a minute." As I turned, I heard a tearing noise and was momentarily snagged by my pocket on a hitching post.

"I smell... I smell..." Rose called out, not looking back.

A man seeing to his horse nearby smiled at me as I rustled free. "The bakery is just around the corner," he said as if to console me.

I took a deep breath and nearly swooned at the smell of freshly baked bread, "Aye, I'll follow my nose."

I found Rose at the bakery with the three McGregor boys. The bread tasted so… Well, words like tasty or scrumptious didn't begin to describe it.

As it turned out, the Reverend had a great deal of trouble finding lodgings for us. We all wished we had taken advantage of the immigration barracks at Lyttelton for one more night. But finally he found a boarding house on Fitzgerald Avenue with rooms to let.

We had the luxury of baths with hot fresh water, which felt almost more delicious than the bread had tasted. Eventually, we had everyone settled in their beds in the boarding house.

I heard Reverend McGregor come to our room. He paused over his young daughters and then opened the window. It was still hot. Rose and I were drifting but not quite asleep, I moved my arm from around her and she pulled it back. Our thoughts joined, effortlessly entwining as we thought about making it this far on our journey. Relief seeped through us both. For a moment we sensed Reverend McGregor watching us, but we felt safe and we were oh so very tired.

Goodnight, LilyRose… Goodnight.

~

Late summer turned into crisp autumn as we adjusted to life in the colony. To be truthful, it was easier for us now. We worried less.

We lived with the McGregors in a big white wooden house on Armagh Street, not far from the Botanic Gardens. We had to share a room with the McGregor's two little girls, but we got used to tiptoeing our way to bed at night. We earned our keep running the household and taking care of the children. We kept very busy cooking, cleaning, doing laundry, and watching the children while we worked.

One thing that did concern me, though, was my cough. I'm sure it was from all the wood and coal smoke in the air. Rose was worried too. She kept telling me I should rest.

"Lily, you have a nap this afternoon. I'll take children to the park." Rose was already settling the two girls, Jessie and Molly, into the large pram.

"But you can't take the new baby; it's far too soon to take him out."

"He'll be fine, better in the fresh air than here with you and Mrs McGregor coughing on him."

Leticia McGregor, true to her nature, had delivered a fine baby boy with minimal fuss not a month before. We all assumed that this would naturally lead to her recovery and she would return to the tasks of everyday life. But this did not appear to be the case.

"Oh, Rose, you'll have your hands full."

"Mick will help me.

Chapter 4

The day was bright. Liam was still not used to the sun here. In New Zealand, no matter how frosty the morning, the sun always tried to shine, as if it were anxious to put in an appearance.

Liam was wandering through the Christchurch Botanic Gardens, catching glimpses of red and gold mixed in with all the green. The gardens had been started a couple years before, and the trees and shrubs were already getting a bit of size. He liked the feel of the gardens and how they gave the city a civilised air. It gave him hope that eventually he might be able to tame the land around his home in much the same way. Liam noticed two young boys eyeing a sapling, as if it might possibly be worth climbing up.

"Jamie and Johnny McGregor, get yourselves back here this instant and help me." Liam heard a sweet Irish voice speaking quite loudly.

Around the bend in the path came a beautiful girl with a head of unruly brown curls, pushing an enormous perambulator with two, or maybe even three, crying children on board.

"Here, take Jessie and Molly, please. Hold their hands and don't let go. I'll quieten down the baby." The girl removed two snivelling toddlers from the pram, who blinked and looked rather surprised that they were suddenly set free.

"Now, don't you dare get out of my sight." The girl moved a loose strand of hair to behind her ear. She picked up the crying baby and gently soothed it by jiggling the bundle on her shoulder and humming. Only then she noticed Liam standing by the young oak tree. Liam smiled and the girl smiled back, a beautiful sparkling grin that seemed to Liam to be a language of its own.

"Hello," she said quietly, while her eyes looked at him boldly, as if she couldn't help sizing him up.

"Good day, my name is Liam, Liam McCann." He extended his hand. The girl shifted the baby on her shoulder to reach for him. He took her hand and looked into her eyes. The attraction was instantaneous and undeniable. Liam felt a wave of movement in his body towards her as they stared into each other's eyes—hers so warm, so welcoming, and so bravely curious.

"Ah," she murmured through her delighted smile.

He would speak, he would say something articulate and…witty. He would ask a question of this beautiful girl, he thought, as he revelled in the feeling of his hand in hers.

Just then they heard one of the boys yelling. "Help, quick, my sister is drowning." The girl's eyes filled with panic.

"I'll go, I'll go." Liam took off towards the screaming. It only took him a moment to fetch the frightened Jessie from the shallow water where she'd landed after tumbling down the bank into the slow moving water of the Avon River.

"It takes two of us, this job. It's impossible to do alone," the girl complained. She deposited the now quiet baby back into the pram, unclasping a tiny hand from a strand of her hair before she stood up. She scooped up the two toddlers and also placed them in the pram, the wet one snuffling and the dry one looking on curiously. "I've got to get them back before Jessie takes cold." The girl pushed with all her strength on the pram, but it didn't go far on the thick gravel path. She wiped her sleeve over her forehead.

"Here, let me." Liam took the handle, angled the pram towards him, then started off down the path. Smiling, he looked over his shoulder, "C'mon, you have to show me where to go." The girl ran to catch up, pulling the two boys behind her.

"I work for the McGregors. They live down Armagh Street, number thirty-two," the girl managed breathlessly behind him. They made their way out of the park and turned down Rolleston Avenue. The tiny baby had miraculously fallen back to sleep. Jessie sniffled, intrigued at the scenery passing by at great speed.

"Excuse me, sir! I'm having trouble keeping up." Liam slowed and turned to see the girl carrying one of the small boys and the other running beside her. She looked flushed and slightly sweaty and very beautiful. Loose wisps of her dark hair curled around her face. She put the child down, wiped her arm across her forehead, and stretched out her hands for the boys.

"Oh, sorry, I didn't mean to… Ah, well, I guess I was thinking about her catching cold." Liam gestured to the pram and started off again at a slower pace.

The girl caught up with him and Liam watched her, breathless beside him, towing the two boys. So many questions coursed through his mind that he couldn't pinpoint the one that was important enough to ask.

Then she smiled at him watching her, knowing she had his avid attention, and all the questions he'd been thinking of seemed meaningless, trivial in the face of her smile.

"Here we are, then." Liam paused at number thirty-two while the girl opened the gate.

"Yes, I must thank you for your…" The front door opened and a boy of about thirteen came bounding out.

"Why didn't you wait for me? We were worried when we found out you'd left without me, and the doctor is coming to see Mother. She's worse again." His words tumbled out, anxious and concerned.

Two men came up the sidewalk and Jamie headed towards one calling out, "Father, she fell in the river, Jessie fell in the river." The man hurried towards Liam and the girl, who was busy pulling the baby out of the pram.

She nestled it into her shoulder and murmured, "There, there now," as if there were a possibility that the baby might stay asleep with all the commotion going on around them.

"What is going on here?" the stern-looking man asked Liam.

"Well, sir, I…"

"He saved Jessie from drowning in the river, Reverend. We owe him our thanks," the girl said over her shoulder as she went through the door into the house with the baby in one arm, towing the wet Jessie with her other hand.

"Ah, well, thank you then, Mr…?"

"McCann, sir, Liam McCann." Liam held out his hand.

"Sebastian McGregor, I owe you…" Just then the front door flew open and the girl yelled out, "Come quick, oh, do come quickly! It's Mrs McGregor."

"Excuse us," Sebastian McGregor said to Liam as he started up the path after the doctor.

Liam stood a moment looking at the girl still holding open the door for the two men. She looked so much paler than she had in the park, quite different really. She smiled at the older boy who was patiently shepherding the other toddler up the path, but did not glance his way.

Liam hurried away, suddenly aware he was likely to be late meeting Frank.

~

Frank McManaway was in good form and anxious to hear how Liam's farm was progressing. Frank and Liam had become firm friends on the ship on their way out. They had stuck together for the past few years as they toiled with picks, shovels, and wheelbarrows and endured rain, snow, and gales clearing bush and building roads. In the last year or so before Liam left to farm, they had both been working their own drays and bullocks, hauling shingle from nearby riverbeds for the roads and occasionally fetching timber from the nearest sawmill for the bridges.

"You can't tell me you miss the camps?" Frank's dark brown eyes sparkled with curiosity as he questioned Liam.

"Couldn't hardly, been sleeping in the same tent till just the other day. Mind you, the air's much fresher now, without you smelling it up." Frank started to question Liam's statement, but then grinned as he realised it was probably true.

"What about the cooking? You couldn't possibly miss that. Remember Shorty? He's still at it, still making the lumpiest porridge. Remember the Scot who tried to get up early and beat him to the mess tent, he was so tired of lumps in his oats?"

Liam smiled, "Ah, I wouldn't half mind having Shorty around to cook my oats."

Frank looked sideways at his friend, "Well, I'm sure you could do much better than Shorty, if someone to cook your oats is what you're after."

"And you, Frank, when are you going to get yourself a piece of land?" Liam changed the subject, although noticing the way Frank was watching the barmaid, he didn't rate his chances.

"Oh, soon enough, I reckon. Looked at some land up north. Just didn't appeal to me; it seemed so far away from everything." His eyes continued to follow the barmaid. "Thinking I might just find someone who likes the idea of being a farmer's wife first." He looked at Liam, "Just so I don't end up with a hankering for Shorty." They chuckled and sipped their beers.

Frank's eyes were still on the barmaid as she rounded the end of the long bar and came towards them with their meals. "You met anyone interesting yet? Any single women around Rakaia?"

Liam waited while the girl put down their dinners, "There you are, sir, one mutton and one pork. Can I get you another beer?"

"Yes, that would be nice," Frank caught the barmaid's eye and held it a moment, "Umm, would you care for a stroll in the gardens after you finish work?"

"Hmm... It would be too dark." The girl eyed him up; Frank was grinning at her mischievously. But liking what she saw, she said, "How about tomorrow, before dinnertime?"

Frank looked at Liam with his eyebrows raised, then nodded.

"All right if I bring a friend along?" The girl looked meaningfully at Liam.

"Fine." Frank kept grinning, his dark eyes twinkling.

"About five, then, at the front gate," the girl said over her shoulder as she sashayed back towards the bar.

Liam started to speak, but Frank interrupted.

"Guess I've organised our entertainment?" He was still grinning.

"Since when did you start...?" Again, Liam was interrupted.

"Made a decision. New country, new rules! For all you know the girl you meet tomorrow night could end up your wife, the girl of your dreams. Just wait. You ask her where she comes from, what she did before she came here, nine times out of ten the lass will turn out to be a farmer's daughter from just outside of Dublin."

"Galway, actually. I'm a farmer's daughter from just outside of Galway... Kate Mahoney." She set down two beers, and with the tray in one hand behind her back she extended the other to Frank first and then Liam, "Lovely to make your acquaintance, gentlemen."

"See," said Frank, with an amused grin, "what did I tell you?"

~

They were there at the dot of five. Kate had undergone a rather startling transformation from simple barmaid in a plain brown wool dress and starched white apron and cap, to fashionable lady. She was wearing a ruby coloured velvet dress, with a large bustle and, what looked like, yards of fabric cascading down the back and trailing behind. She had a matching bonnet tied with ribbons under her chin. Her friend Bridget's outfit was very similar, only in a yellow colour that reminded Liam of the flowers on the kowhai trees that bloomed in early spring. After making introductions, Kate somewhat hastily took

Liam's arm, her other arm still entwined with Bridget's. Bridget reached out for Frank, and soon, they were walking down the lane four abreast.

"You look…" Liam searched for the right words.

"Yes?" Kate was happy to wait for the compliment she felt sure was coming.

"You look very nice, and very different than you did yesterday."

"Why, thank you! Lately it does seem to be one extreme or the other."

"Do you mind it, working at the hotel?"

"Well, your friend," she turned her head towards Frank, "Frank was right. It is certainly not something I would have done in Ireland." Kate turned back and looked closely at Liam. She liked his eyes, so honest and clear. She also liked how his broad shoulders looked in his white linen shirt.

"So why do you do it, then?"

Kate smiled and nudged her friend, "You answer that, Bridget."

"Well, Pete looks after us, and it's better than cleaning out some uppity Englishwoman's chamber pots. That's why." Bridget wrinkled up her nose and then giggled. "And there is another very good reason," she said as she nudged Kate.

Kate laughed too and said, "Yes, there is. We go out walking with the likes of you."

"Oh, the likes of us?" Frank interjected with a question in his voice.

"Yes, the likes of you." Kate turned to look at Liam while she spoke, "Two very fine gentlemen."

Just then they passed the bend in the river where Liam had fished out the dripping toddler. His thoughts turned to the lass with the wild brown curls and how her smile had spoken to him. His mind wandered, reliving the entire afternoon, and wishing he'd made more of an effort to talk to the girl on the way back to her home.

"Liam, you aren't listening." Kate tugged on his arm.

"Oh, sorry, I was just… Well, thinking I guess," he added hastily.

"About what?" Bridget batted her eyelashes and smiled coquettishly.

"A girl I met."

Bridget stopped her manoeuvre midbat, smile frozen in place, "Oh."

"Where did you meet her?" Kate rose to the challenge.

"Right there." He pointed to the tree. "Yesterday, just before noon, but I didn't get her name."

Chapter 5

Leticia McGregor died. The sea voyage, her sixth delivery, and finally a nasty influenza which settled in her lungs all conspired against her. The service was a small affair with the family and some of Reverend McGregor's new acquaintances, who came to show their respect. The three older boys were very distressed at the loss of their mother. That they had already grown accustomed to the lack of her presence in their everyday lives only slightly tempered their distress. An underlying sense of grief now accompanied the daily routine of the McGregor household. Rose worried about Lily, who seemed to suffer from the same cough that wore down Mrs McGregor. Finally, the doctor advised them that Lily's best chance for recovery was to leave the smoky city and try the fresh air of the countryside.

~

Elisabeth Lichfield was reasonably satisfied. As it turned out, she'd married well. At the time, she had thought George was the best she could do, considering her predicament. He had very little money, then, but was educated. She was well aware that she'd taken a risk, but in spite of everything, here she was, the mistress of Avonlea. She wasn't in her beloved England; she'd had to compromise a little. But Avonlea was grand, and it was beautiful. She had servants: maids to take out the chamber pots, a gardener to tend to the grounds, a man in the stables, a cook in the kitchen. She thought back to her life in England. If only they could see her now—Dizzy Lizzy Jamison—mistress of an estate. Oh, they'd never believe it.

But Elisabeth Lichfield wasn't really enjoying herself, and she should have been, damn it. Here she was at Warners Hotel, right in the centre of Christchurch, the closest thing to a city on this entire godforsaken island. She had money to spend—well, her husband George's money—but he didn't seem to mind at all what she did with it, and...

"Ma'am, them girls are here, the ones you were wanting to talk to." Sally stuck her head into the large hotel sitting room that Elisabeth Lichfield had reserved for the interviews.

"Sally, it's 'those girls' are here. But, anyway, there should only be one; there is only one position. Send her in."

The door opened all the way and in walked two young women, two quite beautiful women, Elisabeth thought. The first thing she noticed was their unusual hair. Masses of dark curls, kept barely under control in knots at the base of their necks. The colour reminded Elisabeth of the mahogany table she had just purchased for the entryway at Avonlea. The girls had the loveliest skin, creamy and translucent. Their cheeks were rosy pink. They moved with grace and with elegance, as if they'd been trained in classical ballet. They did not look like common servants. Elisabeth was aware of the difference; she'd spent most of her life studying just that difference—so she could get it right.

"Hello, ma'am, my name is Rose, and this is my sister Lily."

"It is quite obvious you are sisters."

"Yes, well, we do look exactly alike," Rose smiled, trying to maintain a friendly air to combat the woman's frosty one.

"I have only one position as a general housemaid."

Lily looked at Rose questioningly; Rose was biting her lip, thinking.

"My sister Lily would love to take it."

"If I think she is suitable, you mean."

"Yes, ma'am, if you think she is suitable."

~

Lily had a coughing fit after she and Rose dodged a Hansom cab speeding down Colombo Street on the way back to the McGregor's. Rose stopped to pat Lily on the back.

"Your cough sounds worse to me, Lily, but this will work out. When you get out of the city, your lungs will clear in the fresh air. I'll stay here and help the Reverend until he finds someone else or marries again. I wouldn't be surprised if he found an available widow very soon."

"I don't like the idea of you alone in the city." Lily's voice was raspy and she started coughing again. "*Ni neart go curle cheile*," Lily spoke their informal motto between coughs.

"Hah, who is ever alone at the McGregors? Oh, Lily, I don't want to separate either, but we are going to have to eventually, or do you suppose we can find two brothers to marry us and we can all live together?" Rose teased.

"Do you think Mrs Lichfield will be all right to work for?" Lily's voice sounded normal again. "She seems as though she could be really bossy and picky, don't you think? It will be a lot different from helping the McGregors."

Rose told Lily to breathe deep, find her peace, and stop her fretting, but Lily could tell Rose was just as worried as she was.

~

Lily set off the next day, travelling with Mrs Lichfield by train from Christchurch to Rakaia where Ronny, George's stable hand, met them with the buggy for the trip out to Avonlea. The homestead was the largest home Lily had seen in New Zealand. The long sweeping drive reminded her of the large estates that dotted the English countryside. Not that she had ever visited any of them, but when she and Rose had travelled through England on their way to London, she had looked up the long avenues and imagined the splendour and luxury to be found inside. Here there was no lush foliage for homes to hide behind. Everything had a windswept, barren look, although she could make out small oaks, rhododendrons, and even a struggling magnolia in the garden. The homestead was two stories high and painted a bright white. Verandas stretched along the front on both levels. It sat on a natural ridge as if surveying the sweeping lawn below. The view carried on out past the Rakaia River and included a wide panorama of the Southern Alps, which had a light coating of snow on the tallest peaks. They were unlike any mountains she had ever seen before. She shivered, thinking of the winter to come.

Sally enjoyed giving Lily the grand tour through the house and gardens, acting as if she owned the place. A galloping horse made its way up the long drive, kicking up the few autumn leaves that had fallen from the young trees. Sally and Lily watched as the young man on the horse jerked to a sudden stop in front of Ronny, who was working by the stables, not far from where they were standing.

"I've told you, Master Henry, time and time again, you've got to cool 'em down. You don't just go stoppin' a horse dead in his tracks like that. Ain't good for 'em."

"Oh, but Ronny, my man, that's why we pay you. Here," he handed him the reins, "walk him a bit. Cool him down for me. Do your job."

"He's coming over here. Who is he? He looks too young to be Mrs Lichfield's husband." Lily was curious.

"That's Henry Lichfield, the son, and you keep yourself to yourself. He's taken a fancy to me," Sally hurriedly informed Lily and then smiled at the approaching male.

"Mrs Lichfield said her son was at boarding school in Christchurch," Lily whispered as the young man got nearer.

Henry was solidly built—his face boyishly round with an unfortunate prematurely receding hairline. "Well, hello," he said as he extended his hand cordially towards Lily. But she didn't like the tone of his voice.

"Henry Lichfield."

Lily shook his hand, while Sally made the introductions.

"Ah, well..." Henry seemed a little bewildered, "So you'll be staying, then?"

"Well, yes, I am employed here."

"Ah, well, then..."

Henry was confused again. Ever since they'd left England he'd battled this same confusion. How was he supposed to know who he had to treat like a lady? The lines were blurred in this new country. Henry couldn't ask Lily to supper or if she'd care to take a stroll around the gardens with him this evening. It just wasn't done. The most he could hope for was a surreptitious meeting in the linen closet, and he had Sally for that.

It wasn't easy being Henry Lichfield. He had just turned eighteen and was still in school. School, just the idea of it grated on his nerves. He had thought he'd left his schoolboy days behind in England, but no. His father had enrolled him at Christ's College with an ultimatum: study and get a generous allowance, or the alternative—no study, no money. Henry knew that studying would be easier than actually working. He wasn't stupid. He was just tired of being told what to do. Endless hours of lessons, then just when you thought you couldn't sit and listen another minute, you had to go sit in the chapel and listen some more. As if listening to that drivel was actually going to do him any good. Henry knew what he liked. He liked to drink, he liked to play cards, and he liked to have women—not necessarily in that order.

Elisabeth watched Henry talking to the girls on the lawn. She was proud of her son. She always referred to him as hers, and hers only, proud of herself and the fact that George had never guessed the truth. Elisabeth got satisfaction out of giving the boy what he wanted and took delight in his roguishness.

~

Lily settled into her work, her cough clearing quickly in the fresh country air. There was a certain edge to her relationship with Mrs Lichfield, who would not hesitate to find fault if any could be found. But Lily knew how to work hard and so was able, for the most part, to gain her approval. She found Mr Lichfield extraordinarily kind and realised he liked having someone to talk to. She would leave dusting the library until last, where quite often he would be settled with a book by the fire, which he would lower to his lap as they talked.

"Mrs Lichfield is going back to the city for a few days. Would you like to accompany her, Lily?"

"Ah, sir, I'd love to, but I'm sure that Sally thinks she is going."

"Well, you'd like to see your sister, wouldn't you?"

"Oh yes, sir, I most certainly would. I miss her." Truthfully, it was way past just missing her. Lily had a deep yawning hole in the place where Rose usually was. She felt unbalanced without her.

"I'll organise for you to go. Perhaps Sally can go as well."

George watched Lily as she dusted.

"Are you sure you are all right, Lily? You look a little pale."

"Oh, I'm fine, Mr Lichfield, though I am missing my sister." Lily hesitated, "And, well, there is another matter…" Lily didn't know what to ask for. She wanted to talk to Mr Lichfield about Henry, but she wasn't quite sure what to say. It seemed to her that he came home from Christchurch most weekends for the sole reason of making her uncomfortable. Of course, she couldn't tell Mr Lichfield that—it sounded far too dramatic. Still, Henry frightened her. He always seemed to be aware of where she was in the house and purposely organised himself to be in her way. At first, she thought he was just being friendly. Lily was lonely and some company was, after all, better than none, but she soon realised he had more sinister motives. Once, he'd grabbed her arm as she passed him in the hallway, and before she knew it, she was turned with her back against the wall and Henry's mouth on hers. Of course, a well-placed knee in his private parts had put a stop to his attentions, but the whole episode scared Lily. She only relaxed when she knew Henry was in Christchurch or when she could go with Ronny to the river for water.

Just then Elisabeth strode into the library, "Honestly, Lily, you have all day to do the dusting, why on earth do you leave it so late?"

Lily hastened to finish and left the room.

"She really is a fine girl, Elisabeth."

"Too fine, much too fine for a servant, and she knows it."

"Ah, Lily doesn't have a snobbish bone in her body, and she's very unaware of her beauty, I might add."

"Well, you might, but then it becomes glaringly obvious that you are most definitely aware of it, my dear George," Elisabeth answered sarcastically as she settled herself in a chair by the window.

"There's not a man alive who wouldn't notice Lily."

"Did she tell you that she has a sister, an identical twin?" Elisabeth was enjoying having something that resembled a conversation with her husband.

"She's told me about her sister, but I didn't know they were identical." He poured his wife a brandy.

"Spitting images of each other. Honestly, I couldn't see any differences between them."

"Hmm." George swirled his whisky in the glass, "I think Liam might like to meet Lily, don't you?" he said thoughtfully.

Elisabeth sat up in her chair, losing her relaxed demeanour in an instant. "George, you can't possibly be entertaining the idea of introducing our maid...our maid, George. To Liam? Who is our neighbour, George...our neighbour!" She looked at him as if he had completely lost his mind, but before he could speak she started in again, louder than before and bordering on hysterical. "Just imagine, he'd come over on a Sunday and... What, George, what? Would we say to Lily 'Here, let me take that tray, dear. Just have a seat. Here, take mine', and oh, oh... It just doesn't bear thinking about." Elisabeth collapsed back into the chair. "Really, George," she said weakly.

"We don't live in England anymore, dear."

"Oh, and don't I know it, but still we can make it like England. We have to, George, we have to," Elisabeth said, fanning herself with her hand. George could see that Elisabeth was agitated and he knew why. She felt threatened; her background was anything but high society, and after all the time they'd been together, she thought he didn't know. She wasn't aware that it was her vulnerability at times like this that had first attracted him. She wanted so badly to be a lady. He admired her pride and her stubbornness and even her willingness to go it alone, although that was the very thing that eventually came between them. She wanted so much to be someone, and he, at least in the early days, had thought why not? Why not help her? So although he never felt she loved him, at least not how he had once imagined being loved, she needed him. She needed him now.

"Elisabeth... Relax, darling." She looked up, his use of the endearment touching something inside her. "I'm not planning a ball in Liam and Lily's honour that you will be bound to preside over. I'm not inviting them both to dinner so our servants will be obliged to wait on our servants. I promise I won't destroy the order of things."

"Don't do anything, George. Not a thing, promise me." Some of the steel was returning to her voice.

"Ah, well, I..."

Elisabeth reached for his hand and placed it on her substantial cleavage. "Promise me, George."

George promised.

It had been too long, he thought, as he leaned forward to take her lips. She answered him, instantly echoing his need. Moments later he had her moaning, "Oh, oh." She nuzzled her mouth into the skin on his neck while he struggled to undo the back of her dress. Her hands were busy unbuttoning his vest.

"Hurry, hurry," she whispered and lifted his shirt and kissed his bare chest. His breath caught, and he thought to himself, *Slow down, slow down, make this last.* Whatever his wife had been or done in her previous life that she was ashamed of, a conclusion had obviously been reached in her mind that being a lady and good honest sex did not go hand in hand. So it was only on very rare occasions that she lost her inhibitions. This looked like it was going to be one of those times. George was intent on making the most of it. He gently moved them out of the chair and onto the floor. She bathed him in kisses as he pulled the laces completely away from her corset and then worked her dress down over her hips.

"Oh, George, please, please..."

He reached for her chin and tilted her face towards him, "What, Elisabeth, what do you want? Say it, Elisabeth, say it."

She shook her head but then turned and bent, positioning herself on all fours.

"Oh God, Elisabeth." All thoughts of slow, languid lovemaking deserted him as he moved forward on his knees, and with one hand on each of her hips, he pulled her back—hard—towards him, onto him. "Is this what you want, darling? Talk to me, tell me. Say it."

Elisabeth nodded; she could never say the words. She just kept grinding herself against him, losing herself in her need for him, in her need for this feeling that swept through them both…and built…and built…until they could stand it no longer. At last they surged together and lay panting on the floor.

He kissed her, anxious to prolong the rare intimacy. He watched her skin as it paled and then reddened, her strange misplaced sense of shame returning—and, with it, her guilt.

"It's all right, Lizzy, it's all right." He leaned over to kiss her again, ever hopeful that this time it might be different and she'd stay relaxed and pliant in his arms.

Instead, she pushed him away. "Don't call me that," she said and started gathering her clothes, her head bent. She dressed hurriedly and left, shutting the door firmly behind her.

She wouldn't speak to him for weeks, he thought. He smiled, reliving the encounter in his mind. But still, it had been worth it.

~

The dray bounced over the trail. Liam slowed and wiped a splatter of mud off his cheek. He was following the tracks he'd made through the cabbage trees, tussock, and large rocks to the river. This river took a bit of getting used to. It was nothing like the rivers back home that slowly and predictably wound their way through civilisation. This river had no edges, no banks that the water gently meandered past. The Rakaia River was several miles across and lay like a loosely braided rope in its rocky bed. It had a mind of its own. Liam would find a good place for filling his barrels, a spot where the river was moving a little bit more slowly, as if it were trying to catch its breath. A few days later, after a rain, when he would return to the same spot, there would be a wild rush of water sprinting past, carving out a whole new channel. It was always changing.

Liam saw another dray in the distance and two people standing beside the river with buckets. He thought he recognised Ronny, George's stable hand. He manoeuvred his wagon along the river's latest edge and hopped down.

Ronny extended his hand as Liam greeted him.

Ronny looked over his shoulder at the dray laden with barrels and said, "Aye, I've got the new housemaid with me, Lily."

Liam shook Ronny's hand and looked towards the wagon, but didn't see anyone. Then he saw movement as a bucket appeared over on the far side and spilled into the barrel on the wagon. "Oh, hello, just a moment," a muffled feminine voice answered, piquing Liam's curiosity because it sounded vaguely familiar. He supposed it was the Irish brogue reminding him of home. Then she walked out from behind the back of the wagon, her head down, negotiating the rocky riverbed. Liam watched the girl gracefully move over the rocks towards him and the truth dawned on him that this was the girl he had seen that day in Christchurch, the girl who turned up in his dreams, invading his thoughts like she belonged there. He moved a little, a cross between a shiver and shake to make sure he was awake.

Lily, he thought, *Ronny called her Lily. Lily. Her name is Lily. At last I have a name.* "Lily," he mouthed her name to himself just as she looked up, reading his lips.

Lily looked at Liam questioningly. Liam didn't have any answers, any words at all. He just kept looking, looking at her and smiling.

She smiled back.

"Better finish up 'ere," Ronny interrupted their wordless conversation, motioning to Lily, "then we'll help Liam fill his barrels."

Lily turned with her bucket towards the river and bent to let it fill. Liam couldn't keep his eyes off her; it was as if he couldn't quite take her all in, but wanted to. He saw that she kept sneaking glances his way as they worked. She stopped to take a few deep breaths.

"Lily, you all right?" Ronny boomed, noticing her leaning against the end of the wagon.

"I'm fine." Lily moved back into action.

"Well, why were you standing like that with your eyes closed?" Ronny embarrassed her further. Lily shook her head and, crimson-coloured, bent to the river to fill her bucket.

Liam kept working, all the while his mind racing. *How can I talk to her? How can I court her? When can I meet her again? George will help me. Well, maybe he will. She is in his employ though. How do you call on a maid? She won't have access to the drawing room at Avonlea, will she? Do we sit on the back porch? I'll take her riding, that's what I'll do, I'll ask her to go riding with me, on her next day off.*

51

"Been fishing much?" Ronny asked Liam.

Liam shook his head, "Haven't really had the time. What about you?"

"Try to get a bit in on my day off."

"Caught anything?"

"Got one decent-sized trout. Something, isn't it, how they can introduce the eggs and get them growing 'ere. I saw the fish eggs once in Christchurch. Big ponds they built in Hagley Park, next to the hospital."

The wind was coming up. That morning Liam had noticed a nor'west arch over the mountains—a sure sign that strong winds were brewing. Ronny and Lily finished filling their barrels and moved to help Liam with his. Liam caught Lily's gaze once or twice. She would hold his a moment but didn't seem as bold or as brave as she was that day in the park. Too quickly, the barrels on the back of Liam's wagon were full of sparkling river water, and there was no reason to linger in the strengthening wind. Ronny bundled Lily into the wagon and they headed up the track. Liam climbed up slowly onto his seat and turned just in time to catch Lily's lingering backward glance.

He smiled, their eyes met.

She gave him a little wave and smiled back.

Chapter 6

"Hand it up to him." Mrs Lichfield was busy giving orders as Ronny and Lily loaded the luggage onto the dray. George had relented and finally bought her a house in town. She was going there for several weeks to furnish it. Elisabeth kept trying to get George to come as well and take her to a ball, but she wasn't having much luck. He told her there was a series of lectures he wanted to attend later on, but that didn't seem to impress her. Elisabeth was taking both Sally and Lily with her, although she was nervous about leaving the cook, Myra, on her own with extra duties. She'd hate to return to Avonlea and find it less than perfect.

Lily was dying to see Rose. She'd felt so lonely without her.

Lily and Sally listened to Mrs Lichfield complain about the dray all the way to Rakaia—how she would have much preferred the buggy. The train trip to Christchurch was more pleasant; Mrs Lichfield met the Elworthys who were also making their way into Christchurch for some socialising.

"Oh, I am so looking forward to seeing my sister," Lily said aloud but mostly to herself. She and Sally sat on the hard benches in the cheapest section of the train eating their sandwiches and watching the tussock-covered Canterbury Plains roll by.

"We will probably be in town quite a lot now," Sally mused. "Of course, now that the Lichfield's have this house, Henry will be spending quite a bit of time there," Sally finished with a self-satisfied smile. Lily's mood sank, realising she would have to be constantly on guard.

"I think that is maybe why they bought it...for Henry. He seems much too old for boarding school, don't you think?"

Lily had no answer.

~

Rose was delighted to see Lily; they hugged like they might never let each other go. It took very little persuading to convince the Reverend that Lily should stay with them and walk to the Lichfield household to work. Mrs Lichfield was not so easily swayed and relented to the arrangement only after Lily promised that she would still be available every other evening until late.

~

"Oh, Lily, tell me," Rose said as they hugged again the dim candlelight of the McGregor's sitting room, "tell me."

"Tell you what?"

"Something is bothering you."

Rose had just given the baby his late feed and the house was finally quiet except for the slight tinny clatter of the pram that Mick was still pushing back and forth with one hand.

"I think he's asleep, Mick," Lily said. Mick sat down on the settee, his elbow on the arm and his head resting sideways in his hand.

"Tired, Mick?" Lily moved behind him and began kneading his neck with her hands.

"Tired of being a nursemaid; I could get any sort of job so easily."

Rose and Lily were both quiet for a few minutes. Lily kept working on Mick's shoulders.

Suddenly Mick spoke up, "I'm going to leave here soon, make my own way. Just thought I should tell you." Mick sounded determined even though his voice was more peaceful, reflecting the relaxed state of his body.

"Have you talked to your father about it lately?" Rose moved behind Lily and started rubbing her back.

"That feels so good," Lily murmured.

"He just doesn't listen to me; says my place is here. But it makes no sense. I could earn double what we'd have to pay someone else to help with the children. I can't stay here forever." Mick was still seated with his head in his hand, Lily was standing directly behind him, and Rose was behind her. He relaxed even further and the girls, thinking he might be asleep, began their silent conversation.

The Reverend already lost his wife. Can't bear to lose Mick too.

I should ask Mr Lichfield. Maybe he could come back with me.

Mick sat up very suddenly arching his back, "What? What did

you say?" He turned to face Lily and Rose, but neither of them knew what to tell him.

He heard us.

He did.

Somehow he heard us.

Rose spoke first, "You must have fallen asleep, Mick. Lily was just saying that she is going to ask Mr Lichfield about a job for you. Would you like that? To go to Avonlea?"

"What? Wait a minute. You weren't talking. I heard you and you weren't talking. And which one of you was it, anyway? I couldn't tell." Mick stood up, suddenly looking very much like a man, a man who wanted answers.

"All right, then." Lily pointed to the settee, "Just sit back down; we'll try to explain." Mick turned and sat on the floor with the fire at his back, so Rose and Lily both sat down on the settee facing him.

"Well?" Mick wasn't going to let this pass.

"Well, the thing is... Lily and I can talk to each other in our heads."

"Really? You can speak to each other without talking? Read each other's mind?" Lily nodded, not knowing what else to say.

"I've seen you doing it before and thought I felt something different," Mick said in a thoughtful way.

"Yes... Well, we have to be pretty relaxed, and it helps if we are touching each other, but honestly, no one else has ever heard us before," Lily said as she looked at Rose and then at Mick.

"Well, not that we know of," Rose added.

Mick didn't really know what to say. He thought it was pretty strange, and yet, he was curious. "Let's try it again."

"What? No, I..." Lily looked at Mick, her first reaction negative.

"Come on, we'll test it; see if it happens again." Mick was adamant, "Rose?"

Rose thought a moment, "Oh, maybe. Lily, what could it hurt?"

Lily slumped a little in indecision but then took Rose's hand. Mick turned around and moved to sit in front of Rose's knees. She rested one hand gently on his shoulder. All was quiet, except for the fire, which sparked occasionally.

Moments passed. Mick shifted and leaned more heavily on Rose's knees. Lily's shoulders relaxed, and she sighed audibly. Rose started moving her hand on Mick's shoulder, massaging the solid muscle she discovered there. Lily and Rose's thoughts met and mingled; they acknowledged how much they had missed each other. They let certain fragments form into sentences, although there wasn't really any need to.

Tell me... What is it?

Mick, he isn't here?

No. He can't hear us now.

There is this boy, Henry, a man really. He scares me.

Oh, I see.

"Lily, you have to take Mick back with you." Lily startled as the sound of Rose's voice penetrated her consciousness.

"What, what happened? I didn't hear a thing until you spoke. Damn!"

"Watch your language, Mick," Rose reprimanded, her voice determined and slightly angry.

"Well, I... What is this about me again?"

"There is someone at Avonlea who is bothering Lily. We need you to go with her, get a job there, and keep an eye on her. Could you do that, Mick?"

Mick had no intention of being a servant the rest of his life, but being a bodyguard was a different matter entirely. "Well, who is it and what's he done?"

"Lily, tell us."

"Well, it's just... Oh, I feel silly. I think I should be able to take care of myself. Really, I should, but he follows me. He's evil somehow. He wants all the things he can't have."

Mick sat up straighter, concern on his face, and asked seriously, "Have you thought about getting another job?"

"Well, no, it's not that bad, really. It's just that..."

"What's he actually done, then? Tell me." Mick was definitely no longer a child, Lily thought, as he questioned her.

"He kissed me...in the hall. He grabbed me and kissed me," Lily reddened.

"And what did you do?"

"I kneed him in his...private parts," Lily managed, her voice small and quiet.

"Well, good! Good for you, Lily!" Mick smiled and took Lily's hand, "And so, do you think you made your point?"

"No, I think I just made him mad."

~

That Sunday, Liam didn't go to the river for a wash, instead he had a bath. The plough had finally arrived. He had taken the dray to Rakaia to pick it up and bought a few other things, starting with a used set of cast-iron fire dogs and a griddle to set on top of them. The fire dogs sat right in the fireplace, and the griddle was a flat cast-iron tray which effectively turned the fire into an oven—fine for scones and soda bread. The fire dogs also had hooks to hang pots from and so could be used for stews and soups. One day he would get a proper cooking stove, but in the meantime, the fire dogs were quite an improvement. He had also found a copper tea kettle, which he considered an upgrade from his old camp billy, having the added benefit of being able to boil enough water for more than one and a half cups of tea. A large ironstone casserole dish with flowers painted on the side and the pair of rather ornate brass candlesticks made him chuckle. He thought himself a little silly buying things that were not entirely practical, but somewhere in the back of his mind, he knew that it was the extra bits and pieces that made a house a home. After the sweat and toil that he had invested in building his house, he very much wanted it to feel like a home.

The new hip bath was a huge thing made of copper sheeting, beaten smooth. Made in England, it had been in use in the colonies for some time, according to the date stamped on the bottom. The top was an oval shape with one side flaring out further and higher for a backrest. Half circles of copper jutted out from each edge for armrests, and the base was round with a flat bottom. After filling the bath with lukewarm water from his oak barrels and boiling water from his new copper kettle, Liam folded himself into it. He was not in the tub very long before he decided that to strip off and wash in the river was very much more practical, more invigorating, and, in fact, quite a bit more functional—if the degree of cleanliness at the end of the whole process was taken into account. Still, he thought, a woman could hardly strip off and jump in the river. His thoughts then turned to the girl, Lily, whom he hardly knew and yet kept thinking of—imagining her in this bath, in his house. He sat in the tub, in the barely warm water, and felt a longing for…for… He wasn't sure exactly what. Images came to his mind: of Lily meeting him at the door after a hard day's work; stew ready, steaming on the table in the dish with the flowers painted on it; the copper kettle hissing gently over the fire, on standby for their cups of tea. And then she'd come to him and kiss him, welcoming him home. After they'd eaten they would... Liam shook his head, embarrassed at his mental meanderings and his body's reaction to them. He leaned back and took a deep breath, unfolded his cramped legs, rose out of the tub, and dressed.

Today was the day to meet up with George, but hopefully, he'd find Lily, talk to her, and all going according to plan, he'd make arrangements to see her again. Liam smiled and headed out to saddle Smoke.

Liam warmed up Smoke with a fast trot down Back Track and then broke into a gallop after he turned onto the river road. The pace felt good and Liam whooped, an exuberantly loud, almost victorious sound, shouting into the cool crisp air. He smiled as he thought of his farm with its new fences and the newly planted shelter hedges, and his mostly built house, and his horse and his dog and his cow, and the bath and the kettle and the painted casserole dish, and even the brass candlesticks. Things were working out for him, here, in this new land. Fairfield was starting to feel like home. So when he slowed and finally came to a halt outside the Lichfield's stables, and George and Ronny emerged blinking in the bright Sunday morning sunshine, Liam was still grinning from ear to ear.

"Hey, you look to be in fine form." Liam's smile was contagious, and George grinned as he spoke, taking Smoke's reins from Liam and handing them to Ronny.

"Yes, well, I guess I am. What's on today?"

"Fishing maybe. I thought a spot of fishing would be nice, or billiards. What do you want to do? Oh, I do want to show you my new colt...fine looking thing...over here."

They moved back into the shadows of the stables and admired the foal. "Ronny and I were just deciding if we should turn them out." George motioned to the mother and the tiny colt suckling from it.

"Oh, I should think the sun would be the thing for it. Born at the wrong end of summer," Ronny piped in, as he opened the stable doors. "C'mon there, little man, there..." The three men slowly ushered the mare and her foal out into the sunshine. George and Liam leaned against a fence rail. Their view was of the river sweeping by in front of them and the Southern Alps in the distance, the tops lightly coated with early snow.

"I need to talk to the new girl working for you, George." Liam

58

thought the best thing was to be direct, and he had no hesitation about letting George know what he was thinking when it came to Lily, "Her name is Lily, and I would quite like to see her."

George smiled, "Thought you might."

"What?"

"Well, I talk to the lass quite a bit. She's intelligent, borrows books from my library, pretty too." Liam listened intently, desperate for any information he could get about Lily.

"And so…?"

"Well, I thought that you might want to meet her. I mentioned it to Elisabeth, but I have to tell you, she sees it differently."

"What does Elisabeth have to do with it?" Liam asked brusquely.

"Well, Lily is in our employ, you must remember. Elisabeth, well, let's just say Elisabeth has a problem with disrupting the natural order of things. To be perfectly frank, Liam, she isn't happy about our servants consorting with the neighbours."

"Consorting? What the hell does that mean?"

"Settle down, Liam. Lily isn't even here at present." He smiled at Liam in an effort to relieve the tension.

"Where is she?" Liam's voice was hard and he didn't smile back.

"She's in Christchurch. We've purchased a house there. Elisabeth and both Sally and Lily will be there for the next few weeks."

"Oh." Liam's brilliant mood was considerably flattened, but he was used to fighting for what he wanted. "George, New Zealand isn't England and I know your wife has a right to her opinions, but I still want to see Lily. And I will."

"I know, Liam," George smiled. "Why do you think I finally relented and bought a house in town?"

"You bought… So Elisabeth would be away from time to time?" Liam's mind was racing, and he finally smiled back at George. A truly genuine smile, the kind you reserve for your very best mates.

"How about a whisky?" George asked as they made their way to the billiards room. Liam nodded. Then he looked around as if he still had hope he might see Lily today.

"Tell me more about her. What do you talk about?"

"Well, she meets me in the library, usually late in the afternoon. She…"

Liam interrupted, slightly irritated, "She meets you… What do you mean she meets you?"

"Oh, Liam, settle down," George chuckled. "You really don't know her at all, do you?" Liam knew George was right, but did not like being told so.

"No, I don't, for…"

"Just be quiet and listen. I think of Lily like I would my own daughter. If I had one, that is," he added. "She's lonely, desperately misses her sister. She leaves dusting the library until late in the afternoon when I'm usually there, just before dinner. We talk…converse…while she works." Liam relaxed, and George said, "I've had some very pleasant conversations with the dear girl."

"Well, that's just it, isn't it?" Liam mumbled and downed his whole glass of whisky.

"What?" George asked as he watched Liam reach for the bottle.

"I haven't had a single one."

Chapter 7

Liam lost himself in a frenzy of work. He'd been working steadily from dawn until dusk for months, but the intensity increased. The post holes for the fences that used to take him nearly a half an hour each to dig were now done in less than twenty minutes. He finished cupboards and shelves for his bare kitchen and then decided that the sitting room and the one bedroom made a house that wasn't nearly big enough or grand enough. So he hauled more boulders up from the river and laid the foundations for another two rooms out the front. This meant building a hallway and moving the front door, which had only been in place for a couple of months, but nothing would deter him. He also ploughed—long, hard twelve-hour days—turning over the soil in readiness for spring planting. Fortunately he loved ploughing. Sometimes he stopped only to give the horses a break. There was no end to his restless energy.

He entertained thoughts of a trip to Christchurch. He could track Lily down; find some way to speak to her without Elisabeth Lichfield around. But, what then? Only when he was hard at work could he still his thoughts of Lily. Even then, there was the question, always in the back of his mind, 'Would she be his?' He really didn't know her. Was he making presumptions, based on the feelings he felt the one and only time he had touched her, held her hand, in the park? Was he imagining what passed between them could be something lasting, something real?

~

Lily was curious. She questioned the strange feeling of comforting familiarity that had swept over her when she had first gazed up at the tall, handsome man who was mouthing her name as if it were already dear to him. But Lily had no time for daydreaming; she had more pressing matters to deal with, namely Henry Lichfield. Henry, of course, had been delighted with the unexpected arrival of Lily in town, but realised very soon that Sally was going to be a major disruption to the fulfilment of his plans for Lily. What he didn't know was that his mother recognised the predatory look in his eyes as he watched Lily.

"Henry... Really, darling, you must be more circumspect."

"Whatever are you talking about, Mother?"

"Oh, dear, you know perfectly well what I am talking about, the way you look at that girl."

"What? Oh, Lily you mean. Well, she's a sweet thing and I enjoy looking at her."

"Henry, she is a servant, far below our station. But having said that, if you do dally with her, it is imperative that she is willing." Elisabeth spoke to the point.

Henry was taken aback, so involved was he in the fulfilment of his own gratification. He looked at his mother, speechless.

"Really, dear, you must think of these things. I'm sure you have it in you to romance the girl somewhat. At least get her to believe, when it is all said and done and you tire of her, that it was partly her fault." Elisabeth made ready to leave the room.

Henry was surprised at his mother's advice and her willingness to involve herself in his games, but she was right. His eyes hardened and he smiled malevolently. It would be easier and quite a bit more pleasant if he could get Lily to come to him, beg for him even.

For the most part, Lily remained out of his reach. Most of her days seemed to be taken up with accompanying Mrs Lichfield on shopping trips in town; they would visit drapers, furniture makers, and warehouses of private importers. Mrs Lichfield would enter into seemingly endless discussions on the latest styles and trends of home furnishing in Europe and, most importantly, England. Nothing but the best would do. Then, when she felt she was suitably informed, they would return to the same drapers, furniture makers, and private importers to place her orders. Sally would be left at home to do the housework, which left her very disgruntled until she realised that it would be possible for Henry to take time out of his busy class schedule and return home to keep her company. At first this arrangement suited Henry, but he became increasingly despondent at never finding Lily at home and more and more irritated at Sally's overtures.

"Lift your skirts."

"What?" Sally had been kissing Henry in the front room. His hand had wandered to her breasts and she'd loosened her laces, granting him access. She was feeling very…well…good. Henry was showing more interest in her lately.

"Turn and lift your skirts, Sally. You heard me." His voice wasn't the soft, languid voice of a lover asking permission, yet there was something in the way he made his demand that softened her heart towards him—her Henry. She lifted her petticoats and turned. He gently pushed her over the back of the settee and pulled down her underwear, "Ah, Sally, that's my girl," he said now in the soft voice he usually used, and it soothed her. He took her quickly, but hard, with an urgency that spoke of underlying tension, a tension that was not relieved by their quick coupling.

"What is it, Henry?" Sally was sitting on the settee, smugly adjusting her laces afterwards.

"Oh, just the wanting of all the things one cannot have." Henry, still in the haze of sensual pleasure, spoke without thinking, his voice full of longing and strangely vulnerable.

"But, Henry, there would be precious little you cannot have." Sally, eyebrows arched, raised her hands palms upward and looked around the room, well on its way to being very luxuriously appointed.

"What do you know? You are a servant."

Sally overlooked his slight and stared at him. "Tell me, then, tell me what it is you want. What do you want, Henry?"

"More." Henry's voice was small, "I want more." He rose abruptly from the upholstered chair and turned to leave, suddenly aware of his disclosure.

But Sally was smiling at him—beaming—her eyes lit up with wonder. "Ah… But, Henry, I can give you more. I can." She reached for him. "Come to me, take me again," she offered.

"Stop it! Leave me alone." Henry shook his head and shrugged off her arm. "That's not what I am talking about."

~

Henry waited for Lily. He knew she left the house around eleven every second night. She went out through the back door and headed down the garden path to the back gate. It was a short walk down Montreal Street to the McGregors. He had watched her from his window.

"Lily." He stepped into her path. She shrank back, looking from side to side.

"Don't be frightened, Lily, please." There was a different tone to his voice. "I just want to talk to you."

"All right," Lily answered, but moved around him towards the gate. "What did you want to talk about?"

"Well, I just... Stop it, Lily! Stay here." He grabbed her arm.

The gate swung open. "Excuse me, sir, but I've come to escort the lady home, and I think that is what she's wanting to be doing just at present. Going home, that is." Mick spoke clearly but with some nervousness in his voice that contrasted to his stance. He was very muscular for his age, and the way he stood with his fists clenched and poised as he was, he looked ready for a fight. It had an effect on Henry. He let go of Lily.

Mick stepped forward and took Lily's arm, "C'mon then, let's make our way home," he said softly as he held the gate open for her. They stepped through and shut it firmly behind them.

~

"Lily, you cannot live in fear," Rose whispered adamantly as they were getting into their nightdresses.

"Henry will not come to the country as much now, Rose. I will be all right. I like it in the country. I must tell you about the man I met at the river," Lily whispered back. Jessie hiccupped and then turned over in her cot.

"Lily, I feel like you are in danger."

"I felt like I knew him, like I've known him forever."

"Who? What? Lily, you are not listening to me. You must be on guard. You mustn't be alone with Henry. Promise me?"

"I promise," Lily whispered back, crawling into her narrow bed.

~

Lily was back. Liam heard the news from Ronny at the river on Thursday. Elisabeth Lichfield had returned to Avonlea with both Lily and Sally. The news at first delighted him. It was what he had been waiting to hear, but on his way home, he felt despondent. How exactly was he going to go about this courting business? What if Elisabeth put up a fuss? What if Lily wasn't even interested? What if she was spoken for? Liam was filled with doubts and misgivings. He couldn't just bowl up to the front door and ask to speak to her, or could he?

He waited until Sunday, when he was generally expected at Avonlea. There was no point in drawing Elisabeth Lichfield's attention to the fact that he was of a mind to court Lily, and besides, he knew he could count on George's help.

There was a hard frost, but Liam, braving the cold, had an invigorating wash in the river. He entertained fond thoughts of his hip bath and hoped it might turn out to be a useful investment yet. Dressing was a rushed affair. He galloped Smoke along the river road, with Pearl on their heels, and turned down the drive towards Avonlea. Neither George nor Ronny were at the stables. Liam unsaddled Smoke, settled the horse and the dog in, and then headed towards the house.

A quick movement in the corner of his eye caught his attention, and he stopped on the path at the back of the homestead to investigate. Lily was making her way towards the outhouse, in that graceful, elegant way she had. Her wild curls were tied back at the nape of her neck and the long tail swayed as she walked. A 'shee-geeha' she was, he thought. A wind fairy, just like in the old stories. He smiled and kept watching. For a few moments, that was all he needed, just to see her. She disappeared into the small building. Liam waited, his plans of George introducing them faded. He'd call out to her when she returned to the house, speak to her then. She emerged in the exact same moment the sun decided to come out from behind a cloud. She blinked in the bright light and smiled the brilliant smile that Liam remembered from that day in the park. Then she started up the path towards the house with a lilt in her walk. Liam watched entranced.

"There you are, Lily. Help me empty this." The Lichfield's cook, Myra, was standing at the open door leaning heavily to one side, in her hand a very large pot held like a bucket.

"Too stiff, first thing, for this heavy lifting," she grumbled.

"That's all right; I'll help you." Lily's voice was as distinctive as he remembered. It seemed to resonate through the back garden. She quickly darted up the stairs and took the large cast-iron pot from Myra.

Chapter 8

Lily

"Here, I'll help you."

I was startled at the sound of a man's voice from the corner of the house. Last night's dirty washing water splashed onto my dress. "Oh, that's cold." I shivered as it soaked through my stockings.

"Here, I'll take it." The man from the river spoke again. He reached for the handle, just barely touching my hand. For a moment, we both held the pot. I looked down at the water, swishing from side to side. I gathered my courage and looked up at the man standing so close to me. He had been waiting.

"Lily," he mouthed my name silently. My eyes widened and he knew he had my attention. It was just like the first time. He said my name like a prayer, like my name belonged on his lips.

"I'm Liam McCann," he said out loud a moment later.

I stared into his eyes. An amazing blue, or maybe green, or a colour in between. Finally I made a feeble attempt to find my voice. "I know... I'm... I'm Lily." Then I smiled self-consciously. "But you already know that," I stammered and watched the water again, the swishing back and forth much slower now.

"Yes, I do," Liam answered.

Something in his voice made me stop being nervous and shy. I looked up and smiled, not at him, but for him. He recognised the difference and looked at me like I'd answered a question, one that now he didn't need to ask.

"Are you goin' to empty the pot? I need to get it goin' again," Myra interjected. I jumped a little, and the water overflowed on Liam this time.

"Sorry," I said as Liam made his way down the stairs and then dumped the water on the smallest rhododendron in the row next to the path.

"For heaven's sake, Myra, where are you?" Mrs Lichfield appeared at the back door. "Liam, what on earth?" She noticed his wet trousers but didn't notice me standing to the side of the porch, almost behind the door. "What are you doing back here? George is waiting for you in the billiards room. Go round the front. I'll send Sally to open the door," Mrs Lichfield ordered.

"Fine, I'll do just that." Liam started around the house, but he looked back over his shoulder and caught me watching him. He returned my smile. It was quick, but not quick enough; Mrs Lichfield looked sideways down the porch and then tilted her head to see me standing behind the door with my wet skirt and a silly grin on my face.

"Lily, go and change. Put on warm clothes and go to the river to help Ronny with the water," she said sharply.

"But I..."

"Lily, do as you're told."

Chapter 9

Damn, damn! Liam berated himself. He had heard Elisabeth's sharp words. He should have never looked back. He should have been more patient, enlisted George's help, arranged a more private meeting. Still, though, Elisabeth was not going to stand in his way. Not now, not after the way Lily had smiled at him. There might be some challenges ahead, but he'd court Lily. That was all there was to it. He was whistling an old Irish jig by the time he made it around to the front door.

Sally showed Liam to the billiards room. George was seated cosily by the blazing fire, perusing his newspapers. He was always interested in what was going on, both here and back in England.

"Well, hello there." George put down a newspaper to address Liam, "I thought you might come round today," he said smiling at Liam. "What's the plan?" he asked conspiratorially.

"Well…" Liam paused, "I was wondering how you felt about a spot of fishing?"

"What? Lily's here, you know. She's been back nearly a week."

"Oh, I know, but your wife has just sent her to the river with Ronny."

"Has she? Well, let's just see about that. Come on, my boy." George hurried out the door and down the hall. Liam wasn't at all sure about following George to confront his wife, but George took a sudden turn and headed out the front door in his slippers, towards the stables. Liam followed, both curious and amused.

They found Ronny in the stables, hitching up the bullocks to the dray and muttering under his breath. He looked up in surprise at George and Liam.

"Ronny, we aren't short of water, are we?" George asked.

"Well, no. That's why I thought it mighty strange that… Well, no impertinence intended, sir." Ronny's tongue had trouble getting around a word like impertinence.

"No, none taken, Ronny. The thing is… What…" George paused, "Just a minute, Ronny." George turned to Liam. "Do you want her to go to the river? I guess meeting her there would be as good as any place. Or maybe to your house? If Elisabeth thinks she's with Ronny, you could take her home for a few hours. Mind you, you'd have to give me your word you would be a gentleman, Liam."

"The wind's cold. I'll take her home with me. She can go with Ronny out the drive and I'll meet him at the corner, although she'll have to ride double with me on Smoke." Liam paused, imagining Lily on the horse behind him, "Then we'll meet back at the corner in, say, about two hours. All right, Ronny?"

"Well, I…" Ronny was interrupted when Lily stepped from the shadow by the open stable door. She had all three men's full attention when she spoke.

Chapter 10

Lily

"What exactly is going on here?" I asked and surprised myself. My voice sounded a lot more controlled than I felt. I looked at Liam.

"Well…" Liam started and then paused. "Up until now I hadn't had time to ask you," he paused and looked at me like he was acknowledging a mistake, "but I was wondering if you would do me the honour of spending a small amount of time in my company this morning." There was longing in his voice. "Miss," he added for good measure.

His little speech made it impossible for me to be affronted, especially since I was flattered by the invitation. "Well, it is not my day off, and I've been told to help Ronny with water at the river and so…"

"That's not answering my question, Lily." Liam's voice held a note of authority.

"Well, I…" I looked at him. "Well, yes, sir, I would be most honoured to have the pleasure of your company this morning." I looked at Mr Lichfield, "If it is possible?"

"Fine, fine, Liam's plan is fine with me." Mr Lichfield said, shaking his head and smiling as if there were no arguing with fate.

"No, I don't think so." I stepped forward. "I'm not going to your house by myself. I don't even know you."

"But you just said… You'd be honoured to have the…"

"I know I did, and I would…be honoured, that is…but not at your house, sir. I'm not…" My voiced faded.

Ronny climbed into the driving seat of the dray. "If it's all the same to you, I'll be off, then. Lily, are you comin' along?" I started towards the dray, looking down at my feet.

"No, wait! Lily, will you stay with me here, in the stables? Ronny can go to the river. Mrs Lichfield will think you are with him. Please stay."

I hesitated, looking towards Mr Lichfield again. "Oh, for heaven's sake, lass, he's not going to bite your head off. He's a fine man. Stay and have a chat." Then he whacked the bullock on its rear end and the dray lurched forward towards the open door. Mr Lichfield followed the dray, cursing when his left foot, encased in the sheepskin slipper, landed in a pile of steaming manure.

Liam and I were left alone in the dimly lit stables.

It was quiet.

"Umm… Would you like a seat?" Liam turned and pulled a rickety bench out from the wall. I sat down on the end of it. Liam straddled the other end and sat facing me. I turned to look at him and I just kept looking.

Thoughts raced through my head, from *I don't know this man at all* to *Why is it I feel so comfortable in his company?* to *Ah, but look at his fine broad shoulders!* to *Those eyes, those eyes, the way they look at me.* It was this final thought that finally got to me, or that our eyes had locked. My head was already turned towards his, but I moved my shoulders, twisted to face him, and moved almost imperceptibly closer to him. I felt he was pulling me towards him.

The wind whistled through the cracks under the doors, but the stables had a cosy feel. The only light was the pale wintry sunlight shining through the few windows. Liam wiped his brow with his sleeve.

"So, Liam McCann, tell me about you." My voice surprised me again, sounding sure and confident.

"Well, Lily Quinn, I was just getting up my nerve to ask you the same thing." He smiled. I smiled back, not so shyly this time.

"You first."

"No, you."

"All right, then." I started, then paused, thinking about my grandmother and my life back in Creggan. All the secrets I had been bound to keep. "I grew up in County Armagh, a little place called Creggan," I offered.

"Hmm, I was born in Richhill, not that far away. I'll know why you left."

I thought for a moment. There was no way he could know why I'd left.

"No money, no jobs, poor crops."

I just nodded.

"What? What else, Lily?"

"What do you mean?"

"Well, you look like you want to tell me things. Why don't you?" Liam's smile was so genuine. I couldn't look at him and not think of my name on his lips being soundlessly formed.

So almost against my will and most certainly against my better judgement, I began to tell him the truth.

"My Nana raised us, or at least she tried to."

"Why? Where were your parents?"

"My mother died in childbirth, so we never knew her at all. Our father, well, he used to come see us from time to time. He was a sailor. We heard he had promised my mother, that when they had a family, he'd work the land, but once she died, I guess he thought... Well, I don't know what he thought. He kept going to sea and his voyages got longer and longer and, then, he just stopped coming to see us. He was captain of his own ship by then, and Nana Kat heard no reports of it going down."

"How old were you?" Liam asked gently.

"I think about four or five. I can just vaguely remember his visits. He used to pick us up and put us on his shoulders." I had a few nice memories. "But, not much later, Nana Kat started to go funny."

"What do you mean?" Liam moved closer, as if sensing my reluctance to speak of it.

"Well, she...she..." I did not know how to verbalise what had happened to Nana Kat and the impact it had had on me, but I looked at Liam and his kind eyes and decided I could try. "She lost her mind," I said with finality, "only it took her twelve years to do it."

"And all that time it was just you and your sister?"

My eyes filled with tears; one rolled down my cheek.

Liam moved closer and put his hand over mine on the bench, a simple, comforting gesture. I looked down at the large hand completely covering mine and felt the strength I needed to continue.

"She was an herbalist. She knew how to heal people in the old ways. She was teaching my mother when she died. My mother would have carried on and, then, taught us but..." I trailed off. Liam's dog curled up at my feet and I bent to pat its head.

"That's Pearl. You mean she was a..."

"She was not a witch, if that was what you were about to say," I interrupted. I pulled my hand from under his.

"I was trying to think of the word for it. What did she call herself?" Liam asked, maintaining his equanimity.

"She called herself a priestess. She was the most amazing healer, she knew so many things. But it had to be kept a secret, you know. The church thought it had stamped out the ways of Danu and her followers many, many years ago."

"Danu?"

"Danu, or sometimes just Anu, the Mother Earth, the greatest of all the goddesses."

"Ah, I see... I have heard the rumours of old Celtic sects...people who followed the old ways."

I nodded. "Do you see? Liam McCann, do you?" My voice was loud and urgent and I felt a little bit angry, but not with him. "We had this beautiful thing in front of us, this power we knew to be true and good, a treasure store of ceremonies and celebrations, old legends, sacred knowledge meant to be passed on to us, but our grandmother couldn't. She tried, oh, she tried. She knew, you see, knew she was losing her mind. She'd have a good day and spend most of it telling us stories. We believed them at first, just the way she told them, but they started to change. The ending was different, or the goddess of this suddenly became the goddess of something else. She even got confused about some of the herbal remedies, and she couldn't remember the name of the plants or where to get them." I took a breath and carried on with my story. "And then it got really bad, because even though most of the women knew what she was and even went to the gatherings she had led, she...she couldn't keep... She just couldn't stop talking about it. She didn't know how to keep her mouth shut."

"So the secret got out?"

"Well, Rose and I just couldn't take her anywhere, or... Well, it got to the point that if the priest called in, one of us had to quickly usher her out the back door."

"Wouldn't the priest just think it was the ranting of a crazy woman?"

"Well, yes... That is eventually how the whole village saw her...a crazy woman." I had trouble continuing but finally managed, "and we were the crazy woman's granddaughters."

"How did you survive?"

"Just barely. We just barely did, Liam. We were lucky my

grandfather had owned our little cottage and some land surrounding it. We grew things in the garden and kept hens. We trapped rabbits from time to time." Liam was looking at me disbelievingly. "We got by," I said a little defensively.

"Yes, but didn't people help you, two little girls and an old lady on their own?"

"Oh, they did what they could. They would have never let us starve, but no one else ever had much either. You know that." I took a deep breath. "You said you knew why I left, Liam."

We were both silent for a long moment. A horse neighed.

"Thank you, Lily."

"For what?" I looked at him in astonishment.

"Thank you for telling me all that."

I gave a small gasp and covered my mouth, suddenly acutely aware of my confession. I looked to Liam for some sort of reassurance. He was moving away from me, starting to stand. Oh, I shouldn't have said anything. Of course he wouldn't be interested in crazy Katherine Donnelly's granddaughter, no one in Creggan ever had been. Why had I told him? What had I done? I watched the back of him as he left me. "Well, goodbye, then."

Liam opened the door. "What did you say?"

"I said 'Goodbye, then'." I just managed to get it out again.

"'Goodbye'? I'm not leaving, not until Ronny gets back and even then…" He turned, leaving the sun streaming through the door behind him—the wind had died down. Only after he returned to his end of the bench did he look at me again.

"Oh, Lily, whatever did you think?"

I looked up at him and shook my head and then, bending my neck, looked down into my lap. My hands were on either side of me on the bench, stretched out, radiating tension. Liam reached out and covered my hand again, completely encompassing it with his own. We sat like that a few moments, in silence. Then my shoulders relaxed. I moved my hand, turned it over. I entwined my fingers through his and held on.

"So I guess it's my turn."

I nodded, still dismayed with myself and yet strangely buoyed by the feel of his hand in mine and my bravery at taking it.

"I miss my Mam and my Da," Liam blurted out. "I miss my brothers too."

I tightened my grip on his hand. He felt my comfort and looked down at our hands, entwined, between us.

"How many brothers do you have?"

"Four. I was the youngest; they were always looking out for me. I always knew there was someone covering my back, always felt it." Liam looked sad.

"And you miss that now, here, without them."

"Yeah, I do." Liam shifted, moved closer to me on the bench, his knees again on either side. "I didn't at first because everything was so new and different. I wanted to come here. It was part of my plan, and I had Frank. I met him on the ship coming over. He's like a brother now. We worked together for quite a while."

"He watched your back?"

"Aye, Frank's a good friend, but it's different now since I've decided to settle here. I have a farm, you know, Fairfield; it's just up the road." I recognised the pride in his voice.

"I thought you must."

"I've built a house... Well, work is still progressing."

The wind rose a little again and the door swung, increasing the arc of sunshine on the dirt floor.

"Would you be inclined to visit me?" Liam reached out with his free hand to take my other one. I clasped his hand back and nodded.

We heard hoofbeats and creaking wagon wheels and the refreshing slosh of full water barrels. He made to let go of me, withdraw himself, but I kept one of his hands in mine, gently unfolded his fingers, and for just a moment pressed his palm into my cheek. The minute skin touched skin I had to close my eyes.

I just had to feel him. And I could feel him—feeling me.

The strength and the vague familiarity of him swept through me, powerful and reassuring.

"Ah, Lily, Lily," was all he could manage.

Chapter 11

"Yes, Rose dear, what is it?" Since his wife's death Reverend McGregor had begun using endearments attached to her name. Rose was not entirely comfortable with the intimacy this suggested.

"Um…well, I need to talk to you, Reverend." Rose was standing in the doorway of Reverend McGregor's bedroom, which doubled as his study now that it was no longer needed through the day as a sickroom.

"We know each other well enough now for you to call me Sebastian, don't you think?"

"Well, no, I prefer Reverend." She spoke with almost a tone of reprimand in her voice. "Sir," she added as an afterthought.

"As you wish, Rose," the Reverend said, emphasizing the 'Rose' and sounding somewhat disappointed. "Would you like a seat, dear?" He stood, but instead of offering her his desk chair, he motioned to the edge of the four-poster bed.

Rose, slightly unnerved by the Reverend McGregor's demeanour, moved towards the bed. She leaned against it, momentarily forgetting her original mission.

"What was it you wanted?" he asked.

"Well." Rose straightened, her thoughts quickly aligning. "It's about Mick. He is tired of helping me with the children, sir. Johnny is able to help me just fine, sir. Mick really wants to get a job; he's nearly fifteen. I know it's not my place to speak to you of such matters, but he's my friend and I told him I would." Rose's words rushed out, and then she took a deep breath and looked at the Reverend.

"Well, Rose, you are right. It is most certainly not your place."

"But, sir…"

He held up his hand. "I'm not finished yet, Rose. Having said that, I know Michael is unhappy. I've been putting off making decisions about his future, and I guess I should thank you for bringing it to my attention."

"Well, sir..."

"Has he told you what he wants to do?" he interrupted Rose again.

"I don't think he really knows for sure. I do think Lily might be able to find a place for him in the country though. He could try his hand at farming."

"Ah, yes... Well, I'll speak to him." Reverend McGregor rose from his chair and came towards her. He leaned forward, "Rose, dear, there is something else."

"Yes?"

"Well, Mrs McMullan is coming round for afternoon tea tomorrow." He eyed her up as if somehow this news were meant to have an effect on her. "Does that bother you at all, Rose?"

"No, why should it?" Rose answered, a little perplexed.

"Well, she is a widow and I'm sure it has occurred to you that I'm in need of a wife," he answered patiently.

"Yes, well, I supposed you might be looking."

"Did you?" He looked very pleased, then hemmed and hawed for a moment or two, making Rose exceedingly nervous. "Would you be minding if I looked in your direction, Rose, dear?" The last word was emphasized, as if in fact he wanted to make it clear that she could indeed be 'dear' to him.

"Oh, I..." Rose was completely taken aback. She imagined her life stretching out in front of her: Leticia's six children and undoubtedly more of her own, and Reverend McGregor for a husband. She looked at him with an expression of horror.

"Rose, dear, think about it. I am sorry, dear, I have taken you by surprise." He moved forward and took her elbow as if it were time to show her to the door. "It is quite a good offer for someone of your station."

Rose pulled her arm away. "No," she said purposefully, then, after a breath or two, her voice even, she said, "No, but thank you, sir. Thank you for your very kind offer."

"Are you sure, Rose? What about Lily? Do you think she might be interested?"

Rose just stood and shook her head. "I'll make scones and some fresh jam."

"What?"

"For tomorrow, when Mrs McMullan comes."

"Ah yes... Well... Right, dear. That would be lovely." He took a long thoughtful look at Rose.

"And I'll dress the young ones in their best," she said over her shoulder as she hurried out the door.

~

Several days later, Mick sat in his father's study, staring at the bibles and books piled up on the edge of the table that served as a desk. The window was open. Now and then a flutter of fresh air would move the smell of leather and ink away from him, and he could breathe in another smell, the faint undercurrent of something his mother once used—some sort of lavender oil or soap—barely there and yet... He looked around. It was enough to make him think of her. Mick reached out for a prayer book. He flipped through the pages; the thought of the church had never occurred to him before his father's suggestion yesterday. Another Reverend McGregor to add to the long list of clerics that stretched back—well, God only knew how far. But not forward, not with him. There was no question, no wavering indecisiveness; he'd had to bite his tongue not to burst out with 'not bloody likely' when the proposal was first put to him.

To be fair, his father had not forced it upon him. His father had waited patiently for the thought to occur to him. Hoping, like all men hope that their sons will rise to the same challenges and carry on in much the same way as they had. To give them everlasting life? Mick smiled at the irreverent thought—which was the truth as he saw it. No, it just wouldn't do—not for him.

Mick stared out the window, leaning restlessly towards it. Still, the situation left no room for indifference; a man had to make his way. It was all very well to casually dismiss his family's chain of holy men from here to eternity, but he needed an alternative.

His stare turned into a look of intense concentration as he scanned the Port Hills, just visible in the distance. There was in him the slightest sense of yearning. Words and ideas flew through his head as he examined the land. *The earth... Cultivating... Hard... Satisfying... Work...* All fused together with a vaguely familiar sense of longing and a newly discovered sense of hope. He could not yet verbalise his aspirations, not yet claim them as his own. He thought about Lily and her offer to find him a job in the country. He pushed the window open further and deeply breathed in the fresh air. His shoulders squared and his back straightened ever so slightly.

Chapter 12

Lily

I hesitated at the large double doors leading into the Lichfield's library. I could hear muffled male voices deep in discussion. Mr Lichfield was not alone. I was undecided about whether or not I should enter when I overheard my name in the conversation.

"Lily should be along anytime now," Mr Lichfield said to his guest. I peered in through the doors and saw the back of a tousled head and the corner of a strong shoulder. I inhaled sharply, hoping it was Liam. I stepped into the room with the dusting cloth and the beeswax polish in my hands.

"Here she is now," Mr Lichfield said, and I smiled a nervous smile. The tousled head moved as the man turned in his chair to see me.

"Ah, Lily," Liam said my name as if he were savouring it. It was a complete mystery to me how strongly I felt drawn to this man whom I had only met a few days ago. Hearing him say my name set something off inside me. It was as if I already had memories of him from another place, another time. A whole constructed vision of what our lives could be like together came alive in my mind in his presence. Actually, it felt like I came alive in his presence. I smiled as the joy that I heard in his voice filled me.

"Hello, Liam. This is a nice surprise," I said and smiled. Liam smiled back as he looked me over. When I say 'looked me over', there was nothing predatory about the way he looked. I felt honoured by his gaze. It was reverent.

"Lily, you should probably carry on with the dusting. We can talk as usual while you work," George directed. "I would hate to raise Elisabeth's ire."

"Yes, yes, of course." I set the polish on the large oak desk and moved towards the leather footstool. I used it to reach the top shelves of the bookshelves. As I began to move it, Liam stood up. He wore a green linen shirt and the colour of the fabric echoed in his eyes. That was all I could think about as he came towards me.

"Here, Lily, I'll shift that." Liam bent to move the footstool.

"Over here," I said as a motioned with my hand, amused that he was helping me. When the footstool was in place, Liam held out his arm for me.

"Oh, thank you," I said as I placed my hand on the warm skin of his forearm. I let out a sigh.

"What is it, Lily?" Liam bent his head to mine, as he asked the question.

I really didn't know how to reply. I was overwhelmed by the feel of his bare skin under my palm, not only aware of the small amount of warm skin that I touched but also conscious of his entire person.

Oh, I…" I mumbled. "You… you…" I moved my hand on his arm back and forth. "You feel so good," I blurted out.

"Ah, Lily." Liam smiled and then looked purposely at Mr Lichfield. "George?"

"All right, all right." Mr Lichfield stood up. "I'll just go… Where will I go? I'll go check on something. I won't be gone long, mind you." He smiled at Liam and me before he shut the door.

"I wondered how I would go about courting you, Lily," Liam said as he looked around the room, "but this is a start."

I moved my hand on his arm again, and I think I swayed a little with the joy of it. Liam tugged me towards the settee by the large bay window, keeping our physical bond.

We sat down, and he told me more about his farm and the home he was building. "It is not this fancy," he said as he looked around Mr Lichfield's large library. It was crowded with fine English-made furniture. The sofa we sat upon was upholstered in thick soft leather. Hundreds of books lined the shelves around the room, and the bay window had rich crimson draperies of velvet.

"Actually, compared to this, it is not much…" Liam stopped and looked up at the chandelier.

"It is enough, though?" I asked.

"Yes." Liam sat up a little straighter and stated quite firmly, "It is enough. Would you come to visit me?"

I nodded, "On my next day off."

"What is it, Lily?" Liam asked. He seemed to have an uncanny ability to sense my reluctance to say what was on my mind. "You can tell me." His voice was smooth and comforting. I held his arm more tightly.

"Do you think it is madness that I do not want to let you go?" I said. Liam's hand tightened over mine, and the door opened at the same time.

"No," he whispered as Mr Lichfield entered, "I feel it too."

"I see the courtship is progressing." Mr Lichfield was smiling at us. "Only it might be safer not to conduct it directly under Elisabeth's nose."

"Lily's going to come to the farm on her next day off," Liam explained as he took his hand off mine.

I truly did not want to take my hand from his arm. It was irrational, I know, but I felt like I had found something precious and did not want to relinquish it. I squeezed gently and let my hand slowly lift off his skin, and my common sense returned.

"The dusting, I'd better get on with the dusting." I jumped to my feet and scurried over and vaulted onto the footstool. I began frantically wiping the shelves in front of the books. Liam and Mr Lichfield both started laughing, and soon I was too.

~

"You can wait at the hotel. They have a ladies' lounge in the new one."

Liam and I had just arrived in Rakaia. We'd had a slow trip through the winter mud in his large wagon. It was my day off, and Liam wanted to pick up a tank he had ordered for collecting rain water. So, instead of a visit to his farm, I had made the trip to Rakaia with him.

"I don't want to wait anywhere; I'll go with you." I smiled at Liam, "I wouldn't mind having a look around, and I need to call in to the post office."

Liam told me how he had waited patiently for the bridge over the Rakaia River to be built. There had been talk of a bridge before he had purchased his land. His first trip over the river had been a perilous journey on a punt attached to pulleys and drawn by horses on the riverbank. Then, the bridge opened for traffic a few years ago, followed by the laying of rails. And it was opened for trains.

I liked the look of the little town. There was a grocer, a bakery, a butchery, a new school, and several churches. Liam told me the South Rakaia Hotel had been built to replace Dunford's Accommodation House, which had burnt down. He had eaten dinner at the hotel after his first anxious attempt at crossing the Rakaia and thought the fire not an altogether unfortunate event. We passed the brand-new station on the east side of the railway, opposite Rolleston Street. On the west side a large warehouse had been erected. If all had gone according to plan, Liam's water tank should be there now.

"Well, we'll check on the tank first. I'll need to muster up a few men to help me load it. Then we'll go to the post office, then maybe lunch?" I could tell Liam wasn't used to accommodating anyone else in his plans. I nodded.

We pulled up in the yard next to the hotel. He didn't get down from the wagon. He just kept looking at me. I smiled and looked back at him with questions in my eyes.

We felt our closeness growing. We couldn't ignore the easy camaraderie that enveloped us on our trip into town, when the wind made talking an effort. Even the silence between us was comfortable. Being alone with Liam satisfied something in me; the part that was uneasy without Rose was soothed. I felt so relaxed in his company.

Until he touched me.

It was a casual contact. He jumped down from the wagon seat and reached up for me, almost nonchalantly, as if he had helped women out of wagons hundreds of times before. A hand grasped my elbow and the other my waist. I stepped off the high wagon and slid down, one hand on his arm, my other on his chest, all very neat—until the moment he took my full weight. At that moment, all I wanted, all I could think about, was this is my place. I could spend my life in this man's embrace. Almost against my will, my hand on his chest slid up to his neck, and my gloveless hand lingered on the warm skin at his throat. I felt a shock go through him at the intimacy of my movement and the invitation it suggested. He enclosed me with his body. I looked up into his eyes and saw everything I felt. The feelings that swept through us both were too intimate for broad daylight in front of the railway shed. Far too intimate for Rakaia, for any town, for any place or time when there wasn't just the two of us, alone and preferably married. And we both knew it.

~

There was a letter from Rose. Liam and I were sitting in the dining room of the South Rakaia Hotel and the letter was leaning against my water glass.

"Why don't you just open it?" Liam grinned and asked after noticing my repeated glances down.

"Well, I will eventually. Maybe tonight. Just before I go to bed."

"Why not now?"

"I want to savour it, let the anticipation build." I squirmed in my chair, as if the excitement were too much for me.

Liam sat there and looked at me. I wondered if he was thinking about helping me down from the wagon. I was.

"What?"

"You look… You look…" He shook his head and glanced at the letter. "Tell me about your sister, Lily," Liam asked, his eyes sparkling a little.

"Well, she's working in Christchurch for Reverend McGregor, looking after his children."

"But isn't that what you were doing? Wasn't that your job?"

"Yes, we met the McGregors in London and helped with the children on the ship. How did you know?"

"Well, Lily, I saw you…that day in the park. I helped you push the pram back to the McGregors." His voice took on some urgency. "Don't you remember?"

I swallowed and the happiness that I had been feeling completely fled, leaving me feeling a little faint. I took a sip of water.

"Lily, what is the matter?"

"Oh, Liam, I think you must have seen my sister, Rose. The girl you saw in the park, it wasn't me, Liam." I looked down at my hands, not brave enough to look him in the eye.

"No, it was you, Lily. I saw you; I met you there. I held your hand." Liam's voice was full of anguish.

I shook my head again, "We're twins, Liam."

"Identical twins?" Liam asked, his confusion clearly showing on his face.

I nodded. Liam looked at me disbelievingly.

"Why didn't you tell me? Why did you keep that a secret, Lily?" He sounded angry.

"I didn't know. Rose did tell me she'd met a man in the park, but I didn't know it was you." Suddenly I had a memory of her deep connection with the stranger. My mouth went dry and I felt faint. I looked at Liam. Oh, I should have known—the familiarity. I had felt like I already knew him. I should have known. My eyes began to fill with tears.

"You aren't the girl I met in the park, you are her sister."

"Oh, Liam, I'm sorry, I didn't know. I… You know more about me than anyone in all of New Zealand. I thought I told you everything."

"Everything but that." Liam sounded betrayed. He shook his head as if trying to sort it all out. I wiped my eyes. "Lily, it's all right. Don't cry. It's just that I thought… Well, you know what I thought. I didn't know there were two of you."

We ate in silence for a while. I was hungry and the experience of eating in a hotel dining room was new to me. I looked around. There were thick velvet draperies on the windows, a lovely emerald colour, and snowy white linen cloths on the tables. The other female diners were more dressed up, with their bustles, petticoats, and bonnets with feathers. I had worn my best dress, a plain grey wool travelling suit. I knew I looked perfectly presentable, but still…

"Liam, those ladies, are they… Well, what do you suppose they do?"

"Oh, farmers' wives mostly, I think, come to town for the day. Some travellers, I suppose. Why?" Liam seemed happy enough to change the subject.

"Well, I just… Oh, nothing really."

Liam made to rise. "I'll introduce you to Mrs Worthington. She's just up the road from me." Liam stood, hailing a woman just as she walked by. "Excuse me, Mrs. Worthington. I'd like to introduce you to Lily Quinn."

"Hello, Lily! Just travelling through?" She looked me over while extending her hand. I rose.

"Oh no, ma'am. I live at Avonlea." I took her hand.

"Oh, a relation perhaps?"

"Umm… Well, no. I work there, actually, as a maid."

"Oh, I see." But Eloise Worthington didn't look as though she did see, not really. She looked from Liam to me and back again, "Well then, I'll let you get on with your lunch."

I sank back into my chair.

"Lily, tell me. What are you thinking?" His earlier impatience returned to his voice and made it sound hard.

"I think I might be just about finished, are you? I think I would like to go home. I just want to…" My voice trailed off. Filled with despair, I rose from my seat.

"I need to go to the ladies' room."

Liam stood, "Lily, I'm…"

"I'll meet you by the wagon," I interrupted him and felt lucky that he didn't notice my watery eyes before I snatched my letter and turned away.

I took my time. I needed to compose myself, figure out what to say. I knew I had left hastily, but I didn't like the tone of Liam's voice. I didn't like having to tell people I was a servant, even though I knew it was honest work. Working for the McGregors, Rose and I had felt like part of their family and were treated as such. But now, here I was a maid, and apparently looked down upon. I didn't mind the work, but how was I supposed to earn enough to buy suitable clothes to wear courting? And, even if I could afford them, what would Mrs Lichfield and Mrs Worthington have to say about it? And what difference did it make that I had a twin sister? Would Liam want to court Rose instead?

We rode in silence for some time. Liam tried to make conversation, asking me who had taught me to read. I mumbled, "Annie. My mother taught her," leaving him none the wiser about who Annie was or how she fitted into our lives in Creggan.

"Lily, I think I know what upset you, but, well, we can't let people's narrow-mindedness get to us. This is a new country; there are new rules." He was quiet a moment. "But obviously everybody doesn't know them yet," he finished with a smile in his voice.

"Well, I'm sorry I didn't tell you I had an identical twin sister," I answered almost sarcastically. "I told you all along I had a sister. I guess the identical part is more important to everyone else than it is to us. I guess I should apologise for my clothes. They are the best I have and…"

"What on earth are you talking about?"

"I know I looked presentable for lunch in a hotel, like I'd been travelling some distance, but I, well, I can see that I may not be up to your standard." I was looking at my hands again.

Liam reined in the horses. Pearl yelped from the back of the wagon, wondering why we were stopping, no doubt.

"Lily." Liam turned my shoulder so I was facing him. "Look at me, Lily." He put his hand under my chin and raised it gently, "Look in my eyes, Lily, then say what you said again, about my standards." He smiled at me, his eyes piercing me, "Say it again, Lily."

I shook my head and whispered, "I can't." Of course I couldn't. Our eyes were still locked—his full of a beautiful mix of acceptance and desire.

"Lily, I know it's our first real outing, but may I kiss you?"

Still looking into his eyes, I nodded as if there were never any question that he'd be given what he asked for. At the same time I was thinking of Rose and hoping she was going to understand.

Our lips met gently at first, politely. After only a moment our manners disappeared. Liam pulled me closer, needing. Oh God, he needed me. I felt like I had no mind of my own. I was overwhelmed by sensation and so acutely aware of Liam and his need. It sparked and sizzled between us; our kiss deepened. He manoeuvred me closer to him and I conceded. There was nothing to resist, nothing that I didn't want with all my heart. Finally he pulled away just a little, still smiling, still looking into my eyes, still holding me tight.

"Ah, Lily, if ever I had a standard," he paused and swallowed. "You are my standard. Don't you ever forget that."

"And you're not still annoyed that I have an identical twin sister?" I whispered in his ear.

"Hmm… No, not annoyed." He shook his head. "Just, well, it's odd to love a woman and realise there is another one just like her somewhere else."

I gasped.

"Oh, uh…well," Liam blushed, "you know…" I couldn't help smiling as I watched Liam's discomfort. I knew I looked smug. He gently unwrapped his arms from around me and took up the reins to urge the horses back into action.

We stopped where the long drive up to Avonlea left the main road. He helped me down, careful to keep a respectable distance, still thoroughly dismayed at his premature admission. I was buoyant. I felt like his kiss and then his unexpected declaration had infused me with something completely new. I felt all lovely and juicy inside.

"Thank you, I had a nice time." I couldn't keep my voice from sounding mischievous.

"Yes, well, so did I."

"C'mon, Liam, please," I cajoled.

"Please, what?"

"Please, don't look so serious. Smile at me again, for heaven's sake," I reached my hand behind his head and, standing on my tip toes, pulled him down to me. I kissed him, hard but quickly, and then pulled away. I startled both of us, I think.

"I liked what you said, Liam. I did." I grinned and danced away from him in the wind.

He hollered after me, "A shee-geeha, for sure!"

~

On my next day off I walked to Liam's farm, and he showed me through his half-finished house. He was putting a lot of love and attention into the building of it, I could tell. The front door led down a long timber-lined hallway with a half-finished room on each side. The hall ran into a sitting room, where a tiled fireplace waited with a beautiful wooden surround.

"I've got a stew on. I was hoping you would be here for dinner," he said when he saw me wrinkling up my nose trying to discern the aroma that wasn't just new timber.

"My bedroom," Liam said, as I peeked through a door leading off the sitting room. He took my hand and pulled me through another door into the kitchen—with a workbench under the window and an empty space for a large cook stove. The kitchen was at the back of the house with a door leading to the outside and the path to the other buildings. On the other side of the path was a dairy, a laundry with a huge copper washtub, and a storehouse.

"It seems very grand to me." I turned to look back at the house as we headed over to look around the farmyard.

"Do you like it, Lily?" I turned to face this man I was just beginning to know. I looked straight into his eyes for a long moment. He bent to kiss me and much later murmured again, "Do you like it, Lily?"

"Aye, I do."

We tried to meet at the river on my days off, but the weather didn't always cooperate. I would walk to the end of the long drive and start down towards the water. I would hear Liam coming behind me on Smoke, with Pearl trailing behind. At first, he would say something amusing and silly about his luck at coming across such a fine lady out for a stroll. Then he would slide off Smoke in that easy way of his and walk beside me. Later, as the weather got colder, Liam would come up behind me on Smoke and, without a word, extend a hand and scoop me up into his arms. I had to sit sideways, in front of him, and he balanced me with his arms wrapped around me as he took me back to Fairfield for the afternoon.

But when the sun was out, we would sit by the river and talk. I would tell him stories my Nana Kat used to tell us, and he would tell me about his escapades with his friend Frank or what was happening on his farm. We hardly ever ran out of things to talk about, but when we did we were both happy just sitting there quietly watching the river.

Chapter 13

Henry Lichfield thought his life might improve once his father finally gave in to his mother and purchased a house in town. But, no, he had strict instructions that he was to do no entertaining there of his own, not even so much as a card game. He'd made matters worse by impulsively informing his acquaintances that they would have the premises at their disposal before his father had refused him a key. Now his daily life was rife with loaded questions regarding the staging of a break-in and sly innuendos questioning Lily's existence. It was only because they had hounded him that he had mentioned Lily. He wanted to have something good in his life, one thing that they would envy. He had lied, of course. Well, he told the truth about how she looked, like a fairy or a princess—long burnished curls that cascaded down nearly to her rump, clear white skin with a rosy glow. He went on, until eventually they'd asked in their crude way about her womanly attributes, and he'd told them, making up what he needed to—anything to keep this avid attention on himself. They must have sensed the earnestness in his voice, the kernel of truth in his description, and decided to see for themselves. "We'll come to see her, then," they had all agreed. "When?" This posed a problem for Henry; he'd lied about the way she needed him, came to him because of her need. He'd told his friends she loved him.

Elisabeth was in her element. She was busy overseeing the packing of her ball gown for its trip to town. Sally had no experience with organza, so Elisabeth demonstrated how to bunch the tissues around the ruffles to keep them from being crushed in the trunk. George had, after considerable persuasion, agreed to escort her to a ball the following night. He would look so dashing in his evening wear. It had been a long time since she'd had him dressed up and on her arm.

"Will Henry be at the house when we get to town tonight?" Sally asked.

"Oh, no. He is coming out here this afternoon with some of his friends from school," Elisabeth answered.

Damn, thought Sally, and she crunched a ruffle in her hand instead of the tissue paper.

Ronny drove Mr and Mrs Lichfield and Sally to the station in Rakaia just before lunch. Lily was feeling relaxed and happy. The thought of an entire Saturday alone with her list of duties appealed to her. She had plans to see Liam tomorrow for a picnic at the river if the day was fine. Mrs Lichfield did not know Lily was seeing Liam regularly and it made sense to keep it that way. Lily headed towards the kitchen, thinking she might ask Myra if she'd be allowed to make an apple tart to take along on their picnic. Myra was bustling about. There were pots bubbling on the stove and a lovely meaty aroma rose from the oven. She had a rolling pin in one hand. "There you are girl, better get to setting the table."

"What?" Lily asked, "For whom?"

"Henry, he's coming out from town. Any time now. Ronny's bringing them back in the wagon. Coming with four or five friends apparently. Never brought out friends before."

"Oh." Lily thought surely he wouldn't bother her in front of his friends. She'd stay close to Myra the whole time. She'd either be in the kitchen, or with Ronny, or… She closed her eyes. She breathed in deeply to centre herself and said the little prayer for strength and protection that her Nana Kat used to say when she had first realised she was losing her mind. It comforted her with its familiarity, even though it certainly hadn't done a lot of good for Nana Kat, she thought cynically.

Lily watched through the lace of the draperies in the dining room as the wagonload full of overgrown schoolboys came up the drive. She hadn't noticed the pattern before. Close-up, it was an intricate Celtic ring design and in between the three joined rings were tiny serpents turned into figure eights with their tails touching their heads. Lily started when she heard footsteps on the front porch and hastily retreated to the kitchen.

Lily waited as long as she could, dawdling over the steaming dishes that Myra had lined up on the bench.

"Myra, this one needs a larger serving spoon, don't you think? Doesn't this dish have a lid?" She even dashed out to the kitchen garden for some parsley to adorn the platter of freshly roasted meat.

"I don't think those boys will be taking much notice of your pretties there, Lily. Get on with it, lass," Myra finally said, shaking her head.

Lily entered the dining room with a large covered dish in each hand, wishing she would have taken them one at a time. She sat them both down rather quickly and took a quick look at the faces around the table before hastily retreating for another load. *Oh my, oh my,* she thought to herself as she wiped her brow with her apron and leaned against the large table in the centre of the kitchen, taking a few deep breaths. Lily may have grown up in Creggan, the granddaughter of a crazy woman, with very little male attention—if any—but in her short time aboard the emigrant ship, she had learned a few things about men. She was in no doubt that the boys in the dining room were up to no good.

"C'mon there, lass, get on with it." Myra was losing her patience.

Lily turned towards her. "Myra, I'm going to need your help." The determination in Lily's voice surprised Myra. "And you are going to have to give it to me." Myra listened while Lily explained her fears and was sympathetic and supportive of Lily's plans. Lily took one dish in her hands, lifted her chin, and marched into the dining room.

"...but don't speak of it..." Henry was saying and trailed off as Lily entered. The conversation ceased in a way that let Lily know without a doubt that they had been talking about her. She kept her mind on the business at hand, serving politely, making her way to and from the kitchen. Lily did not smile and she did not look at anyone, although she was very aware they were looking at her. The conversation was of parties and card games and who had been lucky enough to go for a spin in Arthur's father's new phaeton.

"Henry, do you suppose we could have more wine?" one boy asked politely.

"Lily, could you get a few more bottles of wine, please?"

Lily raised one eyebrow and looked directly at him.

"I'll ask Myra." Lily was loathe to embarrass Henry in front of his friends, but part of Myra's contribution to the plan was to limit alcohol consumption. When asked just exactly how this was to be accomplished, Myra had shrugged her shoulders and said, "We'll just say I have orders."

Lily returned a few moments later with the dessert, which seemed to take the boys' minds momentarily off the empty wine glasses. But Henry was not so easily deterred and excused himself, following Lily into the kitchen. Lily carried right on out the back while Myra met him at the door.

"Yes, sir, and what can I be doing for you?" Myra's voice was very pleasant. "I hope your friends are enjoying their dinner."

"Ah, well, yes, but I have ordered more wine." Henry tried to sound commanding, but something about Myra's attitude had him doubting.

"Well, that's easier said than done. Y'see, your dear parents left me instructions that the wine cellar was not at your personal disposal this weekend and excepting for a reasonable amount with dinners, I was not to..." She didn't finish her sentence but instead patted her ample bosom, pulling just slightly at a cord around her neck, implying that the key was in a very safe place.

"Where has Lily gone?" Henry looked around the kitchen, not about to be thwarted at every turn.

"She has a lot to attend to this afternoon, sir." Myra's voice held a note of deference that it hadn't a moment ago. "I sent her on her way."

"Where? To where? What is she doing?"

"Ah, this and that. She's around." Myra shrugged her shoulders and started to scrape gravy out of a tureen, as if Lily's whereabouts were not of the slightest importance.

They retired to his father's library. Mitchell and Norm both would have liked to go riding, but then they all concurred they would do that tomorrow. They discovered a decanter full of fine port, fortuitously surrounded by six glasses and made themselves comfortable.

"Ah, I see what you mean, Lichfield." Jonesy didn't elaborate.

"Yeah, she's beautiful," Ricker said somewhat dreamily. "Imagine having that in your bed every night."

"Do you, Lichfield... I mean will she come and see you tonight?" Ernest leaned forward and opened the cigar box on George's desk.

Henry was very satisfied with his friend's reactions and so enamoured was he of this rare attention that the truth seemed of no significance whatsoever. "Probably. It's been at least two weeks. Yes, I should imagine so," he answered nonchalantly. And then, feeling magnanimous, said, "Have one," motioning to the open cigar box.

Norm, Mitchell, Jonesy, Ernest, and Ricker all looked at him with looks that ranged from outright envy to mildly grudging respect as they lit their cigars. Henry had another sip of port, settled back in his father's leather armchair, crossed his outstretched legs on the footstool, and took a long, deep drag on the fine imported tobacco.

Lily saw them looking for her, trying not to be obvious about it. First it was just Henry, upstairs, going from bedroom to bedroom hoping to catch her at work. She'd readied the rooms while they were drinking in the study; Myra had been on lookout for her. Then she'd found Ronny in the stables forking fresh straw into the stalls and broached the subject with him.

"It's not safe for ye…in your bed. Is it, dear?"

Lily shook her head. Ronny pondered.

"Sleep in the loft. We'll burrow you in, in the corner. Nobody'd find ye; I'll be just down here." He motioned with his shoulder to his room, attached to the stables. "Go up there now," he said, looking up at her. "Sit a spell. Looks like you could use the quiet."

Lily watched from the opening that served as a window to the loft. The wooden cover had been left slightly ajar and let in a wedge of bright light. Two of the boys wandered around the house doing a complete circuit, weaving ever so slightly under the effects of the port. Two more of them sat on the front veranda, their shirt sleeves rolled up, enjoying the weak winter sun. Still smoking a cigar, one had a crystal glass, which he perched perilously on the edge of the step. Lily saw an outline of a man in the window upstairs, and she jumped back from the light. She curled herself in the corner behind a bale of straw and drifted off to sleep.

Oh, Rose. Oh LilyRose. If I could just talk to you now. Oh, if only you were here… With me.

Lily woke to the sound of male voices, the creaking of leather and the stomps and movements of horses being saddled. "What's goin' on here?" she heard Ronny ask.

"We've decided to go to the pub."

"Ye what? Isn't it getting a bit late for that sort of carry on?"

"Lichfield, does your help always question you like this?" Jonesy inquired.

"Ah, Ronny, help us here, would you," Henry ordered and motioned to the saddle on the ground.

"Well, and I never." Ronnie paused as if deciding whether to help or not. "You boys put the saddle blankets on underneath, mind you. Planning to tie them up in front for most of the night, are you?" Ronny was not happy but grudgingly saw to the horses. They rode out in a flurry, galloping before they had even turned to head towards Rakaia.

Ronny was shaking his head as Lily made her way down the ladder. "At least you'll have a few hours peace, lass."

~

"Take some of the steamed pudding. I know it's hard to pack; here, wrap it in a piece of cheesecloth." Myra organised Lily, who had just finished a bowl of buttered porridge and was packing the picnic. Lily yawned and stretched. She had ended up sleeping on the floor of Myra's bedroom, thought by both Ronny and Myra to be a safer option than the stables, considering that drunken boys could return at any time during the night. Lily had agreed and felt quite safe in Myra's room, but had hardly slept a wink because of Myra's incessant snoring.

"Nice dress, Lily, you look good," Myra commented as she sliced some mutton and added it to the basket. Lily was not used to anyone complimenting her on her clothes.

"Oh, thank you, I finished it the other night."

"Pretty colour. That deep rose brightens you up." It was actually the first dress Lily had ever owned that was not a dull homespun brown or grey. She thought it was a shame to cover it up with her old winter coat. The sun was shining now, but the winds were unpredictable.

~

"Who's that?" Mitchell pointed to a lone figure on the horizon.

Henry squinted, trying to make out the figure in the distance. "Don't know," he lied.

"I think that might be Lily," Jonesy stated quite excitedly, standing up in his stirrups.

"Let's follow her." Mitchell urged his horse on.

"Ah, I don't think..." Henry was at a loss for words but finally managed, "No, it's her day off. Leave her be."

"Won't she be wondering about you, Henry?" Norm asked innocently enough, but Henry looked at him sharply. "I mean, she might be wondering where you were last night. You know, when she came to your room looking for you." Norm snickered. "We'll just talk to her. C'mon!" They all took off after Mitchell, Henry lagging behind.

Lily was walking on the wagon trail that led to the river thinking of Liam and the possibility of kissing him again when she heard hoofbeats. She knew from the direction that it wasn't Liam and turned to see the riders fanned out, heading straight towards her. She instinctively sped up, but there was no place to run to, no place to hide.

They rode up, and one of them called out, "Hey, Lily." She stopped and turned. They parted ranks. Henry was coming up at the rear. Lily realised that they had no plan, no evil designs already decided upon. She took a deep breath.

They all looked towards Henry. Finally, he spoke.

"Hello, Lily, my dear." There was a strange note in his emphasis and an entreating look in his eyes.

"Hello, Henry." Lily kept her voice even, not really warm but not excessively cold. Whatever did he want from her?

"Where are you off to?"

"Just to the river."

"Who are you meeting?" Mitchell looked pointedly at her picnic basket.

"I don't believe we've been properly introduced," Lily spoke, looking directly at Mitchell, her head held high.

"Hmm... Well... Lily, this is Richard Mitchell." Henry pointed towards Mitchell, "and Arthur Jones, Norm Breckenridge, Ernest Smithers, and..." He pulled on the horse's reins and turned, "John Ricker."

"Pleased to meet you, Lily." John Ricker spoke to Lily, the others had just nodded. "So what are you off to do, now?" He carried on in what sounded like a very friendly tone.

"Well, I'd tell you if I'd a mind to, but I don't particularly. It's my day off, and nobody's business but my own where I'm off to. Excuse me, now." Lily turned as if to go, but the one called Jones quickly moved on his horse, cutting her off. She was surrounded by young men on horseback.

"Wait a minute, there! We just thought we might come with you. Here, I'll give you a lift." He reached out a hand, suggesting Lily might like to climb aboard behind him. She moved away, but there was not much room to manoeuvre between the horses.

"I really do just want to be on my way." Lily couldn't help the quiver of fear in her voice.

"Pull away, boys. Don't scare the girl." Ricker moved his mount back.

"No," Henry answered, as if something in Lily's voice or the situation excited him. He dismounted and moved towards her, his hand outstretched. "Lily, come with me." She shook her head. "Now."

"She doesn't want to, Henry. You can't force her to." Ricker was watching Lily intently. "I don't think she even likes you, Henry," he said quite matter-of-factly. "Does she, now?"

"Of course she does. Lily, come now." His voice was louder and more demanding, as if, by being authoritative, Lily were going to magically throw herself into his arms.

Heads turned at the sound of a galloping horse. "What in God's name is going on here?" Liam yelled, his big grey stallion pushing through the ring of horseflesh.

"Lily." Liam reached for her and she grabbed his hand and launched herself off the ground and into his lap, picnic basket and all. Lily held onto his arm with her free hand. Her heart was thundering in her chest. She was tempted to lay her head on his chest and just close her eyes. But she lifted her chin and looked directly at Henry.

Liam's voice was menacing, "Who are you and where do you come from?" The boys all looked to Henry, strangely hopeful of him showing some backbone.

"Henry Lichfield," he stated with an angry arrogance, "and who are you?"

"Henry? You're George's son?" Liam's voice was incredulous.

"And you?" Henry asked again.

"Liam McCann. I am a neighbour and a friend of your father's. I wouldn't credit a son of George's to be out harassing innocent women." He shook his head and simultaneously tightened his arms around Lily. "You all right?" he murmured. Lily didn't answer but tightened her grip on his arm.

"You boys ought to be ashamed of yourselves," Liam said.

"I apologise, Miss, for causing you distress," Ricker said and turned, shaking his head at Henry.

"C'mon," Liam said, turning his horse.

"Where are you going? Where are you taking Lily?" Henry asked, his voice shrill and oddly petulant, as if his favourite toy were being taken away.

"Away from here. Away from you, Henry."

~

"Lily?" Liam asked quietly and lovingly when they were out of earshot.

"Hmm?" Lily was lost in the warm feel of him against her shoulder and cheek.

"Thank you, Liam."

"Do you think they would have hurt you?" Liam tensed, his tone suddenly not as gentle.

"I'm not sure. Henry would on his own, if he could, but I don't think he'd do anything too terrible in front of the others."

"What do you mean?" Liam pulled up Smoke, agitated now. "Has he tried before?"

"Yes," Lily answered honestly. "He covets me, I think."

"Covets you? What the hell does that mean?"

"He wants me because he cannot have me, Liam. That is all," she answered calmly. "He doesn't love me. Doesn't know what love is, I don't suppose." They rode along in silence until they arrived at his farm.

Lily had to release her hold on Liam as he lowered her to the ground. She struggled with her skirt and petticoats but managed. Liam dismounted and found her waiting. Her arms were ready to go around him.

"But luckily for me," Lily paused a moment and looked him straight in the eye, "you do." She wrapped her arms around him and standing on her tiptoes kissed him softly on the neck. "Don't you, Liam?"

Oh, to have this woman in his arms. Liam bent to find her lips. She was waiting for him, an inviting fusion of warm soft skin and willing lips and caressing hands. He could lose himself so easily in her and know without a doubt that it was the right thing. The true and honest fact was that he wanted Lily to belong to him, in every possible way. Soon, it would be soon, he would ask her to marry him. He'd finish the house first, give her a decent home, buy her a proper cook stove, provide for her. He broke his contact with her lips; she sought him, wanting him back, leaning into him.

"Ah, Lily, dear Lily. Soon, I promise you, soon."

"Now, Liam, now."

Liam was not entirely sure what she was referring to. He had meant marriage, but by the warm, sweet feel of her she had more immediate concerns. She was pressing herself into him.

"Hmm, you feel so good, so strong." She was quiet a moment, "You'd never lay a hand on me, would you, Liam, in anger, I mean?" Her voice had changed with the question.

"No, of course not. Come with me now." She looked up at him, with a look of hopeful anticipation.

"I have to see to Smoke." The look in her eyes changed then, in recognition of the practicalities of life.

Walking hand and hand towards the woolshed, Liam tugging Smoke's reins with his free hand, they made their way to the far end containing his tack room.

"You'll have to stay here tonight, Lily." He turned and looked at her seriously even though she was smiling the most delicious grin.

"I'll keep you safe...from Henry."

Lily and Liam were a match. They fitted together, one of those seemingly rare couples for whom love was no effort. They might have been together ten years or ten minutes, it was irrelevant. They belonged. Lily only had to recall the first moment she had laid eyes on him by the river. He was mouthing her name, silently, like a prayer. She was acutely aware of the depth of his feeling for her. It radiated from him through their lunch and now as they tucked up by the fire. Whatever it was that he wanted, she would give it to him. There were no questions left for her to ask.

Their mutual desire was a palpable thing, alive between them.

She reached out for his hand, gently and lovingly enclosing his. The feel of her skin nearly caused his undoing; it was too much having her here in his home, by herself, as if she were actually his. His heartbeat quickened with the thrill of it all, not just the anticipation of when the first time would be. There was so much more than that at stake. The glorious expectation of forever stretched out before him: Lily at his fireside, night after night, loving, wanting, and needing him. He swallowed and turned towards her, as if there were words forthcoming. She picked up his hand, turned it, and pressed it to her lips. Her lips kissed his open palm. He sighed, then relaxed.

He thought she understood.

~

He watched her breathing evenly in her slumber, the skin of her face glistening in the moonlight. She was curled up with her arm around her knees. Liam was still surprised he had been able to conjure up the strength of will not to take her to his bed last night.

He paced the room trying to take his mind off the woman on his sofa. Henry Lichfield. *The bastard, the bastard! Who does he think he is?* He couldn't take her back there in the morning, not without talking to

George first. He slumped into a chair. Something had to be done. But what?

Lily stirred, uncoiled her legs, and stretched them out full length. She arched her shoulders to elongate her spine, her arms reached out as if they were seeking contact. "Rosie, Rosie?" she murmured and sighed as she curled up again.

Chapter 14

Lily

He was in the rocker, bathed in the early morning light. I think he was still asleep when I started kissing him softly on the cheek, murmuring his name.

"Lily, oh God, Lily..." He reached for my hand, "Stop, please." His voice was soft and held no conviction.

"What, what did you say?" My lips were on his neck, just under his ear. He shivered.

"Lily, you have to stop this."

"I...I don't want to stop, Liam. I want you." I settled myself in his lap, moved my mouth to his.

"Lily, listen. I want you too. Do you understand what I'm saying?"

"Mmm, I certainly do." My tongue explored his lips and darted in ahead of the kiss. I had never in my life felt so generous; I was giving myself to him.

"Lily, don't you want promises?"

Something in the tone of his voice made me pause. Uneasily I pulled away. "I thought..." I didn't look him in the eye. "I thought..." I hastily removed myself from his lap.

"What did you think, Lily?" Liam's voice sounded more irritated than concerned.

"I thought... No, I assumed..." I struggled to find my courage. I took a breath, "I assumed, apparently wrongly, that certain promises had been made."

I turned, gathered up my old woollen coat, and headed for the door.

"Where are you going? Lily, what are you doing?" He sounded a little panicked.

"I'm leaving... I..." I stopped because I didn't know what I really wanted to say. My eyes started to fill.

"Lily, please don't cry." Liam looked lost.

I turned towards him, but then he said in a desperate tone, "I'll get the wagon. I'll take you back to Avonlea for now," as if it were, at least, something he could do for me.

"No, I…" All of a sudden, I was having trouble fighting back tears, "I'd like to walk." When I left, I slammed the door.

I was down the drive and nearly to the corner by the time Liam had Smoke saddled. I heard him coming and hurried across Mitcham Road and ducked between the wires of the boundary fence. By the time Liam got to the corner, I was halfway across the paddock.

I continued my cross-country journey, trudging through the soft dirt of a newly ploughed paddock, and then came to a pasture that was easier to walk on. My thoughts whirled and collided. Promises, what promises was he talking about? I trusted him, I trusted him. He said he loved me. I thought that meant he wanted me. I thought we wanted each other. I assumed—I just assumed—that meant we'd marry. I thought he wanted me, but… He didn't, did he? Not last night or this morning. I snuffled and wiped my nose on my sleeve. I was a mess. A shameful mess. Eventually I made it to Avonlea. My feet were dragging as I rounded the corner of the house. Liam was sitting on the steps.

"Lily?"

I didn't look up. He'd said my name like a cross between a reprimand and question, and I didn't feel like I had any answers. None at all. I went past him up the stairs.

"Damn it, Lily! Please talk to me."

I stopped and turned. "What exactly do you want me to say, Liam?" I knew my voice sounded unbearably sad, but I couldn't help it.

Liam moved towards me, with a pitying look on his face.

"Lily…"

I stepped back.

"Don't." I raised my arms, with my palms facing out as if I could somehow ward him off, "Please, I don't want you to ever touch me ever again." My words echoed through me. Such lies I told, betraying myself. All I could do was turn and run into the house.

Chapter 15

Liam sat back down. He had no intention of leaving until Lily had cooled off and they'd sorted things out between them. He'd found out from Myra that Henry and his friends had left on the late train the day before. George and Elisabeth were still in town, so he couldn't talk to George about Henry. But at least Lily was safe for now.

In time, Liam went to the kitchen.

"Lily didn't look too good."

"No, Myra, you're right about that. Where is she? Has she come down yet?"

"No, haven't heard a thing since she disappeared up to her room. She's going to have to get to work here pretty soon."

"I'm going up; I have to talk to her." Liam's voice was firm, as if daring Myra to question his motives.

Myra shrugged in response, "You got strong feelin's for the lass, I see."

"I do."

"Well, then, it's the fourth door on the right at the top of the stairs. You go easy, gentle like. Our Lily's a good girl."

Hmm. She is a good girl, Liam thought, as he slowly trod up the stairs, thinking of his plans and wondering where he went wrong. It had taken so much determination—getting to New Zealand, working to get enough together to buy land, getting the land, settling on it. Here he was at the next stage. He'd always imagined it in purely practical terms, the finding of a suitable wife, marriage, bringing her to his home, having children. This wasn't going how he had planned. It was all happening slightly out of focus, with all these feelings of need and want that were such an effort to control.

He didn't knock; he just opened the door quietly. She was curled up again, her back towards the door.

Chapter 16

Lily

"Lily?" He spoke softly, "Lily, can I come in and talk to you?"

I sat up slowly and leaned my back against the headboard, my arms still curled around my knees. I looked at Liam and nodded.

He came towards me, taking the only chair in the room and sat in it facing me.

"Tell me what's happening, please."

I looked at him sitting there. He was so beautiful, all strong muscle and…man. Everything about him was so well defined. My throat constricted and my eyes started to fill again.

"Lily, damn it, talk to me." His voice was slightly angry, but he added more gently, "Please, Lily, let's sort this out."

I looked at him curiously now, "You really don't know, do you?"

He pressed his palms together, his elbows extended, as if slightly irritated.

"No." His voice sounded impatient and annoyed.

I saw then that he was on his own edge, just hanging on.

"Well," I took a deep breath. The air in the room seemed thin. "The only person alive on this earth that I ever loved…love, you know, truly love…is my sister."

"But, Lily, I…" He was losing his grip.

"No, let me finish. I love her and she loves me back. No matter what, Liam, she loves me back. She accepts all the love I give her and then returns it. That's the only love I've ever really known." I stopped, thinking he might need a moment for that to sink in. "I don't know how to love you any other way." I swallowed, willing myself to carry on. "And so I need to apologise for… Well, I guess you thought I was…" I couldn't meet his eyes, "throwing myself at you."

He didn't say anything, but his mouth went slack.

"Honestly, Liam, I thought when you said you loved me, it was a promise." My voice wavered, "It felt like one to me anyway. I trusted you, but then I thought you did say it accidentally, before you wanted to, and maybe you didn't want to at all." I was speaking faster and faster, "But I have so much to give you in return." I wiped my nose on my sleeve. "I am sorry…so, so sorry…because it never occurred to me that you wouldn't want it." I lay down again and curled up. "That's the truth." My voice cracked with a sob.

Liam jumped up. I heard him pacing the floor.

"I don't know what to say first."

"You don't have to say anything, Liam. Just go, please." My voice sounded as shattered as I felt.

"Lily, your heart is breaking."

Something small in me wanted to be sarcastic, maybe flippant, say 'Oh, thank you for pointing that out', but the rest of me was in too much pain.

"Lily, I don't want it to. I want it whole."

I heard what he said, but was too afraid to try to make sense out of it.

"Lily, I do love you. Lily, I love you." He got up and then sat on the bed and put a hand on my shoulder. "Lily, look at me." I turned onto my back and moved my hair out of my eyes. I so badly wanted to believe him, but I still felt completely defeated.

"I love you and I do want you. I just wanted to do it right. I want to court you, and finish the house, and then get married…a wedding and all…and then take you home. Lily, I wanted to do it right. I have a plan, Lily. I wanted the time to be right."

My eyes focused as what he said penetrated my misery. I lifted myself onto my elbows.

"Well, there you have it, Liam. I didn't have a plan, did I? My idea of love is bigger than that. Timing doesn't get a look in."

"But, Lily, I just said… I just told you that I want you."

I interrupted, my body still tensing with an angry undercurrent, "Someday, a man will love me the way Rose does. He'll love me so much that he won't be able to hold anything back, ever." I paused, "There will be no deciding if the time is right."

"Lily…"

The door burst open. Liam scrambled off the bed as Elisabeth Lichfield marched in.

"What on earth do you think you are doing, Liam McCann, in

Lily's bedchamber? Out now! This isn't right, this just isn't right. Lily, I'll speak to you later." Elisabeth Lichfield planted herself firmly between Liam and me, determined to shoo him out the door.

He sidestepped her and grabbed my hand. "I'll be that man, Lily. Do you hear me? I'll be that man." He turned and left, slamming the door before Mrs Lichfield had a chance to.

Chapter 17

"Good God, man, what's the matter with you?" Liam had opened the door to George's study and stood leaning against the door frame looking well past dejected. "Come in. Shut the door. Tell me what's going on." George turned and poured Liam a whisky. "Here, it can't be that bad."

"Your wife just kicked me out of Lily's bedroom."

"Oh, I see." George sat down heavily. "Wouldn't have taken you for a man of indiscretion, Liam."

"George, we were having an argument. Lily ran up there. I followed her, wanted to make things right between us. That's all." Liam took a slow sip and closed his eyes, under the ancient misconception that the liquor might possibly improve matters.

"Well, did you?"

"What? Oh, no. No, I didn't." He savoured another sip.

"And so…" George let Liam continue at his own pace, but he was curious.

"I think I broke her heart." Liam's voice caught.

George poured him another shot; there was nothing else for it. After a while, George tried again.

"What happened, Liam?"

"I wanted everything to go according to my plan, George. Lily loves her sister, her sister loves her back. She thinks I should… I didn't tell Lily what my plan was. I held back because I wanted everything to be perfect and right. You know what I mean?"

"No, not really."

"Well, as it turns out, Lily knew." He polished off his second shot, laid his head back, and closed his eyes. "She was right."

"What did she know?"

His voice was quiet and sad, "That it would have been perfect."

~

"Elisabeth has taken her to town."

"What, already?"

"They left this morning, early."

Liam had been up doing chores since before sunrise. All he could think about was sorting things out with Lily, making it right between them.

"Damn it, Elisabeth has done this on purpose."

"Of course she has, Liam. She made it clear in no uncertain terms that her staff and her neighbours were to be, well…" George raised his eyebrows, "You can't say that you weren't warned. Here, you look like you could use some tea."

Liam sat at the corner of the large table in the dining room where George had been breakfasting alone. He sipped the tea silently.

"Do you think she wanted to go?"

"What?"

"Do you think she wanted to go, get away from here, from me?" Liam's voice had the slightest of wavers.

"She had no choice about going, Liam. Elisabeth had decided. She's in our employ after all," George stated firmly, "she has to do as she is told."

Liam rode slowly back to Fairfield, the disorder of his thoughts making him feel unbalanced and very unsure—a state that was entirely new to him. He didn't like it. Not at all. The plan was… The plan was… Well, bugger the plan. What now?

In his confusion he did, however, derive some comfort from his routine. He took care of his stock and spent the afternoon clearing tussock, digging it out by hand, with Pearl cavorting in the sunshine at his side. Eventually, though, the dog quieted, sensing her master's mood. By nightfall, only one thought was really clear: however Lily did or didn't feel about him, she deserved to be safe. He needed to speak to George about Henry.

~

"Don't tell anyone," Rose said, as they sat on the riverbank in the weak winter sun.

"Why not?"

"I overheard him ask her, and I think she said yes."

"So what about your job?" Lily asked.

"Well, I am sure when it's official they won't need me anymore.

Actually, it will be a bit of a relief, I think, although I'll miss the children. Charlotte will be fine."

"Charlotte?"

"Mrs McMullan. We've become great friends." Rose smiled and reached her arm around her sister.

"Now, tell me, Lily."

Lily was quiet.

"You know I'll find out eventually. You might as well just say what…"

"I know, Rose, I know. It's just that I don't even know what to think." Lily closed her eyes and leaned back on the straggly grass of the riverbank next to Rose. The sunlight was weak but still warmed their skin. There was no wind.

"I wanted him to love me like you do," I offered.

"What? Who? Henry?" Rose started to sit up.

"Oh no, no. Liam… The man I met at the river. I told you about him."

"No, you didn't. Not really."

Lily's hand came to her head. "Why haven't I explained all this to you before now? I could have done it in a letter. I could have…" Lily turned to face Rose, "I love Liam McCann," Lily stated quite firmly as she sat up. "I really do."

Rose's mouth dropped open, "Lily… Lily! What are you talking about? Where did you meet him? How long have you known him? Who is he?" Her words came rushing at Lily.

"At the river. He's a farmer. He's kind and smart and so handsome. Oh, Rose, but we had an argument. I think I wanted too much, too much too soon."

"What? Oh, Lily, tell me."

Lily told Rose about Liam, but it took her a while to understand.

"Nana Kat told us that love is worth fighting for, Lily."

"Yes, but I don't think Mrs Lichfield will be taking me back to the country for a while." Lily stood up and straightened her coat.

"No, but you can go yourself on your day off. C'mon." Rose stood up and reached for Lily's hand, "We'll make a plan."

"Plans. Liam had a plan; it didn't work… Well, not so far." Lily turned and smiled at Rose, squeezing her hand.

~

The days dragged on for Liam, leaving him worn out. A conscientious man, he did what he had to do, but there was no undercurrent of anything even slightly reminiscent of joy. He was stalled, like a sailing ship with no promise of wind. He sat there letting God knows what lap the edges; he didn't care. Eventually he'd sink.

A letter came, not exactly a beacon, more like the shaky beam from a lighthouse in a storm, just a flicker at first. Something gnawed at him, too uneasy to be hope, but still the fog lifted a little. Lily was coming to see him. Could he meet the train?

Chapter 18

Lily

I saw him standing on the platform, his easy stance tensed and nervous, his hat clenched in his hands. I hurried towards him, almost within touching distance before he turned.

"Liam, oh Liam." I reached out my hand.

He shook my hand and then released it, "Lily, it's nice to see you."

I stood still for a moment, "Oh."

Liam started towards the wagon.

"No. No, Liam." I reached again, dropping my satchel. I took both his hands, wrapped them around my back, lifted my arms around his neck, pulled his head down, and his mouth towards mine. I called everything to me that mattered and kissed him with it, hoping he'd understand. He took his time.

We bought beer and cheese and some fresh bread and drove down a rutted trail to the river's edge near the township. The winter sun tried its best but I was shivering. We were still not completely at ease with each other, but there was an underlying sense of hope. Liam's mouth turned up at the edges when I caught him glancing at me. I couldn't take my eyes off his strong arms as he controlled the wagon bouncing down the track that had no business masquerading as a road. My hands clutched the seat edges, but still I slid forward.

"Hold onto me, Lily." Liam jutted out his elbow, his hands tight on the reins. I entwined my arm with his and anchored my feet against the buckboard until we were safely down the steep incline.

I unravelled my arm the moment the wagon came to a halt. Liam jumped down in his easy manner and began loosening the harnesses on the horses, implying he planned to stay a while, secluded by the river. I waited for him to finish. He came to me, still seated on the wagon bench. I looked down at him, suddenly apprehensive. "I'm sorry, Liam, I was mistaken. I do want promises," I blurted out on a big exhalation,

"I do." I couldn't help smiling, with the relief of having said it.

"You weren't mistaken." Liam reached for my hand, and bending his head gallantly brushed his lips across my skin, "You were right." He opened his mouth, tasting me, I think.

"Liam?"

"I'd already promised you, like you said. You knew, Lily, without the actual words, you knew." He pulled me from the wagon seat straight into his arms.

"Yes, but I thought about it, and your way is fine with me. You can finish your house and then we can have a little wedding. We can follow your plan, Liam."

"Can we?" Liam's mouth had found my neck.

"Mmm… But the words, you could say the words." I was about to lose my train of thought.

"Oh, the words." I felt him smiling into my neck, "Yeah, those words." He took my mouth, and then, as if the encounter on the railway platform had been only a reconnaissance, he launched his assault. He kissed me with a fervour that resembled barely contained fury. My accusations that he did not love me enough were still lingering and raw. "I love you, Lily, I love you." His voice was fierce in my ear as his hands unbuttoned my coat.

"Yes, Liam, yes, I…" I would have continued, but my mouth was again taken captive. He asked me questions with his tongue and his hands, challenging me. Is this what you want? I answered his questions, and then some, daring him. Is this what you want? The feel of his hand on my bare breast was the final straw. I leaned towards him, silently imploring to be taken.

"Ah, Lily, now. Here? In the riverbed?"

I caught my breath, kissed him again, savouring the delicious feeling of his hand cupping my breast.

I felt our passion being reined in.

Contained and controlled.

It cost us both.

He held me tight as he grabbed a blanket and swung it out with one hand. It hung in the air a moment then landed unevenly on the bed of the wagon. He helped me up and then pulled me to his lap.

"Well, I got a taste," I said grinning.

"What?"

"I got a taste of what it will be like, you know…" I tilted my head, smiling flirtatiously. "When you finally, finally forget your plan." I couldn't help laughing. He wasn't listening; he was staring at my bare breast, inches from his face.

His head bent. "Speaking of taste, I think I may want..." His tongue slowly circled around my nipple; my back arched instinctively. He sucked my nipple into his mouth. I moaned. I couldn't help myself; honestly, I couldn't. He laid me back on the blanket and began undoing his belt buckle.

"Liam." My voice was husky. "No, Liam, it's right we wait." I sat up. "No, don't." I pointed to his hands undoing his breeches. I started putting myself back together.

"I can't wait, Lily."

"Yes, you can. It's me that can't, and I'm leading you into temptation." I tried to speak lightheartedly. I buttoned up my dress. "I think we should do it your way," and I folded my arms across my chest as if that could possibly be the end of the matter.

For the rest of our picnic, I kept my distance. My only consolation was that I knew Liam was aware that all I really wanted was to be in his arms.

"Mrs Lichfield thinks I am at the McGregor's for the day. Did you know the Reverend is getting married?"

"No, who to?"

"Well, he asked Rose, but he's had to settle for Charlotte McMullan, a widow with no children of her own. Rose thinks they'll be very happy."

"Will Rose be out of a job?"

"Eventually, yes. Liam, that reminds me, you know Mick?"

"Well, no, I don't really, but I know who he is." Liam smiled and reached out his hand for my chin.

"No, remember, no touching! Not until I kiss you goodbye."

"I'll be the one kissing you goodbye, my dear wife-to-be, and I'll do it very thoroughly, I might add." Liam was starting to look more relaxed. He stretched himself out in the back of the wagon, cradling his head in his hands and looked up at the sky.

"Oh, all right, then." My eyes kept sweeping along the strong, lean length of him laid out in front of me. "Liam, I have something important to ask you."

He rose on one elbow. "What is it?"

"Mick wants to be a farmer. Rose and I think that, when the

Reverend gets married, he'll let Mick leave. Do you think you can find him a job?"

"I can give him one."

"Really? Really?" I wriggled towards him in my excitement. Liam held out a hand in warning and I stopped.

"I've been planning to get a lad to help around the place; need to finish the hut first, though. He'll need a place to sleep. So I suppose the question is," Liam paused midsentence, "Do I finish the house first or start working on the hut?"

"The house, please finish the house first, Liam," I said firmly, without a hint of humour in my voice.

Chapter 19

Elisabeth Lichfield kept Lily in Christchurch for over a month simply to keep her away from Liam. Having the neighbours and the servants socialising was abhorrent to her; she shuddered just thinking about it. She wanted life to be orderly, nice and tidy, and predictable. It also suited Elisabeth to have someone like Lily at her beck and call. Elisabeth was accustomed to using her position to get what she wanted. Lily never cowered in subservience, and yet she never acted like there was an alternative to Elisabeth's wishes. Whenever Elisabeth demanded, Lily responded with kind acquiescence.

"Henry is coming for dinner tonight, Lily." They were riding back to the house in the new cabriolet carriage after an afternoon of shopping.

"Oh." Lily tensed. "May I please have the night off to visit my sister?"

"Well, I suppose." Elisabeth noticed the relief that swept through Lily's features, like water over sand, smoothing the ridges.

"Thank you, Mrs Lichfield."

Elisabeth nodded and continued, "I don't know about Henry, I just don't know. He's always been so prickly, so hard to… I don't know how to explain it."

Lily was surprised by Elisabeth's words. *No one loves him* was the first thing that popped into her mind, but she bit her tongue. She could hardly tell his mother that. Lily looked at Elisabeth. "It's hard for me to talk about Henry."

"Why is that, Lily?" Elisabeth's question was sincere, as if she really wanted to learn more about her son, finally figure him out. The driver whoa'd the horses to a stop; the road leading into the park was jammed with school children.

"He frightens me." Lily decided to be honest.

"I thought as much. He has very strong needs, you know, for a man."

"It's more than that; he wants the things he cannot have."

"Yes, but that is true of all men, don't you think?" Elisabeth said in a self-satisfied way.

"No," Lily said softly as the carriage started on its way again, but she didn't think Elisabeth heard her.

~

That evening Rose, Mick and Lily and the two younger McGregor boys went walking through the Botanic Gardens. The girls and Mick walked three abreast while Johnny and Jamie trailed behind. The younger boys stopped often to peer down a pathway, examine a footprint, or discuss the height of a garden wall and the injuries that would be incurred if one were silly enough to fall from such a height.

"Lily, I know I could go out to Fairfield and start work for Liam at any time, but I don't want to leave you here in town with Henry. When you go, I'll go," Mick stated decisively, turning to look at Lily.

"But when you both go," Rose looked from one to the other, "where will I go?"

Lily stopped and turned towards her sister, "You will come with us."

"But…"

"There is no reason for you not to. You can work, earn your keep. We'll get more done, and we'll…"

Rose interrupted, "You need to talk to Liam about it, Lily."

"I know he'll say yes."

"How do you know?"

Lily took off skipping, unable to contain herself. The joy at the thought of living with both Liam and Rose and having a home to call their own was almost more than she could bear. "Just do," she called out over her shoulder.

The house was quiet when Mick, Rose, and Lily returned with the children. Although they complained, Johnny and Jamie were sent straight to bed.

"We'll live together again, Rose. You'll like his farm." Lily had her arm entwined with Rose's and both girls sat nestled into the sofa near the fireplace. Mick was sitting on the floor but was leaning back against Lily's legs.

"You still need to talk to Liam about it. He is marrying you, Lily, not me."

"Yes, but you are my sister, Rose, my only family." Lily clasped Rose's hand tighter in hers. Mick turned his face towards them.

"Oh, and you, Mick." Lily put her hand on Mick's shoulder, "You are starting to feel like family."

Like a brother, LilyRose, like a brother.

Mick startled, "I heard that. I heard that, and neither of you actually said it, did you? You said 'like a brother'. Keep thinking; I want to hear some more." Mick closed his eyes, concentrating.

He heard us again, LilyRose.

Every now and then he hears us.

When he's touching us… Or when we are touching him.

See if we can let him in… Think… Think about him working for Liam.

Mick will be a good farmer. He knows how to take care of things.

He knows… There he is… He is…here. Now.

LilyRose, we can draw him in, to listen. Feel that…

"Hey, I heard that," Mick said in a smiling voice.

"Of course you did."

Lily and Rose were strengthened by the fact that Mick could be privy to their unusual communication and still love them. He did not judge or look at them questioningly the way the people of Creggan had, half suspecting that they too would go crazy like their grandmother. Mick's friendship was something solid, something they could hold on to.

~

Elisabeth Lichfield decided to return to Avonlea. She had a restless, aimless sense about her that she thought would be relieved by a change of scenery. She hadn't seen George in weeks, and although she would never admit to missing him, she did wonder what he was up to. Lily tried not to express her delight at returning to the country too overtly, but the thought of being within walking distance of Liam again couldn't help but make her happy.

"I'll have none of it, Lily Quinn." Mrs Lichfield was sitting like a queen on her throne in the railway carriage.

"None of what, Mrs Lichfield?" Lily asked politely.

"I know perfectly well you are sitting there daydreaming about Liam McCann."

Lily sat up straighter, feeling guilty for just a minute.

"You are under no circumstances to contact that man."

"Mrs Lichfield, I am not an indentured servant, nor a slave. I am a free woman."

"And?" Elisabeth Lichfield raised an eyebrow.

"Well, I will contact him if I want to."

"And do you want to?"

"Yes, as a matter of fact, I do." Lily smiled.

Mrs Lichfield seemed to be at a loss for words. She sat back and looked at Lily as though she were thinking about what she wanted and how she was going to get it.

"Nobody defies me, Lily Quinn…ever! Least of all a servant girl."

~

The next morning Lily was tidying the bedrooms. She knocked before entering Henry's to make sure that it was vacant and, receiving no reply, went in. After picking up a few pieces of discarded clothing lying on the floor, she turned to make the bed when, suddenly, the door opened behind her.

"Oh, excuse me! Excuse me, sir." Lily hastened towards the door as Henry pulled it shut behind him. "I thought you were in Christchurch. When did you…?"

Henry stood in front of the door with his arms crossed rather nonchalantly, still clad in his dressing gown. "It's all right, Lily. Don't worry." He extended a hand. Lily stepped back.

"What exactly do you think you are doing?" Lily was more annoyed than fearful.

"I'd like to get to know you better." He started towards her.

"I don't think so." Lily was able to quickly step around him and grab the doorknob. The door was locked. "What? What?" She rattled the knob. This could not be. Lily felt Henry behind her.

He seized her upper arms and turned her to face him. He had a strange smile on his face, "Lily, don't fight me."

She would! She would!

She would fight him until her last breath, but first she'd reason with him.

"Why, Henry? Why do you want this? Why…?" Her voice trailed off, and her eyes began to fill with tears as Henry pinned both her arms against the door. She kicked him hard in the shin, and he glared.

"We'll do it rough if that's how you want it, Lily." He turned her, kicking and screaming now, and yanked her arms behind her hard.

Lily's emotions raced. No, no, no! This could not be happening, but it was, it was. How could it be that no one heard her screams? What could she do? She fought as she could—a kick here and a scratch there—but he had her arms pulled behind her so tight. Soon she was bent over the bed and he was ripping off her skirt. Lily felt so horribly exposed and invaded, and then the pain, the pain came, brutal and vicious, overwhelming her.

Henry thrust harder and harder. He kept saying "Oh, Lily, you feel so good," and words like 'darling' and 'love'. Lily could not accept what was happening to her. She felt dizzy and lost. Even though the initial pain eased, the pain in her heart grew, slithering snakelike through her. *Oh, Liam, oh Liam! Rose, help me, Rose! LilyRose!* Lily shook her head, still trying to deny what was happening to her. She felt faint. She gasped for air, trying to suck it in deep, seeking comfort, seeking any sort of peace.

"Lily, look at me, look at me." His voice was plaintive, almost childlike, in stark contrast to the violence he was wreaking upon her body. But she didn't look, couldn't look, would not give him the satisfaction of even the tiniest acknowledgement. Her eyes were closed and her face was turned. She stopped struggling, gave up fighting him. She realised her fear gave him power, some kind of sick twisted power.

She lay still.

Henry slowly let go of Lily's wrists. He seemed to want to trust her and craved her acquiescence. He slumped down onto her. But the moment Lily's hands were free, she started to wriggle away, her disgust for his sweating body laying draped over hers far outweighing any other thoughts.

"No, Lily, this isn't over yet." He grabbed her by a handful of hair and by sheer force positioned her under him. "I'll have you properly." He jerked her hands above her head with one hand and with the other put a pillow over her upturned face, "Before that bloody McCann ever does."

Lily screamed into the pillow for Liam until she felt herself departing, piece by fractured piece, the edges first. Lily didn't know if she was fainting from lack of air, or dying, but she went willingly.

When Lily woke up, she was in the servants' quarters, in her own room, lying on her own bed, her ripped skirt tucked neatly over her bruised and bleeding body. She didn't cry; she just lay there, with her head throbbing, trying to make sense of… Well… What? There was no logical sequence to anything she could think or did think—just a jumbled, tumbled, swirling assortment of fragmented thoughts and images that she was strangely distanced from.

After a while, her thoughts started to clear a little, and she rose. There didn't seem to be any one around, for which she was thankful. She washed herself the best she could, dressed, and began walking towards Fairfield, towards Liam. Lily trudged out the drive and down the road, with her head bent and her arms wrapped around herself. The road seemed to go on forever.

Finally Lily stood at his door, trembling. She could see Liam sitting still, there, in the sun. She was used to seeing him moving, walking, working, driving a wagon. Not often still. It might have been the first time she'd observed him without his knowledge. It made her pause; there was so much about him she didn't know. What would he be like at the end of a long, hard day? Would he want to talk to her, read with her? Would they laugh together, or would he be tired and grumpy from the tiredness? Did it even matter now? Lily took a deep breath and knocked gently on the door frame, and entered.

~

There stood Lily, in his house. Liam blinked. He'd been dreaming of her. Not a sound-asleep dream, but a daydream, the kind you construct bit by bit and plan down to the last detail. The kind you want to be true. In his dream she wasn't trembling and dishevelled. She didn't have tears drying on her cheeks.

Liam stood up and moved towards her. "Lily, what's wrong? What's happened?" he cried, an undertone of terror creeping from his blood to his voice.

She cowered, he swore she cowered. Her head was bent to her wringing hands. He reached out his hand to tilt her face upwards. Her eyes were brimming with tears.

"God, Lily, tell me he didn't, tell me he didn't."

Lily couldn't speak, but she had the courage to look him in the eye, and he knew. What swept through him was barely containable, making his fists clench uncontrollably. He steadied himself; he'd see to Lily first.

"How badly are you hurt? Should we get Doc Jenkins?"

She shook her head no.

"Come here," he gently pulled her to the sofa. "Sit down." He sat beside her and held her, trembling, in his arms.

"I thought you were still in Christchurch."

"We came back last night, but Henry was in town when we left. I don't know how he…"

"Lily, you can't ever go back there."

Lily's tears were silent.

"You'll stay here now."

"Liam, but what if…?"

"Shh, Lily. It will be all right."

~

But how could it be all right? How could anything be all right again? Lily tossed and turned alone in Liam's bed.

By herself.

She missed Rose. Oh, how she missed Rose. She thought they should have never separated. This trouble with Henry wouldn't have happened if they had stuck together. They would have thwarted Henry somehow. *Oh, Rosie, Rosie.*

Liam had heated water for a bath, and ever so gently helped her wash, made her soup, and tucked her into his bed. All the time his anger was growing, festering—born out of his own agony.

"I'll kill him."

"No, you won't," Lily said as he turned away. She struggled to sit up, "Liam, if you go to jail for murder, you might as well kill me too." Lily took a deep breath. She watched Liam struggling with his anger. She took another deep breath; she knew she had to help him. Even now, beaten and battered, Lily could breathe in peace and find her power. She thought of her grandmother and her mother and took another breath. Lily looked Liam straight in the eyes and with a voice full of conviction said, "I am alive. I can survive this."

Liam stood stock-still, staring at Lily for a long moment, then he slowly nodded, "You can and you will."

Lily reached out her hand, just as he turned away.

"Still, I have to go."

"Be careful," Lily whispered as the door shut.

~

Liam found him towards nightfall, taking shelter in the pub in

Rakaia. The pub wasn't crowded and Henry was seated at the back near the fire. Somewhere in the back of his mind Liam knew he was too angry to be careful, and he needed to be careful.

"You bastard, you bloody bastard." Liam grabbed Henry Lichfield by the collar and jerked him to his feet. He punched Henry hard in the mouth just as it was opening. The other patrons hushed as they turned to watch. Liam hit him again, this time aiming higher for his nose.

Henry knew better than to fight back with his fists. Liam McCann could puree him right here in plain sight and no one would care. "Ruined her for you, have I?" Henry spat out with his blood.

Liam hit him again, this time in the stomach.

Oh, I could kill the bastard, the fucking bastard. Liam's thoughts raged. *He's hurt Lily on purpose, my Lily.* He hit Henry again and again, craving the relief of vengeance, but knowing the consequences.

"Hold onto yerself, man," Liam heard through the haze. "Yer gonna kill 'im." Liam felt hands on his shoulders.

He knew he wouldn't kill Henry.

He couldn't, even though he wanted to.

"It's never as good as you think it's going to be," Henry said, once again pushing Liam closer to the edge. Liam knew that words were Henry's only ammunition. He also knew that if the bastard just punched him in the face, it would hurt a lot less.

~

The morning was clear and crisp, so different from the misty grey, late winter mornings in Ireland. Here the sun shone, like it thought it was summer. Liam had a lot to do. He always had a lot to do. The land he'd bought was good land, but most of it was still covered with tussock and dotted with cabbage trees. There were still water races to be dug, fences to be built, shelter to be planted, and more sheds to be built. He'd spent more time than he should have building the house.

His thoughts immediately turned to Lily, in his house at this moment, perhaps still in his bed. He'd checked on her late last night and watched her sleep in the moonlight. He saw how she'd curled herself up into the tightest little ball imaginable trying to comfort herself. Saw the fresh tear tracks on her cheeks. *Damn that bastard, damn him.* Liam felt his blood pressure rising again. He kicked the gate open.

"Come here, Pearl," he called to his dog. He'd see to the ewes and then check on Lily. He might have time to decide what he wanted to say.

Chapter 20

Lily

It was midmorning before Liam returned. I had woken a time or two and noticed the morning light. Then I would close my eyes and remember. Not what had happened to me, but how I was starting to feel before it happened. How I was starting to imagine myself here with Liam, loving him. It had felt good. I would think, if I just hold onto that, everything will work out. Then I'd doze off again. I was awake, though, when he sat on the edge of the brass bed—awake and afraid to face him. He waited.

"You were gone an awfully long time." I finally decided to talk, but my voice sounded sad.

"It took me a while to find Henry and..." Liam's fist curled and he slammed it into his other palm.

"You hit him?"

He nodded.

"Where was he?"

"Someone had seen him heading to Rakaia. I found him at the pub."

I looked at Liam for a moment. "Did it help?"

"Yes, a little."

"I lay here and thought about what I'd like to do to him."

"And...?"

"Poison."

"Poison?"

"Yes, my plan is to go back there and work like nothing has happened, but poison him, very slowly and very painfully, and watch. I think I would like watching."

We were quiet for a moment.

"There are big flaws in that plan." Liam's lips turned up like he wanted to smile but decided against it. "Firstly, that would be murder. I know I don't know everything about you, but I know you aren't a murderer…" I tried to interrupt, but Liam kept talking, "…any more than I am. And secondly, you can't go back there."

"That is a flaw in the plan, isn't it? I'm no good at protecting myself." I looked at my bruised hands.

"Lily, you're a woman… And not a very big woman. Anyway, there is the third thing."

"What third thing?"

"The third flaw in your plan."

"Hmm, and what is that?"

"Me."

"You? You're a flaw? I don't think so." My eyes warmed as I looked at him sitting on the edge of the bed. Liam noticed, saw something in them. It gave him hope. It made him brave.

"I would be a big flaw in that plan because I won't let you go back to Avonlea. Never." His jaw was clenched and a hard edge had come into his voice, a nuance I hadn't heard before.

"Because I can't protect myself."

"That and…" His voice softened, the hard edge leaving. He smiled and looked a little lost, lost in my eyes.

"And…?" I coaxed softly, just as lost, as the fear and the hope battled within me.

"And I want you. I want you here with me. Marry me, Lily. Tomorrow if we can."

I stared at Liam. After months and months of waiting for him to say it, he had. He'd actually said the words, but things had changed. I couldn't possibly be the wife I had only yesterday imagined myself being. Yet he still wanted me. "Liam, you're a good man."

"Lily, what on earth? Lily, did you hear what I said?"

"Yes, I heard, I heard. I want you too, Liam McCann. I want you. I've wanted someone just like you forever. Forever, Liam!" I was losing my grip. I grabbed his hands with mine, a part of me thinking that if I held on tight enough I might not have to let go. "But Henry… Henry…," I couldn't go on, just couldn't.

"I know what Henry did, Lily. I know. It's not your fault. I'm never going to blame you."

"Oh, Liam, you are such a good man." My eyes were filling. I clutched his hands to my chest, to my heart.

He waited.

"Lily?" he asked softly.

I looked him in the eye and found everything I wanted there. I also knew what I had to do, just in case. "We have to wait."

"What?"

"Wait."

"How long, Lily?"

"A month or so, at least."

There was quiet. Just quiet.

No dogs barking.

No sheep bleating.

Just quiet.

Even the birds were silent.

"Ah, Lily, Lily." I'm sure I heard his heart breaking.

~

Liam drove the wagon in silence. I sat beside him, hugging myself with my arms.

"Are you cold?"

"No, I, I..." I tried to relax a little and took a deep breath. "I just don't want to go back there."

"I know, Lily, but I don't see how I can go in and get your things without you. Henry is back in Christchurch. It will be all right."

We had our backs to the mountains. Liam told me he much preferred driving towards them. He liked looking at them. Liked the way they stood guard over the plains. He thought next time he went to the foothills for firewood he'd take me with him. I said I'd like that.

Liam was quiet for a few minutes. Then he told me how much he enjoyed the idea of having a woman of his own—to think about, to plan with and for. I knew he was trying to make me feel better. Liam said it still seemed too good to be true. Maybe it was.

We turned off onto Avonlea Road and followed the drive as it curved around the huge front lawn.

"Go around the back, Liam."

"Why? I always come this way."

"I need to go around the back."

"Lily, I always come to the front."

"Liam..." I knew I sounded like I was going to cry. Liam took my hand, put it on his thigh, and rested his hand on top of mine while he manoeuvred the wagon to a stop.

I was comforted by the oddly intimate gesture. I waited for him to speak.

"Lily, we have to do this right. Come on." He helped me down, but he kept my hand in his.

Sally answered the door and looked at Liam and me standing there holding hands. "Lily, where have you been? We were starting to worry." She spoke quickly, and nervously greeted Liam.

"Sally, we'd like to speak to Mrs Lichfield. Could you get her, please."

"Well, well, what is going on here?" Elisabeth Lichfield appeared at the top of the curving staircase. She smiled disdainfully as her hand smoothed the satin of her wide skirts, and she started down the stairs.

Something in the tone of her voice made Liam drop my hand so that he could put his arm around me. He pulled me close to him as Elisabeth arrived at the bottom of the stairs.

"Mrs Lichfield, we've come to get Lily's things." He addressed her formally.

"Lily is in my employ. Tell me what is going on here, Lily?" Her voice was stern and demanding.

"I am leaving here. I cannot work for you any longer," I said quietly.

"You are running off with Liam? Just like that?"

"I am not running off, I am..."

"What! What exactly are you doing?"

"I am not staying here. Your son... Your son..."

"What does Henry have to do with anything?"

Liam took my hand again, keeping his other arm around me, an action that did not go unnoticed by Mrs Lichfield, and then he spoke.

"Your son, Mrs Lichfield, has been..." Liam had to stop and steady himself. He took a breath. "Your son has violated Lily in the worst possible way. Avonlea is absolutely no place for a young woman," Liam said with authority. "Lily, go and get your things." He nudged me towards Sally, although I could tell he was reluctant to let go of me.

Mrs Lichfield bristled and grabbed my arm, "How dare you come into my home and start accusing my son of such things? It will be your word against mine, you little tart. I've seen you flirting with him."

"Take your hands off her this minute," Liam commanded, "this minute." Liam took my hand again.

Mrs Lichfield let go of me but didn't stop her tirade. "Am I to assume that the girl will be safe with you, a single man, unchaperoned?"

"Under the circumstances, Elisabeth," Liam enunciated her name clearly, "I don't really think it is your place to assume anything."

~

I thought of myself as brave, but now I felt fragmented and frightened. I missed Rose and I thought maybe I should go back to the McGregors, but Liam would have none of it. 'You are safe here with me' was all he would say on the matter.

The farmhouse certainly felt safe. Though I wasn't sure if it was because it was so beautifully made, or just because Liam was in it.

"Lily, you don't need to cook for me," Liam said, watching me stir the pot hanging over the fire.

"Liam, it is a pleasure, honestly," I said as I ladled up the stew. "I need to keep busy."

"You should be resting."

"I feel fine… Well, I feel like I want to be doing something." I handed Liam a full plate and then sat down at the wooden table in front of my own.

"Mmm, you are a good cook," Liam said after he sampled his first bite.

"I can make a nice stew, at least." We ate in companionable silence. Liam started to speak and then stopped and had another bite.

"How do you go about forgetting what happened?" Liam's voice was gentle, "How can I help you?"

I took a deep breath and shook my head, "I don't know, Liam. I don't know. It just keeps coming to me, over and over. I don't know how to get it out of my head."

"Oh, Lily," Liam laid down his fork and reached across the table to place his hand over mine. I looked down at our hands. "Is this all right? Can I comfort you?" I nodded and looked up at him with my eyes overflowing with tears.

"Oh, Liam." Tears ran freely down my cheeks as I turned my hand over and clasped his, "Your kindness will heal me."

As the weeks went by, we settled into a routine that suited us both. I took charge of the well-stocked kitchen, and Liam was more than grateful to return to the house to find me serving up a hot meal. He changed his routine to include morning and afternoon tea back at the house, when he could manage it.

I began to heal from my ordeal.

Chapter 21

The wind blew. It blew and blew as only a nor'west wind across the Canterbury Plains can blow, angrily sweeping dust and dirt across the flat, compliant land. It irritated or, at the very least, wearied the new settlers. They found it unsettling. After the third day, the wind shifted and blew from the south, bitterly cold, and then came the rain. For three days and three nights, it pelted the ewes, who had started to lamb. Liam spent all his time gathering up the cold, soggy newborn lambs, delivering them to Lily, who warmed them by the fire and fed them sugar water until they stopped shivering and stood up, calling out for their mothers. Then Liam would tie the ewe to the fence and make sure the lamb the lamb was fed and the ewe remembered she was a mother. Over and over, again and again. Some of the lambs had more than one dose of Lily's nursing efforts. Once, in his exhaustion, Liam fell asleep in the rocker by the fire instead of disappearing to the front room. Lily watched him. She curled up with a blanket on the wooden floor, surrounded by the woolly smell of damp lambs. She studied him sleeping there, memorising every detail of his body, his beautiful sleeping form. She sighed and thought, *Oh, please God, to have him for my own.*

Morning dawned and finally the sky was clear. Though it was early, Liam could tell the sun was going to make an effort today. Lily lay sleeping on the floor, in her little ball, which got even smaller as a lamb cried out for its mother. Liam scooped her off the floor. Not quite awake, she was startled for a moment. "Liam, what?"

"Shh, Lily, I'll put you in bed. It's early yet." Lily snuggled into his chest and wrapped her arms around his neck, her head on his heart. Liam walked slowly, relishing the feel of her against him. He had wanted her since he'd first laid eyes on her, and his mind flashed to retrieving the soggy child from the river. He shook his head. Of course, that was her sister. He gathered her closer to him. This woman in his arms was the woman he loved. Lily. All his thoughts of loving and wanting and waiting swirled in his mind. Knowing she needed time to recover, time to heal, time to learn to be at ease with him didn't help. He wanted to marry her, wanted her to be his wife.

When he lay her down on his bed and started to pull away, she murmured, "No, Liam, don't go." She started planting tiny kisses on his neck. Liam could not move. Lost in his emotions, he closed his eyes and felt. Felt Lily's arms holding him tight, felt her lips on his neck, her warm breath on his skin. Liam thought, *this is what a woman can give to a man. Lily is giving herself to me... Lily is giving herself to me...* and then he stopped thinking and accepted her gift.

Let her love flow over him, around him, into him.

He leaned into her, and there was just the slightest hesitation when their lips joined. As if simultaneously they both thought, now?

Now.

The sweetness overcame them and the questions disappeared.

Chapter 22

Lily

I was hungry, hungry for Liam. I tugged at his shirt. "I want your skin, your skin." I undid the bodice of my dress. "Let me feel your skin on me, Liam... Please," I begged because I knew there was a possibility he might refuse me. But Liam pulled his blue serge shirt off over his head to emerge, kneeling there with his chest bare, my breasts just inches away from him.

"Oh, Lily, Lily..." He helped me finish removing my dress from where it clung low on my hips, and he looked, looked at me in my woman's skin, and I saw in his eyes that he wanted me completely and forever.

I saw so much love there.

"Lily, I'm going to take my trousers off," he stated, but I knew it was a question.

"Wait, Liam, what if I'm... What if there is a baby... And then you'll never know." I paused, "Liam, I love you. You deserve to know if it isn't yours."

I collapsed on the bed, my forearm bent to cover my eyes, as if I could shield myself from the agony. I couldn't hold back my tears.

Liam quietly removed his trousers and lay down beside me. He pulled me to him; I felt his warm, smooth skin along the entire length of me. It felt like home.

"Lily, I love you too."

I was quiet.

"Did you mean it, Lily, when you said you loved me?" His voice wasn't strong.

I turned towards him. "Yes, Liam, I meant it, but what an awful way to tell you...the first time. I just wish..."

"Say it again, then," he interrupted, smiling.

It was my turn to smile. "I love you, Liam. The very first time I saw you, that day by the river? I felt it then."

Liam rose on his elbow and then bent his head to kiss me gently. He deepened the kiss, asking me for more, which I gave willingly. As we kissed, I felt myself coming alive for him. "But Liam, I thought we decided…"

"No, Lily, you heard me. I told you I loved you." Then he moved his body over mine, his elbows on either side of my shoulders. "You have to know this, now, about me." He bent his knees between my legs, spreading them apart, positioning himself, and I surprised myself by moving my hips closer to him.

"Liam, but…"

"Lily, listen to me, look at me." I looked into his eyes. "Lily, any baby you have, whenever you have it, will be mine. Mine, Lily. Do you understand?" I nodded as he entered me.

"Liam, oh, Liam," I murmured, just unsure enough to cause Liam to pause.

"Am I hurting you, Lily?"

"Yes… No… Liam?"

"Lily, look at me. Do you want me? Do you want to be my wife?"

I looked at Liam above me, encompassing me so intimately. I looked straight into his eyes and knew exactly what I did want. I, Lily Quinn, did want Liam McCann. I wanted him all to myself. I wanted him all for myself.

"Yes, Liam McCann, I will marry you. I do want you."

"Do you want to get married first?"

The corners of my mouth turned upward, and I moved my eyes demurely downwards, as if any woman in my position could look demur. "First, before what?"

"Oh, well, I…" he smiled, realising, but then moving again, pushing harder, deeper, asking me without words. "Oh, Lily."

"Liam, go ahead." I smiled and felt a new kind of joy surging through me. I reached my arms around him, pulling him to me.

The physical act of love astounded me. The power of oneness surging through my senses was beautiful and brilliant. I vaguely remembered Nana Kat raving on about the sacred power of loving sex, embarrassing Rose and me at the time. But I was beginning to understand now, in giving myself to Liam, I was discovering a deeper part of myself, awakening an earthy rhythm. In giving myself to his mastery, I felt like I was fulfilling an ancient vow.

We dozed in the morning light, completely entwined, totally merged, satiated, or so I thought.

Liam wasn't finished.

He was very thorough in his ministrations—and purposeful. He wanted me to forget Henry Lichfield. He wanted to obliterate him from my body's memory. Gentle at first, his every kiss, every touch was its own gift, its own offering to be accepted and savoured. He watched me, felt me, made sure I knew what he was giving and why. Everything he gave, I received and returned. I think that gave him courage, because the gentleness was replaced with determination, and I think some anger. I had to speak, "No, Liam, it was never this, never this. You, only you."

He shushed me with his mouth, and his tongue dove and delved, urgent and needful. He moved to my breasts. I arched, and everything looked and felt exquisite—the linen sheets against my back, the dappled sunlight on Liam's shoulder, the silkiness of his hair under my hand. Then I began to feel deliciously vague, so overcome with love, that I wanted to disappear into him, a sacrifice for his pleasure.

I abandoned any logical thought. I was a bundle of nerves and need, a curve, a hollow, a bend. Liam's skin, his breath, his mouth, the virile scent of him were all fragments—tiny points of clarity, like individual stars in the night sky. It was all so beautiful, this newfound bliss. I couldn't take it all in. I couldn't open wide enough for him.

~

We needed to get married, and soon. Liam said he knew we understood each other, but people were quick to make judgements. If we were going to have a good life here and enjoy the company of the neighbours, we needed to do something before Elisabeth Lichfield or some other busybody decided to come calling. The sun shone as we walked towards the hills, moving a small mob of ewes with older lambs to a paddock up the road.

"This place feels... It feels so good." I motioned to the fields and smiled at Liam.

"It is your home, Lily," he smiled back.

I let the words he had spoken seep into me. I was behind Liam and watched him—his easy gait as he walked, his broad shoulders. The strength of the man captivated me, my man. My man?

I stopped and stood, shaking my head.

Liam turned and caught my gaze. "Lily?" he questioned. "Lily, come here." He stretched out his hand for mine.

I took his hand and stepped close to him, placing my lips on his beating heart.

"Lily?" he said very softly, "I'll finish the lambing, then let's go to Christchurch and get married."

I couldn't speak, so I just looked straight up into his eyes and let the love I found there shower me, bathe me. I let it soak in like a good hot bath. It felt so right. But what about Rose? Rose, who I had spent every moment of my life with until just four months ago. What would Rose think about me getting married? I knew that Rose would like Liam. She would love him just because I did. But, could this be the start of separate lives?

"Liam?"

"Yes, Lily?"

"My sister, if she wants to stay here with me...?"

"Lily, this is your home. Of course if you want your sister to visit, that will be fine." He turned me, leaving his arm slung around my shoulder as we walked down the drive back to the house.

I looked up into his eyes. "Well, you see, we are very close and I just... It might be more than a short visit." The more I thought about it, the more I had trouble imagining my life without Rose after all the bleakness we'd been through, the isolation we had shared. I knew I couldn't leave her waiting, standing on the threshold, while I leapt for joy.

"Lily, don't worry. It's nice you have family here. I don't have any; she'll be my family too." I turned my head to the hand draped casually around my shoulder and pressed a kiss into it.

Having found each other, the rest of the world was of little concern to us. To be honest, it wasn't all perfect, but Liam and I solved the problems that came our way. Pearl got a nasty infection in her paw, which I treated with mustard and garlic poultices. The poor dog was not happy when Liam tied the sacking around her leg, but her paw improved. I remembered my Nana Kat's recipe for tanning hides and used it to make a lovely sheepskin rug. I enjoyed collecting the eggs and learning different ways to cook mutton. Something always needed attending to. The weather settled and Liam got busy ploughing, so he could get the early spring crops in. I helped him with the end of the lambing. I enjoyed being outside. When we worked together on the farm, I felt I was helping Liam build something. I would look around and see our future here, and the future of our children spread out before me. I'm sure the land itself helped me to heal. I know I felt stronger because of it.

Chapter 23

"My sister... I can't wait to see my sister." Lily smiled her brilliant smile as they came to a halt in front of the McGregor home. Liam was slow helping Lily down from the wagon. They were making a habit of prolonging their proximity to each other when they could. Liam would bend and whisper in her ear, Lily's hand would rest momentarily on Liam's heart, and after a quick glance around to see if anyone was watching she would lift her hand and quickly kiss him.

But Lily heard Rose calling her name and turned from Liam to envelop her sister. Rose was staring at Liam over Lily's shoulder. Liam stared back.

"Oh, Rosie, this is Liam." Lily turned, still holding onto Rose.

"Aye, I know. I think I've met him before." Rose paled and quickly stepped away from Lily.

"Liam said that you had, briefly, by the Avon River. You had all the McGregor children with you."

Rose nodded. She stared transfixed. She had dreamt of this man since their meeting, daydreams far more realistic than her fantasies of Mr Darcy had ever been. She had relived their encounter many times while walking in the park, hoping to see him again. And here he was, standing in front of her. He was more handsome than she remembered. He looked so strong—his shoulders broad and muscular in his white linen shirt. He was staring back at her, his beautiful green eyes confused and questioning. Here he was, so fine looking and...and...belonging to her sister.

Liam's mind was racing, chaotic and unsure. He stared at Rose and then at Lily, looking for differences between them. Rose was looking at him the same way Lily did when... He shook his head. "Ah, Rose," he murmured. He reached out to shake Rose's hand. They clasped hands, trying to ignore the surge of feeling that swept through them both.

~

Promises were made. Promises to honour and obey, in sickness and in health, forever, or until death parted them, made in front of God and the Reverend McGregor. Rose and Mick were the witnesses. Charlotte McMullan and the rest of the McGregor children looked on. The spring weather did not cooperate for the planned picnic in Hagley Park, so they ended up in the McGregor's sitting room for the celebrations. Liam watched his new wife in an animated conversation with her identical twin sister.

"Come now! Please! Tomorrow. Pack tonight. We'll pick up you and Mick tomorrow morning, won't we, Liam?" Lily's voice carried across the room. "The front two bedrooms are finished, and the hut. Oh, wait till you see the house." Lily squeezed Rose's hand and pulled her closer. Liam couldn't hear Rose's reply. He kept watching, though, couldn't stop his gaze going from one to the other and then back again.

"Quite a sight, aye?" Mick stood close.

Liam looked at Mick and then back to Lily and Rose.

"Lots of people look at them," Mick paused, "like you're looking now."

Liam turned towards Mick and nodded as if he understood. "Aye, but one of them is my new wife."

Liam closed his eyes and listened to Lily and Rose, searching for some discernible difference in the cadence, rhythm, or pitch of their voices or in the echoes of their laughter.

"Mick, can you tell them apart?"

"No, not always."

"That's what I am afraid of."

~

"There is a man at the door," Johnny yelled as he tore down the hall to let the stranger in.

"Frank, Frank, how are you?" Liam stepped forward to welcome his friend.

"Didn't quite get here in time, but did my darndest."

"Frank, it's good to see you." Liam grinned as they shook hands. "This is the McGregor family. The Reverend, Mrs McMullan..." He pointed them out one by one and introduced each child separately. "And this is Lily, Mrs Lily McCann, actually." The tone of his voice as he said Lily's name was a mix of pride and passion with an undertone of ancient male possessiveness. "And this is her sister, Rose."

"And so, you are Liam's friend." Rose extended her hand to Frank. He looked back and forth from Lily to Rose, shaking his head.

"It's all right; we're twins. Didn't Liam tell you?"

"No, that's a little detail he omitted from his letter. He didn't tell me about your hair either." Frank was still holding Rose's hand and stepped closer to her, grinning mischievously.

"Ah, well." Rose gently extricated her hand and tried to smooth down her hair.

"I'm just teasing you. It's lovely." Frank gestured towards her head.

"Oh, just look at them." Lily and Liam were turned and whispering, heads close. "They look so happy," Rose commented.

"Forgotten we're here, I'd say." Frank was watching Lily and Liam but kept turning to look at Rose.

"Do you want me to go and stand by Lily so you can look at us both together a little longer?"

"No, stay here, please." Frank reached out to touch her arm.

Rose laughed. "I was teasing you. Who are you, besides Liam's friend, I mean? What do you do?"

"Well, now, I've been working building roads, thinking about buying a farm, but just not quite sure."

"Why not?"

"Well, I just haven't found the right place or the right…" Frank trailed off.

"Molly, don't you dare tip that over," Rose reprimanded the toddler as she reached out to touch the smooth glass of a flower vase. "Excuse me, I might just take the little girls outside." She turned, "Come on, Jessie, Molly. Come with me."

Rose watched the children running with a ball across the garden, glad to have a moment to herself. What was bothering Lily? What had happened to her? What was she hiding? Rose knew there was something nasty hiding in the shadows, but Lily wasn't telling. Frank followed Rose outside.

"I hope I didn't chase you away."

"Ah, no, not exactly, but…" She did want to be left alone. "I just, well, I…" She hadn't expected the tears; she wasn't a teary sort of girl, not really. There were always more practical solutions to problems. The tears came slowly and silently, but still they came.

Frank let her cry. He calmly led her to the rusty garden bench, sat her down, and handed her his handkerchief.

"So, then, I take it you are very close."

"What?" she asked, finally looking up at him.

"You and your sister?"

"Oh, yes, why?"

"Well, why else would you cry on her wedding day?" Frank took a seat beside her.

"Oh, no, I'm happy for her, very happy." She wiped her tears and smiled. Frank found her forced expression of joy endearing.

"Well, then what is it?"

"Nothing. Really, nothing. It's just that…"

"You can tell me."

"Well, Lily's been hurt."

"What? What is the matter with her?"

"I don't know."

"Rose?"

"You said I could tell you. Something is bothering her. There was something violent, something happened."

"What? And you think… No, Liam would never do anything to hurt anybody, least of all his wife." Frank stood up in agitation. "Are you crazy? You saw how they were looking at each other in there."

It was the 'Are you crazy'. He said it with such passion, such belief, and it was so like the taunts from the village children. He watched her pale. A look of what might have been terror flashed through her features. She swallowed and tried to speak.

"Oh, no, not Liam. I…" The words would not come, would not form into comprehensible sentences. "I…" Rose stood up, swaying, but headed quickly for the house.

"Rose, Rose?" Frank started to follow but he had no idea what to say.

"Please, please bring the children in." He heard her clearly, but then she mumbled, and he could have sworn she said 'I'm not crazy'.

~

"Rose, we are leaving now." Lily knew her voice carried down the hall. "Rose, where are you?" She hurried into her sister's room. Lily saw her tear-stained face. "Rose, what is the matter? Rose, tell me."

She said angrily, "No, you tell me."

Lily stood motionless. "Oh, Rosie, Rose." She turned, kicking the door to shut it, but not succeeding. "Rosie." Lily slumped onto the bed beside her. "I wanted to tell you, but I didn't want to ruin my wedding day, and it was all so ugly and awful. I thought that… Well, I never meant to keep anything from you. I…" Lily reached out her hand and Rose clasped it hard. Lily took a deep breath as Rose accessed her memories.

Lily, oh, Lily… You were trapped… He… Oh, LilyRose… You were hurt.

It's all right… Now… Everything is all right.

Liam, Liam loves… Liam loves you.

Liam found Lily and Rose on the bed, holding each other close, dishevelled, and tear-streaked. They sat up together.

He started to speak, but Lily could tell he felt a stranger to their intimacy. He turned to leave, "I'll just give you…"

"Liam, I just told Rose about Henry. It's all right. We're all right. Aren't we, Rose?"

Rose looked at Lily and said, tentatively, "Will be." She clasped Lily's hand tightly as it draped over her shoulder.

"Liam, please." Lily patted the spot beside her. "I need you, Liam." Lily's other arm went around his neck and she pulled him towards her. "I need you both."

Liam's love came straight through Lily to Rose. It flowed, a tangible thing, like blood through arteries, pulsating with power. Only it didn't stop; it overflowed, filling Rose.

Rose's eyes filled with wonder and the most glorious smile spread across her face, all the sadness forgotten.

Lily pulled her arm from around Rose's neck and untangled herself from both of them.

"Lily, what is it?" Liam was looking at Lily's face.

Rose reached for Lily's arm.

It's all right, LilyRose, it's all right.

Lily looked from Liam to Rose and back again. Was it all right?

~

"To love, and life, and whatever else sounds good." Frank held up his glass and clunked it heartily with Rose's. Liam and Lily clinked theirs together, and then all five glasses were momentarily held high in the centre of the table in the dining room of the Oxford Hotel.

"To Fairfield," Mick's voice rang out.

"Here, here," Frank added, "this boy knows what side his bread is buttered on. "To Fairfield.""

"Ah, and it won't be the same after tomorrow," Liam replied as they lowered their glasses.

"Aye, I know," Frank winked at Liam, "having a mistress in residence."

"And a sister's mistress or mistress's sister or... Well, what shall we call me?" Rose giggled and at the same time hiccupped. "Excuse me, excuse me," she added in a singsong voice. Her mood was buoyant.

"Rose, you will be the spinster sister. It rhymes even... Well, sort of." Lily was laughing too, happy finally to be spending time with the two people she loved most.

"I didn't know Rose was going to live with you, Liam," Frank stated.

"I didn't either, but," Liam looked at Lily's beaming face, "she is."

"Yes, I am, as the spinster sister. You have any trouble with that, too bad," Rose teased Frank and reached for the wine bottle, "I like this, I like this very much."

"Me too, fill mine." Lily held out her empty glass. "We've never had wine before, did you know that?"

Liam mouthed, "Nooo," to Frank and they both grinned. Then the dinners came.

Chapter 24

Lily

Finally, in a hotel room on Manchester Street, it was just the two of us, man and wife, alone. There was no polite conversation, no semblance of propriety. He did not leave me to demurely attire myself in my nightgown, and I did not pretend decorum and turn my head while he undressed. There was no bashful hesitation. He was finally my husband. Mine. There was nothing between us but joy.

"Ah, Lily, how do you do it?"

"What, what is it that I do?" I murmured, nestled into his side.

"You love so deeply, I can feel it, Lily. How do you do it?"

I thought a moment before I spoke, "You are easy to love, Liam." I rested my hand on his heart. "It's the same as it is with Rose."

"What?"

"It's easy with you, Liam, as it is with Rose. I love you."

"I love you too."

Much later, he took me again, gently at first, but then he pushed me, pushed me nearly to the edge and back again. Again and again he pushed me—asking over and over is it still easy, is it still easy—as I gave and gave and gave some more. And, finally, when he couldn't take it any longer and lay shattered in my arms, I wanted to whisper so many things, but no words could explain or contain my joy. Even the word joy was not enough. It sounded so mundane, so small and ordinary compared to what I felt. So I kissed his heartbeat and felt its slowing, gentle thud against my lips.

Chapter 25

Their welcome home was a howling southerly blast that swept rain and hail across the plains. Lily and Rose rode hunched under a tarpaulin in the back of the dray between two newly purchased bed frames. Liam and Mick bore the brunt of the storm as they drove the wagon towards home, but the trip was made bearable by the muffled gales of laughter that filtered through the coverings.

"I had forgotten."

"Forgotten what?"

"What they are like together. All the way over on the ship, they were like this. No matter what the weather or the circumstances, they found something to be happy about." Mick was smiling.

Liam smiled back.

They turned off the main river road onto Mitcham Road and went up a rise. "That's the farm." Liam pointed to the right. "There's Fairfield." The wild clouds and southerly wind did not detract from the lush beauty of the Canterbury Plains in late spring. The green of the new crops held so much promise.

There was a lull in the rain. Lily and Rose popped their heads out from under the tarp.

"Look, there's Liam's land," Mick said to Rose.

Liam turned, pausing to make sure he was talking to Lily, "And yours."

"It's our home, Rose," Lily's voice held a note of reverence.

The farmhouse was complete, and Rose was surprised at how well, it fitted into the surrounding countryside. The house sat in a fenced paddock with gravel paths to the front and the back doors. It was larger than Rose had expected and freshly painted a brilliant white that contrasted with the lush green surrounds. A veranda ran the length of the front of the house, the right side closed in with timber halfway up and glass at the top. The corners of the veranda were graced by decorative cast-iron lacework.

"Our home?" Rose asked the question as she took Lily's hand in hers and then answered it herself. "It's yours, Lily, yours and Liam's."

~

Liam loved the company. He spent the days working with Mick building fences, clearing land, planting hedges, and shearing sheep. Whatever had to be done, they did with a cheerful camaraderie. But Liam longed for the nights, alone with Lily. No dream or thought or notion he had ever been fortunate enough to have had even come close to what it felt like to have Lily in his bed night after glorious night. It was a gift.

But he could not deny his unease around Rose. She confused him; she was a duplication, a complication. Liam and Mick would come in at dusk, smell dinner cooking, and hear the girls' laughter. Liam would look at Mick and smile and feel so grateful. At first he thought he was just appreciative of the company, but he soon realised it was more than that. Lily and Rose were a family, and they lovingly encompassed him. He always approached them slowly. Lily would reach out somehow to reassure him. Once confident, he would give her a quick kiss and maybe whisper in her ear. Sometimes he took her hand and pulled her into the pantry. There were many ways to say 'I love you', and they hadn't discovered them all.

Rose was content enough, but for the first time in her life, she saw Lily separate from herself, different. Lily had Liam, and Rose did not. Rose did not in any way begrudge her sister her happiness; in fact, the opposite was true. But she was always in such close proximity to Liam and Lily. Their love was a tangible thing, impossible not to feel. So she felt it. She felt what Lily felt, the problem being that she could not reciprocate; she could only silently stay in the background, containing herself.

~

"Someone is coming up the drive." Lily and Rose were planting potatoes.

Rose raised her head when she heard the hoofbeats on the shingle. She stood and shook the dirt off her skirt. Lily was already walking towards the gate.

"Oh, Mr Lichfield, how are you?" Lily said spontaneously.

"Well enough, my dear, but I've missed you." He dismounted and leaned forward to kiss Lily's cheek. Rose stepped up beside her. "Ah, and the twin sister," he held his hand out to Rose. "How do you do, Miss Quinn."

"I'm..." Rose started to speak but Mr. Lichfield carried on.

"You left so suddenly, Lily, I thought you'd give notice and we'd... Well, I'd have come to the wedding. Elisabeth might not have, but still... Well, I just wondered really."

"I... Well..." Lily paled.

"She left because your son molested her. You are upsetting her now." Rose took hold of Lily's elbow. "Come." She turned Lily towards the house.

"My son, what? What does this have to do with Henry? Lily, dear, what is she talking about?"

Liam strode towards George from the sheep yards. "George." His voice was cold.

"What's going on here, Liam? Why is Lily upset?"

"Ah, well." Liam fists clenched, and he tried to calm himself. "George, your Henry...your son attacked her. Raped her in his bedroom. The door was locked. She swears it was locked from the outside. I'm sure you can see why she doesn't want to talk to you about it." Liam's voice, no longer cold, now quivered with his barely contained rage.

"No, he wouldn't, he couldn't! No, Liam, no!" George slumped, his proud self-possession deserting him. He looked at Liam with sad, imploring eyes.

Seeing his friend's distress, Liam's voice softened, "Ah, but it's true. He did."

"Does Elisabeth know?"

"Yes, I called round there looking for him on the night, then went back again with Lily to get her things."

"But she didn't say, didn't even..." George shook his head and a tear trailed down his cheek. "I didn't know, Liam. I came to congratulate you on your marriage, see Lily. I came to give..."

"It's all right, George. Come in, Lily's all right now."

So George went in and had a cup of tea, but Lily wasn't all right. She was trembling, memories flooding her with a strange, renewed horror. Rose was the only one who noticed. Eventually, George Lichfield left to confront his family.

"How could you, Liam?"

"How could I what?" Liam turned towards Rose.

"Bring that man in here. Look at Lily. Look at her!"

Lily was sitting quietly in the corner of the settee.

"Lily, are you all right? Lily?" Liam sat beside her. He started to take her in his arms. She stiffened, as if his touch were too much of something—too much sensation, maybe—for her overloaded mind. "No, Liam, don't. Rose? *LilyRose?*" Lily reached out her hand for her sister.

Chapter 26

Lily

"Will you come with me to the hills today, Lily?"

"We thought we would."

"No, you, Lily. Just you."

It felt strange leaving Rose behind as Liam and I drove towards the bush line. The day held the sort of promise that only a clear fine day can hold, and there was no wind. That in itself was something to celebrate.

"I'm sorry I invited George in. I didn't mean to dredge it all up for you," Liam apologized.

I shook my head, but I reached for Liam's arm and took hold, not clear if I was asking for or giving comfort.

The memories that had been stirred up by George Lichfield's visit retreated as we spent the day in each other's company. I watched Liam as he chopped down trees for firewood. I helped when I could, gathering branches, tying them in bundles, and stacking them neatly on the back of the wagon. When we spoke, we spoke of small things: would I like to choose the tile for the hearth in the front room; should we get a few piglets to raise for bacon; did I know that Mrs Elworthy had offered him rose cuttings—he could get them now if I liked. Seemingly inconsequential things that wove us together into the tapestry of life. When at last we were back in the yard at Fairfield and the sun was fading from the sky, Liam pulled the bullocks to a halt. He got down out of the wagon and reached up for me, just a hand, a hand out, palm up, turned as if issuing an invitation. I recognised the request. Come and love me, that outstretched hand said eloquently. Then I looked into his eyes. Come and love me, they said. It was as if his body could speak to me; we had a wordless language between us that was all strength and feeling and passion and warm skin.

In Liam's arms, I forgot all about Henry and the violent invasion he had made upon my body. He had not touched my soul. Henry's power was nothing, absolutely nothing, compared to the loving power of this man looking at me now and wondering why I hesitated.

"Lily, you all right?"

I moved then, took his hand firmly in mine, and launched myself into his arms; my feet never made it to the ground. My arms circled his neck; my hands were in his silky hair. He smiled, looking down at me, reading my eyes.

"Ah, Lily…Lily."

He bent to take my lips. I met him, raising up from my legs that were wrapped around his waist. I pressed my body against the long, hard length of him, and we were melded together, lips and bodies and souls.

I lost track of time.

I lost track of myself.

All I could feel was Liam.

Of all my experiences of life up until I met Liam, nothing could compare, nothing was even remotely close to this sweet rush of feeling that coursed through and filled me every time I touched him. Everything bad I had ever known seemed to fade behind, settle back, swirl away like gravel and silt being washed from a miner's pan. All that seemed to be left for me was pure gold. And all I wanted to do was share it, with Liam and with Rose.

"We have to unload the wagon before dark, Lily," he whispered in my ear as I slid down the length of him to find my feet. I nodded and planted a tiny kiss on his heart before turning away.

Chapter 27

Elisabeth Lichfield did her best. She knew that George would, in time, become privy to the knowledge that Henry had 'overstepped the mark', which was how she referred to the incident with Lily. As for any duplicity on her part, well, she certainly was not about to admit anything—to anyone. And so George could only surmise what had happened and believe what Liam had told him. George Lichfield had overlooked an awful lot in the interests of matrimonial harmony, but the truth dawned on him that he may have overlooked too much.

Henry was lying low, in Christchurch mostly. His friends, or school acquaintances to be more precise, noticed the change. There was no longer any pretence at gregariousness. He made no effort to gain attention for himself. If they'd cared to analyse his behaviour, they would have said he was suddenly driven by something—obsessed even—but no one cared quite enough to find out, not even Sally.

~

Frank had been living in Rakaia for three weeks before he rode out to Fairfield.

Liam answered the knock on the door. "Well, hello! And what brings you...?"

"Constable Franklin McManaway at your service, sir. Ma'am... Miss." He bowed to both Lily and Rose, not quite sure who was who.

"Frank, it's good to see you, man." Liam embraced his friend.

"What is this?" He gestured to Frank's uniform, "Didn't get enough in Ireland?"

"Ah, well, yes, but it seems drunkenness and horse theft are the main crimes of any consequence around here."

"Around here?"

"Aye, I'm stationed in Rakaia. Thought it might be good to see you now and again."

"That's great, man, great!" Liam grabbed Frank's hand and shook it again. "Come in, come in." Liam turned and Frank followed him in.

"This calls for a drink."

"Aye, and a toast to me finally settling down. Took your advice, Liam."

"And found yourself a woman?"

"No, not yet." Frank grinned at the girls. "But, seems to me, you have an extra."

The girls looked at each other, one blushing and a little embarrassed. Liam handed Frank a glass of whisky.

"No, I just decided to stay in one place for a while. Policing suits me better than farming."

"Ah, it would. You'd have to check the pubs periodically, and…"

"Yes, there are many laborious duties that call for common sense."

"And a sense of humour," Liam added. "And it's not like you don't have experience."

"What do you mean? What experience?" one of the girls piped up.

"Oh, Lily, Frank was in the Royal Irish Constabulary before he came to New Zealand. I think I told you that."

"I'm Rose, and you didn't tell me."

"Do you always get them mixed up?" Frank asked Liam.

"I try not to." Liam took a large gulp of whisky and shook his head.

Frank laughed, "Ah, to have your problems." He made Liam smile as he looked over at the girls.

"Lily took her apron off. Must have done it just as you arrived. That's what threw me, I think."

"Do you still have to look at our clothes?" Rose asked.

"I want to know for sure. I always want to know for sure," Liam answered somewhat uncomfortably. Lily stood and moved to sit beside him, taking his hand in hers.

~

Sally eventually noticed that Henry was not himself. He had a despondency that she could not help him lighten. He no longer desired her. Oh, he took her all right, but it was always with a sense of indifference. Sally wondered what she could do to recapture his attention.

"Henry, you'll be finished with school soon."

"You sound like my father."

"Oh, has he mentioned somehow setting you up?"

"Sending me off, more like."

"Where? To do what?" Sally sat up straighter in her chair, twisting towards him.

"Oh, if he had his way, I expect it would be the foreign legion, stationed in some god-awful place. That or the army," Henry spoke listlessly.

"And you'd go? You'd leave here and join the army?" Sally's voice held a decided note of alarm.

"Hell, no," Henry said with more feeling than usual.

Sally sunk back into the chair. "And so, what will you do?"

"I bloody well don't know, now do I?"

She felt his frustration and the simmering anger directed at her. "Henry." She moved to her knees in front of him, moved her hands to his trouser buttons. "I can make you feel…" She toyed with him, inciting not his passion but something else, something that also needed release.

He saw in her greedy eyes the planning and manoeuvring, the hopes for their future, assuming so much with her familiarity. He thought of her like a pressure valve, which he pushed and pushed against, finding it barely tolerable. Finally with her hands, or mouth, she eased him. It was somewhat of a miracle, he thought, how good she made him feel. He closed his eyes and imagined Lily. It was her mouth on him, lovingly caressing him. It was Lily, it was always Lily.

Chapter 28

It was Sunday. The river was in a meandering mood and the wind a soft gentle breeze, like it too thought a day of rest was in order. All the necessities for a relaxing day by the river were being unloaded from the wagon.

Frank rode up on his horse. He had exchanged his police uniform for his worsted wool trousers and vest. His dark shiny hair glinted in the sunlight. Rose studied him, his muscular forearms showing below his rolled up sleeves. She entertained thoughts that were not altogether possible to verbalise.

"Hey, how are you all?" Frank smiled as he spoke and surveyed Liam and Mick who were tending to the horses. Lily was struggling with a large picnic basket. He dismounted smoothly.

"Here, I'll help you with that. Rose is it?"

"Thank you, but, no, I'm Lily. Rose is over there, watching you, I think," Lily smiled.

"Aye, well, I see the trouble Liam has. Liam, have you thought to buy the lass a wedding ring?"

Liam came over, wiping his hands on his trousers. "Ask Lily about that."

"Yes, he has, but there are other things we need first..." Lily trailed off.

"Ah... So they play games with you, then?" Frank smiled.

"No, we don't, not ever. Do we, Liam?"

"No, they wouldn't, and they promised not to." Liam took Lily's hand, "I think it would do me in. Come on, come for a walk with me." Liam pulled Lily gently to him and they wandered off downstream.

Frank turned towards Rose, "Ah...and so... Rose, this is nice. At least now I know who I am talking to. How are you?"

"Good, we've been... Oh, here, Mick, let me help you with that." Mick was endeavouring to spread a large canvas sheet on the ground. Rose tugged at the edges.

"Help us get everything out, then we can sit and talk." Rose lifted a bucket from the wagon.

"Here, I'll get that." Frank stepped forward. He reached for the handle and touched her hand. He left it there a moment, lingering a second, just long enough for the feel of her warm skin to register. He took the bucket and glanced at her face; there was no embarrassment. Her eyes were closed and her lips slightly turned up at the edges.

"Rose?"

"Umm." She opened her eyes and the inevitable smile came, "Yes, Frank."

Yes... What? What did she mean? She said it like he'd asked a question, an important question, and he most certainly hadn't. He stood there staring at her smiling face and wasn't altogether comforted by the look in her eyes. He remembered their meeting in Christchurch, her tears and her abrupt departure into the house. He felt vaguely uneasy.

"Would you like to go for a walk?" Rose ventured.

"Ah, yes, all right, then." He extended an elbow. He needed to think. "Mick, are you coming?"

Rose didn't link her arm through his like a decent woman would; she entwined his whole arm and was holding his hand. Then, to further intensify the contact, she laid her other hand on his captured arm, just under his rolled up sleeve, bare skin on bare skin. They walked upriver.

"Do you like living in Rakaia?" Rose asked Frank.

"Yes, so far, so good."

"What is your accommodation like? Do you have a house?"

"Oh, no, in a boarding house for now."

"There's lots of building going on in Rakaia," Mick added.

Frank turned to study Mick. He was still wondering about Rose's line of conversation. "Yes, there is. How are you enjoying life on the farm, Mick?" Frank turned and spoke to Mick who was following along behind them.

"Very well, thank you, but I might just head back and get myself some of that ginger beer the girls made."

"Is that what was in that bucket?"

"Yes, and it was Mick's job to hold the cover on, all the way down here, to keep it from sloshing out." Rose turned her head and watched Mick jump over a large rock.

Frank lifted her hand off his arm and untangled himself.

They were silent for a few minutes, looking at each other.

Finally Rose said, "You touched me when you took the bucket from me. I felt you then, and you felt just right. I wanted just a tiny bit more. That's all."

Frank sat down, leaning against the same rock Mick had just vaulted over. "Sweet Jesus, can you read my mind?"

Rose stood watching the rippling water glistening in the sun. Luckily, Frank didn't seem to be requiring an answer.

~

Liam and Lily sat, leaning back against a boulder, watching the Rakaia River rushing by. The grey-blue colour of the water contrasted with the grey-green of the hills they could see on the other side. Lily leaned back with her eyes closed, her face tilted towards the warmth of the sun.

"I don't get enough of you." Liam pulled Lily closer, turning to see her better, "Not in the daylight hours, anyway."

Lily opened her eyes and looked at Liam. Her spine tingled with pride and pleasure. There was something too big and bold and broad and strong, too sweet, too lush, too precious to name. She smiled. But, oh, what Liam could read in her smile! He saw the solid core of her, coated with all the soft woman-ness of her, the gentle acquiescence, the good humour, the... He bent to kiss her, with a fleeting thought of how useless the words floating around in his head were when he could feel her, anchor himself in the very thing he was trying so hard to describe. She opened to him, as always. Everything he wanted or needed, she gave. He slipped his tongue between her lips. Her tongue met his in welcome. She reached down to tug his shirttail free of his trousers.

She pulled away to murmur, "I want to feel your skin, Liam."

He clasped her wayward hand in his, "Not here." He reclaimed her mouth, probing provocatively in an attempt to find a way to give her what she was asking for, satiate their need for each other. Lily responded to his sweet invasion by arching her body into his as their lips danced together. Eventually they paused, breathing deeply. Lily giggled delightfully. "Oh, Liam, that was..." She trailed off as their eyes met and their gazes held.

"Ah, Lily."

"That one was different, just slightly. I haven't figured them all out yet, but you have quite different 'Ah, Lily's'."

"What are you talking about?"

"Well, they are quite expressive really, although you are saying the same thing all the time," she giggled again. He didn't look like he was in the mood for teasing, but she didn't let it stop her.

"There is a certain 'Ah, Lily' that makes me feel like I am a queen, and anything I ask of you, you would do at my beck and call, almost like you thought you had no choice in the matter. Then there is the 'Ah, Lily' you say and I'll swear you are surrendering; I feel like I have won something. And then there is…"

He interrupted, "I am getting the point."

"Don't you want to hear the rest? There are at least three or four more, and I haven't got them all."

His mouth moved towards her and his body followed. "Ah, Lily," he smiled and captured her mouth once again. She melted into the ecstasy of his possession. A few minutes later he said, "Did you get that one?"

She nodded and whispered, "Shut up and kiss me, woman."

~

"Next time, let's come alone." Lily playfully tugged at his hanging shirttail.

"We could take a trip, a late wedding trip," Liam answered as he brushed a stray strand of hair from her face. They were still by the boulder nestled into each other, but they heard voices and knew they should rejoin the rest of their party.

"We can leave Rose and Mick. Mick can look after the farm and the sheep by himself. Rose will cook for him, keep him company." Liam stood up as he was speaking and held out his hand for Lily's.

Lily was not all his and he felt it, knew it, in the marrow of his bones. However much she professed her love and shared herself with him, there was a part of her that belonged to Rose. He had begun ignoring Rose, though not wanting to. Oh, he was polite enough, cordial, and kind. But he could not really look at her without feeling. And what he felt was not very different from what he felt for his wife. It scared him, in a way that he didn't want to admit.

They returned to find Frank, Rose, and Mick in animated conversation. The ginger beer bucket looked untouched. Frank had brought real beer.

"Well, and how are you two?" Frank smiled, waiting for an answer.

"Just fine, I'll have you know." Liam knelt on the canvas sheet and pulled Lily down to him. "And you?"

"Oh, good," Frank was intrigued as he watched Liam and Lily's easy physical intimacy. He was not used to seeing his friend so…so at home with someone. He looked at Rose. She had an almost glazed expression as she watched Liam move from his crouch to a seated position and then proceed to encompass Lily with his body until it looked like she was sitting on his lap. *Ah, Rose,* thought Frank in a moment of unexpected clarity. Her earlier possession of his arm, his hand, the whole side of his body, flashed into his mind once again. *Ah, Rose, I see.*

He saw all right, but still it gave him pause for thought. On one hand, he very much liked the idea of Rose. She was beautiful. She was intelligent and young and healthy. She had all her teeth—which was no small thing. There was, though, something peculiar about her. Something he couldn't quite put his finger on and didn't really want to, when it came down to it.

"So tell me, Mick, you miss the city at all?" Frank asked to give himself something else to think about.

Mick looked up from the small wooden carving he was working on, "No, sir, I don't."

"You're not getting tired of the wind, or the dust, or the impossible demands of your boss?"

Mick smiled, "No, sir, Liam's a good boss." He glanced quickly at Liam as if seeking permission for such an assertion.

"Well, he's always been a good friend, stands to reason he'd be a good boss, now, doesn't it?" Frank leaned back on his elbows, stretching out on the canvas.

"Well… You good friend and good boss…" Lily reached up and ever so slowly moved a stray wisp of hair behind his ear and then laid her hand on his cheek—which, in itself, would have captured the other's attention—but Liam had his eyes closed and, with a look on his face that could only be described as pure bliss, covered her hand with his own.

Speaking at the exact same moment, Lily said, "Can you get the picnic hamper?" and Rose said, "Good man, you forgot good man."

~

"Tell us a story...Lily... Rose...like you used to on the ship," Mick requested.

They were all replete, basking in the sun, which had pleasant warmth about it. Lily looked at Liam thoughtfully, speculating.

But it was Rose who spoke, "Liam and Frank may not like our stories."

"Now, how could that be? Just what sort of stories are they?" Frank looked interested at least.

"Well, you know, our grandmother..." Lily started to speak.

"Ah, your grandmother, that explains a few things," Liam interrupted.

"I don't know a bloody thing about your grandmother," Frank said good-naturedly and then apologised for his language.

"Well, our grandmother was a... Have you ever worked out exactly what she was, Rose?"

"Well, no. I've never even spoken to anyone else about her."

"Lily told me she wasn't a witch, if that helps."

"Ah, Liam," Lily murmured.

He scrutinised her a moment. "Thank you?" He said softly. "That was thank you."

Lily raised her eyebrows, "Quick, you're very quick."

"And so, where were we?" Frank voiced a little too loudly. "Something about grandmothers and stories, I believe."

"Tell us the one about Iona," Mick piped up.

"You mean Inanna, don't you, the one about the sisters?" Rose answered.

"Well, sometimes you called her Inanna and sometimes Iona," Mick shrugged.

"That is what Nana Kat did too,"" Lily told Mick.

"But still it is a good story, isn't it? It isn't meant to be true." Mick looked at Lily and Lily looked at Rose.

Rose ran her hands down her grey cotton dress and then began to speak.

"Inanna was a goddess, the queen of her world, the Upper World." Rose's voice became more animated as she spoke.

"One day she heard her sister Ereshkigal, Queen of the Underworld, moaning in pain. She decided to go to visit her and see what was wrong. She was dressed in a royal robe with a crown on her head. She had beads of lapis lazuli around her neck, crystals fastened to

155

her waist, and a gold band around her wrist. Carrying a sceptre, she descended to the underworld with her faithful servant."

Rose paused and took a sip of her beer, the others around her in rapt attention. "When she arrived at the outer gates, she commanded her servant to wait for three days and, if she had not returned, to call upon the elder gods for help. But when Inanna challenged the gatekeeper to gain entry into the underworld, he consulted her sister, telling her that a powerful goddess was waiting to enter her realm. Ereshkigal became even more upset and told the gatekeeper to open each gate of the underworld a mere crack and to remove Inanna's royal garments on her way through. So, at each of the seven gates, she was stopped by the gatekeeper, who demanded she give up some part of her clothing. First her crown, then her sceptre, then her jewels, and then her garments. And each time he made a demand of her, she responded in her haughty, queen-like manner, 'What is this?' Each time the gatekeeper's answer was the same: 'Hush, Inanna, the ways of the underworld are perfect'." Rose paused again.

"Is that it?" Frank looked at Rose.

"No, there is more," Mick said. He loved their stories, especially when they involved the underworld, or otherworld, as Mick sometimes called it. He said it was different to his father's version of hell.

"Go on, then." Frank motioned to Rose. But Lily continued.

"Well, finally, quite naked and disarmed, Inanna entered the throne room of her sister. Immediately, she was surrounded by the judges of the underworld, who ruled against her. Then Ereshkigal fastened onto Inanna the eye of death and she was turned into a corpse."

"Great story, Lily." Lily glanced at Liam and then she continued.

"Well, after three days, her faithful servant went to various gods, who refused to help because the underworld was not their domain. Finally, the God of Wisdom helped. He was grieved and troubled. He took the dirt from under his fingernails and created two creatures. He gave them food and the water of life to take to Inanna. These creatures snuck into the underworld like flies, slipping through the cracks in the gates. They entered the throne room and found Ereshkigal lying naked and unkempt, moaning 'Oh! Oh! My inside!' Following the God of Wisdom's instructions, they also moaned 'Oh! Oh! Your inside!' Again she moaned, 'Ohhh! Oh! My outside!' To which the creatures replied, 'Ohhh! Oh! Your outside!' She continued to moan out her agony, and they continued to name her pains back to her. Finally, she stopped moaning and blessed the creatures, offering them any gift they desired. So they asked for Inanna's corpse. They revived her with the food and the water of life. Inanna then arose and ascended to the upper world."

Lily smiled.

"Now, it has ended." Rose looked at Mick and the men.

"I'm not sure about all that underworld stuff. It seems... Well, heathen," Liam said.

"I don't know that it is so much the underworld, like how you might think of hell, as it is the spirit world, the otherworld. You know, maybe just under ours, a little out of sight."

Liam looked at Lily as if he were thinking about what she had said.

"Ah, where the shee-geeha live... The wind fairies?"

"Maybe they do, but it's vast and it's powerful, and all poets know their way there."

"Do they know their way back, then?" Frank reached for a bun.

Rose nudged the basket closer to him. "It isn't evil. I think it is where your soul comes from and where your soul goes. Inanna was just visiting; she had things to retrieve."

"Her sister?" Frank's mouth was full.

"No, no! I see!" Mick sat up and spoke quickly. "There was no other sister. Inanna was missing her soul. She had to go down deep to get it."

"And she had to leave behind all the things that got in her way. She'd never find her soul if she clung to her power or her wealth or her pride," Lily finished for him.

"Or her clothes?" Liam was not going along with their theories. "So if the sister isn't real, then is the gatekeeper?"

"No, the gatekeeper is just her fear speaking. She is afraid to give up all her accoutrements," Rose spoke quickly.

"Well, what about the faithful servant? What's that?"

"The small part of yourself, that knows...knows when you can't do something alone...when you need to ask for help...because everything else is gone."

"And the creatures?" Liam knew Rose would have an answer.

"Your pains, of course."

Lily noted Liam's confused look and said, "The creatures are whatever caused you to lose your soul in the first place. You have to acknowledge them, bless them even."

157

"Bless them?"

"Well, maybe that isn't the exact word, but…"

"What does Reverend McGregor think of all this?"

Lily shrugged, "He'd rather we told Bible stories."

Chapter 29

"Don't you want to go, Lily?" Rose asked as they made her bed. The linens were softer than usual, having dried in the gentle, warm, breeze of early summer.

"Oh, aye, I do. It's just that I don't really want to leave you here. I don't know why, it's just…" Lily paused, a small tremor running through her. "I have the strangest feeling."

"I'll be fine here. Mick will keep me company," Rose said as she continued to fold and smooth the sheets, taking particular care with a corner. "Liam wants you to himself, Lily."

"I know," Lily said, smiling and imagining the joy of being alone with Liam on holiday with no farm work to do.

"He wants to take his bride on a honeymoon trip, and you need to go. I will stay here and look after Mick. It will be the beginning."

"The beginning?"

"Lily, we have to try… We have to try and separate ourselves. You need your own life with Liam and I need… I need to find my own…" A tear slid down her face.

"Ah, Rosie, no… Not yet, not ever. Come here, come to me." Lily's arms were outstretched and Rose did what she had always done to find comfort. They lowered themselves onto the freshly made bed, holding each other tight.

I will go. I will go away with Liam. You can stay.
We will do what we need to do to make him happy, LilyRose.
But you don't need to leave here. You can't leave… Not for good.
I can't watch you love him… Not forever.
But you… You don't watch… Not really… You
Yes, I… Oh, LilyRose… He is here.

Lily's eyes were brimming. She turned and reached out her hand. Liam was there. He stepped forward, surveying them. He did not take her hand, but turned and sat on the edge of the bed, his back towards them.

"Please, Lily, tell me what is going on?"

"Liam, this is just what we do."

"But what is it? What are you doing?"

Rose spoke, "We communicate."

"Without words," Lily added.

Liam had to turn and face them to work out which one of them was speaking.

Lily spoke, "We embrace, or touch. All we need to do is hold hands, and then we…"

"We read each other's minds, talk to each other without words," Rose finished for her. Liam clamped his jaw and shook his head as he tried to take in what they were telling him.

Lily reached out for him, "Liam, Liam, darling Liam, it is not like we…"

Liam raised a hand to halt her speech. "Ah, Lily, enough, I think, for now. Enough for me."

He stood and backed towards the door.

"No, don't go, don't." Lily extricated herself from Rose and moved quickly towards Liam. "You need to understand."

"Pack your bag, Lily. We'll leave in the morning. You'll have two weeks to help me understand."

Chapter 30

Lily

We took the dray. Liam thought we might buy more furniture in Christchurch on the way home. The first stop was Rakaia, where Liam wanted to remind Frank to call in to check on Rose and Mick. After that was done, we made it all the way to Leeston the first night. It was not until three nights later, when we were settled in the Grand Hotel in Akaroa, by the sea on Banks Peninsula, that Liam sat me down on the edge of the bed and got up the nerve to ask me.

"Lily, tell me everything you can about you and Rose. There can be no secrets between us."

I nodded and spoke.

"Ever since the beginning, we have been able to touch each other and know."

"Know what?"

"Know everything… Don't look at me like that, Liam. We are not circus freaks."

"Let me get this straight; your sister knows everything you think."

"Well, not every minute of every day, but well, when we touch, we catch up, I guess. So, yes, the answer would be yes, pretty much, I think. Yes… Liam, please, please, don't look so…so betrayed. I love you, Liam, I love you." I knew I needed to be completely honest with Liam, but I was worried about it. I don't think he found what I had to say very reassuring.

Liam stood. He paced across the room and then swivelled a chair around and, straddling it, sat again. He looked at me, stared for a moment, then slowly closed his eyes and lowered his head into his hands.

"Liam, you are scaring me."

He raised his head, shaking it slightly.

"What have I done, what have I done?" he mumbled. "So your

sister knows everything you think and feel; so she knows everything you think and feel about me, Lily. Everything? Oh, God, help me. Everything? Is there nothing sacred between us, Lily?" His head lowered into his hands again.

I stood and placed my hands on his shoulders and then bent to be even with his face.

"Liam, you've fallen in love with me. That is all you've done."

He raised his head again and looked at me, speculating, considering. Finally, he spoke, "Lily, do you know…can you tell…when you are doing this mind reading with your sister, where exactly you end and she begins?"

I held his gaze. I swallowed. "It isn't really like that." I shook my head.

"What is it, then? Tell me."

Well, we have a conversation, and you might think that we are both speaking, or telling, or thinking at different times but then…but then… There is… We call, we say… Liam, we…

"Tell me, Lily, say it. Look at me and say it."

I started to speak and then stopped, started again, and finally blurted out, "LilyRose, LilyRose… There is just one… One, Liam. I don't end and she doesn't begin. We don't need to."

He closed his eyes for a long moment.

"Ah, Lily, now you'll be starting to understand my problem."

~

We had dinner in the dining room of the Akaroa Hotel, a large room with beautiful chandeliers. The light of so many candles flickering at once fascinated me. There were not many other diners and Liam and I talked about everyday things. Would we get a new cabinet for the hall by the front door? Would we get a proper feather mattress for our bed or leave the ticking packed with straw for a while longer? Oh, and the cook stove. Liam wanted to know if I'd worked out which model to buy. Did he like sponge cakes? Proper light ones with eggs and baking soda, the kind you could make in an oven and serve with cream? Did his mother make them for him?

Before we knew it, the cod was finished, and the potatoes and even the sultana pudding had disappeared, so we walked in the evening light enjoying the sea breeze. Liam held my hand as we watched children fishing off the jetty. Eventually we returned to our room.

"I am here." I stood by the window, facing Liam. "I am here for you." I stretched out my arms out wide. "I am Lily; I am not Rose." I spun and my skirts swished. "I want to…"

"I want you to take off your dress." His voice held an underlying note of tension.

I disrobed. Liam didn't help but once again sat straddling the chair, his eyes attentive, devoted.

"Now, arms out, twirl again."

"Naked?"

"Naked." He nodded as he spoke. "Go on."

I moved for him, dancing in the silence, feeling so bare and yet beautiful in the moonlight—his fairy girl, his wife. I willed him to forget about my mystical other half, Rose, who was me but was not me.

I danced openly and precisely. I danced explicitly and yet demurely.

I danced warm skin and soft touches. I danced dark nights and deep kisses.

At first, his eyes spoke of possession.

He wanted to confine.

I danced expansion, unfettered, refusing to be shackled.

I saw the moment he looked past what he could see and saw what was possible.

I saw love's liberation.

Here I began. He caught my hand and stood, pulling me towards him. He'd take me to the end.

~

"Do you think I am a selfish man, Lily?" We were walking arm in arm along the edge of Children's Bay. The evening was a gentle one.

"Ah, Liam, no one could call you a selfish man."

"You could though, if you wanted to."

"Because you want me all to yourself, like this, all the time?" I loosened my arm and slid my hand in his. I wanted the feel of his skin.

"Aye, we need to marry off Rose. Don't you see?"

"Rose might go eventually, Liam. She might marry Frank even. But I won't love you more because she's gone." I stopped and was looking right at Liam. "She's… Well, she's just part of me, Liam."

Liam looked out across the sea, quiet for a long time. The waves lapped at the shore making a soothing sound.

"So what is this then, Lily, all this about not knowing where you end and she begins? Tell me, what am I supposed to do?"

He let go of my hand.

"Tell me, how I love you with all my heart, with everything. Love you, Lily... YOU... Protect you and honour you and cherish you. How do I do that, Lily, and not...and not..."

I interrupted, "Love Rose too?"

He turned to see my face and found my eyes brimming. He kicked at the sand and stomped off. I followed with my tears.

We walked in silence for much longer than we should have. My heart ached, ached from what? Too much love? Selfish desire? All the old feelings of uneasiness and worry came crashing in on me. Finally, I sat down on the damp sand in the moonlight. I watched Liam's back as he walked on. I felt abandoned, deserted. Eventually he turned and, when he had seen my shape on the beach, I knew. He came back and sat down beside me. My arms were crossed in front of me, my hands tucked in, head bent. I was afraid. Finally I spoke. "I am the selfish one."

Liam didn't say a word.

I went on, my voice cracking. "I am the selfish one because I want both of you. I love you both so much, but Rose has to go, doesn't she?" I shook with emotion as I sobbed. Liam sat for a long moment and, eventually, he spoke.

"You know I am a practical man."

I nodded.

"Well, there is one fact that I can't deny."

I looked up at him.

"I love you, Lily McCann." He said it softly in my ear.

I raised my face, couldn't help brushing my lips against his cheek, couldn't help opening myself for him. "And I you, and I you."

We had ten days. He used those ten days to make me his. We forged something between us as strong as metal. Something, at times, red hot, then white hot, then tempered in water—the sea at dawn, the bath in the afternoon. We grew trust, nurtured it, and tested it. It wasn't easy.

It was, though, exquisite.

He demanded.

I offered.

He challenged.

I bestowed.

He toughened his easiness; I questioned my pliancy. We both gave everything we had to give, but neither of us ever gave in. Here I am, I said; this is what I have to give you.

Ah, fine, but this is what I want; this is what I need. Can you give me this?

Surely, my body answered. My confidence grew and I started to do some of the asking. Together we taught our love to be defiant.

Chapter 31

Henry was running out of time. He felt the relentless movement towards whatever it was his father was planning for him—some far-off post with a trading or shipping company. If that did not eventuate, it would be the military. Men were needed and he'd be roped into whatever place they found for him. There was only one thing that brought him joy, only one thing that brought him any sort of peace. And he focused more and more on that one thing.

Lily.

Oh, he knew she had married McCann, an inconvenience to be sure. But at least he knew where she was. She was at Fairfield, and she was waiting for him.

~

It was strangely hot for so early in the summer. There seemed to be no relief from the blistering sun. It beat relentlessly down on the plains, sucking the moisture out of every living thing. Mick and Rose spent the morning hauling water from the river and hand-watering the potatoes. The only shade to be found was under the odd cabbage tree, or under the wagon, or at the edge of the house when the sun wasn't straight overhead. They worked for as long as they could, but eventually retreated to the riverbed, not for another load, but because they hoped the cool water might refresh them.

"Here, Pearl! Come 'ere, girl."

"I swear even the river looks lethargic."

"Well, it is warmer than usual, isn't it? Pearl, come 'ere." Mick watched the dog as it rounded the bend in the river. "What's down there? Something's got her attention; she usually listens to me." Mick started to stand.

"You stay, relax. I'll go. Have a nap if you want."

"You be careful if you're thinkin' you might go in, Rose."

"Oh, aye, to be sure. I'll just sit at the edge, but, oh, I'm so hot."

~

It couldn't be this easy, could it? Henry sat in the tussock with the dog muzzled and tied beside him, limp in the baking heat. She had looked for the dog, called out in her engaging voice, but then she'd gone to the river's edge and started to undress.

There she was, alone, in a very thin layer of something flimsy and white—a fairy, no, not a fairy, an angel, his angel. She had her bottom in the water, her elbows on the shore. Her head was thrown back, and her eyes were closed. She was thinking of him, he knew, because her nipples were jutting out and she was smiling. Oh, Lily. He took a few deep breaths to get control, but his hand moved to his crotch. There was no help for it. It only took a minute, or a few minutes maybe, but now he could think straight. He had to move slowly, carefully.

Rose let herself drift tranquilly inward, finding the peace within herself, barely aware of the blissfully cool water. Henry's eyes never left the back of her head as he crept up behind her. Oh, he wanted to look around. He kept feeling like that damn hired boy would be coming around the bend any moment or that bastard McCann would come flying out of the bushes back from wherever the hell he was. *Serves the bastard right leaving Lily by herself,* he thought, as the river rock in his hand struck her temple. He stepped into the water and stooped, gathering her up as the current threatened to pull her limp body away from him. "No, no, she's mine." He tightened his hold and kissed her forehead. "Mine."

Chapter 32

"Home! Sweet, sweet home." Lily smiled at Liam as they turned and started up the drive. But by the time they had reached the house, their cheerfulness was gone. It was as if someone had cast an evil spell, a spell that left only stillness.

"Something has happened." Lily spoke quietly, not moving off her seat. "To Rose, I think. Oh, Liam." She reached for him.

"Lily, you don't know. They could have gone to the bush line for the day, or the river, or…" A tremor ran through Liam; his shoulders shook.

"What was that? Liam, you feel it too, don't you? You feel this."

Liam looked up at the clear sky. "Does feel oppressive, like just before a thunderstorm." He turned to look back up the drive. "Lily, here comes someone."

He helped Lily down and they waited, strangely immobile, for the rider to make his way down the drive. His head was bent, but it looked like Frank.

Liam started forward. "Come on, it's Frank." He pulled Lily along.

"He has bad news, he has bad news."

"Lily, whatever has got into you?" He dropped her hand and went to greet Frank.

"Rose is missing," Frank said, even before dismounting.

Lily gasped and crumpled.

"Missing?"

"Missing, presumed drowned. You'd best come down to the river."

Lily rose slowly, first feeling like something was seeping into her or maybe out of her, and then she stood, inexplicably reinforced. "Yes, take me to her. Take me to her."

"There is no body, Lily," Frank said solemnly.

"Of course not! Take me to where she last was. Quickly, please."

"Go with Frank; I'll see to the dray. Be right behind you. Where is Mick?"

"Hasn't left the riverbed since yesterday. Won't."

"Since yesterday... She's been missing since..." Liam shook his head.

"Frank, please, let's go," Lily interrupted.

Frank turned and mounted. Liam gave Lily a hand up.

~

Mick saw Lily clinging to Frank's back and shouted, "Rosie, Rosie, where were you?" He started towards them and then fell in an awkward stumble. He stayed on the ground.

"Mick, Mick, are you all right?"

It took all his effort to turn over, turn his face to the light.

"I thought for a minute, more than a minute, that my prayers had been answered, that my fervent appeals to the God of my fathers had been satisfied. Oh, Lily, where is she? Where is she?"

Lily was beside him in an instant. "Take me to the place, Mick. Show me."

He stood up and took Lily's hand, pulling her towards the river.

"I was here." He pointed to a boulder. "But she was down there." His arm moved in a sweep, and he started walking purposely downriver. "She would have yelled; she would have come floating past me. She would have let me know she was in trouble. Rosie would have let me know."

Lily hurried to catch up to him. She took his hand. "Of course, Mick. Of course, she would have."

"So why didn't she, Lily?" Mick paused. This hollow here, we think, is where she sat. Her apron was here, but no shoes. Her shoes would be here, wouldn't they? And then Pearl wasn't well. I found her over there. She was laid out panting, trying to get to the water, then she drank and drank."

Lily looked around. "Mick, go and get Frank for me, please."

Mick returned with Frank and Liam. Lily called to them from the scrubby bushes back from the river. "Come here, quick, come here! Look, look at this!" Lily pointed to the smashed-down bushes she'd found—the perfect little alcove, with views to the river and Rose's position. The men found footprints and hoofprints. Pearl started growling, a low menacing growl at nothing but the bushes.

"I'll be damned, a kidnapping. We should have..."

"Oh, Frank, it looked like a drowning. Who would stalk her like

169

prey and then pounce when she... Oh, my God... Oh, my God! Oh, Danu, mother of all, please help us find her. Give her strength." Lily rushed back towards the river, searching the bank, overcome with a new terror. She dropped to her knees, crawling along and feeling the stones.

"Lily, darling, what are you doing?" Liam's voice was anxious.

"It's here, just here. Just a minute, I'll find it... I'll... Ah, ah..." Lily's hand stopped in midair, poised above a grey fist-sized stone. Her hand hovered. She stretched out her fingers and with some effort touched the stone.

She moaned, an uncontrollable, low, agonising moan.

"Lily, please." Liam sat down heavily beside her. Her distress was almost unbearable for him. But what could he ask her not to do, or to do for that matter? He gathered her to him.

"It's... It's Henry...Henry Lichfield. He used this rock." It was clutched in Lily's hand—a heavy, sucking, violent weight.

"He had it in his hand, and he hit her on the side of her head." Lily moaned again and closed her eyes. Her body went slack in his arms.

"Lily, Lily, wake up! Where are you going?"

"Lord, we've got to get her home. Liam, lift her up. I'll help you get her to the horse." Lily heard Frank's voice.

She struggled. "No, NO! We have to find Rose. We have to find Rose."

"We will. Here, give it to me, Lily." Mick took the rock out of Lily's hand and then suddenly jumped back, dropping it and nearly losing his footing. "Ah, Lily, I see," he said with a frightened expression on his face.

"Put me down, Liam, put me down. I'll be all right. Mick, you felt it too! Did you see it? Did you see Henry?" Lily reached for both his hands.

"No, I just felt it. I felt Rose. Lily, she's hurt. I don't think she's... She's still not awake, is she?"

Her arms went around Mick, "No, I don't think so."

"All right, you two, now tell us what is going on here!" Liam pulled Lily out of Mick's arms, "Tell me, Lily." Liam's voice held both fear and anger.

"Sit here and tell us. The bastard, the fucking bastard... I'll kill him this time. Tell me, tell Frank. We'll go after him."

"No." Lily yanked her arm away from Liam. "I'll ride with Frank. I'll tell him on the way."

"The way to where, for God's sake?"

"Avonlea! That's the first place we have to look."

Frank followed Lily as she made her way to his waiting horse.

"You all right, Mick?" Liam asked.

"Yeah."

"Lily, I'm sorry, I..." Liam hurried up behind Lily, grabbing her hand as he spoke and lifting it to his lips. "We'll find her."

"Oh, Liam." Lily's hand went from his lips to his neck of its own accord. "I cannot lose her."

"I've heard them before, you know, when they talk to each other without speaking."

"Oh, have you now." Liam paused and turned back to look at Mick as he spoke.

"This was different though. I felt... I felt the violence...and space." He caught up to Liam and Lily. "A void, it was. A hole, exactly where Rose is supposed to be."

~

George was home but not in the mood for visitors, not at all. Elisabeth was less communicative than usual, which was saying a lot or nothing, as it turned out. She wouldn't tell him where Henry had skipped off to. Taken the gig and one of his best horses, no less.

One close look at Liam McCann and the constable at his side, and George knew this wasn't a social visit. He hurriedly ushered them into his library. Lily got right to the point. The story didn't startle George as much as it sickened him. It filled him with dread, and as the facts unfolded, left him disgusted and horrified. And one more emotion was there—a feeling at the edge, creeping in slowly—oh yes, guilt. Guilt, that a child he raised could stoop to this sort of carry on—rape and now what? Murder? Charges for abduction, at the very least, and jail.

Guilt and shame, hovering around disgust and dread, tried to consume him. Deep down, he'd always felt he was a good man. He was a man with some honour or decency, at the very least. "So what can I do to help? What do you need?" he finally managed.

"We need to know where he is, or the places he would be likely to go." Liam McCann's voice sounded like what molten iron would feel like if you had the guts to touch it. His voice singed the air. Lily turned, eyes wide and slightly stunned, but then, surprisingly, she smiled. Not a cheerful smile; there was no joy. But a grim recognition of his rage and the effort it took to contain. She stepped closer to him.

"Ah, well, if we only knew. I, for one, do not know, that I can tell you, but there may possibly be someone in this house that does know." George rang the servant's bell.

"Who do you think might know and why do you suspect them?"

George looked at Frank, "You are…?"

"Constable McManaway from Rakaia."

"Well, Constable McManaway, my wife… She usually seems to have some idea of what her son is up to, not that she ever tells me about it." George shrugged his shoulders. "I would give you permission to question her."

"I would not need your permission. No disrespect intended, sir. Anyone else?"

"Yes, there's Sally, a housemaid. She and Henry, well, there was something going on there, but again, I am privy to very little that occurs around here, or so it seems."

~

Mick and Lily returned to Fairfield to pack supplies hurriedly for what might turn out to be an extended journey to find Rose, although they hoped not. Frank and Liam stayed to interrogate Sally and Elisabeth. Elisabeth did not feel the need to cooperate, so Frank went to her room himself and threatened to arrest her as a suspected accomplice if she did not tell him what she knew. Sally, on the other hand, gave them much more information than they really wanted about Henry and his deviant behaviour. But neither had any concrete information on where Henry might have taken Rose or why.

Frank headed straight back to Rakaia, thinking that the only answers would be found questioning people who may have seen the Lichfield's gig on the road. He hurried; the culprit had a head start. He felt personally responsible that the avenues of escape had been left open for nearly two days while he had wrongly presumed Rose had drowned.

~

Henry held Rose's hands and talked to her. He tried to will her back to consciousness.

"Lily, can you hear me? Lily, open your eyes. Lily, come to me."

Over and over.

Several times it looked like she was trying. Her head would move back and forth and she'd attempt to speak. Her words were incomprehensible, and she'd drift off again, leave him.

They made good time as they travelled north. She was an inconspicuous lump on the seat beside him. He'd planned to book a sea passage from Lyttelton to Auckland and, from there, set sail to England. He wanted to get as far away as he could from any threat of Liam McCann finding them. But he could hardly carry an unconscious woman on board a ship and not be noticed. And, then, what would happen when she did wake up? He needed to apologise, explain why he had to do it this way. She'd understand, wouldn't she? Understand he could not deny his love. In the meantime, he continued north, stopping only to buy provisions and to rest the horse.

Henry slept intermittently through the night, his arms wrapped around his precious Lily. When he woke it was to pull her closer, into him, as if he were trying to tell her where she belonged. Even in her profoundly deep sleep, he wanted her to know he had a place for her.

"Ah, Lily, here now." Henry dampened her forehead with a wet rag in the early morning light. He opened her mouth to drip water in. She sputtered but finally swallowed. "Ah, Lily, do you remember the last time we were together? I had to show you then, take you." More drips, more sputtering. "But Lily, now you know, don't you? You need me. I'll take care of you, Lily. I'll protect you. I'll keep you, Lily. There, there…" He carried her to the gig and adjusted the blankets around her on the seat, kissed her forehead, and continued on.

~

Frank gleaned some information on Henry's probable direction, but it was Lily's intuition that finally led them to Rose. Mick watched Lily. She was tucked in front of Liam on Smoke, her face alert, eyes darting from side to side, pinned down like some small nervous bird. He thought she looked like she would fly away if Liam relaxed his hold—fly straight to Rose.

"It will be getting dark soon, Lily. We'll find your sister. We'll find Rose and that goddamn bastard. I should have…" Liam was nearly choked with rage.

"No, we can't stop, Liam. She's close, Liam, very close." Lily strained forward in the saddle. "Come on, Smoke, just a little further. Rosie's... Rosie, ROSIE!" Lily grabbed at the reins, trying to turn Smoke.

"Lily, damn it!"

"Let me down! I'll run. She's...she's..."

"Where is she, Lily?" Frank rode up. "Tell us where she is."

Lily pointed through the golden light of the sunset to a rocky outcrop just ahead. "There."

Liam had the reins firmly in his hands and Lily gripped between his arms. "Listen to me. Listen, Lily. You and Mick have to stay here while Frank and I..." Liam held Lily tighter. "We'll apprehend Henry. Are you listening, Lily?" He gave her no time to respond but went on. "Promise me, Lily." He tightened his grip on her. He bent his head to whisper in her ear, the sternness so evident, but also yearning. "Promise me you'll stay here; you have to be safe. Lily, please." She took several deep breaths. He felt her take them, felt her accept his command.

She turned and kissed him quickly. "I'll wait here with Mick and the horses. Please get her, Liam. Bring back Rose."

Frank and Liam went on foot through the tussock towards the rock outcrop Lily had pointed to. Frank laid a hand on Liam's arm, "I'll arrest him. Take him back to Christchurch for trial, Liam."

Liam shook his head. "After all this, you think he deserves to live?"

"In prison."

Liam didn't agree.

~

The makeshift camp was on the other side of the outcrop, sheltered from the prevailing wind. Liam and Frank made their way around the side of the rocky hill. Henry had built a fire. He was stirring something in a pot.

"Ah, Lily." He turned to the girl propped against the rocks near the fire. "You've slept long enough, really you have. Wake up now, Lily darling."

It was the way he said 'Lily darling' that inflamed Liam, igniting the anger and despair left over from the pub in Rakaia when Henry had taunted him. All the agony that Henry had inflicted on Lily inflamed him. The rage that came upon Liam was dark, but not cold and calculating. It was a powerfully hot and violent feeling that sought some sort of resolution. Blood—he wanted blood. He bounded towards Henry in his fury. Henry had time to turn and scoop up Rose, and then he inexplicably started up the rocks.

"No escape up there," yelled Frank.

Liam was able to catch up to Henry after just a few steps. "Come down, Henry. Give me the girl." Liam slid a little on the loose rocks and grabbed a tussock to pull himself upright. Henry kept on, slowly defying the incline. Frank started up further over.

"You'll fall, hurt her," Liam yelled as he followed, knowing a tackle could result in disaster. For a few minutes, only two sounds besides heavy breathing were heard: boots on gravel and Rose's sudden low moans. The slope flattened off a bit near the top. Lily and Mick could see everyone as they appeared at the top of the rise.

Frank dove sideways at Henry, yelling, "Get the girl."

Liam was behind Henry and tried to get around and under Rose to cushion her landing, but she flew as though she'd been hurled. Her limp body sailed through the air.

"ROSE!" Lily screamed from the ground, and Mick grabbed her hand as they watched in horror. Liam saw Rose's shoulder hit the ground first and then her head. Momentum took over and she rolled, and then slowly slid. Liam scrambled after her, trying to control his descent and still overtake her relentless trip downwards.

Liam got a grip on Rose's flaccid hand and slid another foot or two before he was able to tenuously anchor them both to the side of the hill. Lily and Mick were yelling up to him, but he couldn't hear what. Very slowly he pulled Rose to him. By moving his hand up her forearm and then getting a good hold under her arm, he was able to drag her onto his lap. He finally had her in his arms. Secure for the moment, he rested, head bent low over Rose. He gasped for air, and his heartbeat settled from the exertion and rage that had turned so quickly to fear.

"Ah, but you are safe now in my arms," he whispered. She was breathing. "Rose, Rose, can you hear me?" Liam slid his hand down her arms and legs to check for injuries.

There was a slight stirring on his chest, then something cool on his neck. A hand, Rose's hand was there, as if to offer comfort.

"Ah, Liam," she mouthed. She opened her eyes. "Ah, Liam," she said soundlessly again. Her eyes were filled with the whole of it. All the anguish and terror, the misery of it all, but also the elation, the rapture of survival, the bliss of knowing she was saved. He recognised it all.

Thankfulness.

Love.

Oh, he could see the love, feel it. It was something akin to a homecoming. It washed up against all the anger and rage and softened him. She was safe. He bent to her, all other rational thought lost, and kissed her tenderly on the lips. "Ah, Liam," she murmured one more time before her eyes closed.

"We should go up, help them down," Mick said as he and Lily started towards the back of the rocky outcrop.

"LILY, you are all right?" an incredulous Henry bellowed.

"Shut up or I'll gag you," Frank spoke sternly, tugging on the rope he was using to tie Henry's hands behind his back.

"Lily, how did you get down? How did you... What... What?" Henry craned his neck up at the rock, trying to see where he had thrown her. Liam and Rose were on the other side of the crest. He sat down in the dirt shaking his head. Frank motioned Lily and Mick to continue on.

"How did she...?" Henry started to sway from side to side. He sidled nearer a boulder, keeping up his rhythmic motions. Frank watched him. Henry didn't so much lose his mind as very slowly let go of it, as if life would be easier without it. He said, "Lily woke up, Lily woke up," again and again. Then the gentle sway turned into a periodic thud, almost metrical, his head against the boulder, his head against the boulder, his head against the boulder.

Rose struggled in Liam's arms. She heard the voice, the kind voice that had called her, called to her over and over, when she would have gone for good if she could. It was the voice that kept pulling her back.

Rose opened her eyes, raised her head, and tried to speak. "I'm here, I'm..." Liam tightened his arms around Rose just as Lily and Mick got to them.

"Rosie, Rosie, are you...?

"She'll be all right, Lily, she'll be all right," Liam said hopefully as he carried Rose down towards the horses. Lily and Mick scurried behind.

"Lily woke up. Lily woke up." Lily gasped at the sound of Henry's voice saying her name and clung to Mick's hand.

"Frank, get him to stop that," Liam shouted, and Rose moaned in his arms. "It's upsetting both Rose and Lily. Get him out of here or I'll..." Liam stopped and shifted Rose in his arms again. "Oh, I'm sorry," he murmured in Rose's ear and she quieted.

"Mick, you'll have to go back and get the Lichfield's gig. Make sure the fire is out as well." Liam said in a softer voice. "Lily, can you get her water?" He sat down, his back against a boulder, Rose still in his arms.

Lily got the leather water pouch from the bags on the tired horse.

"I can't let go of her, Lily, I can't." Liam looked up at his wife as he hugged her sister close to him.

"I don't want you to," Lily smiled as her eyes filled with tears. She sat beside Liam and took Rose's hand in hers. "It was so close; we could have lost her," Lily said. She wiped her eyes.

Liam craned sideways towards his wife. "Come closer." She moved her face towards his.

"Thank you, Liam, thank you." She reached to kiss him. When their lips joined, Liam tasted her tears. They felt the fear and tension dissolve a little. Rose stirred in Liam's arms and Liam had to pull away. "Liam, Liam," Rose mumbled, her eyes flickering. Liam readjusted Rose in his arms and then looked deep into Lily's eyes, "How did you know how to find her?"

"We are connected." Lily smiled, and she lifted Rose's hand and placed it on her heart.

Chapter 33

Lily

"Ah, ah, that feels so good," Rose murmured as Liam and I lowered her into the copper tub—her first complete sentence.

"Wake up, Rosie. Wake up and talk to us," I gently cajoled.

"Lily."

"Yes, I'm here."

"No, no." She waved a limp hand and opened her eyes, although it looked like it was a struggle to do so. "I'm Lily." There was something in her voice, some honest conviction that stunned us. I started washing her hair, my eyes locked on Liam's, both of us full of questions.

Liam sat by the tub. He put his hand on Rose's arm and squeezed it to get her attention, "Do you know what happened to you? What do you remember?"

Rose's eyes were closed; she was drifting again. He squeezed her arm, shaking it gently.

"Wake up! C'mon, answer me."

Rose made an effort. She tried to sit up straighter in the tub, "I kept drifting away, not like now. Now I'm just tired." She closed her eyes again.

Liam moved his hand to her chin, lifting it slightly. She opened her eyes and looked at him in a way that made me gasp. Liam's voice caught in his throat, "What else, what else do you remember?"

"Well, Liam." Rose swallowed. "You ought to be very thankful, because when I thought one more breath and that will be it, I'll just go... I would hear him. He would be calling me. 'Lily, Lily, wake up. Lily, come to me'. And I thought of you, calling me. You, Liam." Her hand reached out for his. He let her take it, and she pulled it towards her and kissed his palm. "You."

Liam looked at Rose in the tub and me standing behind her, soaping her hair.

"Ah, but you are Rose," he said to her.

She nodded and whispered, "LilyRose," then smiled a small contented smile.

We tipped her back and rinsed her hair. I washed her bruised back while Liam held her steady, and she floated to wherever she needed to go to heal.

"Annie made us decide."

"What?"

"When we were about eight, she came to teach us to read. Annie said our mother taught her and she was going to teach us." I reached for the flannel sheet and spread it out on the floor by the fire.

"What did she make you decide?"

I didn't look at Liam, who was holding Rose up in the tub. Instead, I fiddled with the edges of the sheet, "Can you lift her out and lay her here?"

"Come hold her, I'll take my shirt off first. What are you telling me?" He reached under Rose, bending and scooping, and then stood with her over the tub while the water dripped off both of them.

"Lay her down, here. I'll show you." I wrapped the fabric around Rose and dried her.

"Turn her on her tummy for a minute." I trailed my hand down Rose's back. "Here, see this." I gently touched the birthmark on her lower back. It was just a little to the right, pinky red and shaped exactly like a rosebud. "Because of this mark, she was Rose and I was Lily."

Liam didn't speak. In silence, he watched me dry Rose and get up to fetch a nightgown. He helped me put it on her.

"And until that day, when you were eight years old, you truly did not know who was who?" he finally said.

I nodded. "She's shivering. Will you carry her to bed?" I asked, and Liam gently manoeuvred his arms under Rose and then stood up.

"She shouldn't be alone, Liam."

"No, she shouldn't." He followed me down the hall to our bedroom. He lay her down gently and then pulled the rocking chair over to the bed while I tucked her in. He sat down and watched me as I fussed with the blankets and pillow.

"Come here." He patted his lap. "Please."

I came around from the opposite side of the bed and stood before him. A tremor passed through me; I took a deep breath. I was worried about Rose and exhausted from the search. Liam took my hand in his, studied it a moment, then pulled me to his lap.

"Whatever happens to Rose, we can't have you forgetting where you belong, now can we?" he said as his arms enveloped me.

"Ah, Liam, Liam." My hands were in his hair, pulling his face towards me. "You… I belong to you." My mouth was on his, no shy-girl kisses. I was past asking; I was doing the telling. Take me, I ordered with my lips and tongue, as relief washed over me. Take me.

"Ah, Lily, let's go back by the fire." He lifted me up and carried me out past my sister's sleeping form.

There on the wooden floor by the coals that glowed orange, we let our bodies comfort us. We took all of the anguish, fear, and uncertainty of the last few days with us into the bliss.

We returned much lighter. Ah, but we were left wondering, could love solve everything—could enough love?

After I checked on Rose, Liam and I bathed together. I was tucked between his legs in the tub as he washed my lower back. His hand faltered, then he stopped completely, and after a moment, I turned.

"So you were eight years old."

"Yes, we were somewhere around eight, and Annie made us decide. She said you both can't be LilyRose forever. She said, 'I was there. Lillian wanted one of you to be Rose and one to be Lily, and anyway, it just ain't right… Causes confusion'."

"If she only knew." I could tell Liam was smiling as he spoke and I craned my neck to see.

"So you told Rose she could be Rose because she had something that looked like a rosebud on her back."

"Well, it wasn't that simple. We both wanted to be Lily."

"What?" Liam, soaping my back again, paused. "Why?"

"We just both thought we were." My shoulders slumped, "And then I had the idea that her rosebud was a sign, a mark."

"How did she know it was there? She couldn't see it, could she?" His fingers stilled on my lower back.

"No, I told her. She believed me though."

"I'm sure she did."

I craned my neck again, something in the tone of his voice made me need to see his face. "Of course, she'd believe me. She'd know if I was lying."

~

It just seemed right. There was no hesitation, no moral dilemma. Rose needed watching, comforting, when she woke only half-aware. I, at least, needed to be there. So when I took Liam's hand, as we started down the hall, and pulled him into our bedroom, I wasn't asking for a debate. Together we nudged Rose to one side. Liam blew out the candle. I crawled in and took Rose in my arms, then Liam did the same to me, his warm body completely surrounding me.

His arms were long enough to wrap around both of us.

Chapter 34

Dodging traffic—hansom cabs mostly—an overloaded wagon, and the odd bicycle made it feel like a long way from one side of the street to the other. Elisabeth made it to safety and glanced down the long flat road. It looked depressingly endless, stretching to nowhere. She couldn't help comparing everything in New Zealand to her beloved England. Oh, for a curve, a bend in the road, and around the bend a meadow with an ages-old stone fence, lined by ancient oaks. But, no, here she was, stranded on the Canterbury Plains, in the monotonous flatness and the unceasing wind, breathing dust.

No wonder Henry had been driven to... what? George had called him depraved, said her lack of love had corrupted him. She had defended Henry as always, made excuses for him, but George would have none of it. He said he wasn't going to lift a finger, said he trusted the legal system. Henry would get what he deserved. She'd said no son of hers was going to jail, whether he deserved it or not. As it turned out, Henry was a little smarter than she gave him credit for. She smiled, thinking of the letter they'd received from the judge.

She was shown into a small room. "Have a seat, madam. I'll get the prisoner."

The room was stuffy. Elisabeth took off her gloves and removed her bonnet. The door opened and shut very quickly and there was Henry, unkempt, swaying unsteadily on his feet. His hands were bound behind him.

"Henry, good Lord! What has happened to you?" Elisabeth clasped her gloves and her bonnet to her chest and scooted back in her chair. "You look awful, absolutely awful! I realise you are trying to get out of this by pretending to be insane or something, but really, this is carrying it a bit far, don't you think?"

Henry didn't answer.

"Idiotic... That is what I think... Absolutely idiotic behaviour! What are people going to think? Henry? Henry, are you even listening to me?"

Henry tried to focus on the woman and the voice speaking so sharply. It wasn't Lily's sweet voice. It bit into him, tore him, dug in through scar tissue. There was a faint glimmer of recognition, a fleeting memory. Idiot... Idiotic the voice had said, and he smiled, grinned at what seemed to him like a familiar endearment.

Elisabeth stood, clutching her gloves and bonnet. "Henry, HENRY!"

The voice was loud now, insistent. He heard it quite clearly. All the other voices in his head took refuge in dark places and abandoned him.

"Henry, listen to me. I'll not have this. You will not behave so...so... Henry!"

Elisabeth moved closer and took hold of Henry's lapels. She shook him, and his head came forward and back and forward again, in a familiar rhythm. Ah, something recognisable, with words to go with it. "Lily woke up, Lily woke up, Lily woke up."

She dropped her hands and peered into his face. "Henry, you really are... Henry... Good God, you are an idiot." Elisabeth Lichfield stared at her son. "A crazy idiot."

Henry looked at the voice, softened in recognition of the truth, and grinned, bending towards it. He shifted his feet and shuffled forward, searching instinctively for some vague longing for comfort, "Moth..."

"DON'T! Don't you dare come near me, you fool, you idiotic fool." Elisabeth pushed at his chest, forcing him to step backwards. She edged herself around Henry towards the door. She didn't look back.

~

There was not a thing Liam could do differently, as he and Lily nursed Rose back to health. He had to be present for both of them: his wife and his wife's sister. He could not separate the inseparable; there was no dividing the united. They had to start slowly with calm reassurance. He was able to soothe Rose, ease her into well-being. Lily was always there, knowing what he offered and why.

"Rose needs to sign this." Frank stood in their kitchen, holding out a document.

"What is it?" Liam looked up.

"Mr Lichfield is divorcing Mrs Lichfield and she is taking Henry back to England." Liam and Lily looked at Frank, "To an asylum. The authorities are more than happy to see him go. There just aren't places for people like him here."

"But prison... What about prison?"

"You saw him; you saw what happened. He hasn't gotten any better, Liam."

"Here, give it to me. I'll sign it 'Rose Quinn'. I can do that." Lily reached for the papers. Frank looked like he wasn't sure he should give them to her.

"I'll not have her bothered by all this. Not now, Frank. She's just starting to get better."

"Can I see her?" Frank asked.

Lily looked at Liam for a moment. "I'll see if she's awake." She headed down the hall.

Liam cleared his throat. "She's getting stronger, awake longer, headaches aren't so bad."

"And?" Frank queried.

"Well, she's still confused in one very important area." Liam took a bottle off the shelf.

"Go on." Frank was curious.

"She thinks she's Lily."

"She what?" Frank's voice was raised.

"Here," Liam pulled out a chair with one hand and put the bottle on the table with the other. "We'll have a whisky."

"It's all right, you can come in." Lily's voice filtered in from down the hall.

"Ah, we'll have it in a minute." Liam turned, ushering Frank ahead of him. "It's a twin thing, well, a lot stranger than most twins, I think," he said as they walked down the hall. "They seem to be able to share their memories. So when Rose got hit on the head and Henry kept calling her Lily, over and over..." They were at the door. Liam shrugged his shoulders and looked at Frank as if he hoped his friend might have some answers.

"Rosie-girl, I hear you're on the upswing?" Frank was jovial. Rose looked at him and squinted her eyes as if thinking very hard.

"Everyone is calling me Rosie, but I'm sure... I'm sure that I..." Frank saw her distress.

"Oh, well, the thing is, you do feel better, don't you? You do look a lot better, if I may say so."

"I am healing." Rose smiled a little. "Are you busy with all the…" She stumbled on her words as if reminded of things she desperately wanted to forget.

"Oh, you mean all the drunks and horse thieves and louts I contend with on a daily basis?" Frank answered. Rose smiled again. "Actually, things have been kind of quiet lately, since we managed to get you home."

"I need to thank you for that, for getting me home." Rose looked up at him again.

"Ah, but it was your sister who saved you. She realised what happened before I did. And I still don't know how she knew where you were. It's a mystery to me, Rosie-girl."

Rose flinched ever so slightly at the 'Rosie-girl'. She remembered a clear evening on a ship with Sean O'Hennessey whispering sweet nothings in her ear. She tried to recall… remember… summon…

"She's tired, I think. Let's let her sleep," Lily said softly.

They went back to the kitchen and sat down quietly.

"Ah, well, time will tell, I guess. What does the doctor say?" Frank inquired.

Liam and Lily exchanged a glance. Liam shrugged then spoke, "Doc Jenkins doesn't really know the extent of her injuries. It seemed too complicated to explain and we…"

"Time will heal her; you are right, Frank," Lily interrupted. "Liam, I'm just going to get some potatoes for dinner, listen for her."

Liam nodded his head and reached for the whisky bottle.

"What's really going on here, Liam?"

Liam didn't say anything while he got two glasses and poured them each a drink. Frank waited, and eventually Liam spoke. "Well, you know it started out complicated, Lily having a twin and all, and their strange upbringing. They are so entwined." Liam sipped at his whisky. "But lately, I just don't know. I can't go on like this. It's too confusing. We have to nurse Rose back to health and then… Well…"

"I don't envy you," Frank said thoughtfully.

"What?"

"Well, you have Lily, but then Rose." Frank shook his head. "Does she want you? Does she really think she is Lily and she has those rights?" Frank took a long swig of his whisky, as if he needed fortification before he heard the answer.

"Well, in the first place, however tangled up I am in those two, I am not an immoral man, Frank. You know that." It was Liam's turn for several long swallows.

"And secondly?" Frank prompted.

"I'm thinking."

Frank poured them each another glass while they thought.

Finally Liam spoke. "We've got to get Rose to realise the truth."

They continued to drink quietly. Then Frank spoke, "Anything you think I can do to help?"

"Visit often and keep calling her 'Rosie-girl'. I could tell that was making her think about it. Maybe you could…" He turned, hearing a noise in the hallway.

"I thought I'd try to get up." Rose looked pale as she leaned against the doorframe. Liam jumped to his feet.

"Rose, here, here." Liam reached out for her and collected her up. He carried her to the sofa, put a pillow behind her back and a quilt over her, all the while murmuring, "Are you all right? Are you sure you should be up? I'll get your sister." Rose reached out for his hand when he started to move away.

"Stay here, please." She weakly pulled him towards her. "Please." Liam sat down beside her. She snuggled in, and he let her.

Frank watched Lily as she entered the room, struggling with a bucket of potatoes.

"Rose is up," he said softly.

"What?" Lily turned quickly and took in Rose, her head now on Liam's lap, eyes closed and her hand entwined with one of his.

Liam met Lily's glance but didn't speak.

"She just came wandering down the hall, like she was looking for him, really," Frank observed.

"Aye, and she found him." Lily turned, picked some potatoes out of the bucket, and reached for a knife. "You'll stay for tea, won't you, Frank?"

~

That Sunday a southerly blew through. Frank came back to the house after a morning fishing trip with Mick and Liam to take shelter. Lily had the fire going and Rose was sitting on the sofa enjoying the warmth. "Thank you for the fish, Frank. It makes a lovely change from mutton," Lily commented.

"For some reason I always think of Fintan when I eat salmon," Rose added.

"Fintan?" Frank questioned.

"Fintan mac Bóchra. He survived the flooding...you know, Noah's flood...by turning himself into a salmon," Rose said thoughtfully.

"So, what? You think you may be eating his relatives?" Frank grinned as he spoke.

"No, she doesn't. Do you, Rose? You must know Fintan's story, Frank?"

"Ah, Lily, isn't he the one who went with Noah's granddaughter, Cessair, on the expedition to Ireland just before the great deluge?"

"Yes, that's him. There were only three men on the trip and about fifty women."

"Yes, I always wondered about that. Each man had sixteen or seventeen wives," Frank commented.

"How'd that work?" Liam asked.

"I don't think it did, not at all. The other two men...Bith and Ladra...both died and Fintan found himself with all the women. He fled." Frank shrugged his shoulders. "I should imagine he thought he might get henpecked to death."

"Frank, honestly," Rose laughed.

"Anyway," Lily continued the story, "Cessair died of a broken heart six days before the flood. She must have really loved Fintan."

"And then," Rose picked up the story and carried on, "All others drowned in the flood, except for Fintan, who turned into a salmon. He lived under the waters in a cave called Fintan's Grave."

"Is he the one that turned into an eagle and then a hawk? You told us about him on the ship." Mick had moved from the table to the floor by the fire.

"Yes, he survived and became an advisor to the kings of Ireland."

"Sort of a mythical repository of all the knowledge and history of Ireland." Frank was thoughtful, "You would wonder why it is we make up such things, wouldn't you?"

"Or, if it is made up." Lily was now seated close to Rose on the settee.

"Some of it has to be." Liam joined the girls on the settee and took Lily's hand.

"I'm not so sure." Rose snuggled in closer to Lily, as they made room for Liam. "Not everything can be explained."

Liam turned and smiled at Rose. "That I know, that I know."

Frank looked puzzled.

"So this Fintan fellow, whatever happened to him?" Mick enquired of Frank in a sleepy voice.

"Oh, well, he buggered off."

"Well, yes, but he had reasons." Rose relaxed, leaning into Lily.

"Which were?"

"Well, it isn't really written anywhere, but Nana Kat says…said," Rose sat up straighter, "that he met a magical hawk, and they recounted their lives and then decided to leave the mortal realm."

"Because?"

"Well, it was sometime in the fifth century, after most of Ireland was converted to Christianity."

"And?"

"And, well," Rose swallowed, "Nana Kat told us that he left because the magic was gone. Nobody believed in their own power anymore." Liam's arm went behind Lily's shoulders, his hand touching Rose.

"And what power was this?" Frank's voice was slightly discordant, as if the questions he was asking somehow weren't the right questions, weren't specific enough.

Lily answered, looking straight at Frank, "The power to transform, of course."

There followed a companionable silence, warm and sleepy, only ever found late on Sunday afternoons with good friends.

Ah, Liam, I can feel you.

The hand Liam was just resting against Rose moved to grasp her shoulder. He turned to peer at Rose, then took Lily's hand with his free one.

I hear you, I hear you.

Lily's eyes opened wide and she looked at Rose.

Liam is listening… He can hear us.

I love you, Liam.

Liam jumped up from the sofa, startling the others. He reached back and took Lily's hand again. "Come with me." He pulled Lily along as he spoke. Lily looked confused. Rose started to get up. "No, just Lily," Liam said sternly. "Sorry," he nodded to Frank and Mick, "we'll be back." Liam led Lily down the hallway to their bedroom.

The bedroom was cold; the fire had not been lit. The weak late afternoon sun shone through the lacy curtains. Liam shut the door and turned Lily towards him.

"I heard you, Lily, I heard you. Tell me that again, like you did before, in your mind." Liam held Lily close to him and smiled as he spoke.

"Oh, Liam! Dear, dear, sweet man." Lily shook her head. "You did hear us, and we heard you," she said sadly.

"We?"

"Yes, all three of us were touching, and somehow, you were able to enter our private world, like Mick does sometimes. You felt the beauty of it, didn't you?" Lily smiled and reached up and kissed him gently on the lips. "It feels like a blessing to me that you can hear us." She paused, "I love you so much, Liam, but I would never say so under those circumstances, not with Rose there."

"Oh, God, that was Rose? Rose loves me like that? It felt like you, Lily. It felt like you." Liam dropped his arms from around Lily and raked both hands through his hair.

"It felt like me because she still thinks she's me. She's using my memories of you. She can't tell they are mine. Oh, Liam, sometimes it feels like she is stealing you from me." Lily shook her head. "But she doesn't mean to. She isn't well. She just isn't well."

Chapter 35

Lily

Liam sat down on the edge of the bed, his shoulders uncharacteristically slumped. "I am running out of patience with all this, Lily."

I took off my shoes. I didn't know what to say. I climbed onto the bed behind Liam and began to massage his shoulders. After a while I told him, "Well, it's important that you don't touch us both at once again. Not unless you want to hear our thoughts, and…and…" My eyes started to fill and my voice broke.

"Oh, come here, dear Lily." Liam turned around and pulled me into his arms and we lay down together.

"I don't know what else we can do for her, I really don't."

Liam tightened his arms around me. "She'll get well, I'm sure of it. It's early days yet." I knew Liam was making an effort to be optimistic for me. "She'll marry one day, have her own husband."

I stretched and nestled my face into his neck. "Yes, she will," I said, and for the first time ever, I imagined Rose and I happily separated, living with our own husbands and children. We would be fine by ourselves. I kissed Liam in celebration of my awareness. I felt the hard warm muscles of his shoulders under my hands and I explored them in jubilation. "Mine, you are mine," I whispered triumphantly.

"Yours, only yours, Lily." Liam captured my mouth with a hungry urgency. My response was deep and sure; I sought his strength. Tingling sensations cascaded through my body as I arched against him in invitation. Our kiss was long and absorbing. We gave each other the reassurance we needed. My hands reached for his trouser buttons. His hand came down on mine.

"The others?" he murmured, at the same time his other hand snaked up my dress.

"Mmm?" I purred, beginning to undo the buttons of his shirt. Liam shifted beside me and then made to get off the bed. "Where are you...?"

"Just a minute." Liam got up and went to lock the door. He paused above me. "They will wonder where we are. But, you know, I just don't care." Liam smiled a devilish smile. "Turn over so I can get at your laces."

Liam started to undress me in the dim twilight and then stopped to light a candle. "I want to see you, Lily."

"And I you, Liam." I sat up to kick off my stockings as Liam divested himself of his underclothes. Fascinated, I examined the muscles that rippled down his arms, his flat stomach and narrow waist, his long muscular thighs. Our eyes caught, and for a few moments, we lost ourselves in silent communion. "Mine," I mouthed, "Only mine."

Yours... His lips formed the words as he embraced me.

Chapter 36

Liam and Lily believed that time would heal Rose, and her body did strengthen. But the effects of her head injury lingered.

"Oh, my head is throbbing again," Rose said to Lily. They were out walking alongside a paddock of wheat rustling in the warm evening breeze. It was almost ready to harvest. They stopped near the gate to rest.

Lily took Rose's hand. "Henry hit you, Rose, with a big rock, and then you fell again on your head. I saw you."

"I know I was hurt, and I know you think I am Rose, but I just... I just..." Rose struggled to voice her thoughts.

"He thought he'd kidnapped me, Rose. The whole time he had you, he called you Lily," Lily explained once again.

Rose shook her head and tightened her grasp on Lily's hand.

"You have to understand, Rose, Liam is my husband. He is the..." Lily suddenly had an idea. "Do you know where Liam and I were, Rose, when Henry took you?" Rose shook her head in confusion. "Think about it, Rose." Rose was silent.

"We were on our wedding trip." Lily paused, caught up in her memories. Suddenly Rose murmured and, then, gasped in awe.

"Ah... ah... Liam," Rose said and smiled in delight as all Lily's memories flooded into her.

"No! No! He is not yours! Liam is not yours, Rose," Lily cried out in anguish and pulled her hand away.

"But I, I..." Rose said in a small, lost voice. Lily could not stop the tears that came streaming down her cheeks. She leaned against the wooden gate.

"Rosie, Rosie, we've got to sort ourselves out. When we were small, we had no choice. We shared everything and it helped us to survive," Lily said through her tears. "But now, Rosie, we have to grow up. We have to learn to live without each other." They were both quiet for several long moments. Finally, Lily shook her head and dried her tears with the corner of her apron. She squared her shoulders and reached for Rose's hand again, and this time, she placed it on her stomach and covered it with her own. "I am going to have a child, Rose. Liam and I are having a child." Lily's voice was filled with emotion, "I need a husband to call my own."

An incredulous look worked its way slowly over Rose's face. She shook her head as if wanting to deny some elemental truth while her hand gently caressed her sister's belly. Suddenly she stood straighter and cocked her head, seeming to listen. She moved her hand on Lily's stomach. The look on her face changed. She looked inquisitive and curious. She spoke knowingly.

"There are two," she said softly, "there are two."

Lily's mouth dropped open, and her other hand flew to her stomach. She was afraid to speak. She watched Rose, who was deep in thought. It was like watching someone wake up.

"Lily," Rose spoke slowly, looking deep into her sister's eyes, "you must be Lily, and you have a husband." Her voice broke and she swallowed, "Liam is your husband."

Rose sank to her knees in the grass beside the gate. "I am so sorry, Lily. I am so sorry." She sobbed and sniffled. "I'll go. I cannot stay here. We are causing so much confusion, within ourselves and for Liam. You and Liam need to be together without me."

Lily sat down beside Rose and hugged her sister close to her. "Shh… It's all right; it was the injury, Rosie. There is nothing to apologise for. Everything will be fine now that you know who you are." Lily smiled, hugging her sister. "But you can't go just yet, Rose. You'll stay until you're truly well, until after the baby comes."

They turned and saw Liam striding towards them. Lily could tell he was worried.

Lily waved and hollered, "Rose remembered!"

"Tell him about the babies later. There are two, Lily. Tell him when you are on your own," Rose whispered, as Liam came towards them.

"What happened?" Liam looked from Rose to Lily.

"Oh, she just finally got it through her thick skull that she's Rose." Lily surprised herself by laughing, suddenly in a better mood than she'd been in since Rose's abduction.

"Really? Rose…?"

"Yes! I'm so sorry, Liam. I'm so sorry. I had all Lily's memories,

and I don't know where mine have gone. I'll go soon, I will, after..."
Rose paused and bit her tongue.

Liam reached for their joined hands.

Tell me. You two... No secrets.

They both startled and tried to pull their hands away, but Liam
held on.

Tell me.

Last time he was just listening.

Not like this... Not so strong.

I am here... There is no point in talking about me like I'm not here.

He held their joined hands in both of his. His grip radiated
warmth and power mixed with tenderness and undeniable strength.
Until now, there had been barriers to cross, conscious attempts to
hurdle certain obstacles, unspoken impediments, tiny things in the way.

But now, here was his voice, right inside their heads—their
hearts—speaking with such confidence.

Lily? Rose?

No, Liam.

LilyRose.

Just when everything felt safe and they felt like they knew where
they stood, they were swept one step further. They would ask, again, is
love able to be defined? Confined? And if so, how? What happens
when love is not ordinary or traditional? What happens when love isn't
what the world expects it to be, assumes it to be? Because the truth is
that sometimes love can burst its banks, overflow in a wild rush of
feeling, and those who stand on the edge, just dipping their toes, are
swept away with no time to ask for permission and no time to seek
authorization. It is more a matter of keeping your head above water
and not breathing in too many of the sparks in the air.

Chapter 37

Lily

"When are you going to tell him?" Rose asked me, as we were finishing our evening meal.

"Oh, well, it's just that…"

"What's this, Lily?" Liam asked.

"Come on, Mick, come with me." Rose grabbed his hand. "We'll be back in a few minutes." They made their way out the back door.

Liam turned to me, "What is it, Lily?"

I looked at him—not a glance, nothing fleeting, nothing at all superficial. Rather I gazed, considering the man in front of me, the man I loved. I hid nothing from him. He saw what I saw, seeing himself in my eyes. He reached for me, "Lily, don't do that."

"What?"

"The way you are looking at me, it makes me nervous."

"Nervous?"

"You look too… I'm trying to think of the word… Ah, adoring… sometimes." He was smiling. His hand, firm on the top of my shoulder, moved to the side of my neck seeking bare skin. Then his hand wrapped my neck and he tilted me. Moving towards me, he saw the exact moment I lost focus, let love overpower me. Yet I kissed him with a strength, a slightly different intensity than usual. He murmured, "What is it, Lily?"

"It was in Akaroa, I think, by the sea."

"Lily?"

"Oh, Liam," I spoke softly and moved my hands to my stomach. "Here, in here, your blood is mixed with mine."

"Lily, a child, our child? Yours and mine? Why didn't you say so?"

"I did. I am. I'm…"

"You're what, Lily. Tell me." He saw it cross my face, I think—the elation that could change to something bleak in an instant. He pulled me closer to him, as if there were something he could save me from.

"I'm scared," I whispered into his chest. "My mother…"

The door opened. Mick came in and reached for the bottle on the table. "Time for a toast?"

Behind him, Rose paused. "Maybe not just yet, Mick."

"No, no." Liam smoothed my hair back and smiled. "We've got a lot to celebrate, don't we, Lily?"

I took a deep breath, my eyes not leaving his and nodded. "We do."

"Did you tell him there are two?"

Liam looked from me to Rose. "Two," he said slowly with some perception of my shadowy fear. He reached for his wine glass then, pausing, turned and reached for the whisky bottle.

Liam and I came together that night with an almost reckless intensity, as if there was some unmentionable time limit to our joy, and it was our intention to defy it. Our awareness of each other was heightened, nothing was overlooked or unobserved. Instead, everything was perceived, discovered, and attended to.

Much later in the timeless space between midnight and dawn, our bodies completely satiated, we talked about it again.

"How do you know there are two? How can you tell this early?"

"I can't. But Rose…"

"Rose?"

"Rose knows."

Liam was quiet.

"She can sense them. She put her hand on my belly and just knows. Two… a boy and a girl."

"Oh." Liam readjusted his hold on me. "That's good news, isn't it?"

"A son? You wanted a son?"

"The fact they aren't identical twins is a relief."

"A relief?"

"I like knowing what's what," he murmured, drifting off.

"Who's who, you mean." I turned and kissed his heart, tiny kisses, in perfect rhythm with the beat.

~

Once Rose recovered her identity, things got a little easier. It seemed the three of us formed an unspoken agreement to accept the emotional confusion for the time being. I wanted Rose to stay with us until the babies were born, and she was fully healed.

For Rose and me, life seemed to become fuller, richer, and deeper. We slid into each other like we had when we were children. We gave up any pretence of who was first or second, or in front, or behind, or in the middle. Nothing needed defining. We just were. Everything expanded to hold all that needed to be held. To be fair, we pulled Liam into our circle. The love he had for me had naturally expanded to include my sister. He fought it when he could, but he didn't really have a choice.

Liam never faltered. He was true to me, his wife. But I also knew he could not deny what he heard and felt with his heart. There was only one, LilyRose.

Oddly enough, for the first time in our lives, Rose and I were physically different, easily recognizable as separate and distinct. Liam had the comfort of always knowing who was who.

Our relationship wasn't a triangle or a circle. If I had to name it, I would call it a sphere.

But, sometimes, to name is to belittle. Words are not good containers for conveyance; the meaning leaks and sloshes over the sides of language.

Does it seem, sometimes, there is more to be felt without language?

Love expands and imparts. We listen and feel. We breath, touch, hold.

All is provided.

What I can say is that when Rose, Liam, and I were together nothing was vague. I noticed every small thing in sharp focus. Magic occurred when I saw so singularly. Everything became exceptional—brilliant even—obviously and vividly connected.

So her became him, and I became she, and me became you, and you became he.

Until there was nothing left but we.

Chapter 38

The land was bountiful. The slender stalks of wheat shimmered in the summer heat—the seeds of civilisation. Mick's mind wandered as he sharpened the scythes. He'd read about it in the history books. He didn't think it was in the Bible, although he'd spend a fair bit of time reading that. No, somewhere, he'd read about grain, the growing of it. How it changed things, let everyone settle down and stay in the same place, how everyone learned to read and write instead of just hunting and surviving.

Mind you, there was still a pretty strong element of survival about it all, perched here on these plains. Oh, they were fertile enough. The green gave you confidence to cultivate, promised you in all the right ways. But, still, if it didn't rain, or it rained too much, or the wind blew too hard, or the frosts came too late or too early, it wasn't like farmers could just relax, was it? No, there was always something that could take them to the edge and, there, they would teeter.

Mick supposed it did reduce the men on the front line, so to speak. Everyone wasn't out hunting and gathering. While the farmers farmed, some people were busy building courtrooms and libraries, writing the books to go in them. All of them confident they would be fed. He finished his sharpening, oiled the scythe to a shine, stood up, and swung it a few times.

"Go lower, Mick, or your back'll be aching before noon." Liam bounded down from Smoke, waving a handful of wheat. "It's ready. Could you hitch up the horses to the wagon? I'll tell the girls."

Mick had the wagon loaded and parked by the house as Lily emerged with a large basket. Mick jumped down, "Here I'll…"

"No, I'm fine. You get the water jugs; they're just inside the door."

The men cut the wheat with the scythes, stopping only to bind large bundles with twine. They stood them in the sun to continue ripening and await the arrival of the threshing machine. Both Mick and Liam worked zealously—almost obsessively—cutting, binding, and stacking. A feeling of anticipation mixed with fear drove them. Here, this is what we've done. We've managed this, almost. It still isn't safe, though, from the wind or the rains, God help us.

It took them twenty-seven days, harvesting about two acres a day. There was one serious nor'wester, followed by a drizzly morning, to remind them it wasn't meant to be easy.

Lily and Rose kept the men fed and took turns helping in the fields. Liam told them not to overdo it and Lily agreed, saying Rose still got headaches easily and was not completely herself. Liam and Mick laughed, and Liam replied, "Was she ever?"

Chapter 39

After the intensity of the harvest season had passed, they resumed their habit of going to Rakaia every few weeks for supplies. It always seemed a bit of a holiday. Rose and Lily would hurry to the shops. Sometimes they found something eminently useful (although they would later admit they had been getting along quite happily, in their ignorance, without it). Other times they looked at something frivolous—imported things they wouldn't buy—and would stand and marvel at the lace collars or beaded bonnets and wonder what sort of occasion would require a person to wear such an article.

Other times, they would meet someone new, someone from the Emerald Isle, who spoke in a brogue so familiar they felt transported. If they closed their eyes, even for a moment, they would open them expecting to be surrounded by green hills and foggy mist. Or they would meet a family of German immigrants, passing through, surveying before they settled, or a family from the Scottish Highlands heading south with no need for scrutiny, intent on joining their clan.

After doing their jobs and shopping, they would make their way to the pub for dinner. One evening George Lichfield came over to their table. He said he was sorry the way things had worked out for Lily and Rose, but he did not want to spend the rest of his life feeling guilty. He admitted that he questioned himself relentlessly. What could he have done differently with Elisabeth and Henry? Had he contributed to the situation? Could he have seen it coming? All he could say was that, at the time, he did what he thought was best. He apologised once again. Liam, Lily, and Rose admired the courage he demonstrated by telling them this. Liam invited him to sit down and ordered him a whisky.

"Here's to friendship," Liam said as he lifted his glass.

"And forgiveness," George replied quietly.

"Ah, but we've nothing to forgive you for, George." Liam clunked his glass on George's. "To friendship." George smiled, blinking, his eyes suddenly moist.

"You've got your harvest in," George stated after a moment.

"Yes! What about you, George? Did you get enough men?"

"Just." He paused and drank. "Terrible shortage of good men about. Most of it was done by a travelling gang."

"It's good to have it done though, isn't it?"

"Yes."

"We have more than a good harvest to celebrate. Lily is with child."

George raised his glass again. "Congratulations, Liam, you'll make a fine father. And Lily... Oh, what a mother you'll be."

They had another drink, because it was easier than talking about fatherhood. George was saying his farewells just as Frank and Mick joined them, already deep in conversation.

"And, well, I had to sort him out. He's in jail now," Frank was saying as he took a chair and nodded towards the others.

"Can you put him in jail for that?" Mick asked.

"Ah, well, no. Not technically, no. But he is in jail thinking about it. Well... Thinking about not doing it again, to be precise. That's what I told him, 'You sit here and think about what you've done'."

"And will it help?" Mick asked.

"Always does. Some people just need the fear in them a little. You know, feel the consequences of things. There is nothing like having all your freedom taken away."

"Yes there is. You could rough him up a bit; let him know you mean business."

"Ah, Mick, that's called bodily harm, and no, I can't really do that. Not, at least, as standard procedure." Frank smiled. "Now, let's talk about more pleasant subjects. Rosie-girl, your head's all healed?"

Rose nodded. "I still have headaches, but certain important things have become clear to me." She smiled at Lily.

"And, Lily, you sweet thing, what is this bump you've acquired so suddenly?" Frank asked.

"Aye, they are growing all right." It was Liam who spoke, putting his arm around Lily's shoulders.

"They?" Frank inquired.

"Oh, haven't you heard? Apparently there are two." Liam smiled as he answered.

"And you know this...?"

"Rose."

"Oh, Rose… That explains everything. Now, speaking of Rose…" Frank turned towards her, and Rose looked at him. "Might you like to come with me, maybe, next Sunday afternoon? May I pick you up? I'll hire a gig. We'll go for a drive. Maybe back here. Dinner, maybe?"

"An awful lot of maybes." Rose smiled.

"Well, maybe I…"

"Oops, another one."

"Rose, for heaven's sake, answer the poor man." Lily elbowed her sister. Liam's hand that was resting gently on Lily's shoulder moved to Rose's. It was not a calculated move; Liam gave no thought to the consequences of linking them all together in public. But now Rose was healing, and her voice was stronger. He felt them both and heard Rose's confusion.

Not now… Not yet… I'm not ready.

Lily saw the confusion on Liam's face; he tightened his grip on Rose.

Lily then heard Liam say quite clearly.

You don't have to go, not yet…

"And so, Frank, tell me…" Mick struggled to fill the awkward silence. Frank stared at Liam's hand grasping Rose's shoulder while Rose looked at Liam like she had found something that had been lost for a long time. Lily sat between them looking strangely uneasy.

"Frank, which stables do you normally hire a gig from?"

"What?" Frank turned towards Mick. "What did you say?"

"Which are the best stables in town?"

Liam… Let go now. It's all right. It's all right…

Lily covered Liam's hand with hers and lifted it from Rose's shoulder. She uncoiled it from behind her and settled it in her lap, contained between both her hands. Lily could tell Liam felt misplaced, adrift, but her whispered words anchored him. "It's all right."

Rose slid off the bench and stood up. "I'll be back," she said quietly. They all watched her go.

~

Rose came back a few minutes later with none other than Sean O'Hennessey in tow. "Look, Lily, what turned up. In Rakaia of all places!" Rose laughed as she spoke, pulling on Sean's arm.

"Aye, Rose, I must have known you were here is all I can say." Sean shrugged his shoulders. "And probably still not married."

"And why do you say that? I could have been, twice over, counting your pitiful proposal!"

"I managed it. Sean, this is my husband Liam McCann and his friend Frank McManaway." Lily beamed as she spoke.

Mick had already stood and embraced Sean. "What brings you here?"

"Looking for land. I'm visiting a small holding up Mount Somers way tomorrow. And you, Mick, you're looking... Well, good... And grown." Sean smiled. "Can I buy you a beer?"

"Sit down, sit down with us." Rose sat down next to Lily and Sean sat across from her next to Mick.

There was reminiscing to be done. Sean wanted to know how they had all ended up in Rakaia. But then the conversation moved to more general deliberations. Frank and Liam joined in. What do you think of New Zealand, now that you've been here a while? Is it what you expected? Do you miss Ireland? Think you'll ever go back, even to visit? How long will it take, do you think, for this to feel like home?

"It does for me." Lily squeezed Liam's hand in hers. "Can't imagine," she shuddered, "I don't want ever to go back."

"And you, Rose, are you as settled as Lily is?" Sean asked.

"That's a good question. Rose?" Frank looked at her inquiringly.

Rose's hand moved to Lily's, who was still touching Liam.

Ah, feels like an inquisition.

"I agree with Lily. Our life here is much nicer than it ever was in Ireland."

"But do you feel settled? Do you?"

"Oh, what's with the inquisition, Frank? You know she's still recovering." Liam's voice was sharp.

"What? Rose, what happened to ye?" Sean was worried.

"Oh, Sean, it's a very long story, and half of it happened to Lily. We're fine now, really." Her free hand went to her temple, her fingers gently rubbing in a circle, her thumb anchored under her chin.

"You sure?"

Rose nodded, not looking at all sure.

Liam, let's go home. Take us home.

Liam stood up. "It's time we were heading back. Mick, do you want to get the wagon?"

Frank and Sean watched from the window as Liam bundled the two women into the wagon. They waved their goodbyes.

"He is very…"

"Another beer?" Frank interrupted. "Lily is his wife, and just a few months ago, they almost lost Rose, her sister, her only other family." Almost thinking out loud, Frank said, "I was wrong to put her on the spot."

"Well, no single woman would feel entirely settled living with her sister and her sister's husband, would she now?"

"Ordinarily you'd think so."

"Aye, Lily and Rose aren't what you'd call ordinary, though, are they?" Sean smiled first then chuckled. "Have you ever seen them dance?"

"No."

"Well, on the ship we'd have the occasional little do, knees up. You know the kind of thing. The first time I saw them, it was… Well…" Sean closed his eyes.

"Tell me." Frank sounded impatient.

Keeping his eyes closed, he said, "I swear they were possessed by the music somehow. You know how most of the time they look like, well, sort of angelic, all soft and sweet?"

Frank nodded.

"Well, when they dance, it's different." Sean lowered his voice. "It's like I said, they are possessed…by the music, the movement… I don't know." He shook his head. "Whatever it is, it looks like it is on the verge of overwhelming them."

"And?" Frank wanted him to go on.

"And…?" Sean looked up at Frank, questioning.

Frank nodded, "Go on."

"Whatever this power is that has a hold of them, well, you can see they battle with it a little, then it's like a decision's made or something. Does this sound like nonsense?"

"No."

Sean was silent.

"And…?" Frank prompted.

"I can't really say."

"Can't or don't really want to."

"Little of both."

"Would a whisky help?"

"Never has hurt."

Frank waved to the barman. "And so, you say it's like a decision is made, then what?"

"You realise this is just how I see it. But there were others there. They noticed too."

"Yes… And what were they doing?"

"I don't think I can really explain it. You know what you should do? Organise a dance, a ball, right here in Rakaia. You could do that, raise money for something, do something for the community. Do that, and you could see for yourself."

Sean and Frank sipped on the newly arrived drinks.

"I could organise a dance," Frank said thoughtfully.

"Do. I'll come. We might argue though."

"Maybe, maybe not."

Sean raised his eyebrows.

"Rose might not want either one of us."

~

"We have to sort this out. We can't be doing that in public." Liam's hand ran through his hair. They were home and Liam was watching Lily as she poured a kettle of boiling water into the tub in the middle of the kitchen. "Why did I even reach for Rose? I want her to go, damn it all."

"You sensed her confusion, Liam, her fear. You were just comforting her, Liam, nothing more." Lily put down the kettle and walked over to him. "Like you would do for me."

"Oh, oh." Liam shook his head as he thought about what Lily was saying. He looked from Lily to Rose, who was now busy lifting a heavier pot off the stove and pouring it into the tub.

"No more. I can't do this anymore." Liam gestured with his palms up as his hands swept the room and he shook his head.

"Liam." Lily's voice was nervous and fearful.

Liam carried on. "No more of this silent communication. You have to promise me you won't do it in front of other people again, and you won't let me do it. Please!" Liam looked from Lily to Rose and back again.

"Well…" Rose acted like she was thinking about it.

"No, really, I mean it. Not ever. Maybe you two can say small things in emergency situations, but don't you ever pull me into it and pour all that love over me like you did today. You can't just expect me to sit there, nonchalantly, absorbing it all. Bloody hell, I am not...not a sponge." Liam threw the sea sponge into the barely filled tub, and the water splashed up onto Lily's dress. Lily jumped back.

Liam reached for her. "I'm sorry, Lily."

"It's all right." Lily stood facing him. "I promise." Lily smiled tentatively. "I promise. Oh, Liam, you are so good at putting up with the confusion we cause you." Lily stepped closer and ran her hand down the hard muscles of his arm and whispered, "It's the least we can do for you, my dear man."

Liam stretched down to get a hold of Lily's wet hem, "I didn't mean to get you wet. It's just..."

Rose interrupted, "Liam." She started to reach out for his hand and then stopped, "I promise too."

"Sit down." Lily pulled out a chair for Liam. He sat down and she started to massage his shoulders gently. Lily freed Liam's shoulders of tension. Rose continued to fill the copper tub. They hummed while they worked, picking up and letting down parts of the tune at different times, so that the separate strands entwined and the whole melody seemed a lot more than the two parts.

"Bloody typical," Liam mumbled when he realised what they were doing, "Bloody typical."

They all accepted that Rose would leave after the babies were born. But Liam had to admit that within this certainty, another truth emerged: Lily and Rose were happy together, safe and secure at last. Their love simply radiated out of them and pooled at their feet, and all he had to do was soak it up. They relished his attention, savoured it, as if to be loved and accepted together, whole, was a gift they had never expected to be given.

Chapter 40

Winter was setting in, but there were no heavy fogs or mists that clung to the earth for days on end. Winters on the Canterbury Plains were often oddly bright. It could be bitingly cold after a hard frost, but the sun was surprisingly generous. It confused them. In the old country, dazzling sunlight came with an expectation of heat or, at least, a little warmth. Here, the sun might shine brightly on a winter's day as if understanding that a bright outlook was helpful, regardless of the exact details of the situation or, maybe, in spite of them.

"It will be a nice surprise." Rose surveyed the row of tiny gorse bushes stretched out along the length of the fence line and shivered.

"Oh, I can't believe we got them all planted." Lily moved her hand to the back of her hip in the classic pregnant woman's pose. She was nearly six months along.

"Liam might be mad that I let you help, though."

"I'm fine, really. The more I do the better I feel, though I'm tired now."

"Let's go back. I'll make some soup for tea, and you can put your feet up." Rose took Lily's hand and pulled her along. They stopped once again before turning onto the track that led to the house and admired their handiwork.

It was dark when Liam made it back from the bush line with a full load of firewood. The fire in the house was almost out. Only glowing embers remained, and the lantern had been dimmed. The room was bathed in a soft golden glow. Lily and Rose were asleep on the sofa, draped like lovers, over and around each other. Liam watched them sleep for a few minutes, but soon he could no longer bear not touching his wife. He was embarrassed that he still looked for her belly, still needed confirmation. He gently picked up her hand. She stayed in the land of dreams, exhausted from the day's hard work. Liam was tired too and let his thoughts flow, uninhibited.

Oh, I love you. Wake up, Lily. Wake up and look me in the eyes. Let me see the love in your eyes.

Rose teetered on the edge of consciousness, feeling delicious warmth.

Lily, you look so beautiful lying here.

Rose didn't move.

Oh, Lily…

The things he was imagining were continuing to warm Rose. Her skin started to tingle with a vague sense of anticipation. "Wake up, Lily," she whispered in her sister's ear. "Wake up, Liam's home."

Liam heard Rose, but his eyes were on Lily. She stirred, her mouth forming a drowsy half-smile. He couldn't help himself and bent to capture her lips with his own.

A moan escaped, not from Lily, not from Liam… but from Rose.

A soft, yearning moan that spoke of want.

"Oh, Rose, I forgot. Oh, shit. I'm sorry, Rose."

"I'll just get up. I need to sit up." Rose struggled, still encumbered with a drowsy Lily. "Lily, move. Please… Please, I have to get up." Rose hastily removed herself and made her way out the back door into the night.

She leaned against the side of the outhouse for a moment, breathing in the cold air, then crumpled to the ground. "Oh, Liam, Liam," she cried as she hugged herself. She is so loved; Lily is so loved.

After Rose left them so quickly, Lily pulled her husband towards her. He moulded himself around Lily just as Rose had moments earlier. They were there asleep when Rose eventually returned from the cold night. She reached out to touch them, to shake them gently awake, so they could make their way to bed.

She stopped herself just in time.

~

Several weeks later, Liam stared out the window at a row of tiny pine trees in the moonlight. One day they would make a hedge and shelter the garden from the cold southerly wind.

"Liam, how is it your skin looks so golden in the moonlight?" Rose said softly. "Mine looks pale, white, like a ghost."

He turned and Rose took his hand in hers and murmured, "Lily sleeps." He tugged his hand, but she held firm. She thought it would be easy. She tried to find him, in her mind, but couldn't. At first she thought there was something in the way, blocking her, but then realised there was something missing.

Oh, Lily... Lily...

Rose turned and whispered to Liam, "Come, come with me." She moved towards the door and gently pulled him behind her. He looked back at Lily stretched out on the sofa. "No, come, please," she urged.

They made their way to the kitchen and lit a candle; they sat with the glow between them.

Rose looked at Liam, her face unreadable. Finally she spoke, "She fears... She fears for the lives of her children."

Liam started to speak, raising a hand towards Rose. Rose shook her head and continued, "She thinks... She thinks she knows..." Rose swallowed and carried on, "She thinks that if they do survive, she quite possibly won't. Like our mother." The final words rushed out of Rose in one compressed breath; they landed dense and heavy.

The hand Liam was reaching towards Rose fell to the table. Rose took it in hers. For long moments, the candle flickered, making shadowy shapes just outside the golden glow. Liam bent his head, shook it several times. His hand moved from its soft cradle and shifted to surround Rose's hand. He clasped it hard. Liam raised his head, looked straight into Rose's tear-filled eyes, and spoke powerfully, "We cannot let her go."

Rose shook her head and bit her lip. She reached out with her other hand. She wanted Liam to hold it; she wanted his strength. He held both her hands, and as they looked into each other's eyes, there was much more than the table between them.

Liam had never felt consciously aware of individual moments like this before. They paraded, each one coming in unhurriedly, and then doing a slow pirouette on the table in the candlelight, and then slowly fading just in time for the next one's entrance. Rose's hands loosened in his, and she slowly, very purposefully started to remove them, yet lingered, and he felt a tiny caress, a loving stroke. It seemed she was giving and taking fortification. For the briefest of moments, her eyes spoke of misery, sacrifice, then suddenly there it was—her tenacity and a resolution. That one moment pirouetted with a peculiar flourish, drawing attention to itself, and Liam saw what she was doing. Liam saw what he needed to see.

The next moment he grasped again for her retreating hands. She saw his need and relented, gave in to a goodbye. The feel of his hands in hers gave her the courage to speak. It was only a whisper with tears in the way, but she declared, "She must not think that I can take her place."

~

The Policeman's Ball was held at the South Rakaia Hotel. The name embarrassed Frank, the only policeman stationed in Rakaia. He had mentioned the idea of a ball to his new landlady, Mrs Rouse. She was a formidable woman who had run with the idea, galloped with it to be more precise, although the image of Mrs Rouse either running or galloping was not one to be pondered on for long. She organised leaflets, sold tickets, sorted out musicians, and arranged supper in the most efficient manner.

The day was cloudy and cold. Not yet the deepest part of winter, but getting close enough to it. Lily and Rose were bundled up in the wagon for the late afternoon journey. They had taken rooms with Mrs Rouse to save coming home late.

Lily reached under the blanket for Rose's hand. "Tell me, Rose."

"Tell you what?"

"Everything! Talk to me."

"Ah, well, we need to do more shopping tomorrow, more muslin and wool, for tiny things." Rose smiled. "Are you going to do more knitting?"

Lily nodded.

"The cradle Liam is making is beautiful, isn't it?"

Lily nodded again.

"He's making it extra wide, says if it is twins, he's sure they won't mind sleeping together."

"Rose, stop it."

"Stop what? You just said…"

"You know, all this chatter. Tell me. What is going on?"

"There is noth…"

Lily interrupted, "You know very well what I am talking about, Rose Quinn. You and Liam are skirting around each other, like planets orbiting the sun."

Liam slowed the wagon. "I'll tell you, Lily, but not here." His voice was resolute, definite. "I'll tell you tonight." He smiled at her, and then, after Rose had turned, mouthed, "Ah, Lily," and then "Later."

~

Sean had been right. Frank watched Rose and Lily dancing together. They seemed magical, mystical, like they had entered another dimension, as they moved to the music. Their combined energy seemed almost combustible. They simmered with joy. Frank reckoned he could just about see it radiate out their pores.

"Come dance with Rose," Liam said to Frank as he walked past on his way to Lily.

"Lily, don't overdo it." Liam took Lily's hand as he spoke.

"I'm well. I'm having so much fun, I..." Lily gulped for air between words.

"Come with me now."

"But... Rose?"

"Rose can dance with Frank." Liam nodded over his shoulder to Frank, as his hand moved to the small of Lily's back to guide her forward, kneading the muscles there without thinking.

"Oh, now that feels nice." She closed her eyes, stopped walking, and leaned back into his hand.

He whispered in her ear, "People are watching."

"Hmm, well." She opened her eyes, looking tentatively around. "I am not used to people; I forget."

"I know." He guided her out.

Liam found a table in the corner of the supper room, sat her down, and then brought food and watched her eat. Watched her breathe, in and out, in and out, waiting for the rosy glow to fade, the sheen to settle, but it didn't.

"Liam, you have to stop looking at me like that."

"Why?"

"As you pointed out earlier, there are people." She glanced around. "And unless you want me sitting on your lap, well..." She shrugged her shoulders, smiled, and sighed.

He kept looking.

She looked right back and said softly, "'Later'... It's later. Tell me."

"No." He shook his head, looking around, "Tonight, when we're alone."

~

Rose danced with Frank, Sean, Mick, and others too numerous to mention. It didn't seem to matter whether it was a waltz or a polka, she danced with her particular mix of grace and defiance. She created a tension, but overflowed with joy. It was intriguing, yet confusing.

"Rosie, the offer still stands."

She had to back away and look up, remind herself whose arms she was in.

"The offer?"

"You know, on the ship." Sean pulled her close again, bent his head to her, whispered in her ear. "Just let me know if there's a chance."

Oh, she thought, there was every chance, every chance and no chance, no chance at all. Rose was happy and sad at the same time. Something about not being able to have what she really wanted made her feel reckless, and it was Frank who eventually caught her attention. When he took her hand and gently tugged her towards the cool night air, she went. She sized up the broad shoulders in front of her and the thick dark hair, curled at the back of his neck. She pulled herself closer.

They went out the front door and around the building, passing other people chatting in the night. The music floated out; the lantern lights glowed; the atmosphere was warm, defying the cold.

Around the corner, Frank stopped. Their hands parted, and he hesitated very slightly before he turned towards her.

The light from the windows was barely enough. He wanted to see her.

"Yes?" She asked because there were questions in his eyes.

Frank acknowledged her with the slightest movement of his head. *Just a moment, please. I need a moment*, he thought. What do you say to a woman you desire, desperately desire, who you don't have any reason to believe desires you? "Rose, do you..."

Her hand went to his chest, found a hold in the vee of his woollen jacket, pulling him ever so gently towards her. Then she kissed him.

Small, soft kisses.

It took him a moment to realise what was happening, stop the questions that had been forming with such rapidity, filling his head, making him nervous.

His arms wound their way around her, tentatively at first, but she moved closer to him, inviting his embrace. He took a step, moving her in front of him until her back was resting against the wall. Still, it was she who kissed him.

Finally, he dared to kiss her back.

And when he did, it was with bravado, as if he were hurling himself off a cliff, happy to free-fall, feel the rush of it all and damn the consequences.

Rose happily went along with the ride, curiously exploring, experimenting.

Liam rounded the corner and saw their embrace. There was a collision in his mind: what he saw and felt crashed into what he knew he couldn't feel, couldn't express. He had seen Rose leave with Frank and he knew he shouldn't follow them, but he felt compelled to protect her, make sure she was all right. He clenched his fists tight and turned, unable to comprehend the conflicting emotions coursing through him. Somewhere there must be air available for breathing, somewhere there must be... where?

Rose saw him, saw his face, just as he turned. She saw the devastation she had wreaked.

"Oh, ah..." She moaned. Frank pulled her closer in his ardour and pushed her back against the wall in his mounting excitement.

"No, no, Frank. Please, I..."

Liam turned at the low sound, knew her pain.

"What is it, dear sweet Rose?" Frank murmured in her ear.

"Frank, please stop. You must let me go. I'm sorry. Please let me go."

He slid his hands down the length of her. He did not want to let her go. "Why, Rose, why?"

"I'm sorry, Frank, so sorry. I just... Well, I'm sorry." She took his hands off her, looking past him. He turned.

"Liam, bloody hell! How long have you been there?"

"I came to get Rose. Lily wants her," Liam lied. Rose stepped forward and took his arm. They turned and headed for the door.

"I'm sorry, Rose. I..."

"It's all right. I'll go, Liam. I promise I'll go after the babies are born, and I'll go far away from here," she replied.

~

"It's later," Lily whispered when they were tucked up in bed at the boarding house. Lily was burrowed into Liam, seeking warmth. "Tell me."

"I'd rather show you." He kissed her hard, but pulled back quickly, then again.

"Liam," she said between the kisses and the breaths. "Liam!" she said, more impatiently.

"I don't seem to have the words."

213

"Find them."

He stilled, and the moments marched past this time, no pirouettes or flourishes. Steady and determined, they gave him the silent treatment. He kissed her again, and then again, and watched the parade. Would it go on forever? His words, when they came, startled them both.

"I want you to hear me, without Rose."

Lily was silent.

"I love you, Lily."

"I know, Liam, but you also…"

"No, Lily, you, just you. You're all I want."

Lily was quiet again.

"So, try. Summon up whatever it is you need to summon up; I'm waiting." He held her tighter.

"But why?"

"Try."

Liam thought he felt a glimmer for a moment, a tiny misstep in the march of time.

"There is nothing without Rose."

"There is everything, Lily, everything! A lot more than most people have. We have our farm and our children, Lily." His hand left her shoulder and travelled down, caressing the swell.

He moved, shifting in the bed, his mouth wanting to follow where his hand had been.

"Only you, you are the only one who will do." His hand gently parted her legs.

"But, Liam…?"

He claimed her mouth, silencing her.

"You," he whispered as he moved his mouth to kiss her neck. "You," he whispered as he lowered his lips to her sweetly curved breast. "You," he whispered as he took the rosy pink tip into his mouth. Lily arched her body involuntarily against the long hard length of him.

Yes, you, dear Liam.

Lily? Lily?

Yes…

Liam raised his head; he was grinning foolishly, "I heard you, I heard you!"

"You heard me." Lily smiled and laughed with the joy of it.

Chapter 41

Rose and Mick made the fortnightly trip to Rakaia for supplies, choosing what looked to be a clear, fine day. The weather in New Zealand was a constant source of curiosity: one minute the wind could be blowing from the nor'west and then suddenly it would come from the south, degrees cooler. Mick reached behind him for the blanket and handed it to Rose.

"Looks like they are going to fight it out," Mick stated.

"Who?"

"The warm tropical winds and the cold southerly ones."

"Ah," Rose shivered.

"Didn't see this one coming."

"We're almost there," Rose said, wrapping the blanket around her shoulders.

"Let's hurry with our jobs, then head back. It's looking nasty." Mick turned his head slightly, motioning to the bank of black clouds stacked on the horizon behind him.

Rose did the grocery shopping and then meandered through the dry goods store, forgetting Mick's anxiety about the weather. She enjoyed being away from Liam and Lily. The strain was oppressive. Oh, it wasn't like she had an alternative, she knew Lily needed her until the babies were born and then, perhaps, for a while longer. But her days could not go on indefinitely like this. She could not continue to deny her true feelings; her heart was not strong enough.

"It's getting worse." Mick approached her and waved towards the front windows of the shop. "We should stay in town."

"Liam will worry."

"Liam will take one look at the storm and know exactly what we decided to do."

By the time they had stabled the horses and started on their way to Mrs Rouse's accommodation house, the rain was pelting down. Mick and Rose ran in the dust and mud with the blanket held over their heads, flapping behind them.

"Hang on tight, or the blanket will blow away," Mick warned.

"Feels like we could fly, lift off." Rose's voice was breathless and she jumped in the air, giving the wind the chance to take her. She ran a few more yards and launched herself again.

They arrived at the boarding house to find Mrs Rouse, Frank, Sean O'Hennessey, and two other gentlemen sitting down to their midday meal. Mick and Rose burst into the hallway next to the dining room on a current of energy—laughing and moving—a wet and muddy tangle of blankets and coats and laughter. Rose leaned against the wall opposite the door to the dining room. She was completely dishevelled and made a feeble attempt to straighten herself.

"Now, that was fun!" Frank and Sean heard her say, her voice vibrating with mirth.

"Hello, sorry to interrupt." Rose waved to the men through the doorway while Mrs Rouse helped her with her wet coat.

"It could never take ye away, not really." Mick was taking off his own soaking jacket.

"Ah, but it felt like it just might. You have to admit there was a possibility."

"Sorry, Rose, no chance." Mick had laughter in his voice. "None at all." He shook his head and the water flicked around.

"Here, I'll get you a towel," Mrs Rouse bustled off down the hall.

"Sorry, didn't mean…" Mick shrugged apologetically, as Mrs Rouse waved her hand behind her dismissively.

"Oh, but, Mick, it was lovely, wasn't it? Just knowing that maybe, any moment, up you'd go…away?" Mrs Rouse returned with a towel.

"Rosie, come on, let's have some dinner. You weren't going anyplace; I had a hold of you."

"Rose, Mick, this is Mr Harding and Mr Somerton." Mrs Rouse motioned with her hand. "Lily…sorry…Rose Quinn and Mick McGregor." She sat down. "And Constable McManaway and Mr O'Hennessey you know, of course."

Rose and Mick sat at the end of the table and ate mashed potatoes and gravy. Had she known they were coming, Mrs Rouse would have cooked them each a mutton chop—still could for that matter—but no, the potatoes and gravy would do very nicely they assured her.

Rose sat there, storm-ravished, everything about her tousled. Frank looked at her, slowly chewing his mutton, and remembered kissing her and how Liam had interrupted them. Although warmed by seeing her, he felt a sense of hesitation. The thought that came to his head was shipwreck. *She looks like she's just survived a shipwreck and enjoyed it.* He took another bite of his mutton.

Sean's emotions were no more articulate but rather more pointed, centred as they were on one particular area of his body, where they coalesced most uncomfortably. "So you will be waiting out the storm?" he managed.

"No point heading back now, not with the dray, we'd be going straight into it." Mick took a sip of warm tea.

"I am going to read," Rose stated.

"You are?" Sean's mind was still not on the conversation.

"Yes, I am going to snuggle up somewhere, preferably very near the fire, and read a book from Mrs Rouse's shelf. And, if at all possible, without interruption," Rose added, then noted Sean's expression, "well, maybe some conversation, but it must be scintillating, though, or humorous, at the very least."

He recognised the tease in her voice and a thought came to him, the first clear one since she had stormed into the boarding house. "Rosie, I can always make you laugh."

~

It took a while to get settled. Mrs Rouse was adamant about not sitting around in wet clothes. Rose wasn't cold. Her wool coat had deflected or absorbed most of the rain, but the bottom of her skirt was wet and the moisture had travelled up like a wick.

Sean found her sitting with her bare feet propped on a footstool in front of the roaring fire. Her petticoats were arranged for maximum exposure to the heat, fanning out like a rose in full bloom and steaming.

"Aren't your feet hot?"

"No, it looks hotter than it is." Rose didn't look up from her book.

Sean took the chair beside her. "What are you reading?"

"*Pride and Prejudice.*"

"What is it about?"

Rose finally looked up. "Oh, it's a love story. The girl, Elizabeth Bennett, falls in love with a man, Mr Darcy. She has a sister, Jane, who falls in love with a different man."

"I should hope so."

"What?"

"That her sister falls in love with a different man."

"Oh, yes, well…" Rose paused, looking pensive, and then carried on. "There are quite a few misunderstandings and it takes them all the way to the end of the book to…"

"But you've only just started it."

"I've read it before. On the ship. Remember that English girl, Mary? The one in first class with all the brothers?" Sean nodded, and Rose continued, "She had it."

Sean looked at the fire; Rose's gaze went back to her book. After a few minutes of companionable silence, she put her book aside and leaned over to rearrange the bottom of her skirt. She sat up and turned towards Sean and smiled. "Sorry about that." She waved her hand at the book. "Tell me about your land."

"Well, I don't know if I'll get it or not. It's way out, behind Mount Somers. I'm waiting to hear if they've accepted my offer."

"Are you excited?"

"No, just nervous." Sean sat up a little straighter in his chair. "My offer is unusual. I want to make a payment and then work the rest off by profit sharing. I don't know if they'll go for it or not."

"But it's the people you have been working for, isn't it?"

"Yes."

"Well, they know you then, know what you're like."

"Yes, they do." He smiled a little, "But if someone else has the cash…" He shrugged.

Sean told Rose about the homestead, the way the morning light crept slowly through the half valley, and how it disappeared so quickly behind the hills at night.

"Do the hills make you feel safe?" Rose questioned.

"What do you mean?"

"They feel to me like they are standing guard."

"Yes, I kind of know what you mean."

"Liam thinks so too. I think they help when the wind blows."

"How's that?" Sean raised his eyebrows.

"Well, no matter how hard the wind blows, or has ever blown, there they are."

"What? You mean because the hills haven't moved?"

"No, no…well, maybe. It's more like there is a border, an edge.

No matter how hard it blows on the plains, you won't be blown off."

Sean chuckled, "No, Rosie! According to you, you'll be flattened against a hill first. Your theory is pretty faulty." He smiled, "The worst wind is the nor'west, which blows away from the hills anyway."

"So?"

"Well, there is nothing stopping you being blown into the sea, is there?"

"All right, all right," Rose smiled. "The hills help somehow, I know that. I just don't know how to explain it."

"Rose, can I take you out to dinner tonight, at the hotel?"

Rose folded her arms across her chest and thought a moment, "Well, Mick…"

"Mick can stay here and eat," Sean interrupted. "Just you and me, Rosie, for once."

His voice held a note of just barely explicable longing, some ancient yearning that ricocheted right off her heart, but left something small and recognisable, familiar.

She said yes.

~

The South Rakaia Hotel on a cold southerly winter night was a place where you could ask for mercy. It was filled with travellers of all sorts, coming and going. There were farmers and sheep herders, drifters and drovers, bakers and butchers, a tinker, several teamsters, and a gang of railroad men. There were men with no occupation to call their own; their only desire being to make their way, any possible way. There were a few women, dressed in crinolines, with lace collars. There were wives and mothers, mostly travel-worn, or maybe just worn out with the effort of adjusting to the newness of the land.

So the travellers gathered, some just starting, others ending their journeys, and some with no perception of any transition at all. All of them were glad to have a roof over their heads in the storm, glad to have something warm to fill their bellies and a pint to lighten their hearts.

The smells of the people, open fires, lantern oil, roasting meat, and the yeasty aroma of the ale mingled with the clamour of conversation. It was punctuated with laughter, high shrills, and low rumbles that formed an oddly comforting human harmony.

Rose relaxed on the wooden bench, resting her back against the wall, replete after a hearty meal. Sean sat across from her, leaning towards her with his elbows on the table, wishing he was sitting beside her. Rose's hand rested idly just inches from his. He wondered what she would do if he touched her and, without further contemplation, brushed his fingers across the top of her hand, almost indolently, as if it were a casual, thoughtless movement. Rose shifted slightly and turned her head and looked at his hand on hers for moment. She closed her eyes and moved her hand slightly.

He kept up a gentle massage.

"Rosie?" Sean's voice was gentle.

"Hmm?" He saw more than heard her response.

"Have you thought about marriage… To me?"

She nodded, her eyes still closed.

"Hey, you two!" Sean's hand retreated quickly as a loud jovial voice interrupted their exchange.

"Good dinner?" Frank sat in the gap beside Rose.

Rose sat up, pulling her back away from the wall. *Paying attention now*, Sean thought.

"Yes, delicious, but this beer," she picked up her mug and took another sip, "is making me sleepy."

Frank put his hand on hers and lowered the mug to the table. "Don't drink anymore, Rose. You know it goes straight to your head." And then, as if he didn't quite trust her, he took the mug from her hand and drank the rest. "You're not used to it," he said after the last gulp.

"Frank McManaway, I'll not have you treating me like a child." Rose was smiling. She picked up the empty mug and turned it over. "I'd have liked to douse you with it. How are you? Any news since lunchtime?" Rose asked with feigned sweetness, "Any drownings, presumed or otherwise?"

"Rose, Rose, Rose." Frank shook his head.

"Or kidnappings? You haven't overlooked any kidnappings, have you?" She looked at him with mock horror.

"Rose, stop it." Frank and Sean were both laughing.

"I'd just hate to think of some poor woman being whacked on the side of the head, or something, and then bundled off to heaven only knows and…and…"

"Rose, I'm leaving." Frank stood up, still laughing. "Shall I get you another pint?"

"Yes."

"Do you really want another one?" Sean asked after Frank left.

Rose shrugged. "A sip or two. I was enjoying it, feeling all lovely and soft and... Sean, weren't you proposing again, or was I dreaming?"

Sean looked at her teasing smile and decided to join the game. "I think you must have been dreaming, Rosie-girl."

He took her hand again.

"Ah," she smiled, "maybe I was, but I'm sure I saw myself in a valley of sorts, with mountains at my back, watching the sun rise." Rose's eyes were on Sean.

His grip tightened for a moment. "And the wind would be blowing?"

"Always. Well, on and off, you know." Rose shrugged, still smiling, full of teasing tension. She held up their joined hands, "But somehow..." She took a breath, "I don't think you'd let me blow away."

Sean was thrown off balance, his mind instantly filled with possibilities that included her, as if there could be no equilibrium in a world with so much potential. He let go of her hand and, in his confusion, the best he could manage was a long swallow of the last of his ale.

Frank returned with Rose's mug. "Drink up, and I'll walk you home."

Rose nudged the mug towards Sean. "You need it more than I do."

Frank sat back down, "Sean, you all right?"

"Yeah, yes! I'm fine." He sat up straighter and smiled at Frank. "Never better, Constable, never better." He smiled at Rose. "You must have better things to do on such a nasty night than escorting us."

"No, it's pretty quiet."

Rose stretched, lifting her shoulders and rotating her neck a little. "You could find something better to do, Frank, a fine mind such as yours would eventually work out that..." Sean's hand was on the table making a beckoning motion to Rose's. Frank watched as Rose slipped her hand into Sean's.

"Oh! Umm...all right." He took a long gulp of the beer he had brought Rose. He looked at Rose and Sean's joined hands a moment longer. "You'll make his life a misery, won't you, Rose?"

Rose laughed. "Of course I will."

Sean grinned.

~

They talked about living, all the tiny things that make up life after survival has been fought for and won. What did she like to cook… what were his favourite things to eat… what was his family like… did she read a lot… did he miss Ireland? They seemed to mesh. There was a sense that an amalgamation was possible and might actually be very pleasant.

"We'd better go," Sean murmured.

Neither of them wanted to leave the cocoon they'd so carefully spun in the dim, warm corner of the hotel. Sean stood up suddenly and took her arm. "Right, let's get moving."

They hurried through the rain, a few dim glows from windows guiding the way. Mrs Rouse had left a lantern burning on the porch, a beacon in the dark.

Just inside the door, he pulled her close.

"I'll know soon about the land."

"I won't go until the babies come."

Why did it sound like they were talking to themselves, and not each other?

"After, though, after her confinement, you'll come with me, you'll leave your sister, then?"

"I…" Rose faltered, unable to form words, or even the ideas behind the words, to describe the abyss that formed in her mind at the thought of leaving Lily. There was only blank space. She leaned limply into him, ineffectively trying to gather her thoughts.

She had to leave Fairfield. All right. She had promised she would. All right. She couldn't bear to live with Lily and Liam, live and not love. All right. So she'd turned to Frank at the dance. Not all right— too close, much too close. She'd go far away. All right. Get away, fly away with Sean. All right, all right, it should be all right… It will be all right.

"All right," she muttered weakly. "All right." Rose turned and hurried down the dim hallway. Sean had the strange sensation that she was escaping—a fading apparition—her muddy layers of skirts, wafting, swirling, lifting, like the wind was blowing straight through them.

Chapter 42

Lily

Liam leaned back on the pillows, hands behind his head, watching me. He closed his eyes and sighed. I watched as his whole body fell into a deep tranquillity. Once he'd figured out that Rose and Mick would not be braving the storm and returning, he had moved our mattress in by the fire. I was still on the sofa, trying to finish my knitting.

"What are you making?" his voice was languid.

"Another little undershirt."

"It looks bigger."

"Well, I thought I'd done enough tiny things for two, but maybe I should do more." My needles paused as I thought.

He turned on his side, "You're sure now?"

"Yes, I can feel them both; they move at different times. One will kick, and I swear it wakes the other one up." Liam was quiet.

"Do you think...?"

"Liam, I know you are worried, so am I, but Myra and Rose will do. Myra's delivered lots of babies."

"Not twins though."

"No, just a few, and..."

"And what?" Liam said as he propped himself up on his elbows.

"Nothing."

"Lily, put the knitting down. Come here." He patted the mattress beside him.

I smiled at him and felt the worry disappear for a moment, slide off my countenance like rain off our roof.

"Just a minute," I finished the row and stuck the needles into the ball of wool. I stood and stretched, my arms up high, then, down to my lower back. I arched and leaned into my hands, stretching out my spine. Then I slowly brought my arms forward and touched my belly.

"What do you tell them?"

"That I love them, always will, and…"

"And?"

"To not be afraid, they mustn't be afraid." I knew he heard the small but vivid note of dread I tried to hide.

"Lily, I'll take you to Christchurch, to the hospital there, with doctors."

"No, no, Myra and Rose will be fine, and you…you could help." I looked at him, measuring him up. "I think you might really be able to help, Liam."

Liam nodded.

"And Mick, Mick hears us sometimes; Mick might help."

"Lily, what are you talking about? Mick is not going to help deliver our child, our children, certainly not."

"No, no, I don't mean the… well," I faltered.

"Well, what?"

I took a breath, "When I imagine it all, I think of Rose…LilyRose first, and then you, you especially, but Mick too. Mick definitely could help."

"Help what?" Liam's voice held a note of annoyance.

"Liam, listen to me. You know exactly what I am talking about. The power we create in our minds when Rose and I communicate and, then, when you join in and, sometimes, Mick. It's that… That is what I am going to need most of all." I sat down on the edge of the mattress.

"Oh, I see."

"Do you? Do you see why I can't be left alone in some hospital with strange men who think they know what's best for me?"

Liam nodded slowly.

"And why if it gets difficult, and I think it very well might, Mick might have to be there?"

"I'm having a little trouble with that one."

"Oh, Liam." I moved towards him, crawling across the mattress. I lay beside him, facing him. He raised himself on his elbow; his other hand went to my waist and then caressed his children.

"Liam, you mustn't forget about my Nana Kat, my mother Lillian, and what they were."

"I don't know that we ever had a very precise definition," he smiled.

"My mother and grandmother and her mother before her and her

224

mother before her, back as far as you can imagine, were women of knowledge, wise women with ancient wisdom so powerful that it became necessary to keep it a secret."

"Because?"

"Well, I don't know all the details… But because their knowledge was so powerful that it frightened people… People in high places. And the circle has been broken, severed by my mother's early death and my grandmother's insanity." My voice was beyond sad, "Nana didn't blame anyone or anything, not really; she just said what is, is."

"Does that help?" Liam asked gently.

"Not particularly, but what I know is…" I emphasised the word 'is' and covered Liam's hand with my own, "is that the wisdom has power, extreme and possibly unimaginable power."

"Magic?"

I nodded only slightly. "Yes, but that word trivialises it somehow."

"Miracle?"

"Much better, but the priests would never call the power behind a miracle 'magic', would they?"

Liam chuckled. "So, Lily, you think you are going to need a miracle?"

"Maybe, but that word is almost as bad as magic, isn't it?"

"Well, it conjures up all sorts of dire situations needing divine intervention."

I rubbed my stomach. "We may need intervention, Liam, and the powerful sort I'm talking about will most assuredly be divine."

"And so, we are back to Mick?"

"You see now, don't you, how everyone who loves us, who knows us… Their power will help, their energy… If we all say no, no…" My head shook vehemently.

He pulled me close to him. "No, to what?"

I had tears gathering in the corners of my eyes. I tried to find words.

"No, to what?" His hand went under my chin. He lifted my face to his. "Tell me, Lily." He watched me struggle, "Say it."

"No, no, I am not going… NO!"

He held me, but couldn't get close enough. He turned me so his arms encompassed me from behind. I wriggled back into him, finding my place, settled but still tense.

"No, no, we won't let you go," he whispered in my ear over and over. I let his words soak into me and eventually went limp and pliant in his arms.

"You and Rose," I murmured sleepily, "you and Rose."

We both drifted off to sleep, he with one arm completely encircling his family.

~

Liam and Mick worked long, hard days through the winter. There was no sense of respite on the plains. The snow didn't fall and settle for weeks; the ground didn't freeze solid for months; not a thing seemed to hibernate. There were no excuses not to carry on.

They built fences and hauled firewood, planted hedges and dug out tussock, painted the house, and built grain storage next to the stables. Liam moved the mobs of sheep from one paddock of grass to the next one, secretly still awed that the sheep needed so little shelter.

Rose and I cooked and baked, sewed and knitted, and we read, sometimes to each other and, sometimes, by ourselves. My belly had long been at the point where it looked like it could stretch no further. The first thing anyone said to me was 'Lily, shouldn't you be sitting down?' And if I was sitting down, it was 'Lily, shouldn't you be lying down?'

I was lying down, draped sideways along the settee in front of the fire, but still I wasn't comfortable.

"Rose, can you rub my back?"

"Hmm, just a minute, I'll get the pie in first."

I turned and tried to reorganise the pillows under me.

"How much longer do you think?" The door on the oven clamped shut.

"The sooner the better I think," I said with some certainty.

"Lily, tell me again, what I should do." Rose reached to massage my lower back.

"Just don't let me go."

Not for a moment, you know.

Like this... This is all? This is enough?

It has to be, LilyRose. It may not be enough, but it is the beginning. It is the only place to start.

And Liam... Liam must help... He must... His strength will...

Rose took her hands off my back; I turned to face her.

"You can't be afraid of him."

"I am not afraid, that's silly. Why would I be afraid of him?"

"Rose, Rosie," I said her name softly and shook my head. "You think you keep secrets, but you know you can't."

"All right, then, I'll say it." She paused and gathered her strength, looking me straight in the eye. "You think you are going to die, don't you, Lily? And if you do, you think everything here will be fine, because... What do you know? Rose will be here."

Rose's hands were clenched, and she turned, pacing towards the fire. She stopped and looked back at me. "That's what you think, isn't it, Lily?"

We held each other's gaze.

"I'll not have it, Lily. I will not be your replacement. I won't!"

"Rosie." I held out my hand to her, "Rosie, come here."

Rose stayed, hands still clenched.

"Ah, you daft girl," I sighed. "I know, I know, Rose... because I would do it for you."

Rose stared at me, her eyes filling with tears.

"And I would love whoever needed loving twice as fiercely because you weren't there to do it."

Rose stepped forward and, wiping her eyes with one hand, reached out and took mine with the other.

LilyRose... LilyRose... The pie!

I stood slowly and started towards the kitchen, but Rose rushed ahead to rescue the pie. She plonked it with some force on the table. "All right, then, all right. But you need to promise me one thing."

"What's that?"

"Don't die."

"Rose Quinn." My voice had a smile in it as I looked down at my hand on my belly.

Rose reached past the steaming pie and put her hand next to mine. "You won't go, I know you won't. Besides I've already told Sean I'd marry him after the babies come."

"No, I won't." I smiled at Rose's news and moved my hand to cover hers just as we felt a kick. "Not if I have any choice in the matter."

Chapter 43

George Lichfield tried to heal. He worked towards some sort of redemption. He found the strength to forgive himself for his own transgressions, whether real or perceived, and made an effort to understand Elisabeth and Henry and the choices they had made that had led them to such dark places. But barely an hour would go by when he wouldn't think of them.

The image of them boarding the ship was seared into his consciousness: Henry's blank stare, his drooling foolish grin when he recognised his mother, her inability to mask her disdain, her disgust at the sight of her own son. Then Elisabeth's condescension towards George, contempt almost, at the way she was being treated. Had the woman no shame at all?

George's mouth formed into a wry grin on its own. Of course she had shame, had it in abundance, but if only she had let her defences down, lived a little. Why was Elisabeth so afraid of living, of loving? Oh, the effort it must take to maintain such distance—that was it, wasn't it? She had spent her life and most of his maintaining a distance. What comfort did she find in that? Had it never occurred to her just to open her arms, to him or to Henry?

Well, she was getting some distance now. He thought of the expanse of the sea between them, mile after mile of nothing but aloof, cold Southern Ocean. Maybe her notion of safety would finally be satisfied.

"Excuse me, sir, breakfast is ready."

"Oh, yes, all right, then. Thank you, Sally." At first, he'd wanted Sally to go, but he'd noticed something in her, a fragmenting of sorts, when he'd told her about Henry. He let her stay as a housemaid while she recovered. Later he recognised his kindness as camaraderie. After all, she too had tried to love Henry and failed.

"You'll sit with me today?"

"Certainly, sir."

Their conversation was simple—simple questions and simple answers—with George doing most of the inquiring. There were long quiet spaces that brought comfort to them both in ways that neither of them could articulate. She was truthful with him, and he was kind to her. It was enough.

"Who's that?" Sally pointed out the window to a rider on the drive.

"It looks like Mick." George turned towards Sally. "It must be time. Lily's babies must be on their way."

"Oh!" Sally's hand went to her mouth. "Myra, I'll go and get Myra. She's packed a case already."

"Sally, it will be all right, no need to panic." George reached for her arm and touched her with a fatherly pat. "Really, it will."

Sally looked down at her arm and a fleeting smile crossed her face. She put her hand on top of his, briefly and almost surreptitiously. "Have you seen her lately? Her belly is huge, and she's…she's…"

George shook his head. "It will be all right."

They all went—George, Myra, and Sally. Ronny drove them over. Thought he might even stay and wait for the good news.

Chapter 44

Lily

"Lily, Lily, it's like there is a knife in your back, and someone is twisting it at regular intervals!"

"Rose," I gasped for air, "you don't need to explain it to me...ee...eee." The 'me' was a wail, as another contraction took hold.

Rose had one of my hands in hers and Liam had the other. Another pain came sneaking in, slow but relentless, building, cresting in an agony so intense that I almost lost consciousness.

"Lily, Lily!" Rose called out in a panicked voice.

"No, Rose, relax. Remember what Lily told us. Hold her, hold her." Liam tried to keep us calm.

Rose rubbed her own lower back with her free hand and took a deep breath.

LilyRose, LilyRose... Can you hear? LilyRose... Liam... He is here.

My body relaxed. I looked from Rose to Liam.

Hold me here... Hold me here... Hold... Hold.

Another pain came—striving, clutching, clasping—and then reluctantly went on its way. Just in time for another to creep in, plant itself, be recognised.

Hold... LilyRose... Liam... Hold.

This was the way I weathered the onslaught, possibly the only way this battle could be fought. My sister, who was more than a sister, and my husband, whose love I had tested and found limitless, formed a triadic union, creating the strength I needed.

Mick burst into the quiet room. Sally and Myra were right behind him. "What, what...?" He instinctively stepped towards Rose and took her free hand.

Myra was all action and began her examination and assessment of the situation.

"Good progress, Lily, you seem to be coming along." She looked at the concentration on the faces surrounding her and our fiercely clutched hands. "Whatever are you doing?"

"Don't ask." It was Liam who answered.

Myra shrugged, "Sally, can you get some more towels, please?"

It was the last thing that anyone said for quite a while.

Childbirth felt to me like orchestrated chaos, a terrible wrenching and tearing, agonising and merciless and unending, but somehow familiar and expected. Something deep and primal in me was not surprised that the effort to bring forth life was so tormenting.

I battled and fought the pain, but eventually, I was forced to accept the inevitable suffering. Liam chose to fight it, although he wasn't sure what 'it' was. Rose's distress was not separate from mine, but my acquiescence confused her.

LilyRose, do not give in. You have to fight. Listen to me.

No, no! We cannot fight this. Let the babies come. Let it sweep over me and take them.

"That's it, Lily! You've got to relax and push with the pain. You can do it." Myra's words rang out, clarifying. "Can you see, Sally, the baby's head? This time, this time."

I readjusted myself on my elbows, knees bent, and my legs spread wide. I united with the anguish. "I will bear these children. Danu, mother of the all, help me, please," I said as I pushed.

The baby burst forth with far too much force, riding on a river of blood. His father turned him. Myra wiped the mucous from his mouth and handed him to Sally.

"Lily, the boy has been born."

I felt myself going. My head lolled for an instant, but then I held steady. My eyes locked with Liam's.

"Myra, you have to get the girl."

"Lie back now, dear. She'll be coming along, just wait."

"No! There is no time! You've got to..." I spoke to Liam, "You have to save our daughter." Liam, Rose, and Myra all looked at me in stunned silence, trying to imagine what it was I was asking. "Please." My voice was desperate. "There is no time."

"Liam, you must rescue our daughter." My voice found some firmness. "My love, we have no choice." Liam closed his eyes and swallowed.

"Myra," he said, his voice firm and strong, "tell me what to do."

Mick held out a kitchen knife. Myra was holding a towel between my legs trying to stop the incessant flow. "Just here." I felt her finger, damp and warm. "Keep it low and light. Once you're through the skin, you'll see the womb."

"Hurry, Liam." My voice was very small, but definite. "There is not much time." Liam's eyes darted from mine to the knifepoint, seeking nonexistent assurances.

I clung to LilyRose, my sister Rose, who seemed anchored to the edge of the great deep crevasse that was the pain. The pain was trying to own me, pull me from Rose's hold. It reached up for me out of the chasm, grasping for me. I dodged.

"There, see, Liam, the hand, take the hand, take it. Now the shoulder, work your hand in and under, twist a little." Myra instructed while pushing the towel against me.

Liam freed the baby from her entrapment.

"Is she... Is she...?" I strained to see, my eyes blurring.

"She is alive, Lily! She is alive, thank God." Liam said the word 'alive' like it was a promise he would keep.

He held our daughter up to me for a moment. She looked me straight in the eyes before he handed her to Mick.

"Ah, ah." I relaxed and tried to smile. I felt myself letting go as the pain receded.

Rose shook my hand, still clutching it tightly. "Lily, Lily." There was panic in her voice. "You promised me, you promised."

"We both made promises, and you are going to have to keep yours," I murmured weakly.

"Lily, Lily, don't leave us..." Liam's voice was filled with anguish and his words trailed away as he looked at the gaping wound on my belly.

A tiny stirring, a question, formed in the face of death. Was there something love could do in the face of the devastation? Could I say no, rebel?

"Liam, hold my hand."

"I am, for God's sake, I am."

"Rose?"

"Yes, I am here, Lily. Right here beside you."

Come, then. Come and hold me here.

LilyRose... LilyRose...

Mick... Mick will help.

Mick moved to put his hand on Rose's shoulder, his other hand still holding my daughter to his chest.

There was complete stillness for a long moment.

Then a surprised silence.

What? Who... It's the girl.

My baby girl... Caitlin, her name is Caitlin. And the boy... He is William.

Minds met and mingled in a sorrowful dance, none of us able to admit to farewell or commit to goodbye. But I felt it, knew without a doubt the moment, the critical point, when my life blood lost the ability to keep me conscious. I saw the road, a wide path that narrowed in the distance, illuminated by a mysterious light. I wasn't beckoned, felt no compulsion, but ambled ahead, curious.

Chapter 45

"LIAM!" Rose's voice grew strong and sharp. "Liam, take my other hand."

He wiped his eyes and reached across Lily's bloody body, finding her hand. "Now, Liam, now."

LilyRose, can you hear me? Lily?

Rose shook Lily's hand quite violently, moving her sister's shoulder and head.

Lily, listen… You said you wouldn't go. Come to me… Come to me… LilyRose, come here, now!

There was confusion. The path curiously divided and presented a question, which required a decision. Lily was too tired to decide anything. She was happy just floating, meandering. The lights were pretty.

"Liam, you have to speak. She hears my voice as her own. Liam! LIAM!"

"Rose, dear, she's gone." Myra wiped her brow.

"NO! NO!" Rose twisted in position, but wouldn't let go of Lily or Liam, who started to pull away, tears running down both cheeks. She yanked Liam towards her. He momentarily lost his balance, stumbling against the edge of the bed, "Liam, tell her to come to me. Please, now!"

Rose shut her eyes in concentration. Liam shook off his despair and followed her, grasping and grabbing at what he thought felt like the receding Lily.

LilyRose… NO, Lily. LILY! Listen! Go to your sister. Find LilyRose… Lily… LILY! Don't go… Find Rose!

The voices were very faint at first, but their familiarity made her pause…and listen. She heard Liam calling.

Ah, to be cherished.

And something besides him.

Exquisite and tiny.

Reaching for her.

Ah, to cherish.

LilyRose? LilyRose? Here, here I am. Come now... Home... LilyRose, home to me...

Help me, help me... Rose... Liam... Mick... Help me...

She had to traverse an abyss, a huge chasm. The leaving had been gentle, but she might have gone a little too far on her way, because the effort required to pull herself back was monumental.

Lily's body twitched. Then she mouthed the word, "Liam."

Liam saw it. He stared in amazement. "Lily! Lily!"

Lily's eyes opened, looked at him with love, and then she let go of his hand, let go of it. Rose let go of his other one, tossed it away, and grabbed Lily's. She bent her forehead to her sister's.

Now, Lily. Come to me now. NOW!

Liam heard Rose's command as surely as if she'd said it out loud, but what followed and passed between them was not for the fainthearted. There was an ancient confluence, a convergence of energy as spontaneous as it was deliberate. For several moments, time stood still or did not exist at all. There was an indescribable opening, an almost unbearable wrench, yet it was welcoming. It left a huge rift, which settled a little, feebly attempting to heal, but leaving an open wound all the same. Over and around and through it all there was infinite sorrow, laced with all-encompassing joy. There was inexpressible happiness entwined with unspeakable misery. There was a sense of other spirits in the room, helping and supporting and lending their knowledge.

Interwoven were familiar voices: Liam, *Can this be happening? Well, we mentioned the word 'miracle'.* And Mick, *Nothing surprises you, does it?* And Caitlin... dear, dear Caitlin... *Who would have thought...* and William... *Wake up, sweet boy, mummy's here.*

Rose slumped, in a dead faint, her body poised momentarily on the edge of the bed. Mick reached out for her, but he still had Caitlin in his arms. Rose slipped further, as both Myra and Liam tried to catch her, knocking her head on the edge of the dresser on her way to the floor. Liam followed her down and gathered her up, cradling her, but he couldn't seem to find the strength to raise them both up.

"We should put Rose in bed." It was Mick, his voice steady, but his body sagging. He slumped to the floor beside Liam, the baby in his arms making noises that reminded him of kittens.

"Look at her."

Liam raised his head. Caitlin looked right at him, his tiny girl who had introduced herself so unmistakably, already capable of loving so thoroughly. He reached out a hand; he needed to touch her. He stroked her cheek, and she turned her head as if seeking his touch and closed her eyes.

"Bring me the boy."

Sally came, leant against the wall, and lowered herself and the child slowly. She sighed when she hit the floor. "He's awake now."

William looked at his father with curious eyes.

Liam reached for him, his finger tracing his cheek line.

The baby blinked, intrigued, but exhausted, and his father watched him as he drifted slowly and safely off to sleep.

The three of them sat there, leaning against the wall, each holding another being in their care. Liam looked down at Rose, her head cradled in his lap, an insipid ghostly version of herself and his dead wife. What had just happened?

He tried to think logically.

Reason or remember?

He tried to sequence the events in his mind, to order things. But his thoughts wouldn't sit still, not long enough to be counted.

Mick shifted his position. "There are things we have to do."

Liam nodded.

Still they stayed where they were for as long as they could. To rise up meant facing the aftermath of the bloody battlefield. Liam would have to face the fact that Lily was dead. He would help lift and turn and clean his beloved wife, prepare her body for the worms. Could they… Dare they decompose her beauty? Ah… There was a tiny shard of clarity. Because no, most certainly not, came the answer.

"They've had well enough time," Myra said to George as they came through the door. Liam winced, grasping at the fleeting thought he'd been thinking and knew he should remember, but it faded, blended in with the rest of the chaos.

The battlefield had many trenches to check. First, there was Rose; they must attend to the living. Liam gathered her up and got to his feet in one strong rush of energy that startled Mick and Caitlin. Mick soothed the baby, and she hushed at the sound of his voice. Liam took Rose to her bed and had some trouble disengaging himself from her warm body. Something in her wanted to cling to him for comfort, and something in him wanted to let her. He left Myra organising a compress for the swelling on the side of her head.

George was in charge of the sugar water for the babies. Sally bathed them, dressed them in soft gowns, and wrapped them in knitted shawls.

Liam and Mick put off facing death, until it could no longer be avoided. They went into the coppery, yeasty smelling room armed with a tin bucket full of warm soapy water and a pile of cloths as if there were things that could be washed away and then forgotten. They started by cleaning up the blood on the floor. Liam pondered briefly on the inexplicable number of footprints before he wiped them away. Mick took the bloody towels and cloths out to the washhouse. Liam stared for a while at the sheet covering Lily before he got the inclination to lift it. He looked at her face. Had her death not been grim? She lay there, sweetly, serenely, not luscious or alive by any means, and yet her death mask...?

"She is still trying to tell us something." It was Mick looking over his shoulder.

"What?"

"Well, she doesn't look afraid."

"She doesn't look a lot of things."

Liam pulled the sheet down further. "Do you know what to do?"

"I think you just clean and tidy the best you can."

"She'll need a clean dress."

After the babies were fed, Sally helped them. Ronny returned from Avonlea with a large wooden box. It was George's idea. The box had encased his grandfather clock on the trip out from England. It would be big enough for Lily and more solid than anything they might make in a hurry.

Liam did what was required of him, as if moving forward with deliberate activity was the only possible option. They washed her and dressed her in a clean dress and lifted her into the box.

Eventually though, night fell and, with it, the proposal of stillness. Liam turned inward and found his thoughts were no more ordered or rational, or for that matter understandable, than they had been earlier. What had he told Lily to do? Where was she now? How could she be anything but dead? He'd cleaned her body, saw the devastation. He'd felt her torment, but he couldn't feel her now, could he? Gone, she was truly gone. His thoughts held still, and he whispered to himself, "Lily has gone."

A wave of grief washed over him—so forceful that it took away everything that was memorable and good, so potent that it stripped away the possibility of anything ever being right again. There was nothing to hang on to. The anguish was dense and weighty, yet dynamic enough to fill every nook, every cranny. It turned every corner, found every niche. There was no room left for his heart to beat. He cried, and the grief filled even the minuscule void his tears had made.

Chapter 46

Lily was buried at the beginning of a new row in the Rakaia cemetery. The priest told the parable of the lost coin, which Liam forced himself to listen to, trying to make sense of it through his numbness.

"Either what woman having ten pieces of silver, if she lose one piece, doth not light a candle, and sweep the house, and seek diligently till she find it? And when she hath found it, she calleth her friends and her neighbours together, saying, 'Rejoice with me: for I have found the piece which I had lost'."

Puzzled, Liam looked at the priest as if he were offering some kind of hope for lost and scattered pieces.

"Likewise I say unto you, there is joy in the presence of the angels of God over one sinner that repenteth."

Liam looked questioningly at Frank, who shrugged. Certainly the angels would be joyful, but Liam didn't think Lily had much need for repentance.

He didn't sleep. He cried for Lily, for her kindness, for her grace, for her laughter. He cried for her delight. He cried for her passion. He cried for her incandescence.

He cried for her.

There was, however, no relief from the aching, cloying, throbbing, nauseating sense that the world, his world, was empty—empty except for the grief.

He heard what sounded like a lament in the distance, a funeral dirge carried on the wind. There was something oddly comforting in the sound, some vague feeling of assurance that there may be something firm enough for an anchor.

He stood up to go to the babies.

William and Caitlin, his son and his daughter.

They were so beautiful, so perfect and, yet, so small, so needy. Their neediness saved him. He'd hold one or the other, and things he could not name would well up inside him and, ever so briefly, edge out the heartache, nudge it sidewise. He felt a fleeting joy, with guilt hot on its tail.

"That child spends more time asleep in her Papa's arms than she does in the cradle."

"Do you think? I try to make sure they have turns."

Sally smiled. "I'm teasing you, Liam."

"Ah, they are good babies, aren't they, Sally?" Liam readjusted Caitlin on his shoulder, savouring her warm silky hair and her breath on his neck.

"Except for when you take them in there." She pointed to Rose's bedroom down the hall.

"What do you mean?"

"Caitlin cries. Doesn't seem to matter if she's just been fed or changed, or she's just fallen asleep. She cries like her life is depending on it."

Liam sat up a little in the rocker and put his hand on Caitlin's back. "What does the boy do?"

"William... He joins right in. They make a terrible racket."

Liam stood up.

"I leave them out here, now, when I see to Rose. Liam, where are you going? Oh no, don't! She's so sleepy and settled." Sally called after Liam, who was already halfway down the hall with Caitlin on his shoulder and a candle in his hand. Rose had lain unconscious since she had hit her head three days ago. Liam pulled down the quilt and laid the baby next to Rose in the crook of her arm. Caitlin opened her eyes and her lungs at the same time. Her cry was not full of anguish and despair. Liam listened carefully. Caitlin was not absolutely desperate for anything; she was merely trying to be heard.

"Can I take her now? She's going to wear her little self right out." Sally bent to scoop up the baby as Liam nodded, deep in thought, still watching Rose.

He sat down heavily in the chair beside her bed. He had largely ignored her existence for the last few days. There was something too strangely anomalous about the whole question of Rose and Lily's death. He took her hand. He smiled at the thought of his four-day-old daughter already telling him what to do.

"Rose, Rose, wake up! Come back to us, Rose." He gripped her hand tighter.

Rose... Rose, we need you. Please wake up!
Wherever Rose was, she wasn't listening.

~

Liam took the babies in twice a day, ensconced them in Rose's limp arms, and let them howl. Sally was horrified. Liam said not to worry; it was good for their lungs. On the second day, Liam thought he saw Rose move her arm and, then, wasn't sure, until he heard a moan.

"Rosie, Rosie, there now, that's it. Make your way back." But Rose drifted off again.

It was Mick's idea to join forces, so to speak. Liam still didn't quite know exactly what the forces were, but he knew what Mick meant. They tried a circle firstly with both babies, but William howled so loudly they couldn't hear themselves think, let alone find Rose. Caitlin, on her own, fell instantly quiet.

Rose, Rose, are you there? Rose...
Liam was sure there was something.
Rose... Rose... Can you come back to us? No... No?
Had he heard a 'no?'
No.
It was definitely a 'no'.
LilyRose...
What?
Maybe... LilyRose... LilyRose can...

Mick and Liam stood with their hands held together tightly. Liam lifted his other hand from Rose's shoulder to brush her cheek. "What do you think she meant?"

"Well, you know, when Lily died, she didn't really... Well..."

"You can say it, Mick. I'm as confused as you are."

Mick took a deep breath and finally let go of Liam's hand. He sat on the bed by Rose. Caitlin stared up at him with fascination. He reached out to her, and she grabbed his finger.

"I think they..." He finally turned to look at Liam. "I think that, when we call, we need to call them both."

"Ah, LilyRose."

Mick nodded.

Rose's eyelids flickered, but nobody noticed.

~

Time seemed stretched. It languidly and quietly slipped by, elongated and distended by sorrow. Sally stayed to help with the children and Rose. Myra sent food with George or Ronny. Mick and Liam took turns attending to the animals and the farm chores. Spring was in the air, but its promises were not loud or clear enough to be heard. The ewes started to lamb, and there was some consolation to be found in the achingly hard work and the gift of new life.

Rose took her time healing. They could wake her now, sit her up, and feed her soup while she viewed them all from a distance. Liam held her hand and tried to call her to him in his mind, but he found only devastation—a ruinous, fragmented rubble that threatened to pull him under. He would persevere, and every now and then, there was a wisp of something soft and gentle and loving. He would put William or Caitlin in her arms, and Rose would clasp the baby to her breast, bend her head, and whisper incoherently.

~

Liam had felt the upsurge in the wind on his rounds the night before, a determined freshening. The southerly that emerged was open and candid about its proposed escalation. Liam and Mick got up early to check on the ewes and new lambs and moved what animals they could to shelter.

"Hey there, Liam!"

Liam and Mick were in the sheep yards trying to lamb a distressed ewe when Sean O'Hennessey rode up. They turned—wet, muddy, and tired—towards his voice.

"Frank told me Rose was hurt?" Sean looked worried. He dismounted and held out a hand to Liam, "My condolences for your loss."

Liam looked down at his own hand, with its coating of bloody mucous. "I..."

"Oh, never mind..." Sean waved at Liam's hand, "I need to see Rose."

There was something in Sean's voice that alarmed him, something he couldn't name or maybe was afraid to.

"She's not up to visitors; I'm sorry."

"What do you mean?"

"She's in bed, can't talk, very ill."

"I'll just sit by her bed. I'll do the talking; maybe hold her hand." Sean's voice was yearning and hopeful.

The idea of Sean holding Rose's hand did not sit well with Liam. He turned to Mick. "Let's get this finished."

The lamb's head came out, its tongue swollen and bluish.

"Might still be alive." Mick circled the neck with his hand and then arched his fingers and then his hand into the opening, circling in deeper and deeper until he had the shoulder. He strained to wrench it out. Liam pushed on the ewe's bulging wool coat from the outside. The ewe moaned in pain, the sound surprisingly humanlike. The lamb loosened and was born; it flopped lifeless to the ground.

Mick's hand disappeared back into the warm. "There's another one." Mick pulled, his elbow moving in and out a few times as he tried to get a hold. "Here it comes."

Mick pulled the tiny lamb from its mother and quickly wiped the thin mucous tissue from its nose and mouth. "Come on, little fella," he said gently. The lamb snorted and coughed. His mother turned her head and called, interested and concerned. She tried to stand and faltered. Mick pulled the lamb in an arc around to the ewe's face and she licked it vigorously, her body still heaving from the effort of giving birth.

"They should be all right. We'll leave them in the stables tonight, though," Liam said as he stood—the cold, wet morning's work evident in his stance.

"C'mon, then." He motioned to Sean, "We'll clean up, then go and see if Rose is awake."

~

"Oh, Rosie, Rosie-girl, my Rosie-girl," Sean rushed to Rose's side. With one hand he began caressing her, a gentle sweeping movement from her forehead to her chin. "Oh, Rosie," he said in a broken voice. Then he knelt, gathering up her hand, enclosing it in his own, and he started praying.

My God, what on earth? Liam's tired mind was reeling, *When did this… When did she…did they…?* Liam sat down heavily in the chair on the opposite side of the bed and watched in stunned fascination as Sean gently kissed Rose's finger tips one by one and murmured, "Rosie, my Rosie-girl," completely oblivious to anything else.

Liam's bewilderment quickly gave way to a simmering and confused anger. What could he say? What could he do? He clenched his fists and watched Sean's uninhibited adoration. His wife was dead. Lily was dead. Gone. This was her sister laying before him now. Rose. Rose, who was not his, was not married. Rose, who could never be a replacement for Lily. He had promised himself that. Rose herself had said it could never be.

He chewed the inside of his lip and tried to breathe more deeply. Somewhere there had to be something to grab hold of. He unconsciously reached for Rose's other hand.

Her head turned towards his almost imperceptibly, awakening to his touch. "Liam, Liam," she mouthed slowly, soundlessly, her eyes locked on Liam's, alert and clear. "My love, my love," she croaked, just audibly, and swallowed, dryly and painfully, then closed her eyes again.

Liam started to say, "I'll get you wa…" but was interrupted.

"Did you hear that?" Sean said excitedly. "She spoke to me! She spoke!"

"Sean, she…" Liam didn't know what to tell him, how to explain the mystery of Rose, of LilyRose. There was so much he didn't know himself. Had there been some magical occurrence, some mysterious merging that he needed to believe in? And what if there hadn't, and Rose was still only Rose? Ah, there… She was never only Rose, was she? No, she was always more. He held her hand tighter, watching and thinking. His children needed a mother. If he and Rose could… It would be like giving them Lily again. Lily to love them. His thoughts ran fluid and flooding through the chaotic debris, but snagged. Lily. Lily.

In the ruin was Lily.

The memory of Lily.

He knew he couldn't ascend out of the mire and leave her there.

He gently set Rose's hand back down on the bed and left her with Sean.

He stood at the door to the kitchen. His hand rubbed his eye, and then both hands went behind his head as he stretched and sighed.

"Ah, Liam, come sit." Mick pulled a chair out from the table and motioned to the tea cup, "Have some?"

Liam nodded on the way to the table and sat, seemingly burdened by a tremendous weight.

"She went to dinner with him once," Mick offered.

Liam didn't say anything.

"It was that night a couple months ago when we were stuck in town, bad southerly, remember?"

Liam nodded and reached for the tea.

"They went to the pub; I stayed at the boarding house. Mrs Rouse made a lovely beef roast. I don't know where she got the beans, tasted almost fresh..."

"Mick," Liam interrupted him.

Mick smiled and shrugged, "They must have talked. Did you know he proposed to her on the ship?"

"Heard."

"Well, actually he asked Lily first, accidentally. Thought she was Rose." Both Liam and Mick were quiet a moment, then Mick started to chuckle. He desperately tried to contain himself. It wasn't a laughing matter, or was it? Liam's shoulders shook, and then he gave way and smiled.

"Lily had to kick him in the shins to get him to stop kissing her," Mick's chuckle turned to laughter. "And then Rose came upon them, and well, she must have let him have it. He stalked around for days afterwards, glaring at the both of them, like this." Mick impersonated Sean's angry glare.

The lighthearted moment was oddly merciful; it somehow released them both from their sad tension, gathered up goodness in a pile, and plopped them on top of it. For the first time since Lily had died, Liam felt all right about his vantage point. There was the tiniest sense of lightness.

It might be possible to manoeuvre.

"We need to keep Sean away from her, until she's herself again."

Mick looked at Liam with mock incredulity on his face, "Which is?"

Liam shrugged and smiled wryly. "Well," he held up both hands and comically raised one and then the other as if weighing the possibilities. He shook his head while Mick laughed again, tears welling in his eyes. "The thing is... I think, well..." Liam was still smiling, but thought there was something important to point out. "Do you remember, Mick, the last time Rose hurt her head and she thought she was Lily? We had to convince her she was Rose."

Mick nodded, wiping his eyes.

"Well, we can't have Sean in there telling her who she is, you know, trying to convince her, because, you know…" Liam faltered.

"Something happened, Liam. I know Lily isn't gone, not all of her."

"Well, we won't know that until Rose can tell us, will we?"

"No, we won't."

"Tell you what?" Sean appeared at the kitchen doorway.

Liam wondered how much Sean had heard.

"How was she?" Mick interjected quickly.

"She didn't speak again."

"She's not well at all. It's much worse than last time," Liam said solemnly.

"Last time?"

"She was whacked on the head pretty hard by Henry Lichfield. Took ages to come right." Mick took a sip of his cold tea.

"Oh, I remember. Well, I… How long was she like this last time?"

"Months." Mick plonked his tea cup down on the table as if to accentuate the word.

"Months?"

Liam and Mick both nodded.

Wailing started in the parlour, then intensified. Sally called out, "Mick, can you warm the bottles?" She came in through the door with a baby in her arms.

Mick stood up to see to the bottles, and Liam held out his arms for his child. "There, there now, Will." He held the baby out from him and looked at his face. "Lunch will be here presently." William snuffled and looked back at his father with bright eyes.

"He understands?" Sean leaned in towards the baby.

"Oh, maybe. Might just be the sound of my voice." Liam smiled and moved the baby to his shoulder. William seemed to snuggle in, happy to wait.

Sally returned with Caitlin.

"I'll take her." Mick held out his arms.

"Oh, and don't I know you will." Sally gave him the tiny bundle.

"She likes me, I think."

"Of course she does! You helped rescue her." Liam shifted William's weight and moved slightly in the chair as he spoke.

"Rescued her?" Sean mind was whirling with questions regarding Lily's children, now so obviously motherless, and Rose. Would Rose ever leave them?

"Aye, but it's a long story, and one I may never feel like telling." Liam reached out as Sally handed him the milk. He deftly transferred William to a lying position in his arms and brought the bottle to his lips. "Here you are, Will, dinnertime." William latched onto the rubber teat and began sucking vigourously.

Sean turned to watch Mick who repeated the process with Caitlin. "You boys look like you know what you are doing."

"Didn't take us long to catch on. Mick's the one with experience," Sally piped up as she peeled potatoes. "Would you like to stay for dinner, Sean? It'll be ready within the hour."

Sean looked at Liam, "Well, I don't know. I came to talk to Rose. Had good news, but..." Sean's voice wandered off.

"What sort of news?" Liam asked, watching his son making short work of his milk.

"I...um...wanted Rosie to be the first to know, but I..."

"Come back in a month or so. She'll be better then."

"Do you think that's what I should do, Mick?" Sean looked very confused. "We had plans, Rosie and I, before... But I don't know now." Sean bent his head and made a halfhearted, almost dismissive, gesture towards the babies. Both Mick and Liam responded by tightening their holds on the bundles in their arms.

Liam spoke slowly and with some effort. "I agree with Mick. I think you should leave Rose to heal, and when you come back, she'll be able to speak for herself. The truth is, Sean, none of us knows what she wants."

"I know what she wanted." Sean raised his head to speak and looked Liam straight in the eyes, "She wanted to come to Mount Somers with me and be my wife."

Liam's whole body went tense, trying to contain his raging emotions. William, who moments before had been relaxed and sleepy in his arms, squirmed and whimpered, although his mouth remained firmly latched on to his dinner. A wave of emotion swept through Liam and, with it, a promise of liberation. At first, he welcomed it as something he deserved; all the grief-filled anxiety was about to be furiously released. He could feel his control slipping away as he tumbled, descending under the accumulation of angry confusion.

Caitlin coughed–a wracking, milk-spluttering sort of cough. "Give her to me, Mick," Liam said as he stood up and quickly handed William to Sean, who took him awkwardly. Liam clutched his daughter to his chest. His whole hand covered her little back as he patted her and cajoled her breath back to normal.

Finally he sat back down and leaned back with her curled over his shoulder. Caitlin's knees were bent under her and her head was buried in her father's neck. One of her arms curled around under his chin and rested, fist unfurled, under his ear. To Liam, it felt like she was hugging him. He closed his eyes and took deep breaths.

"We'll send a message if she improves enough to talk to you, Sean." Mick went around the table and held out his arms to take William.

"Oh, yes, right." Sean handed Mick the squirming boy then looked again at Liam. "I'll just go and say goodbye, then." Sean started for the hallway, and Liam's heartbeat quickened. Caitlin shifted slightly, and Liam felt the warmth of her tiny palm as it pressed flat against his skin.

Chapter 47

The spring storm intensified, and they awoke to an icy layer of snow covering the earth. Liam spent most of the morning reviving newborn lambs. He remembered how much Lily had loved helping him last year. He tried not to sag under the weight of thinking about her. Some of the memories surged in unannounced, unwelcome in their intensity, while others drifted in, wafting through his mind. He'd grasp for them, while they soared just out of reach, teasing him. He knew he needed to focus on saving his flock, making a go of his farm, yet, at times, his love for Lily seemed like a dream he wanted to fall back into. The memories, at least, made him feel alive. They were something to cling to.

For several weeks after Sean's visit, Liam looked in on Rose only briefly, late at night or early in the morning, and saw that she was sleeping more peacefully. He heard Sally and Mick's reports of her growing coherence, her simple sentences, and the delight she found in the babies. He asked them if she responded to 'Rose' or insisted on 'LilyRose'; they said that 'Rose' didn't seem to worry her.

There was no lessening of his slump, and there could be no healing without the acceptance that Lily was completely and irrevocably gone. And if she was, Rose might heal and go too, like she'd planned, up into the hills with Sean.

But what if some miracle had occurred, and there had been some blending or mingling, however jumbled, between his wife and her twin sister? What then?

Liam McCann would have never admitted it, not even to Mick, but he was afraid to find out.

~

Sally softened, taking care of Liam's babies. There was something so insistent in their demands of her, so pervasive. She didn't make a conscious effort to love them. It was more a case of they asked and she answered. Love materialised, emerging pure and untarnished. She was enamoured, Mick thought, besotted. He mentioned it, and she only replied, "Oh, and what about you?"

George realised he missed Sally and their quiet conversations. His trips to Fairfield to deliver Myra's cooking and to check up on Rose became more frequent. He would sit in the kitchen sipping tea with a small warm bundle on his lap and talk to Sally as she went about her duties.

"I think we should get Rose up today, bring her in here, and let her sit by the stove."

Sally looked thoughtful. "Oh, aye, George, I think that would be a good idea. She needs pushing a little, and Liam's not going to do it."

"What do you mean?"

"Oh, it's just that he misses Lily so much, and he has the babies and the lambing. He's so tired when he comes in. Some days they don't even stop for lunch."

George stood to put William, who had fallen asleep in his arms, back in the cradle. "We'll do it then."

"We?"

"We'll get her up. She'll be wanting to be a mother to these babies, Sally."

"Oh, aye, she will." George heard the dejected note in Sally's voice. He walked over to where she stood at the bench mixing dough. The spring sunlight shone through the kitchen window and onto her hands.

"Sally, Sally." His voice was gentle and understanding. His hands encircled her waist from behind. She turned quickly, at first surprised and then strangely heartened. The bowl and the wooden spoon were forgotten and her hand sought his shoulders. She could see he needed some reassurance from her, a sign that his advances were welcome.

"George, tell me what you are thinking."

"I've been missing you, Sally. I know you are needed here for now, but I had grown accustomed to your company, to our conversations… And I…"

Sally smiled a shy smile in encouragement. "Go on."

"I would like to give you a child. I would like you to have my child, maybe more than one." George's polished English voice was quick and excited. "Sally, I want a family, a real family this time, with love and respect." The surface of his countenance cracked, "And truth and honesty." His words came out with a sob, but Sally heard him clearly. "Can you love me?"

She looked him straight in the eyes. There was an unspoken discussion, and eventually, she nodded.

He bent to kiss her. First his lips touched her forehead in an almost fatherly manner, and she closed her eyes to let his love wash over her, fill her. Then she raised herself up onto her tiptoes to seek his mouth. She sought some passion from her friend, knew that was what she needed. He answered her, letting her see and feel his desire.

They stood embracing and kissing, reaching and touching. Sally's heart warmed with the heat they generated. They found there was tinder and some kindling, enough to burn. Together they gathered up the jagged, broken pieces of themselves and, like a child's puzzle, made what they could, fit. And the leftovers, the stray pieces they wanted to forget, were joyously flung into the roaring fire.

~

Liam and Mick returned for a hot meal at lunchtime and found delightful disarray. William was on George's lap, chortling. Sally was setting the table with an unusually wide and silly-looking grin. The stew was bubbling on the stove, filling the room with an aroma of what could only be described as 'home'. And there was Rose, sitting in the rocking chair, holding Caitlin on her lap. She had the baby turned towards her and Liam watched spellbound as he heard her say, "Mum, mum, mmmmm, mummy," and the baby cooed back to her.

Rose smiled at Caitlin with her wide and embracing smile, the one that could pull him in and not let him go. He felt a sharp pain in his heart as he thought of Lily. Then Rose shifted her gaze and her smile in his direction, and another thought superimposed itself, flashing through his head. It was of Rose the first time he saw her in the park. She was smiling that same smile, brilliantly, just like now, invitingly, looking only at him, just like now. Liam exhaled loudly. He didn't feel like he was walking over to her; he was gliding, pulled towards her as if he had no choice but to be at her side.

"You are up."

She nodded, still with her dazzling smile.

"Does your head still ache?" Mick asked as he took a seat at the table.

"Just a little now and then, but all and all, it's much better."

Something cumbersome and complex swirled through Liam, questions that wanted to be asked. *What do you remember? Did Lily come to you? Stay even?*

"Sally and I have news," George stated with a broad grin on his face.

Liam looked to George and Sally with detached dismay. Mick paused with the stew ladle in midair.

George took Sally's hand. Liam saw it then, before George spoke, the possessiveness that would protect and defend. "This may not really be the right time, but Sally and I have some happy news in the midst of all this sadness. We are engaged."

Even Sally was surprised and shrieked, "We are? We are?" There was a question in her voice as if she couldn't quite believe it. George let go of her hand to stand and give Mick the baby in his arms. He turned and took Sally's hand again. "Yes, Sally O'Bryan has agreed to be my wife."

"Aye, I have," answered Sally with a note of defiance that seemed to dare anyone to disagree.

"Oh, but, George?"

"Yes, Rose?"

"Isn't...aren't you...?" Rose struggled, "Aren't you already married...to Elisabeth?"

Everyone was quiet. William was asleep, and Caitlin in her uncanny way seemed to know it was a moment of truth.

George's countenance was wistful, and he sighed, "Oh, dear Rose, it is a long story. Elisabeth and I have divorced."

"Ah, well." Liam put his hand on Rose's shoulder as if to comfort her. "Let's eat, and then we'll talk, you and I." Rose looked up at him, and he swallowed. "About what you remember and what you don't." Liam's hand tightened on her shoulder, seeking something from her. She nodded and then bent to kiss the baby in her lap.

Liam chewed slowly. There was so much to face and they were all still so wounded and raw. Every now and then he would catch Rose's glance. She looked at him questioningly, concerned. He would lower his head and take another bite.

After they cleared away the meal, he finally approached her. "We'll go down the hall to your room." He took her arm and helped her up. She swayed and her hand went to her temple. "Are you all right?" His grip on her arm tightened, and she leaned into him.

"I'm a little dizzy."

His hand moved from her arm to her back, and he stooped and scooped her legs, holding her close to him. "I'll carry you, then." He walked slowly down the hall, with her arms around his neck and her weight against his chest. He didn't look down at her, and he didn't see or feel her lips against his shirt, right over his heart.

He laid her down, and she didn't let go. Her arms tightened, pulling him closer to her. She whispered, "Where have you been, where have you been?"

He was overcome. There was no other way to explain it. A fresh onslaught of sorrow and grief was tangled up in this live woman—this warm, living, breathing, speaking woman.

This woman who was not his and yet, in some strange way, was or could be, maybe.

This perfect wife, perfect mother for his children.

A second chance.

Is that how he thought of the woman clinging to him, a second chance? Is that what he wanted with her, from her? He bowed his head, shaking with emotion. He let her hold him.

Moments drifted on; he couldn't tell if they were coming or going, enveloped as he was in her arms. There was peace to be had here, a fragmented thought announced rather timidly.

He reached around her, feeling like he should be gathering her up, helping her collect all her parts. She pulled him closer to her, and he stretched out beside her on the bed. She squirmed until she fitted as close to him as she could. Her hand moved to his chest, and he felt her unbuttoning his shirt. He felt her warm breath first and then her lips. She kissed his heart, just once.

He felt it race.

Lily?

No...

Rose?

No...

Ah... ah... LilyRose.

And she kissed each beat.

Liam lay there and felt his grief rhythmically subsiding with each heartbeat, leaving clear space. He relaxed, exhausted, drifting peacefully, and knowing that the woman in his arms had the answers to his questions.

~

They were startled awake by the knock at the door. The door opened. "Almost dinnertime." Mick smiled broadly as he pulled the door shut again. Rose and Liam sat up, self-consciously untangling themselves.

Liam stood up next to the bed and stretched. Rose watched, sitting—her arms wrapped around her legs, her knees curled up to her chest.

"Do you want me to carry you to the rocker?"

She shook her head no.

"What is it? What's wrong?"

She looked at him with such an overwhelming love in her eyes that he had to sit back down on the bed. "What is it?"

When she spoke her voice was not strong. "I need you..." she hesitated, "I need you to call me by my name."

He looked at her. What made him think she was going to make it easy for him, answer all his questions? Hah! No, here she was, asking him.

"Which is?"

Tears welled in her eyes.

Liam's thoughts raced, twisting and turning and hairpinning back on themselves. She cannot be only Rose because that means Lily is truly gone, and she cannot be only Lily because where, then, is Rose? She has to be...must be...LilyRose. The building tension in his body, in the whole situation, just left. Careened off one of the tighter corners into a deep gully. He reached for her hand.

"You haven't minded that everyone is calling you 'Rose'."

"No, but you haven't been calling me anything, nothing at all."

"Ah, well, it's a very long and complicated story, and I find it all very confusing. I think... Well, I think, LilyRose, that it is time to go and eat." Liam lifted up her hand and kissed it.

The tears welling in her eyes spilled over and ran into the edges of her smile.

~

Everyone gathered around the wooden table in the kitchen. George had stayed all afternoon to help Sally with the babies while Mick attended to the sheep. Liam felt strangely refreshed. When was the last time he had slept during the day? Caitlin and William were both awake and were shuffled from one lap to another so that everyone had a chance to eat. Caitlin smiled and squealed when she was passed to Mick's outstretched arms.

"They will be three months old tomorrow," Sally commented.

Liam shook his head. Three months had passed since the children had been born and Lily had died. He looked down at the woman beside him at the table. Rose looked back at him and managed a small smile.

She looked around the room and took a breath. "I can't remember very much, but I know my sister died." Her voice was full of something, but it was not sadness or grief. "She died giving birth to these two beautiful little babies." She reached for William, took him from George, and snuggled him into her lap. "She told me, right before she went into labour, that, if this should happen and I was left here, I was to love..." she looked down at William and over at Caitlin, but could not raise her eyes to Liam—not yet, not quite yet—there was still too much unsaid between them—"...her family, twice as much, because she would not be here to do it." Rose looked around the room as if she expected some questioning. "I said no at first, but she told me I had to, because, well, because..." Rose struggled to speak. "She said she knew I would do it because if things were the other way around she'd do it for me." Rose bent and buried her face in the back of William's neck.

Liam's arm went around her without any conscious thought. He bent to her and whispered, "Is that all?"

She slumped a little but then raised her head to him. "You, of all people, must know that is not all," she whispered back, and she sounded slightly irritated.

~

"Did she tell you what happened?" Mick sat on the sofa by the fire. Liam was stretched out in the rocker, his hands behind his head.

"Not specifically, no."

"Did you ask?"

"Not specifically, no."

"Well, what happened in there?"

"We met in our minds, just for a moment. I asked if she was Rose and got back 'no' and then Lily, and again I heard 'no', and so then, of course, the only answer left is LilyRose, isn't it? And then later, after we slept, she told me that I needed to call her by her name and I said it. I called her LilyRose."

Mick sat back, readjusting the length of his growing legs. "I'm just going to ask her straight out what the hell happened. See what she says."

Liam looked thoughtfully at Mick, "I think if she really knew, she'd tell us. She's still healing, still confused."

"Ah, maybe, but…"

"You want to know?"

"Yeah, I do."

"You know already, Mick. You were there. I know too. We just want her to tell us, reassure us that what we saw and felt actually happened."

"I guess so." Mick was starting to look sleepy. "I thought the babies might wake again."

"You hoped, you mean." Liam smiled. "Off to bed with you, boy."

"Yeah, I'll be going." Mick unfolded himself and rose from the sofa, his cheeky grin finding itself at home on his face, "Seeing as I had no time for an afternoon nap."

Liam sat a while longer and watched the firelight dancing with the shadows on the ceiling. It was very late when he finally felt tired enough to sleep.

~

He smelled her first, the clean smell of soap and warm woman's skin. He nudged her over to make room and to see if she would waken.

"Oh, hello there," she said sweetly and drowsily.

"Rose, what are you doing here?"

"LilyRose, to you mister. LilyRose. Got that?" She didn't sound so sleepy. She reached for his arm and wrapped it around herself, snuggled in, and found her place, "I'll not be without you. I won't."

He let her fall asleep in his arms, relishing the warm sweet weight of her. But it was too soon. His soul was still wounded. There was a thin skin over the wound— alive and growing, he knew, but fragile and easily torn all the same. He got up, gathered her in his arms, and returned her to her bed.

Chapter 48

Liam and Rose were both very aware of the distance between them. Yet, because this space was reasonably full, there didn't seem to be any immediate need to explore it. Rose slept a lot as she struggled to regain her health. When she was awake and feeling well, the babies captured her full attention. As for Liam, the farm work piled up as the days lengthened and the grass grew.

And the grass did grow. It was a luxurious spring. Just when things looked to be getting a little dry, a southerly would sweep through, usually at night, leaving a trail of moisture in its wake. The sun would shine again by midmorning, creating a humid fecundity. The land felt rich—rich with promise. Liam took it at its word. He worked up more land, planting more wheat and another paddock of oats. He enlarged the vegetable garden. His farmer's heart knew that bounty could only be bestowed on those who made ready.

Rose mended little by little, day by day. There was still something quiet and sad that she couldn't push away or quite get on top of. It leaned on her, occasionally tried to surround and smother her. She kept fighting for air. She spent a lot of time with one of the children on her lap and the other close by. She would tell them stories, and they gurgled and smiled at the sound of her voice. Eventually her thoughts would turn to her sister, her twin. All her memories of their childhood seemed to be anchored in the smiling face that used to look back at her, reflecting all she thought. Her face. She had thought it was hers.

She started to understand how their strange upbringing had influenced her thinking. Her sense of self had never been clearly defined. Who was she without Lily? She looked down at Caitlin in her arms. There was no choice there. No decision to be made yea or nay. From the very first moment she had laid eyes on them, she had loved these babies. Ah, but even before that. She closed her eyes and breathed deeply the sweet air emanating from the back of Caitlin's neck. From the moment of their conception she had loved them.

What?

The memories mingled and mixed. Liam in Akaroa by the sea. They had snuck out in the moonlight, she—nervous and shy—and he—bold and insistent. She could see and feel it all so clearly, and then it dimmed, fading from her reach. She remembered that hot day by the river and how, after that, everything was warped and cloudy except for a voice insisting she wake up. Then she remembered being in Liam's embrace.

What?

Caitlin squirmed, uncharacteristically unsettled. Rose stood up to walk with the baby, cradling her in her arms. *Who am I? What is mine?* The questions, clear and audible in her head, were disconcerting, and yet, she had no recollection of thinking them. They had appeared fully formed and determined to be answered. *Who am I? What is mine?* They came again, tenacious and purposeful.

She kissed Caitlin's forehead, and the baby snuggled closer.

~

After Sally returned to Avonlea, Mick and Liam took turns doing household chores and watching the babies while Rose rested.

"I need you to tell me some things, Mick." Rose was sitting in a wicker chair on the front lawn in the sun. William and Caitlin were both lying on a blanket at her feet.

"Like what?" Mick looked at her quizzically and then sat down on the blanket. He made faces at William, who had caught his eye.

"Well, it has occurred to me," Rose began earnestly, and Mick turned to look at her, "that I am somewhat confused."

Mick's chuckle started low and then let loose. Caitlin and William kicked and chortled.

"I don't know what is so funny about that."

"Ah, Rosie, Rosie, you've always been confused," he managed through his mirth.

"Mick, stop laughing at me," Rose said with a smile.

"All right, all right! What do you want me to tell you?"

"Well, the thing is... I think it would help me if I figured out..." she paused, then began again, "Out of all my memories, I think I need to know which ones are mine and which ones are Lily's...were Lily's." Rose slumped a little, as if the admission had cost her more than she had bargained for.

Mick sat up and took her hand. "Where do you want to start?"

"Well, it all confuses me; I don't really know what's what. Lily always told me things, in our minds, and then I saw and felt what she saw and felt. And, well, it's all mixed up in my head now."

"But if you always did that, how would you know now? I mean, now that she's gone?"

"That's it, you see, it's all so tangled up." Rose detached her hand from his and reached up and rubbed her temple. "I need to know who I am, and what I think."

Mick leaned back on the blanket and pulled Caitlin to him. He dangled his hand over hers and she reached and grabbed at his fingers. "All right then, tell me about growing up with Lily and your grandmother. Tell me what it was like from your point of view."

Rose sat back in the chair and gazed up at the sky. Mick looked at her and thought the memories probably weren't all that good.

"Go on, then."

Rose, still looking up at the clouds, began to speak. "All and all, it was...difficult." She looked at Mick as if waiting for something.

"Don't judge it. It doesn't matter if you think it was good or bad, or difficult or easy. Just tell me what it was like. Tell me your earliest memories. Can you remember your parents at all?"

"Not my mother, you know she died giving birth." The pause was long and painful. "Just like Lily did, but my father..." Rose's voice rushed onward as if to outrun the grief, "My father used to come visit us, now and then."

"I can remember one time, when we saw him coming to the house, my sister ran ahead of me. I watched her being swung up into the air by this giant of a man who we really didn't know. He was kind, though, very kind to us. He worked very hard cutting firewood and stocking up all our supplies, and he left money for us. Anyway, I watched as he spun her around. They twirled and dipped, dancing on the path in front of our cottage. I felt her joy, but I wanted it to be me. It was such a strange notion; I think it was the first time I thought of myself as someone separate from her. I used to wish he would stay, but he always left again, and Nana Kat would say, 'The only thing he loved more than the sea was your mother'."

Mick pulled William by the foot over to him and tickled his midriff until he giggled. "Go on."

"So I always wondered what the sea was like, and the power it had to pull him away from us." Rose was quiet for a few moments. "When we first thought about leaving Creggan, it was me who wanted to go somewhere very far away. It didn't really matter where, I just wanted to go by sea."

"So that you…?"

"I wanted to see what the mystery was."

"And did you?"

"Well, you were there." She smiled at Mick. "I liked the adventure." He smiled back and nodded.

"I felt brave setting out like that, by ourselves. I think it was easier, though, knowing that it was what our father did. He took voyage after voyage, didn't he?"

Mick nodded.

"I wonder though, now. I don't think he could have loved it more than he loved Lily and me. I think maybe he did it because he couldn't face life without my mother." Rose sat up quickly and looked straight at Mick. "He was afraid. He was afraid, Mick! That is what it was. Once I fell asleep in his lap, and I woke up and he was looking at me with the saddest, most sorrow-filled look. Well, I didn't know what it was, then, but it was longing. He wanted to stay there and love us, but he was afraid to."

Mick nodded as if she'd made a point, but there were still things to resolve.

"I wonder what he was so afraid of?" Rose said thoughtfully.

"Ah, well, there are mysteries, all that goes on between you and Lily."

"You think that could have scared him?"

"Scared me at first. Well, I wasn't so much scared, I guess, as intrigued."

"Tell me what you thought when you first met us."

"Not yet. Finish with your father first."

Rose looked down at the babies, both dozing now in the shade of the house. She looked pensive, "I want to think that he didn't love the sea more than us, like Nana Kat said. I think that, without my mother, it was just easier for him to go away and leave us there." Rose smiled tentatively. "He may have even thought my mother might have wished it, you know, so that Nana Kat could teach us things."

They sat quietly.

"I don't think he ever knew that Nana Kat was losing her mind."

Rose tipped her head onto the back of the chair and closed her eyes.

"When I first met you and Lily, I kept staring at you, trying to work out which was which. I'd never seen anything like you two, people who were exactly the same. Then I felt...whatever it is that runs between you. Sometimes it would feel like just before a storm, and I could feel there was about to be lightning, as if Lily were the sky and you were the earth."

"Always?" Rose raised her head to look at Mick.

"What?"

"Was I always the earth?"

Mick had to think. "Yes, you were. Everything came down to you, Rose."

Liam strode towards them. Rose glanced up at him but didn't smile.

"You all look very...well, settled."

"Mick's helping me. I'm trying to figure things out."

"What things?" Liam asked, although he thought he probably knew.

Rose motioned for Liam to sit down and waited until he did. "I decided that I needed to figure myself out."

Liam smiled and nodded.

"Don't you dare laugh! I've already had to put up with Mick's amusement at the idea." She waited for his smile to fade. "My memories and Lily's are all so strangely blended together, and it bothers me, Liam."

"It didn't before; you used to like it."

"Well, then I knew, didn't I?"

"Knew what?"

"That she was Lily and I was Rose."

They were all quiet, watching Caitlin, who was asleep on her back. She turned herself over and tucked her knees under her chest, so that her little bottom was perched in the air. Then she stuck her thumb in her mouth.

"That's the first time she's ever done that," Rose murmured.

"She sucks her thumb all the time," Mick stated as he stretched.

"But she's never turned over by herself." Liam's hand went to Caitlin's back and her eyes opened for an instant.

"Tell me about the birthmarks," Liam asked Rose.

"What?"

"Well, Lily told me her version. You tell me yours." Liam caught her gaze and held it in his own.

Rose looked slightly worried. "Well, all right, then."

"Nana Kat always called us 'LilyRose' together, just like that, and we came or went or did whatever it was she told us to do."

"She didn't ever have one of you do one thing and the other another?"

"Not that I can remember."

"I think, at first, it was 'Lily and Rose', but as her memory got worse, it just became 'LilyRose'." Rose paused. "For a while, at the end, we had no name, no name at all." Tears began to gather in Rose's eyes. Liam took his hand off Caitlin's back and shifted himself so that with his other hand he could reach for Rose's hand.

"But when we were, oh, I'm not sure, about seven or eight maybe, my mother's friend, Annie, started coming over to teach us to read. Apparently my mother had taught her. Well, she wanted to know who was Lily and who was Rose."

"And you really didn't know?" Mick asked.

"No, we didn't." Rose took a weary breath.

"This is tiring you." Liam's hand tightened over hers. She nodded but went on.

"We talked about it, but we both wanted to be Lily. We both actually thought we were." Rose was deep in thought. "No, that isn't right. What we thought was that we were LilyRose, together we were LilyRose. It was only when Annie insisted one of us needed to be 'Lily' and one 'Rose' that we thought about ourselves as different people, each needing a separate name."

Liam and Mick looked at Rose first and then at each other.

Liam said quietly, "Ah, it goes so deep."

Rose nodded, thankful for his understanding. She went on, "Once we got around the idea that one of us needed to be one name and one the other, then we disagreed. I'm not sure why. Maybe it was just that 'Lily' came first in 'LilyRose', and it seemed to both of us that was more our name than anything else. I'm not sure. Then one night we were getting ready for bed, and Lily said, 'Look at you! There is a rosebud on your back. That's it—a sign. You are meant to be Rose'. I didn't speak, and she carried on all excited, 'You see, Rose', calling me for the first time by a name of my own, and I just…" Rose shrugged, "I decided to go along with her theory."

"Even though she had the exact same mark on her back," Liam said in a quiet, gentle voice.

Rose's head nodded, and she tightened her grip on Liam's hand. She raised her eyes to his. "Well, I guess I thought it had to be decided, and that since we truly did not know..." Rose shook her head, "No one really knew. I thought her idea would work. She looked at my birthmark and knew I was Rose, and when I saw her birthmark, I knew I was Rose."

"Was it hard, keeping track?" Mick stretched again.

"Yes, because, for days, there would be no need of names, and we'd slip back into our old thinking."

Liam tugged Rose from the rocker towards him. She curled in front of him on the blanket and he stroked her shoulder. "Before this, before Annie asked you to decide, what did you call your sister? When you wanted her attention, what did you say?"

Rose was quiet for so long that both Liam and Mick thought she might have fallen asleep.

"Nothing," came her voice, the voice that could be Lily or could be Rose. "There was no need for names. Back then, we didn't even need to be touching to share our thoughts."

"Ah, Rose," Liam said, feeling her aching sadness.

"She would turn when I thought of her, when I needed her, when she needed me." Rose's tears came and her voice trembled. "There was no beginning and no end to us."

Mick sat up quickly, "How did she not know about her own birthmark then?"

"Oh, she saw the birthmark very clearly on my back. When she saw her birthmark in my mind, she thought it was her thought and my birthmark. The birthmarks didn't look any different, Mick."

"Yes, but didn't she sense you weren't being entirely truthful?"

"Yes, I think she did, but at the same time, we were trying to call each other by different names and separate. We were trying to separate ourselves. We had to make some effort to think a little differently." Rose wiped her tears. "Something had to be different, and so much was going on. Nana Kat's mind took a turn for the worse around then." Rose's tears turned into sobs. "And our father stopped coming."

Liam's arms went around her. He scooped her up and stood. "Enough for now, enough for now."

"But your father..." Mick had to ask, "What did he call you when he came? He must have wanted to know who was who?"

But Liam was striding towards the house, and Mick's questioning voice woke Caitlin. He picked her up. "Now, now, sweet girl," he said, and she snuggled into his chest and fell back to sleep.

Chapter 49

At first I huddled like an orphan in the dark. I slept, unaware of any dreaming. I waited, but I didn't know what I was waiting for. I thought I might hear a familiar voice that would cajole me from my tiny space, invite me to stretch out and make myself at home. But nothing came, no voices at all. There was a glimpse once; I'm sure I saw some loving eyes, familiar, loving eyes. I tried to speak out then, but I couldn't hear the sound of my own voice. I waited like that, huddled and quiet, a long time. Eventually I got up the nerve to set out.

I wandered.

I had no sense of any place I needed to go or be. There were rifts, steep inclines to be scaled, and deep, deep ravines to be explored. There was nothing flat or calm or easy. Everything made my heart beat faster. I seemed to be always gasping for breath. Beautiful, exquisitely intricate patterns and designs were on all the hills in front of me. They were colour and light and texture and shape, like some secret language that I kept thinking I should be able to understand. What is this telling me? But all I could say with words was 'it is beautiful', or some other useless adjective that did not describe it well at all. As I climbed each hill, I seemed to understand what it meant. It would match something in me and feel right, but still no words came.

And then there were the dark, deep places I went to, with their own rapture. Something sensuous called to me and eventually convinced me that it was indeed beautiful too. This I understood, but again could not explain, not with words. Once or twice I heard something, a rhythm in the silence, steady and familiar. I reached for the rhythm, but I was not fast enough, and it faded. I travelled; I know that. I travelled far, so far and so wide that I thought I would surely fade to nothing being spread so thinly. There was no hope of any consolation. How was I to gather myself in?

Chapter 50

"Rest until tea time," Liam murmured, putting Rose on her bed. He took his time as if he wanted to stay. Rose entwined her arms around his neck and looked into his face. He saw it in her eyes, her almost overwhelming urge to pull him to her and never let him go. He bent to her and kissed her forehead.

"Oh, Liam, Liam, please." She struggled in his arms towards him, seeking him.

He held her tenderly, but did not let his passion spark. "Rose, you'll figure things out. Come to me when you know, Rose. Either, or…or both, Rose. You have to know." He slowly untangled himself and left her to sleep.

Rose dreamt memories. There was a clearing and they were gathering nuts. It was late in the season, but still they found the walnuts in their slimy skins under the wet leaves. They peeled them to the shell and put them in their basket—bite-size treasures.

The men came upon them suddenly. "Oh, and what have we here?"

"Lillian Donnelly's brats?"

"No, she'd married. Quinn, his name was. Died birthing them, Lillian did."

"What a beauty she was! Pity—a pity that. All for nought. No remedies or potions strong enough to save her. You'd think they could have mustered up something, wouldn't you?" The men chuckled, leaned their traps against a tree, and sat to rest.

Rose saw it all very clearly, but her point of view kept changing. She would see from one direction in the dream and then see it all from a slightly different viewpoint. Was she even dreaming? Or just remembering?

"Ah, but look at them. For all the dirt and grime, they've their mother's good looks," one of the men said, and then he paused as if thinking. "Remember Lillian at the festivals? She'd dance with flowers in her hair."

They dared to look at the man as he spoke of their mother. She danced, did she? And with flowers in her hair? The man's words swirled through and filled them. The thought was nearly too much that this mother they had never known had expressed such joy.

"Look at them," one of the men said. "Can you tell any difference between them?"

"Oh, no, but I'm sure after a bath ye could."

"No, my Betty says no. They are exactly alike."

The girls kept searching for walnuts in the decomposing forest floor while the men spoke, as if they were not there in front of them listening to every word.

"Not easy," said one of the men, "gathering your tucker, one mouthful at a time."

"I would have liked Lillian for mine, eh?" one man said and the others turned to him. There seemed to be some consideration of this particular thought; something was being weighed up.

"Hmm, but then these girls would be yours."

The man shook his head, "Oh no. No."

"And don't forget the crazy old lady, eh, Parker? You wouldn't want an old witch for a mother-in-law, would you now?" The men laughed, and Parker didn't say anything else. They soon gathered up their belongings and crossed the clearing without having said a word to the girls.

But look! They saw it at the same time—a rabbit, skinned and ready for the pot, sitting where the man Parker had been.

What could have been hours or might have been minutes later, Rose smelled something cooking, a delicious rich smell. Ah, rabbit with stuffing, walnut stuffing, and gravy it was. She woke and, after pausing by the babies asleep in their cradle, made her way to the table.

"Ah, Rose, did you rest well?" Liam asked.

"Hmm, I dreamt or, maybe, remembered. I'm not sure."

Liam finished ladling up the mutton stew and watched Rose take a deep breath of the meaty aroma. "Pass muster?"

"What? Oh, yes! It smells delicious. Did you make it or did Mick?"

"Joint effort," Mick said, just before he popped a bite into his mouth.

"Do you know where we could get some walnut trees?" Rose questioned Liam.

"I could ask George; he has some. There might be seedlings underneath. Why?"

"Oh, I dreamt about collecting walnuts. There was a grove of them in a clearing near where we lived. I'd like to have some here, I think." Rose ate her stew slowly.

"Well, I'll see to it, Rose." Liam's thoughts raced. Had she ever before wanted something for herself, for the future? Had she ever asked him for anything? Oh, she'd asked him to distance himself from her, so Lily wouldn't think she had a replacement in waiting. She'd asked him that all right, and he'd been only too happy to oblige. But, other than that, was there anything? No, not until now and the walnut trees.

It was Mick who asked, "This dream, tell us about it?"

"Oh, Lily and I met some men in the woods, and they spoke of our mother. Nana Kat never really did. Oh, sometimes she'd say something like our hips were narrow like hers, and we'd surely meet the same fate." Rose's shoulders shook off the memory. "Or when she was having trouble remembering something important that she wanted to tell us, she'd say 'If your mother was here to teach you this, you'd know it by now'."

"What did the men say about your mother?" Liam asked.

"Well, they talked about how beautiful she was and how she danced with flowers in her hair, and one man said she should have been his."

"Ah, I see," Liam said gently.

"I like thinking of my mother dancing." Rose's look was faraway, "And that she wore flowers in her hair."

They were all quiet as they chewed.

"I like knowing that sometimes she was happy."

"So we'll plant walnut trees, and when they are big enough, we'll dance under them. Is that it, Rose?"

Rose looked at Liam like she didn't understand his question.

"Oh, no, no," she said and shook her head, looking confused. Liam's smile faded.

"I'll gather the walnuts when they fall. They make nice stuffing."

Chapter 51

Rose's memories made her feel like she was looking out the same window, but always finding a different view, another perspective. She spent hours quietly reminiscing to either Mick or Liam, or sometimes, she even told the babies her stories.

"People used to come to see our grandmother all the time, sometimes people from the village and sometimes people from far away."

"How did they know where to come?" Liam and Rose were sitting on the front veranda. The night air was warm and they'd taken chairs out from the house. They could see across the paddock of young green wheat to the road.

"Surely you knew of women who could heal? People talked, told others."

Liam nodded. "So what happened when they came?"

"Well, Nana Kat helped them. She remembered her remedies more easily than other things. She'd send us away to collect what she needed: dandelion, wild chamomile, different lichens. Sometimes it was something as simple as flax or butter. I remember one mother that came with a tiny dot of a child. Said he was refusing to grow. The woman said, 'My mother-in-law put a curse on the child the moment he was born; said he'd never be as strong as his father'. Anyway, Nana Kat gave the boy broth made from vegetables and told the woman to feed him nothing but broth and well-cooked meat for twelve months, and he would grow again."

"Did it work?"

"Oh, aye, it did. They came back in a year. The boy was bonny and almost fat-looking. But he got sick every time he ate bread or oats, and so, Nana said, 'Your mother-in-law's curse is powerful'. She gave the woman a charm to say at sunset every day to counter the mother-in-law's power, but then she told her she must keep the boy on his broth and meat until he was full grown, to be on the safe side."

"Do you believe in all of that?"

"Well, she helped the boy. He grew. I saw that with my own eyes."

"You have to wonder about the mother-in-law though. Do you think she really wished him ill?"

Rose shrugged her shoulders. "I could tell you all kinds of stories. Nana Kat could always help the old people with the achy bones. She made them knapweed tea, sometimes with willow bark. She showed them how to make it themselves and what to say while they stirred."

"What to say?"

"Oh, there was always something a person could say to make it work better, or longer. The time mattered too. Some potions could only be made on certain days of the week or just after sunrise or while the sun was setting."

"It sounds, well, complicated and very illogical."

"Well, what did your mother do when you got sick?"

Liam thought of his mother and her tender ministrations when any of her sons fell ill. "She cared for us, tucked us up in bed, and brought us hot soup and tea. Sometimes it was chamomile or willow bark tea. A couple of times I got sick in my chest and got a horrible hacking cough. She made mustard poultices then." Liam was quiet for a moment, remembering. "The mustard seemed to burn right through my skin." He rubbed his hand up his chest, until it was around his throat. "And then when I coughed, everything would come up, all loose and slimy, but I didn't care, I was so glad to be rid of it."

"Your mother was not so very different."

"She didn't say any charms."

"No, but she let you know she loved you."

"Do you think that is the same?"

Rose shrugged and rocked in her chair. "There is something in that...some power...in knowing you are loved. I think it helps a person to heal." Rose's eyes locked with Liam's. "Don't you think so?"

Liam wanted to hold her gaze, not just for the next few moments but always. Always and forever, like this, on this porch, with the two sleeping children safe inside. His thoughts raced and careened sideways into each other as he tried to keep them on track. What he truly wanted to say and what he did say were not the same things at all.

"Rose, do you think you are getting better?"

Rose was momentarily lost, left hanging by the practical tone of his voice, devoid of the emotion she saw in his eyes. Things did not match. It seemed there was a purposeful deception being carried out. She thought he was waiting for them both to heal. She thought it was just a matter of time.

When she spoke she was careful to keep her truth to herself. "My head is much better, thank you."

Liam shook his head. "I know. But I mean you. Are you better? All this…" He held his hands out to the sides, palms up, as if he were surrounded and maybe engulfed by her mystery. "Is this helping? Are you figuring out which memories are yours and which are Lily's?"

The way he said Lily's name seemed like he wanted something from Lily's memories. There was some deep longing and yearning hidden in the syllables, but not contained there. Whatever was in his voice echoed in his eyes; pain and grief vied for centre stage and sorrow was not far enough away, not long enough gone.

Rose didn't know how to answer him.

Liam kept looking at Rose sitting in the moonlight.

"You don't grieve for her," he said finally.

"Not the way you do, Liam." Rose sounded agitated.

"Why not?"

"Because… Well…" Rose put her hands on the armrests of the rocker and stood up rather abruptly. "I want to yell at you very loudly, Liam, but I won't because I'll wake the babies. But let me tell you, I could scream at you, really scream, and you know what I'd scream?" Rose was speaking in a violent hiss, her face contorted, and her eyes had turned into slits. Liam was shocked into silence as she carried on.

"I would yell at you that I don't grieve for her because she's not dead. She's not dead, Liam. But then you would want some proof, and I can't give it to you. I can't, because of course, she has to be dead. She's not here, is she? There is a grave with her name on it, and you have no wife, and the babies have no mother, and I, Liam… I have no sister." Rose pushed the rocker out of her way and stomped across the lawn. "So just leave me alone, just leave me alone from now on."

A slightly unnerved Liam stayed seated, oddly satisfied by Rose's outburst. There was something familiar in her anger. He recognised her confusion, even though he could not make any more sense out of it than he could his own.

He could see her outline leaning against the fence. He walked out to her.

"Rose."

"Don't."

"Don't what?"

"I'm tired of being mollycoddled, sick and tired of it. My sister is gone, dead and buried, isn't she, Liam?"

"Well…"

"By God, speak the truth."

"Her body is gone; she died in childbirth."

"Your wife is dead. My sister is dead." Rose sobbed as her eyes overflowed with tears. She snuffled and used her sleeve.

"My wife is dead," Liam repeated as if he still needed to convince himself.

"I am here," Rose said bravely.

"You are here, but you are not my wife."

"No, I am not Lily. I am Rose."

Everything was very quiet, and the moon went behind a cloud.

Rose had nothing left to say.

They both turned at the sound of a baby's cry, but it faded as the child settled again.

"Rose?"

"Yes?"

"I feel that there are things I should say."

"There are at that, Liam McCann, there are at that."

"Well… Well, the thing is," Liam swallowed audibly, "I am not ready to say them yet."

Rose's shoulders slumped and she wiped her eyes. She turned and started walking towards the lamplight glowing from the house. "The thing is, Liam McCann," she said softly over her shoulder, "love would heal us."

Chapter 52

I was exhausted. I was tired of wandering, although the textures and designs, the patterns of light and darkness, were all starting to feel more familiar, like an ancient wisdom that I once had access to. I still did not understand the music, the language, or the code; whatever it was supposed to be. The thought dawned on me that I could find a niche, a place in the pattern that I liked and just lie down on a nice colour. I chose lavender. I thought I would rest there completely unnoticed. I blended in very well.

At first I felt at ease. My heart finally slowed and I was no longer gasping for breath, but then I had the strange sensation that I could just disappear into the weave, into one tiny strand of whatever was making up the whole.

What did make up our whole, Rose and I?

Ah, finally, words started to come to me. Ah, sweet, sweet language. It all came surging through me and I felt.

What did I feel?

I felt wood under my hands, the top of a wooden railing, and my sleeve against my face. But why was I crying? Why was everything so dark? And the words, someone else was speaking. I tried to lean into the other world, where the words were. I wanted to hear, but couldn't. Then it all faded, and I settled again. I felt relaxed, familiar, like it was all right to let someone else do the talking. Rose could do it.

Rose, had that been Rose talking?

The patterns and colours started to vibrate, and again I felt there were things I should be able to understand but didn't or couldn't. The vibrations felt good though, invigorating.

Chapter 53

George decided that Sally deserved a proper wedding, and maybe he did too—a celebration with their friends that would mark a new beginning. He loved how she gasped at his suggestions. "Oh, George, really?" she would say when he took her to the dressmakers in Christchurch. "Oh, George, are you sure?" she asked when he showed her the guest list. "But I served them tea and scones, George, right here. They were sitting on this very sofa!" George would smile and kiss her and say between the kisses, "Tea and scones, you say, you served them tea and scones." Then he would tickle her or slip his hand under her petticoat, and she would laugh or feign modesty.

There was always a single moment when the giggles or tickles turned to passion, and they both knew it. They would look into each other's eyes and simultaneously offer up silent prayers of gratitude that they had been lucky enough to find each other.

At first George did not believe his good fortune. How could she possibly want to love him? And it was not too late, not too late for a real family.

George saw her delight in her surroundings. Sally checked on the magnolia blooms, commenting on how far they had opened and how sweet they smelt. She hand-watered the vegetable garden. Anything looking slightly wilted in the hot summer sun had her full attention. She moved the litter of barn kittens to the garden shed. "I like to watch them play," she said. She went with him to the stables, fed the horses apples or carrots, and figured out which one liked what better. She gradually accepted her role as mistress of the house, organising menus after asking Myra for advice. She would arrange flowers for the dining room and apologise for the lack of form. "The flowers don't really like holding still," she'd say. She continued some of her old chores, more artfully than before.

George would say, "No, no, Sally, we'll get another maid."

And she'd reply, "No, George, it is my privilege." Her privilege?

He watched her change, gracefully accept abundance, and yet remain so grateful, aware of all the goodness surrounding her. Wasn't it funny that it was the exact same abundance that had surrounded Elisabeth?

The exact same things.

Ah, his dear, sweet Sally! George smiled, not only did she delight in his company, she had never once asked him to take her shopping.

~

Rose didn't know what to wear to the wedding. She gathered up Lily's clothes and moved them to her room. Most of them she'd worn or seen Lily wear, but there was a satin dress she'd never seen before. It was a buttery cream colour, with a pattern on it. The design looked like watermarks on paper, swirling randomly across the fabric. She held the dress to her cheek, then ran her finger along the light purple ribbons stitched up the bodice. When had Lily worn this dress?

"Lily... Lily... LILY?"

Her cries frantically echoed throughout the house. She was desperate because, suddenly, somewhere inside her she felt that Lily might answer her. There was hope, hope that if she called loud enough and long enough...

"Rose! ROSE! What are you doing?" Liam ran in and shook her and, then, held her. "Stop it, Rose, please stop it."

"Oh! Oh, Liam! Liam? What?" They stood in Rose's bedroom with the satin dress crushed between them. "I...I... What was I doing?"

"You were calling for her, for Lily. You were hysterical for a minute there."

"I wanted a dress to wear to the wedding tomorrow." She looked at the dress still in her hands. "Can I wear this one?"

"Of course you can, Rose. Lily bought that in Akaroa, on our trip, on the last day. We came back and you were gone, and we...she got... I don't think she ever wore it, Rose." Liam let go of her and put his face into his open palms. He used his finger tips to massage his eyes.

"I'm sorry, Liam, I'm sorry."

Liam's shoulders sagged.

"I don't know what came over me, I really don't. I was looking at the dress, the way the design in the fabric loops around on itself. And the light shimmers on it, doesn't it? Then I felt the ribbons. Look how finely... See here, you can hardly see the stitches."

Liam's hand left his face; his look was quizzical.

"All right, all right. I am not explaining myself very well. My thoughts still get so confused." Rose rubbed her temple, "But I thought I heard something, like I used to when...when... I thought I heard LilyRose. Liam, I really thought I did." Rose's tears were sudden and swift. He reached out for her; he couldn't deny her comfort. She dropped the dress and her hands flew to the buttons of his shirt.

"Rose, Rose, what are you doing?"

"Quiet, just be quiet." She pressed her ear to his chest. "Ah, yes, yes," she murmured and then moved her mouth to a place on his chest. Tiny kisses, they were, and she had to hurry them to keep up with the surge that occurred when he realised what she was doing.

~

Ah Lord, what a blessing! A still summer day. George's neighbours and friends gathered on the front lawn as he watched them from the house. The sweep of the riverbed was evident behind them and even the mountains sitting in the background looked contented. He smiled when he saw Liam dressed in his best. Beautiful Rose was beside him, leaning over the baby carriage. He couldn't look at her and not think of Lily. Mick stood with his hands on the handle of the carriage, rocking it gently back and forth.

The wedding went according to plan. The travelling vicar commented that although marriage was a serious undertaking, there was joy to be found in becoming man and wife, and he was pleased to find that joy so evident in Mr George Lichfield and the new Mrs Lichfield.

Sally looked radiant in her cream satin wedding dress. At first shy when introduced to Mrs Elworthy and Mrs Langford and other neighbours, she found strength in her husband's presence and looked them straight in the eye when she extended her hand. She glowed with the look of a woman who knew she'd found her place in life and wasn't going to make any apologies for it.

After dinner and the speeches, George and Sally finally made their way to Liam, Rose, Mick and the babies. Sally picked William up out of the carriage and hugged him to her breast.

"Ah, you sweet, sweet boy," she murmured, "I've missed you."

George noticed. "Sally...my wife," he said smiling to the others, "got very attached to the babies after they were born."

"Congratulations, George!" Liam said, extending his hand. They started to shake hands, but then pulled each other in and were soon patting each other on the back in an embrace of sorts.

"Thank you, Liam, thank you."

"It does my heart good to see you so happy, George," Liam said quietly in his ear.

They separated, and George quickly wiped a hand across his eyes. "Rose, you look well."

"Oh, George, thank you. I am much better." Rose smiled.

"Rosie! Rosie-girl!" came a voice from behind them. "Do my eyes deceive me?" The voice turned into none other than Sean O'Hennessey emerging from the bushes, not exactly dressed for a wedding.

"Sean O'Hennessey!" Rose looked at him in astonishment. Liam watched as her glorious wide smile started slowly and then spread across her face as if it had no choice whatsoever. Sean reached out, looking to take her hand, but Liam stepped forward and Sean paused, cleared his throat, and let his eyes roam over Rose.

"Mr Lichfield, my apologies for interrupting your party. I called into McCann's place and found it deserted. I carried on my way to Rakaia, but seeing the people gathered on the lawn, I thought, surely, this is where they would be and I…"

"It's a wedding, Mr O'Hennessey, our wedding." George put his arm around Sally as he spoke.

"Oh, aye, I figured that out. Congratulations to you, sir," Sean held out his hand to George, "and to you, ma'am," he nodded to Sally.

"You are welcome to stay, sir. We count our friends' friends as our own," Sally offered.

"Well, thank you kindly, Mrs Lichfield. I would be most honoured." As Sean spoke his eyes went back to Rose, who was still smiling, and he thought he saw a questioning look in her eye.

"Rose, it is good to see you looking so well."

"I'm busy trying to remember the last time I saw you, Sean. I have memories of a dance and then of a pub."

"Ah, good," Sean's grin was hopeful. "You look so much better, Rose. I came to see you just after your sister died. You weren't well at all. Did no one tell you I was there?"

Rose looked at Liam and then at Mick, who chose that moment to poke something in the lawn with his foot, "No, I don't think it was mentioned… Not that I remember."

"We should move on, darling," George said to his new wife. Sally kissed the top of William's head before she handed him to Mick. Caitlin started to cry, and Rose and Liam both reached down to the buggy at the same time. Liam did not defer to Rose and picked the baby up.

"She'll be hungry," he said almost to himself. He squatted down with the baby on his shoulder and searched through the bag at his feet for their bottles.

"Rose, could you come for a walk?"

"Um, I'll help Liam feed the babies first, Sean."

"Mick and I are fine, Rose." Liam looked up for a moment and caught Rose's eye, "Go ahead. We'll be fine."

She heard it in his voice, a vague hard edge. She looked questioningly back at Liam, and he gestured with his hand for her to go. Rose turned towards Sean and they moved away.

Liam fell back onto the lawn, moving ungracefully from his squat to a seated position. He jarred Caitlin and had to shush her whimpering. Mick sat down beside him with William and watched Rose walk across the lawn with Sean.

"People are looking at us," he said under his breath.

"Oh, aye." Liam looked around. "Not used to seeing grown men feeding babies."

"Yes, there is that, I suppose."

The men were quiet as the babies drank their bottles.

"Everyone is wondering what Rose will do," Mick said quietly.

Liam turned his head towards Mick. "Everybody?"

Mick nodded. "Some people think how wonderful it is that she is here to step into her sister's shoes and be a mother for your children. Others are more judgemental; think it unseemly and that you should marry her before people start to talk."

"It sounds like they already have."

Mick smiled and nodded.

Liam saw Sean and Rose talking at the edge of the lawn. Rose was smiling at Sean, laughing, waving her hands. He saw there was something high-spirited about her, something of her old self. He watched and became restless and tense. Caitlin fretted in his arms.

"Liam, my good man, how are you?" Liam looked up and saw Frank standing in the sunlight.

"Oh, Frank, all right, I guess. Haven't seen you in a while."

"Been pretty busy, and I thought you'd be too, with the children and all. And Rose, how is she?" Frank knelt on the lawn beside Liam.

"Fine, just dandy." Liam nodded towards Sean and Rose. Frank followed his gaze. "Oh, Liam, my man." Frank shook his head, "What on earth are you waiting for?"

Liam rose and started to tuck Caitlin back into the carriage. He didn't look happy. "Mick, you watch the children, I'll just be..."

"I'll go with you," Frank interrupted. The men started across the lawn. "Liam, you look a little wound-up."

Liam turned to look at Frank. "Do I now?"

"I think you should save it. Save it for tonight, for God's sake. You'll have her to yourself, in your own house."

Liam kept walking.

"It beats me," said Frank, "why you haven't sorted this out before now. Surely you must have talked about it."

Liam stopped walking. "Frank, we've been grieving, and Rose hasn't been well. I wanted to give her time to decide what she really wants. I know she told Lily she'd take care of the children, but that doesn't mean... Well, it would be nice to know what Rose really wants. Oh, hell, I don't even know what I really want. Well... I do. I think I do. But then I feel so disloyal, and so I..."

"Liam, let's get a beer, or better yet, some of George's whisky. C'mon." Frank shepherded Liam towards the French doors that led into the billiards room.

Rose watched Liam and Frank rise and walk towards her. She hoped that Liam was coming to join them and they might get some of the afternoon tea that was being put out on the tables. She thought about kissing his heart and how it had felt so right and so... She'd felt so...full, doing that, like all of her was present, pulled together at last, content. And he'd reached for her, for just a moment, held her to him like she belonged there.

"Rosie, are you listening to me?"

"Oh, Sean, yes. Yes."

Sean took her hand and pulled her towards the shade of the garden shed. She hesitated and got a last glimpse of Liam's back, and then let Sean guide her.

Rose leaned against the rough wood and wiped her brow with her hand.

"Does your head still pain you, then?"

"No... No, not much. But I do get confused easily."

"Right then, what about your memory? Do you remember our conversation in the pub?"

Rose looked at him thoughtfully. "I do remember a very pleasant evening." She was quiet a moment and then said without thinking, "I very much liked being the centre of attention."

"What? Oh well, yes, Rosie-girl, that's just it really. I want you to be the centre of my attention. You know... Always, permanently." Sean reached out and took her hand. His words rushed out. "Do you remember? Do you remember that you said you would come with me, marry me? Do you remember, Rosie-girl?"

Rose clutched his hand as a wave of something fearful swept through her. She needed something to hang on to, anything.

"Oh." Sean pulled her closer. "You do remember."

"No, no, I..." Rose moved further along the wall and tried to disengage her hand. "I don't."

"But you did. You said to me that you would marry me, Rose, and live with me up in the foothills. You were going to come with me. Think about it, Rose. It was a cold southerly night, and we were in the pub in Rakaia and I was holding your hand. Like this," he held up their entwined hands. "You promised me. You told me how the wind bothers you, how sometimes you feel like it would sweep you away, right off the plains." Sean swung his free arm wide. "And then you said, 'But you'd keep me safe'. You wanted me to keep you safe."

Rose remembered a sweet feeling of something decided. The memory wasn't solid at first, the edges quivered, but the feeling kept spreading and it solidified. It was her memory; there was no Lily there. She had decided to go with Sean. She had said she would marry him.

She studied Sean.

Sean waited with her hand clutched to his breast.

"Aye, I think I did."

"Oh, Rosie-girl." He bent and kissed the hand he held in his, "You'll come with me, then?"

"Come with you?" Rose stood up straighter. "Oh, I..."

She looked into his eyes. Her decision hung between them. It had been a good decision, but that was then. There had been reasons to leave Lily and Liam. Did they still hold true? She searched in her mind for the answers and kept coming back to that night in the pub. *That was*

me, Rose, thinking on my own, planning my future for myself. That was me. Me.
She nodded as if trying to affirm herself in the midst of her confusion.

Sean pulled her to him. "Oh, Rose, Rose, you don't know how happy that makes me."

She let herself be held. There was comfort to be had in the warm strong arms around her. Sean kept saying 'Rose', 'Rosie-girl', and she liked how he said her name. He said it like it meant everything to him.

"I'll come for you on a Saturday, in a month."

"But I..." Just then, Sean bent his head to kiss her. His hand gently tilted her face up to his. She closed her eyes and felt his rough calluses on her smooth skin. His lips found hers, and for a moment, she melted into the offered tenderness.

~

Mick garnered smiles and nods from the wedding guests as he circled the lawn with the baby carriage. He knew exactly where Rose and Sean had disappeared to and spotted them through the bushes periodically. He tried to work out why he felt so annoyed with Rose, disgusted really. He thought of them as a family. Well, Liam and Rose and the babies were a family. He was... Well, he was their friend. He looked down at Caitlin asleep in the carriage. She was on her side facing William. She had one arm over her brother's chest, as if she were trying to gather him up for a hug.

Anyway, what was Rose doing? And where was Liam? He saw Sean bend towards her, saw Rose accept his kiss. He shook his head; obviously they weren't a family. Not like he wanted them to be.

"Rose! Rose!" he called out, pretending to look around.

Mick was calling her. Rose pulled away from Sean and looked towards the voice. He was coming to her with the carriage; he had the babies. The babies. Lily's children. Her children?

The children. Are you forgetting the children?

The voice was angry and loud in her head.

"How are the babies, Mick? Did they drink all their milk? Did you change them before they fell asleep?" Rose's voice was anxious.

"Oh, they are fine, contented. Look at them." He motioned to the pram. "Sound asleep."

"I thought... Well..." Rose stopped and took a breath. "Why were you calling me?"

"Oh, I do want you to watch them. I want to find Liam. He said he'd teach me to play billiards. I thought I'd go and see…"

Rose took the handle of the carriage. Mick looked warily at Sean and walked towards the house. Sean looked down at the sleeping babies; they looked like tiny angels or cherubs. He'd seen a postcard once with a cherub on it. He thought about telling Rose about it, but then saw how Rose was smiling down at the babies as she adjusted their blanket. He was suddenly full of questions he was afraid to ask. Finally, he spoke to Rose, and his voice sounded like he had something else, something serious to attend to. "I'll go now, Rose. I'll see you in four weeks."

~

"Mick! Mick, my boy! Where on earth have ye been?" Liam's accent was thicker than usual. Mick had found him in the billiards room.

"I've been seeing to the babies mostly," Mick said, "and watching out for Rose."

"Oh, aye." Liam looked like he might be thinking up some sort of excuse and then said, "I don't think our Rose needs much looking after." Liam bent over the table and lined up a shot.

"Well, she won't be our Rose for much longer if you keep going off and leaving her to Sean O'Hennessey, will she now?" Mick picked up a cue stick.

Liam stood up quickly and stepped towards Mick. "What do you mean by that?" Liam's voice sounded angry, and Mick looked at him, wondering just how much he should rile him up.

"The whisky's been flowing pretty freely." Frank waved his arm around the room and looked at both Mick and Liam.

"Ah, well, he had her in his clutches. He was kissing her, he was, and she didn't look to be minding. Not at all."

Liam grabbed the side of the billiards table as if he needed something to steady himself, "What did you say?"

"I told you what I saw. You heard me."

Frank put a hand on Liam's arm; Liam shrugged it off.

Liam glared at Mick.

Mick held his gaze unflinchingly.

"You'd never lie to me, would you, Mick." Liam didn't say it like a question; it was a statement.

Mick shook his head. "No, sir, I would not."

"The babies are with Rose now?"

Mick nodded, then quietly said, "Yes, they are."

Liam cleared his throat, instantly more sober. "I think we'd better go and get them; take them all home."

Mick and Frank followed Liam out the French doors to the veranda and scanned the garden for Rose. She wasn't immediately obvious. Liam strode around the lawn with his fists partially clenched, looking from left to right. They found her with the babies, on a rug, tucked in the shade of a hedge.

"Well, hello, I'd wondered where you'd got to. Frank, it's nice to see you," Rose called out cheerily. "Here, sit down."

"I was thinking we'd be leaving about now."

"Oh, Liam, whatever for? Everyone is settling in for the afternoon. There is tea and plates of cream buns." Rose gestured to the tables. "I haven't had one yet, have you?"

"No."

"Why ever would we go home now?"

Liam glanced around and then sat down close to Rose. Frank and Mick turned towards the babies, who were both on their backs on the blanket.

"What did he want from you?" Liam's voice was low, yet intense.

"What?" Rose was startled. "Oh, Sean." She bent closer to Liam and smelled the liquor on his breath. "You've had a lot to drink."

"A lot to celebrate."

"Liam McCann, you don't sound like a man who has been celebrating."

"Are you going to answer me?" His voice had that hard edge again; he sounded almost mean. "What did he want from you?"

"I don't know. He confused me. I am still having trouble remembering things. Let's go and get some afternoon tea." Rose stood.

Liam caught her hand as she stood up and she paused for a moment, but didn't turn back towards him. He let go.

"Sort it out tonight, man," Frank murmured as he watched her back.

"You said that before and she... I still can't believe she would have kissed him." Liam shook his head and made to stand up.

"Sean's gone, Liam. I saw him leaving as I came to get you." Mick propped Caitlin up and kept one hand behind her back. "Look, she can just about sit up."

Liam sat back down and reached out as the baby swooned sideways. "I think it will be a while yet."

"Oh no, she's a fast learner."

Rose came back with a tray of tea and buns. She handed a cup to Liam and sat down beside him.

Liam turned and studied Rose. What could there be without her? What was he waiting for? He thought he needed time to heal, to get over Lily, and he did. They both needed time. But what if they took their time together? There was no imagining Rose anywhere else. How could he live with the thought of her in another man's arms? How could his children be anything less than her own?

Rose looked back at him and slowed her chewing, "What are you thinking now, Liam?" she whispered.

"Oh, that I cannot bear it, Rose, to think of you in another man's arms."

Rose dropped her eyes. Shame flooded through her. She turned and put down her cup and saucer. *Oh, and there I was, there I was, leaning into Sean, accepting his kiss, plain as day. There I was.*

"What's the matter, Rose?" The sarcastic note in Liam's voice echoed his hurt.

The tears overflowed despite her best efforts. Rose wiped her hand under her eyes. "You know, I think you know."

"Well, Mick saw you, he saw you kissing him." Liam tried to speak softly, but had trouble keeping his voice down.

"Liam, maybe you should…"

"No, Frank, it's all right," Rose said. "Let's finish our tea and go home."

Liam nodded in agreement.

Chapter 54

Liam and Rose kept their distance. What was unresolved between them was swollen and seething. It was easier and safer to stay apart. There was no bridge building or discussion from opposite sides of the divide. The days came and went, and the only joy to be found was in the children.

Liam felt the baby's warm breath on his neck while his small warm body lay curled on his chest. It was William he'd plucked from the cradle by the fire tonight. He had developed a habit of relaxing in the evenings like this, the warm soft weight of his child giving him the only comfort he could find. He'd read with his book poised over the sleeping child to catch the flickering lamplight. He read because it kept him from thinking. Eventually his arms would tire, exhausted after a day of hard work, and he would set down his book and stare out the window. Tonight, there was a full moon and he could see out into the night. The night was unusually bright. He could make out the tiny gorse seedlings he'd planted in hedgerows next to the fence line. The shingle he'd hauled up from the Rakaia riverbed made the track linking his farm to the main road look like a stream in the moonlight.

Little Will stirred on his chest, nuzzling his face closer into Liam's neck. Liam, with one hand on the baby's bottom, moved in the rocking chair to make himself more comfortable.

Rose was sitting on the sofa. She looked past Liam to see the full moon out the window and realised another month had passed since Lily's death. Lost and unsettled, she still grieved for Lily. Her only anchor was knowing the babies needed her. Liam worked from dawn to dusk in an effort to farm this land of his, and she spent the days lovingly caring for Lily's babies. She knew Lily would have hated this wall of silence between them. But Liam had been determined to cling to the quiet, perhaps believing there was a possibility it could bring him peace.

Caitlin stirred, starting her small distressed sounds that signalled hunger. Rose went to retrieve the two bottles left warming in a pan on the embers of the stove in the kitchen. She handed one to Liam before she collected Caitlin from the cradle. Liam shifted William in his arms as the baby began to suck noisily. "Hungry tonight, are you, William?" Rose looked up at the sound of Liam's voice and their eyes met, held for a moment, and then a moment longer.

They both looked deeply, as if they were searching. Liam swallowed.

"Liam, please." Rose's voice was soft. Liam shook his head and looked back down at his son.

Sometimes Liam just wanted to dive into Rose. No, not dive. Dig—slowly, painlessly, gently, and yet ever so purposefully, with tiny tools and brushes, like an archaeologist.

He wanted to take Rose apart, piece by piece, until he found something, one tiny little thing, that made her different from his wife. He wanted to see the part of her that made her Rose, made her more than a replication. Something that wasn't just physical. It had to be more than that. And when he found it, he would raise his hands and possibly his voice in jubilation. He would cry out, "Here you are! Here you are!"

He thought it was only fair that, if he loved her at all, he should love her for herself.

~

It started out like an ordinary Saturday. Liam and Mick left early and headed to the top of the farm. They were going to dig out tussock for most of the day.

Rose was busy with the babies. She was a little worried about Will; he was congested, but not feverish. Rose finally lulled Will to sleep, but he wasn't well-settled. She heard a wagon coming down the drive and went to the door, expecting that Liam or Mick had returned for something.

"Rosie, Rosie-girl!" Sean called out as he jumped down from the wagon.

"Sean?"

"Rose, it's so good to see you smiling. Are you ready? Have you packed?"

Rose tried to think what it was she should be ready for and why on earth she would be packed. Her face must have shown her confusion.

"Oh, Rosie-girl, it's your head still. Your memory isn't up to scratch, not yet. Never mind!" He reached out for her and took her hand.

"You promised me at the Lichfield's. You said you'd come with me, be my wife."

"No. I..." Rose stared at her hand in Sean's, as her mind tried to dredge up any fragments of memory she could find from that day.

"You are coming to Mount Somers with me, to my farm. Well, it will be mine eventually. Ours, Rosie-girl! It will be ours."

"No, Sean, I don't think... I was confused." Rose tried to gently extract her hand from Sean's, but he wouldn't let go. She heard a sound from the babies' room and moved in that direction, pulling Sean along with her. "I have to see to the..."

All of a sudden there was a scream, a bloodcurdling wail of agony. Rose shook loose from Sean and ran into the room.

Caitlin was deep red and shrieking as Rose lunged into the cradle to pick her up. Her tiny legs came up and kicked Rose's hands and at the same time her arms came down, as if she were trying to shove Rose away. She turned towards her brother.

Everything slowed.

"Oh, William! Will!" Rose reached out, and it seemed to take her forever to get to him.

Will was turning blue and gasping for tiny breaths. He was wheezing painfully in and out, in and out—slow, shallow breaths that weren't enough, weren't enough, weren't nearly enough.

"Oh! Oh, Will, sweet boy." Rose held him close, taking deep breaths herself, trying to think clearly about what needed to be done.

"Sean, you must stoke up the stove and get water boiling. We must have steam; we need steam."

"Shall I find Liam?"

"No, he's too far away. Go! Do it now, please."

Sean left, and Rose stood there holding a barely breathing William. *Oh God! Oh Danu, mother of all, help me, help us.* She looked at Caitlin, quiet now in the cot, her eyes wide open and trained on her brother's back.

They waited for the water to boil. Then Rose held William over a cup of the steaming liquid, willing his lungs to relax and take in more precious air. At first it seemed to be working, they were sure he took a few deeper breaths. But soon he was wheezing again—rattling, barely in, barely out.

"I'll go for the doctor. There's one in Rakaia."

Rose looked at Sean. A doctor with some wisdom beyond her own was definitely needed. Yes, a doctor. "No, it will take too long. You'll have to take us there."

Rose handed the baby to Sean. "Hold him up; it seems to make it easier for him. I'll gather our things."

There was no rhyme or reason to her packing. Rose took the valise from under the bed and shoved in anything she thought they might need. She grabbed a wicker basket full of clean nappies and snuggled Caitlin into them. She found the bottles and took a large jug of milk.

All the time, her eyes never strayed far from William, willing him to breathe more deeply. She wanted to push air into him, give him her air. *Take it, take it. Breathe, child, breathe. Live, live.* All the time there was terror lurking, death threatening her with its proximity. She would not relinquish him. "No, you cannot have him," she mumbled as she reached out to Sean for the baby.

"Rose, what did you say?"

"Nothing, nothing. Please put our things in the wagon. We must hurry." She took a stone crock filled with the hot water and sat under a blanket with William all the way to Rakaia, hoping that the steam might serve some purpose. They found the doctor's rooms and, thankfully, he was there.

The doctor was kind, and Rose was relieved to see his competency. He kept up the steam treatment, but added some sort of mixture to it, and made a poultice for Will's chest. He worked calmly, but with a sense of urgency as Rose and Caitlin watched. Rose didn't know if it was hours or days later, but finally, little Will was breathing easily on his own, and she started to as well.

~

Twilight hadn't turned to darkness when Liam and Mick turned off Back Track and headed up the drive. Liam hurried the horses when he noticed there was no soft lamplight glow from the windows to welcome him.

"Rose?" he shouted as he jumped from the wagon seat, startling the tired horses. He threw the reins to Mick and shouted again, "Rose! Rose!" Liam entered the dark house. There were no candles lit, no fire in the stove, and no bubbling stew in the cast-iron pot. No Rose and no babies. He found a candle and the matches and stood in the middle of the kitchen. *She would have left a note, told me where she was going.* He started searching the table and the sideboard in a panic.

There was no note. He went into the children's bedroom. The valise was gone from under the bed. The bedclothes from the children's cradle and all their nappies were gone. Where had she taken his children? Why had she left?

Liam sank down on a chair at the kitchen table and his head slowly lowered to his hands. *Rose, Rose! Where have you gone with my children?* The house was more than just empty; it was a miserable void.

"Good God, man, where are they?" Mick burst into the kitchen.

Liam raised his head quickly, "I don't know. I don't know."

"Well, you'll never find them sitting there."

"I know." Liam rose. "She packed, Mick. The valise is gone, the children's clothing. She's gone."

"What do you mean gone? Rose wouldn't leave you, Liam. She wouldn't leave you. Where would she go?" Liam started to speak, but Mick interrupted him, stepping closer. "She wouldn't take the babies, she wouldn't! We have to find her, we…"

Liam took Mick by the shoulders and set him back. "I know, I know." A tremor ran through him, making his shoulders shake. "Mick, go and saddle the horses."

They stopped at Avonlea. No, they hadn't seen Rose, but Ronny had seen a wagon. It was the man who turned up at the wedding, the O'Hennessey fellow. Yes, that was the one. He'd passed by quickly, in a hurry going somewhere, but no sign of Rose. No, not a sign of Rose. She would have called out, waved, wouldn't she?

They followed the road to Rakaia. They would talk to Frank—he would help—and find Sean. Liam's mind was a crashing, banging cacophony of unwelcome thoughts. Visions of Henry Lichfield abducting Rose from the river stormed in, and he urged his horse into a faster gallop. *William and Caitlin gone! Not at home in their warm cradle by the fire!*

Ah, the… The what? Who should he be angry at? What had happened? Such mystery surrounded their disappearance. In his darkest moments he had questioned whether Rose would eventually leave and go with Sean to live far away in the hills. When she wasn't looking, he had studied her, watched her with Caitlin and William. She would not go; he had convinced himself. She would not leave Lily's babies without a mother. The thought had never occurred to him that she would leave and take the babies with her.

They wove their way through Rakaia. Something was going on; the main street was cluttered with wagons, gigs, and horses tied to the railings. Frank was not at the police station. Mick went to one pub and Liam the other to ask after both Frank and Sean O'Hennessey. Mick was the first to get any news. Frank had been sent for by the doctor; seems there was an urgent message to be delivered quite a way out of town. Mick headed for the doctor's rooms. Liam found Sean O'Hennessey eating dinner and having a pint in the Railway Hotel.

"Sean, what's going on?"

"Liam!"

"Do you know where Rose is? She's taken the babies." Liam's words were hurried and anxious.

"Frank just left to bring you word; knew you'd be worried sick."

"Where are they? What's happened?"

Sean looked at him. "Relax, man, everyone is fine. The babies are fine."

"Goddamn it! Tell me what you've done with them!" Liam grabbed Sean by the shirt collar.

"Whoa, hang on! I told you everyone is fine. I went to your farm. I thought Rose was coming with me. She promised me, agreed to it last month. The babies... Well, that was another matter. Let go of me and I'll tell you."

Liam slowly let go of Sean as his words sunk in. She was leaving him. Rose was going to a new life, somewhere else. He sunk into the seat across from Sean, his isolated valley of sorrow becoming an island surrounded by deep darkness, and no way out.

"...but the girl... she screamed, and Rose raced in and the boy was blue. He couldn't breathe."

"What? What?" Liam's whole demeanour changed as he stood up again.

"We brought him to town, to the doctor."

"Where? Where are they now?"

"Still over at Doc Jenkins's place. He thought they should stay the night. He's breathing easy now, your boy." Liam was out the door of the hotel before Sean's sentence ended.

The lights were low at the doctor's house when Liam rapped on the door. He heard a muffled voice and stood shifting his weight from leg to leg waiting for the door to open.

"Liam McCann, Doctor. My son was brought here earlier."

"Oh, yes. Did you not get the message? All's well, I'm pleased to report."

"I need to see him…them…both of them."

"Well, I believe they are very well-settled. The whole ordeal was exhausting. The dear baby girl didn't close her eyes to sleep once the whole day."

"I'll be quiet."

Doc Jenkins looked at the man in front of him. Anxiety seemed to be oozing out his pores—anxiety and something else, something sad and forlorn.

"Ah, well, come in, then."

He showed Liam to the room and handed him a candle. "Please don't wake them." He paused and looked Liam over. "I'm going back to bed. Show yourself out."

"Um, Doc?"

"Yes."

"Thank you."

"You're welcome, Mr McCann."

The room was still with just an occasional splutter from the banked fire. Liam smiled a little as he made his way slowly to the cradle positioned near the fire, but his heart skipped a beat when he found it empty. They were all in the big bed. There was Rose, with William snuggled in next to her. Liam watched the rise and fall of his little chest. He was breathing normally. Rose's arm was over his legs and her hand rested lightly on Caitlin's back. Caitlin was sleeping on her tummy with her knees up under her, her head turned away from William, thumb firmly in her mouth. Liam looked more closely and realised her other hand was holding her brother's.

Liam raised his sleeve and wiped his eyes. Tears of relief? They were all safe, safe and well. Tears for his family, the family he wanted, but now with Rose's decision, a family he had no hope of having. Was this to be the last image of them all together? His eyes wandered to Rose, all tousled, warm and lovely, and then darted away. No, he wouldn't look, wouldn't torment himself. He'd think of Lily instead. Lily had been his; she'd chosen him. He silently pulled a chair to the side of the bed and sat, quiet tracks of tears forming on his cheeks.

Liam woke before Rose did and stretched his chair-shaped body.

Caitlin had turned herself over; she opened her eyes and raised her arms up to him. He picked her up and carried her to the window. He opened the dark draperies a little and saw that the day was bright.

"Ah, Liam, hello there," came a sleepy voice from the bed.

"Don't act like you are glad to see me," he said without turning around. Caitlin squirmed in his arms.

"What?" Rose sat up. She still looked half-asleep, "Of course I'm glad to see you. Yesterday I... He wasn't breathing, Liam." Rose turned in the bed and lay back down with her arm around William. "He couldn't get any air in, I thought... Oh, for a little while, I thought he might die." She shuddered and tightened her hold on the sleeping baby.

Liam walked over to the bed, "Thank you for taking care of him, of both of them. I know there are other things you want to do."

"What?" Rose sat up more quickly this time, and William stirred. "Liam, what are you talking about?"

"Sean told me about your plans."

"Sean? Oh, Sean. We had a misunderstanding, Liam. But I don't know what I would have done if he hadn't been there. We owe him our thanks." William started to fuss. "Oh, he'll be hungry. He didn't have much at all yesterday."

Rose rustled for her clothes and clean nappies for the babies. "You'll have to go ask Mrs Jenkins for the milk I brought with me."

Liam laid Caitlin back on the bed and went in search of their milk. They fed and dressed the children without speaking.

"I'll take them now; Mick will help me. You can go."

"I can go?"

Liam nodded at the valise on the floor, "With Sean. I believe he is still waiting."

Rose turned pale. Suddenly her heart felt too heavy, and she had to reach for the bedstead to hold herself up. "Do you want me to go, Liam?" she barely managed.

"You've made it clear."

"What exactly have I made clear?" Rose took a few deep breaths. A moment of confusion showed in her eyes. Then she threw her shoulders back and let go of the bed. Where was the strength coming from? When her voice came, it was strong and determined. "If you think for one moment that I would leave these children, well..." She paused, staring at him, and then her voice changed. "You don't really know me at all, do you?" She shook her head and started putting their belongings in the valise.

"Were you planning to take the babies with you?"

"No, I was... Is that what you thought of me?" She choked on her words, but turned to face him, and when she found her voice, it was venomous. "You think that I would run off with another man and take your children with me?" Both babies started crying.

"Sean told me he was coming to collect you, Rose." Liam's voice was cold.

"So Sean told you I was going to run off with him, and you believed him. And I was going to take the children with me, was I? Steal them away from you. And this is something you want to believe to be true?" Rose stamped her foot and continued yelling, "I have asked you in a hundred different ways if you want me, Liam."

Liam tried to quiet Caitlin. His thoughts were dark and ugly. God, he hated Sean O'Hennessey. And Rose, how could she think of taking the babies, the only thing he had left of Lily. Lily, oh God, Lily. Lily was truly gone, wasn't she?

"And still, still, you have no answer for me? Fine then, fine." Rose tossed her hair over her shoulder. "So is that it? Do you want me to leave? Will you banish me, then? Tell me. I'll go if you want me to. Do you think it will be easier for you without me, raising the children on your own?"

Liam heard everything she said, and the words slid into his wounds like vinegar on a sore, itching and burning at his already confused and angry thoughts. Lily was gone. Lily was gone, but she would have wanted Rose here, with the children, with him. Oh God, Lily was really gone.

Liam wrapped Caitlin in a blanket. Rose threw more of their belongings into the valise and, then, viciously punched them in.

There was a loud rap at the door and then it opened.

"You had a very sick baby yesterday and this carrying on will not be doing him any good at all." The doctor glared at them from the doorway. Mick stood behind him.

"We'll go now. My apologies, sir." Liam nodded to Mick.

"I am not the one you should be apologising to." The doctor looked at Rose, who was lifting William into her arms. Liam lowered his head.

There were practical considerations to deal with. They had to get the babies home, and they didn't have the wagon in town. Mick went to the livery stables to hire one, but Sean turned up and offered to take them home. Rose accepted before Liam could get a word in edgewise.

"That would be lovely, Sean," she said and looked over at Liam. "We can chat on the way. I believe there are things we need to sort out between us."

Liam and Mick rode slowly behind, in silence.

"Sean, I am so grateful for your help yesterday. I don't know what I would have done if you hadn't turned up when you did."

"Well, I'd said I'd come, Rose."

"I know that now, but I need to apologise about that too. I know I said I'd marry you, but that was before Lily died. I am sorry, so sorry for all the confusion I've caused you these past few weeks. I'm obviously still not thinking clearly. I'll not be going with you, Sean."

Sean reached for her hand as he breathed out a deep, sad sigh. "I figured as much Rosie-girl."

"You did?"

"After yesterday, watching you. You couldn't ever leave Lily's children. You are their mother now."

Rose squeezed his hand. "Aye, I am."

"And… Well, you know I'd take them if they were orphans, but they have a father." He turned back to see Liam and Mick riding close behind. "Two even."

"Oh, Sean, I…"

"You don't need to say anything else, Rosie-girl. I should have known when I accidentally asked Lily to marry me that you two were nothing but trouble." Sean's smile was wry.

Rose smiled and chuckled. She kept his hand in hers and bent her head close to him. "Thank you, Sean, thank you."

The minute the wagon pulled to a stop, Liam was all business. He removed the babies from the wagon, one at a time, and took them into the house. He gathered up the valise and the wicker basket and dumped their contents in a pile on the floor.

"Whatever are you doing, Liam?" Rose asked as she entered the kitchen.

Liam had begun to put the clothing into piles. "Sorting out your things."

"Because?"

"It will be easier for you to pack."

"I'm not going with Sean."

"I saw you all cosy, making your plans."

"Liam, stop. Look at me."

"You can go now. Take whatever you need. I don't care. Just go."

Rose walked over to him and reached out her hands to cup the sides of his face. He baulked, pulling away. "No, look! Look at me. I will not leave my children. I will not go." Her voice was different, angry and determined.

Liam stared at her, his voice dull and lifeless, "That's exactly what Lily said; then she went."

Rose shook her head—no, no.

"Sean's leaving now." Mick burst into the kitchen, "He wants to say goodbye, Rose."

"Oh." Rose moved slowly as if there were more to gather up than she could possibly manage. She made it out to the wagon and found her manners in the mess that was her mind.

"Thank you again for yesterday, Sean. I don't know what I would have done without you."

"Oh, glad to be of help, Rosie. I'm leaving now though; don't expect I'll be coming this way much." He shrugged his shoulders.

Rose reached for him; they embraced. A long last embrace and she kissed him.

"Farewell, Sean."

Rose made her way back to Liam. "Come with me, now, to the river." She held out her hand.

He stood, but didn't take her hand. "Why do you keep kissing that man if you've no intention of…?"

"Liam, let's go."

"No, I've chores to see to."

"After the chores."

Mick stood behind Rose. "I'll see to the babies."

Liam looked at both of them and slowly nodded.

Chapter 55

"You are walking awfully fast," Liam said after he followed Rose out the door.

Rose stopped and turned. "I wanted to get away from the babies so I could raise my voice."

"Ah, it's to be like that, is it?"

Rose shook her head. "I don't want it to be, and it doesn't seem like it should have to be, but I... Well, I just don't know." Liam started towards her. "No, don't touch me, I don't want you to touch me," she said as she gulped in air. "Let's go to the riverbed. Let's walk for a while."

So they walked in the still afternoon silence towards the water. Liam felt something in her calling out to him, and he kept feeling like he wanted to reach for her hand. If he could just touch her, maybe he could still his swirling thoughts and think about what he should say. There was so much that he needed to tell her.

"So," Rose finally said, as they neared the river's edge, "you've said several times that you can't bear the thought of me in another man's arms."

"No, I can't."

Rose stopped walking and faced him, her back to the river. She swallowed several times before she spoke, "Well, then, does that make you think... Does it, Liam? About where I am supposed to be?"

What? What? He'd been watching the sunlight glint off her hair. He shook his head, as if to wake himself up.

"No? Well, I can't see how it can be that you can't bear to think of me in another man's arms, but then again, you don't particularly want me in yours. How am I supposed to stay and take care of the children?"

She put her hands on her hips and stamped a foot. "You know I'd never leave them. And so... I am supposed to live with you in your home and take care of the babies and do the washing and the cooking and be what... the housekeeper? The nanny? Is that what you want me for, Liam?"

Liam opened his mouth to speak, but Rose carried on.

"You never did ever really want me here, did you, Liam? Lily and I confused you so terribly. Oh, I know you tried. You tried to love and accept me because Lily wanted you to and it made her happy, but it never made you happy, did it?" Rose paused and took a breath. "You felt guilty and torn because I wasn't your wife, and the love you had for me wasn't that different from the love you had for Lily. But I can tell you this, Liam, you were never disloyal to Lily. You were never unfaithful. You never loved me for myself, Liam. You just thought of me as more Lily, which, in a way, I was." Rose stopped speaking again and, trying not to feel defeated, looked Liam over. He was silent.

"I think I see." Rose wiped away tears. "You can't want me, really want me, because it would mean that you love me, Rose Quinn. You can't ask me to marry you, because you would feel disloyal to Lily. Does loving me now, just me, make you feel like you were disloyal when Lily was alive? Is that it? Is that how you feel?"

Liam stood there in the early evening light, watching a tortured Rose bare her soul, as she tried to strip his.

"What about you?" he finally said. "How did you feel then? You never said, not one word. Were you happy, Rose... Then?"

She sniffled and shook her head 'no'. She straightened her spine and wiped her eyes. "I was happier than I'd been in a long time. To be with Lily again was something, and you..."

"And me... What about me?" Rose heard the note of yearning in his voice.

"I wanted... I wanted you." She stared at Liam, her voice full of emotion. "What I really wanted was to have you all to myself."

Liam reached for her hand, and she let him take it. He led her to a large rock and they sat.

Liam started to speak and then stopped.

Rose waited.

Liam cleared his throat and turned towards Rose. He didn't speak until she met his gaze. "The truth is I really only wanted one of you. It was easy for me because Lily was my wife, but you... You were different, Rose. You are different. You are not your sister."

~

297

I heard those words. He said to Rose, 'You are not your sister'.

It broke free and then it flew.

I cannot tell you exactly what 'it' was, but 'it' had held me a prisoner of sorts—for a long, long time. I had been wandering, waiting for someone to give me the answers. Then I grew tired and lay down. I'd chosen a stripe in the pattern where I thought I could fit, be what I needed to be, a martyr of sorts. I rested and dreamt, heard the rhythm, and recognised Liam's heartbeat. But then Rose thought about leaving the children and I awoke. It crossed her mind and I saw it. Maybe it was only the challenge that she asked herself—could she do it?—that I heard.

I woke up a warrior, willing to fight for what was mine.

But I saw no road to travel down—no destination I could head to without her, without Rose. There was no horse to ride, no fine carriage, nothing to take me where I needed to go. I was not a magician. But then the words came, because he finally saw Rose as herself. He said to her, 'You are not your sister'. He acknowledged her.

Ah, I could speak. Now I knew I could speak. Liam had seen me and loved me. He had seen LilyRose and understood, and now—now—he sees Rose.

He sees everything there is to see.

And that was how the freedom came, swept through me—me.

Rose, Rose, I am here.

LilyRose?

Lily. It's just Lily.

LilyRose.

~

"Rose?" Liam saw the emotion flood her face when he said her name. He reached for her hand and bent to her; her eyes went unfocused, glazed over.

"Lily?" she questioned out loud.

Yes, I am here.

"Lily, are you really there?" Rose sat up straighter and her voice went from dreamy to strong.

"Rose, what are you doing?" Liam questioned, his eyes wide.

"Lily, talk to me. Oh, LilyRose, are you there?"

I am here, but you must calm down. Take a deep breath. I am here.

"Where have you been all this time? Where have you been?"

Liam fell to his knees. "For God's sake, for my sake, for the children, please don't do this, Rose. Just stop. Stop it, please."

Rose?

Yes, Lily.

There you go. That's it. You don't need to speak out loud.

I'm upsetting Liam.

Yes, you are.

I'll take his hands.

Please do. Take his hands, Rose, and pull him to you.

Us, Lily, I'll pull him to us.

~

Liam let Rose pull him towards her, wondering all the time… Why? Why? His thoughts were not clear. They were a tangled, wretched mess. A great gaping hole still remained where his wife had been and climbing out was slippery and unsure.

It was like burning stubble. There was a roaring blaze, but it eventually reached its peak and died down, and what was left? The area he'd so carefully burnt was all bare, desolate, and smoking.

He was tired of trying to keep it all contained. What had Lily told him once about loving? 'I love her and she loves me back'. Could it possibly be that simple? 'She accepts all the love I give her and then returns it'. Lily had been talking about her sister; she had been talking about Rose. 'That's the only love I've ever really known'.

Liam raised his head; Rose looked deep in thought.

He cannot hear us.

No, we aren't strong enough.

Comfort him, Rose.

Chapter 56

Rose tightened her arms around Liam, and I felt her shiver, as her hands crept up his forearms towards his shoulders. I felt the warmth.

I felt myself coming alive.

"Ah, Lily," she murmured, welcoming me home.

Liam jumped, "What did you say, Rose? What did you say?"

"Quiet, Liam. Just let me touch you, please."

"No, I…" Liam pulled away and he stood up, "Damn it, Rose. Goddamn it all to hell! Just let me love you. You, Rose. Goddamn it. It is you I want." Liam grabbed Rose's hand and pulled her towards him.

She fell against his chest. "Say that again. Oh, please, say that again," she said.

He was saying it again, over and over, "Rose, I want you. Marry me. Oh Rose, I want you." He kissed her.

It happened then. I… We… Rose and I… LilyRose… Both of us together, united, answered him.

Our kiss was intense and powerful, as if by joining our lips we were joining our hearts. The passionate sensations threatened to overwhelm us. Liam paused to breathe and said again, "I want you, Rose, I want you."

To answer, I smiled wide, I felt the love within me radiate out. Liam stood transfixed as he looked at me smiling before him. He searched deep into my eyes. "Ah, Rose, Lily… LilyRose?" He whispered the question, not losing eye contact.

He sensed our merging, felt our magic.

At first, all I could do was smile, the elation was so intense. I felt the joy in me expand. It stretched and lightened me, made enough room.

"Rose," I mouthed back carefully, "I am Rose."

His eyes never left mine. He nodded slowly as if he would accept that one condition.

We started walking in the direction of home, stunned I think. We were holding hands, but we didn't speak. After a minute or two, I started skipping beside him because the internal conversation between my sister and me was so lively.

Where have you been?

I could ask the same of you. I called out for you, I called.

My head, I hit my head.

I remember. I had just barely reached you.

You came. I still can't believe you came when I called.

We started reminiscing, back and forth, back and forth. We both felt the blending and the stirring. Our thoughts fused and combined as we shared our memories. She saw the chasm, the gap I had crossed to get to her, and she stopped and gasped. Liam turned, "Rose, are you all right?"

I nodded and told him, "It's all coming together. Everything, Liam, everything that we tried so hard to keep separated."

He put his arm around me and urged me up the hill, "It will be easier now," he said, "there is just one of you."

Did you hear that?

Of course... One... Of course...

I pulled free of Liam and skipped ahead. I held out my arms and closed my eyes and spun like a child. I spun and spun and everything blurred, and I felt it mixing and blending. I spun until there were no lumps or uneven places left. Everything felt smooth and flowing. Then I had to collapse to the ground and let the earth help me find my equilibrium. I sat there dizzy, but oh so happy, with my arms wrapped around my knees, my smiling face towards the heavens. I looked up at the sky and felt like I wanted to breath it all in.

Liam was leaning on a huge boulder, his arms crossed in front of him.

"Ah, Rose," he said and my name seemed to linger on his lips. "Would you like to explain that?"

"Let me see... The 'Ah', sounded happy, the 'Rose'... amused, and I think a little..." I held out my arms, "Liam, come here."

Laughing, he came and picked me up. He carried me to his boulder and sat me down facing him. I hitched up my skirts a little. I wrapped my legs around his waist and my arms around his neck. I felt like that was the only place in the world I truly belonged. I couldn't say what was there that hadn't been there before or even if something was missing that had been there once—some remnant of fear or guilt or

301

CHERYL IRWIN

even shame, maybe. I just don't know. He wanted me, oh, he wanted me. He had seen all of me, all the hills and all the shaded valleys, all the oddly duplicated nooks, and all the crannies. He'd seen me twist and take sudden turns, and still he held on.

My face was buried in his neck. I kissed his skin and tried to breathe the scent of him into the depths of my being. I arched my back and leaned away, my breasts firm and high in his face. "Ah, Liam," was really all I could say, but I said it with a desperation that echoed his own, because he started to undo my buttons and then his belt buckle. "Oh, it has been so long, so long," I moaned and writhed on the rock with my skirts around my waist. Liam came to me fast and hard.

I wasn't ready.

Oh, I was ready in my mind, in a wife-craving-her-husband and-knowing-what's-coming sort of way. I was well and truly ready. But the pain made me arch and cry out, "Stop, no! No, no!" I guess that the fusion that was my body and my mind still lacked harmony.

"Lily?" he started to ask, "Rose, what is it?"

I sat up, and when he would have pulled away, I pulled him closer into me. I squirmed and breathed deeply.

"Rose." Liam took my shoulders in his hands and made me look at him.

"Ah, you," I said.

"What made you cry out?"

"The pain... I wasn't expecting the pain."

We both looked down to where we were joined and saw the blood. Liam looked at me incredulously, but his voice was filled with anguish when he spoke.

"I'm sorry, Rose, I didn't think... I didn't think about it being your first time."

"It's all right, neither did I," I said, again pulling him to me.

He was gentler then, but I didn't really want him to be. I wanted him to take what I had given him, as if it were his right. I wanted to feel the strength of his love pulsing through me. The feminine in me wanted to belong to the masculine in him with every fibre of my being.

There were a few twinkling stars in the dimming light by the time we headed home. Ah, home. I hurried my steps. The children: William and Caitlin, our children.

Mick was all grins from the moment we walked into the house, his eyes glued to our entwined hands. "So, it looks like you two..." he started to say and then stopped and looked at me funny. "I'm feeling that strange... like before-a-lightning-storm... feeling again."

Liam looked towards the window. "No storms coming, Mick, none at all," he said grinning.

Caitlin squealed. I picked her up and she kicked her little feet, chortling with delight. I held her close and whispered, "I heard you. I heard you calling me, little Cat." William was quieter, but he looked deep into my eyes. He looked like he was remembering something, or possibly deciding whether to forgive me. We spent the rest of the evening rocking and feeding our babies. We could have put them to bed a lot earlier, but I liked the feel of them in my arms.

"So, Rose," Liam said, long after Mick had retired to his hut and we had the babies settled. "Rose," he said again, and my name lingered on his lips, and I realised he was saying it aloud just to hear it.

I tried to tell him what it was like, what had happened. He wanted to know exactly, and there was no 'exactly'. I couldn't say one 'exact' thing about any of it. I told him that on the walk up from the river I was having a conversation with myself, with LilyRose. I told him I didn't know who was speaking, but there was a voice that asked and a voice that answered.

"I do that all the time, in my own head. I ask and I answer."

"Really?"

"Yes," he said. "I carry on conversations with myself."

"Well, who is the other voice?"

He shrugged because he had no answer.

"Sometime today we just stopped caring who was who, or what was what. It just stopped mattering."

We both thought about this for a minute, then I smiled at him and felt a surge of joy. My whole body felt like it must be glistening.

He stood up, took my hand, and drew me out of the rocker. He looked like he had something to say, but thought better of it. He pulled me towards him, where I belonged.

After a few long moments, he nudged me towards the bedroom. Once we were inside, he undid the buttons at the back of my dress and nudged me again, this time away from him. I turned, curious, and saw that he was seating himself, straddled on a chair. He folded his arms across the top.

He looked at me...with...with... "Ah, Liam," I murmured as it struck me. I started to pull my dress down, "You want me to dance."

His eyes were burning, and I mean burning, into me. He nodded slowly and waited.

I slipped free of my clothes and held out my arms, and I danced for him.

I can dance.

Author's Notes

As a young woman, I moved from the United States to my husband's family farm on the Canterbury Plains in New Zealand. The original farm house was still there, although in a state of disrepair. I walked in and immediately started imagining what the lives of the people who first settled here would have been like. There were many clues to how they lived: the huge cast-iron cook stove, the butter churn, and the copper urn for heating the washing water were all in their original places. Fragments of lace curtains hung in the broken windows and wafted in the breeze over the abandoned brass bed.

I immediately knew there was a story that needed to be told and I would tell it. I knew some of the history. My husband's great-grandfather had emigrated from Northern Ireland to New Zealand in 1863 and worked building roads until he had enough money to buy land. He purchased Fairfield in 1873 and, soon after, married a maid from a neighbouring farm.

So I started my story based on these facts and created a credible storyline by researching sea voyages to New Zealand, what the Rakaia Township was like, and other details. What I wasn't prepared for was the strength of the characters to create their own story through my imagination. All I had to do was listen and write as the story unfolded. *Another Word for Sister* is a love story and yet also an exploration of individuality, the body/soul relationship, the lost divine feminine, and the reality of death.

Another Word for Sister is my first novel.

I am also an artist. You can see my artwork at:
www.cherylirwinarts.com

Questions and Topics for Discussion

Warning: These questions are spoilers! Don't read them until you have finished the book!

1. How did Lily and Rose's difficult early years mould their personalities? How did it affect their relationships with others?

2. The mother figures in this story are complex characters or have had difficult lives: Lily and Rose's mother dies in childbirth, the grandmother who could raise them loses her mind, Elisabeth Lichfield is too self-centred to know mother love at all, and Lily dies in childbirth as her mother did before her. How does this affect the children of these mothers? How does this reinforce the importance of mothering?

3. What are the characteristics of the male characters? What do they have in common? What are their strengths and weakness?

4. All three main characters left everything they knew behind and set off on a sea voyage to a land they had only heard about. What kind of people were able to do this? Can you think of any comparable situations that people undertake today with the same lack of information and inherent risk?

5. What draws Liam and Lily together? What are some of the strengths of their initial attraction and partnership? The challenges?

6. How did Lily and Rose deal with the evil of Henry Lichfield? Why do you think facing the darkness and consciously choosing to heal is important?

7. Lily and Rose both had a sense of the importance of knowing

what their ancestors before them knew and were aware of what they had lost. Do you ever have a sense that there is ancient knowledge that you should or could know, but don't?

8. What does life with Liam offer Lily that she hasn't encountered before? What are the risks?

9. How do you think Liam handled living with both Lily and Rose? Describe the dynamics between the three main characters.

10. How do you feel about the metaphysical parts of this story? Do you think there is a possibility of soul travel actually happening?

11. Did you enjoy the shifting viewpoint of the story? Did you miss Lily's voice after she died? Were you happy when her voice returned? Why do you think the author chose to tell the story the way she did—and what difference does it make in the way you read or understood it?

12. What are the main ideas—themes—of this story? How are the main ideas reinforced throughout the story?

13. Do you have favourite passages? One that strikes you as insightful, even profound? Perhaps a bit of dialogue that's especially poignant or that encapsulates a character?

14. Is the ending satisfying? If so, why? If not, why not? And how would you change it?

15. Do you think this novel changed you in any way or broadened your perspective? Have you learned something new or been exposed to different concepts?

16. If you could write the sequel to *Another Word for Sister*, what would you want to happen?

17. If you could ask the author a question, what would you ask?

Send your question to cheryl@cherylirwinarts.com for a reply.

www.ingramcontent.com/pod-product-compliance
Lightning Source LLC
Chambersburg PA
CBHW052020240626
47153CB00006B/1892